PINO
89

Dear Reader,

We at Zebra would like to welcome you to a wonderful reading experience. From the publisher who consistently brings you the best in historical romance come two memorable, magical novels— *Masque of Jade* by Emma Merritt, and *Masque of Sapphire* by Deana James.

There may be no relationship more demanding, more fragile, or more rewarding than that between sisters. Emma Merritt and Deana James capture the essence of such a relationship in their separate but interwoven stories of Laura and Judith—strong-willed, beautiful women who struggle to understand and trust each other as each learns what it means to love the man who has claimed her.

Separately, each book stands alone as a spectacular sensuous historical romance in the best-selling Zebra tradition. Together, *Masque of Jade* and *Masque of Sapphire* create an evocative and very unique tale.

In the prologues, interludes, and epilogues of the books, you will watch the sisters argue and agree as passionately as only sisters can. In *Masque of Jade*, you will discover Laura's secret thoughts and dreams; in *Masque of Sapphire*, you will see Judith's side. And when you have finished both, you will have a very special understanding . . . of sisters, and of love!

Happy reading!

Carin Cohen Ritter
Senior Editor and Product Manager
Zebra Books

PASSIONATE NIGHTS FROM ZEBRA BOOKS

ANGEL'S CARESS   (2675, $4.50)
by Deanna James

Ellie Crain was a young, inexperienced and beautiful Southern belle. Cash Gillard was the battle-weary Yankee corporal who turned her into a woman filled with hungry passion. He planned to love and leave her; she vowed to keep him forever with her *Angel's Caress*.

COMANCHE BRIDE   (2549, $3.95)
by Emma Merritt

Beautiful Dr. Zoe Randolph headed to Mexico to halt a cholera epidemic. She never dreamed her caravan would be attacked by a band of savages. Later, she refused to believe that she could love and desire her captor, the handsome half-breed Matt Chandler. Captor and slave find unending love and tender passion in the rugged Comanche hills.

CAPTIVE ANGEL   (2524, $4.50)
by Deanna James

When handsome Hunter Gillard left the routine existence of his South Carolina plantation for endless adventures on the high seas, beautiful and indulged Caroline Gillard learned to manage her home and business affairs in her husband's sudden absence. Caroline resolved not to crumble and vowed to make Hunter beg to be taken back. He was determined to make her once again his unquestioning and forgiving wife.

SWEET, WILD LOVE   (2834, $3.95)
by Emma Merritt

Chicago lawyer Eleanor Hunt was determined to earn the respect of the Kansas cowboys who openly leered at her as she was working to try a cattle-rustling case. The worst offender was Bradley Smith—even though he worked for Eleanor's father! She was determined not to mistake passion for love; he was determined to break through her icy exterior and possess the passionate woman who lurked beneath her.

Available wherever paperbacks are sold, or order direct from the Publisher. Send cover price plus 50¢ per copy for mailing and handling to Zebra Books, Dept. 2956, 475 Park Avenue South, New York, N.Y. 10016. Residents of New York, New Jersey and Pennsylvania must include sales tax. DO NOT SEND CASH.

MASQUE OF JADE
EMMA MERRITT

ZEBRA BOOKS
KENSINGTON PUBLISHING CORP.

ZEBRA BOOKS

are published by

Kensington Publishing Corp.
475 Park Avenue South
New York, NY 10016

First printing: April, 1990

Printed in the United States of America

Prologue

Calmly regarding the defiant nine-year-old girl standing in front of her, Laura stood in the center of the room, her arms folded across her chest. She found it difficult to believe this was her baby sister, that this was the four-year-old child she had left behind five years before when she and *Grandmère* had traveled to Austria to visit Great-Aunt Sophia. At the moment Judith Claire looked more like a street urchin than a daughter of an aristocratic English family.

And from the way Judith Claire glared at Laura, it was evident she found it difficult to believe this seventeen-year-old stranger was her older sister. And even if she was her sister, Laura was not going to dictate what she would or would not wear.

"I am not, and you can't make me!" Judith exclaimed spitefully.

Despite her exasperation, Laura said calmly, "All right, Judith, but you're cutting off your nose to spite your face."

Judith's head tilted upward, and her chin jutted at

a defiant angle. "It's my face. You go on and be what *Grandmère* wants you to be, but nobody can make me do anything." Judith flounced across the room, stopping in front of the mirror, her thin arms akimbo. "And don't think *she* hasn't tried."

Home only two months, Laura was already tired of the child's obnoxious behavior and despaired of teaching her manners. She pointed to the cheval mirror. "Judith Claire, turn around and look at yourself."

Judith glanced up, a mischievous grin spanning her face before she turned her head to look at her reflection in the mirror.

Softly, Laura said, "Now tell me truthfully you don't want to do something about the way you look."

Judith whirled around, the skirt of her light blue batiste dress billowing around her legs to reveal scabby knees in the holes of her stockings and drooping lace on her pantalettes.

Laura moved until she stood behind Judith, staring over the child's head at her reflection in the mirror. Until this moment Laura had not been aware of the difference between them. Now she was. Her auburn hair was pulled into an immaculate chignon at the nape of her neck, short curls framing her face. Her Lincoln-green bolero—the same shade as the tiny leaves that dotted her white dress—was a deliberate and thoughtful contrast for the rich color of her hair.

Laura reached out to pat Judith's riotous red curls into place, but Judith jerked her head away. She stuck her fingers in the sides of her mouth and thrust out her tongue at the reflection in the cheval glass. Her eyes danced with devilish delight.

"Judith Claire, behave yourself!" Laura admonished.

The nine-year-old tossed her head, the mane of long red hair falling over her shoulder. Dropping her hands from her mouth, she wiped wet fingers down the skirt of her dress.

Laura grimaced at such atrocious manners. That five years could make such a difference in Judith was hard for Laura to believe. *Dear Lord, what had she been thinking when she decided to bring Judith down to dinner tonight? What would Grandmère say if Judith should choose to do this at the dinner table? What would George think?* Unable to bear the answer to the question, Laura closed her eyes.

Judith said, "I think I look just fine the way I am."

Wondering if she heard the slightest hint of pleading in her sister's voice, Laura opened her lids. She peered into the narrow face but saw no softening in the glittering blue eyes. She sighed wearily and reached into the pocket of her dress to withdraw a blue velvet box which she opened. "Yes, you do look fine. That's what I'm trying to tell you. You're a beautiful little girl."

From her fingers dangled a gleaming gold chain and a heart-shaped locket. In the center of the heart gleamed a sapphire—its color the exact shade of blue as Judith's eyes.

"Hold still." In the fragile silence that descended, Laura undid the clasp, hardly daring to breathe lest she frighten Judith. With satisfaction she noted the impudence disappear entirely from Judith's countenance.

The child seriously contemplated herself from her face to the toes of her shoes. When she finally lifted her head, startling blue eyes caught Laura's. They softened as a little hand lifted and gingerly touched the tangled mass of red hair; blue eyes lovingly caressed the locket.

7

Laura moved closer and circled Judith's throat with the chain, the brilliant gold heart coming to rest at the neckline of the faded blue batiste. For the briefest of moments Laura's hands rested on Judith's shoulders, and the two of them gazed at their reflections in the mirror. "But you can look so much better."

Laura waited eagerly for a response. When she had learned that she would be returning home, she had begun searching for a special gift for Judith. When she had seen the sapphire she had known that was the perfect choice. Fiery blue Judith!

Perhaps, Laura thought, she could breach the years that had separated them and succeed in establishing a real sister relationship with Judith. Perhaps she would gain her trust and confidence. Laura had so much she wanted to give to Judith, so much she wanted to share with her.

Laura reached for the hairbrush. Now to do something with those curls. Such a shame! How truly they reflected the nature of the child. They, too, refused to be tamed. Laura moved closer to Judith and with two fingers lifted a curl up to Judith's crown. "It's time to put your hair up when you come to dinner."

"No!" With a twist of her head, Judith darted away. "Cook doesn't mind what I wear."

For a moment Laura stood, the hairbrush poised in air. How mercurial Judith was! And without provocation! Intimacy of any sort seemed to frighten the child. But Laura could not give up in defeat. Someone had to take Judith under wing before it was too late. It was quite evident that Mama was not. Already the child had been left to her own devices too long, allowed to stay in the dower house without supervision other than that of the servants, who

8

really cared little about her. They had allowed Judith to persist in her hooligan ways. When Mama had not exerted the energy to discipline Judith, no one else had either.

During the two months that Laura had been home, she had often been exasperated with Judith. No matter how friendly had been Laura's overtures, the child had rejected them. But Laura laid no blame on Judith. She blamed their parents, who did not take the time for either one of them, especially Judith.

Although Papa loved them both, he had been busy for the past three years establishing his shipping firm in Louisiana, and Mama . . . poor Mama . . . loved no one but herself and refused to grow up. She wanted to remain the lovely debutante Charlotte Mary Harrow for the remainder of her life. She was a social butterfly, flitting from one event to another. And much to *Grandmère*'s dismay, she was an outrageous flirt.

On her return home, Laura had been saddened to discover that Mama was jealous of her youth and beauty and did not wish her to be around. Rather than having a mother and daughter relationship, Laura found herself in competition with her mother. Laura also discovered that she was the only one who cared about Judith, the only one who *really* cared.

Mama was too busy with her social calendar; Papa was busy with his shipping in America. Uncle Harry, *Grandmère*'s oldest son and heir to Harrestone, had taken an interest in Judith until Cybil, his wife of fifteen years, had finally gotten pregnant. Then his interest had been Cybil and now was his only child and heir—little Harry.

Amelia Harrow had waited for a grandson and a direct heir to Harrestone, and only his birth brought her home from Austria. Now that Little Harry had arrived, George Beckworth, Viscount Chichester, a twice removed nephew of Amelia's late husband, would become the heir presumptive.

Laura felt a surge of happiness when she thought of George. She was not concerned that he would no longer inherit the vast Harrow estate, because he was a wealthy man in his own right. He had made two trips to Austria to visit with her while she and *Grandmère* visited Sophia, the Countess Von Aushwerg—*Grandmère*'s older sister and Laura's great-aunt, and it was during one of these visits that he had proposed marriage to her. How marvelous he was and such a dashing man and so romantic. She did love him.

Although Laura's heart felt lighter, her resolve was strong. Judith would come to dinner tonight and meet George. "You're not eating with Cook to-night," Laura said, slipping her arm around Judith's waist. "You're eating downstairs with the family."

"I don't want to!" Judith jerked away again and fled across the room toward the door.

Judith's obstinacy was taking its toll on Laura. Laura's temperament, a pendulum swinging from one extreme to the other, was becoming as mercurial as Judith's. Now she was beyond exasperation, well on her way to anger. Darting after Judith, Laura caught the end of her dragging sash.

"Stop right there! You're going to eat downstairs if it's the last thing you do." Doggedly, she began to reel her sister in by the tattered piece of material. If it were the last thing she did, Laura would see that no sister of hers would be a social outcast in her own family.

"You let me go!" Judith kicked backward at Laura's shins, but Laura sidestepped the flying heels and managed to grab the other end of the sash.

10

"Come back here." Laura caught one of Judith's wrists.

"Ouch." Laura knew she was not hurting the child, but Judith seemed to take pleasure in pretending that she did as she struggled to free herself. When she could not, she kicked even more furiously.

A surge of confidence rushing through her, Laura bowed her body to escape the flying heels. In the past she had tried to reason with Judith, and that did not work. The only way she could get the child's attention was to react in the same brash manner. "You're not getting away from me. I'm bigger than you are, and I know what's best for you."

"You're not my mother."

Laura heard the break in Judith's voice and knew tears were not far away. She recognized the stark hurt that underscored the words; she heard Judith's heart cry *I want a mother.* It had not been Laura's cry until recently, not until she and *Grandmère* returned to England and she found herself replaced in *Grandmère*'s affections by Little Harry. But even then her cry was not as desperate as Judith's because Laura had George and his love. And she was older. She understood *Grandmère*'s desire to have the estate remain in the immediate family.

"You can't make me." Judith spun in Laura's arms.

Laura released her sister, but one faded blue sash wrapped around Laura's arm. The other landed under her foot. Laura moved back to free the material just as Judith flung her hand out. With eyes widened in disbelief, Laura saw the ragged nails as they came toward her like claws to catch her dress just below the bolero. She staggered back, but not in time. The delicate fabric tore from the waistband. Judith looked at her sister. The beautiful dress was ruined.

The sisters stared at each other in paralyzed silence.

Then, unable to contain her anger any longer, hurt gnawing at her insides, Laura shouted, "You little hellion! Look what you've done."

"You made me do it!" The blue eyes glittered dangerously. "It's nothing but a stupid dress anyway."

"It was a Madame Bernice. *Grandmère* chose this material and design especially for me."

Judith shrugged her shoulders and picked up the hem of her faded blue batiste to mince across the room toward the mirror. She poised her left hand as if dancing the minuet. "Why, sister dear, she did this for me too."

Before Laura knew what was happening, Judith rushed to stand inches in front of her, caught up the skirt, and waved it in the air so vehemently that it popped. Her voice quavered, then escalated into a screech. "This was your dress five years ago!"

Perhaps the dress had been handed down. Laura was not sure. But she knew Judith had been well provided for and had wardrobes full of new clothes that the child stubbornly refused to wear, much preferring her old ones. Cook often threw her hands up in defeat when it came to the child, but Laura recognized the anger and hurt in Judith. Her obstinacy and rebellion were a cry for attention.

Laura drew in a deep breath. Patience! That was what she needed in order to deal with someone as obstinate as her sister. Laura felt the flush of anger fade from her cheeks as her eyes moved over the worn batiste to the locket that lay amid the frayed lace. Knowing she would argue no more, she held out her hands and smiled. She had other dresses which she could wear—not as pretty and certainly not as special, but any one of them would do.

"But I have one for you that is new. I had it made especially for you."

"You did?" Judith's eyes widened. "Is it a Madame Bernice?"

Laura moved to the divan of chased maroon velvet, where she sat. "Actually, yes, it is. Come and see." Sitting, she patted the place beside her and lifted a striped dress box onto her lap. She lifted her hand and beckoned, her heartbeat quickening when Judith took a step. Quickly, she lowered her head and concentrated on opening the box. She must not let Judith know how much the giving of this gift meant to her. Already the child knew exactly how to manipulate Laura's emotions. The tissue paper cracked as she brushed it aside to reveal a bundle of glowing chintz with sapphire-blue stripes.

Judith reached out and touched the lush folds. "Is this really for me?"

"Yes, it's really for you."

Quickly, the hand retracted and two fists jammed against Judith's eyes.

"Don't you like it?" Laura lifted the dress from the box and held it by the shoulders. The material shone with a luster like silk, and the square neckline was ruffled with delicate Irish lace. A sapphire-blue silk ribbon marked the high waistline.

Her head bowed, Judith mumbled, "Why?"

"I want you to meet George."

"Who's George?" Her voice was stronger now.

"Who's George?" Laura laughed softly. "He's the man I'm going to marry. He's George Beckworth, Viscount Chichester."

Judith's head jerked up, and she stared at her sister. "Viscount! Humph! Is he made out of some more of *Grandmère*'s special material just for you?"

The sisters laughed together, and Laura believed

everything would be all right. Finally, she had cracked the shell in which the child hid. Given time, she would pull Judith out altogether.

"He's quite a famous whip of the *ton*," Laura said. "And I've known him for ages."

"And you've never brought him to see me before?"

The smile faded from Judith's face. "Well . . . no . . ."

"Why?"

To cover her embarrassment, Laura spread the dress onto the divan and rustled through the tissue paper in the box. She felt heat diffuse her cheeks. She could not tell Judith that she was hardly presentable, that her social graces were considerably lacking.

Laura finally said, "You . . . you needed some time to grow up."

"You didn't bring him because I'm ugly." The anguished cry echoed through the bedchamber.

Laura shook her head furiously, curls dancing around her cheeks. Little fists tightly clutching the faded material of her skirt, Judith backed across the room to the door.

"No!" Laura leapt to her feet, grabbed the new dress, and hurried after Judith. "You can be as pretty as anyone."

Judith shook her head, the mane of red hair flying, blue eyes glinting with anger. "But not pretty enough for George! And I don't want to be. George is probably just an old stuffed shirt anyway. Who'd want to meet him!"

"Judith, that's not the way—"

"Oh, yes it is." Judith ran to the door.

"You don't understand . . ." Laura pleaded with Judith, the shimmering folds of the dress draped across outstretched arms.

She turned and screamed, "I understand. Take

14

your old dress and go back to *Grandmère* and George and Madame Bernice."

Laura moved toward the door, and for a moment Judith remained where she stood. Then she took a step forward. And another. Grubby hands darted out, fingers digging into the blue striped material which she yanked from Laura's arms.

In horror Laura watched one fist close over the skirt and twist, the other twisted in the bodice. The delicate material could not withstand such an assault. It split, the soft sound serrating the more delicate fabric of their momentary accord. The frayed material landed on the floor. As if her deed had not fully expressed her intentions to Laura, Judith stamped on it with her dirty black patent shoes.

The blood drained from Laura's face.

"You leave me alone!" Judith shouted, and slammed the door.

Tears of exasperation running down her cheeks, Laura stood there, her sister's words echoing through the silent room. She knew she ought to chase after Judith and try to make amends or, at least, insist on her coming to dinner. But she could not, not tonight. Too frequently since Laura had returned to Harrestone, the two of them had enacted scenes similar to this, although not quite as vicious.

She walked to the window and stood looking down on the finely manicured lawn and formal gardens that stretched so elegantly in front of Harrestone. Bracing her hand against the casement, she laid her forehead on the cool windowpane. Still, the tears ran down her face. She could not have stopped them if she wanted to.

When she saw George's carriage bounding up the drive, her lips tipped in a tremulous smile. He was indeed a handsome man! Thirteen years her senior, he was a marvelous choice for a husband, and she did so love him. And he loved her. She would always be first in his life. He would take care of her . . . and of Judith. She would marry George . . . she would . . . and become mistress of her own home.

Then she would bring Judith with her and would teach her to be a lady whether she wanted it or not. Yes, she would do just that!

As she straightened her back, Laura sniffed and wiped the tears from her eyes. She walked to the wardrobe. Now she must dress for dinner. The family . . . and George would be expecting her.

Chapter One

September 1813
New Orleans, Louisiana

The air hung heavy over the city. Moonbeams, deceptively strong and determined, weaved through the thick, sultry darkness to splash their silvery light into the courtyard below. Delicate color glimmered on the festoons of vines that clung to the moldering walls. In the center of the court, water gurgled softly from the fountain, the brim of which was circled with a vast array of potted flowers. At one side stood a tall white marble statue, ghostlike and surrounded by a tangle of vines. Across the way, at the back, a narrow flight of stairs rose a full three stories, stopping now and again at small landings, then curving and continuing upward. The railing was twined from bottom to top with a magnificent wisteria vine. In the summer it was heavy with purple flowers; now the leaves were changing their hue.

Gently, the moon touched the woman who gazed at the fountain. An autumn breeze stirred softly to blow the pale green silk against her body and to outline supple, rounded breasts and long slender legs. Short auburn curls escaped the bondage of an elaborate ostrich-plumed hat to wisp around her face.

"Beautiful night for a stroll, isn't it?" The masculine voice, loud and clear yet seductively lazy, drifted across the courtyard.

Startled, Laura turned. In the shadowed corner of the garden, beyond the spill of light from moon or upstairs windows, a man leaned against the outer brick wall. He wore a western-style hat with a low crown, the broad brim pulled low over his face. Chin and cheeks were illuminated in the sputtering glare of a match held to the tip of his cigar. Yet he was masked by a seductive haze of smoke. He pushed away from the wall, and without breaking his gaze tossed the lucifer to the ground. He moved toward her.

He was not over six feet, yet the closer he came to Laura, the taller he seemed. Tucked into black boots were close-fitted trousers, their tawny color a beautiful contrast to the rust tailcoat which he wore. Tailored to perfection, it molded his broad shoulders and hinted at a physically fit body. In the muted light that filtered through the windows to mingle with the moonbeams, his features were quite clear. His face, a smooth composition of masculine planes and angles, was framed by a high white collar and blue and tan cravat, a stark relief to his thick black sideburns.

So handsome, he could have been Lucifer himself walking straight out of the bowels of hell! Laura knew she ought to go back but could not.

"I'm glad you joined me." The western drawl, such a contrast to the refined accent of the Creoles among whom Laura had lived for the past nine years, wrapped around her like an invisible thread and

18

pulled her closer to the stranger. He smiled, displaying beautiful white teeth. Then he laughed, the sound setting Laura's blood to running through her veins like liquid heat. "The evening is far too lovely to spend it cooped in a house with a bunch of yakking stuffed shirts. Mamas choosing bridegrooms and setting wedding dates. Papas extolling their glorious French heritage and repudiating the barbarous American invaders."

Laura laughed breathlessly; the man was right. His deep, mellifluous voice sent a shiver of excitement down her spine. She drew the cashmere stole more closely around her and stepped back. He was one of the most virile men she'd ever seen. Not handsome in elegant sophistication like Roussel; rather, he was rugged and powerful.

"But let's not discuss Maurice Dufaure's autumn ball," the seductive drawl suggested. "We have no time to waste on boring subjects; let's talk about ourselves."

The man was altogether too familiar. "I enjoy Monsieur Dufaure's balls, sir." With a scant twinge of guilt the small social lie sprang to Laura's lips. "I don't find them boring at all. I merely came out to get a breath of fresh air."

Again the man laughed—the sound gentle but mocking. He shifted his shoulders, the lines of his coat emphasizing the ripple of muscle. The movement startled Laura. She backed up a step, a step that brought her closer to the corridor. Her gown whispered around her feet.

"Please . . . Miss Talbot—" He resettled his shoulder against the wall. "Don't go in yet."

Although spoken softly and framed as a request, the words were a command—a command that kept Laura's feet firmly in place. She turned and through muted light again stared at him . . . at Lucifer. The fringe of her gold-shot white cashmere shawl frolicked in the breeze. Curls danced around her face. "I'm afraid I'm at a disadvantage, sir. I don't know who you are."

"If I tell you who I am, will you stay and talk with me for a moment?" Low and cajoling was the plea.

Such audacity! Laura's heartbeat quickened; her blood raced; but her voice remained steady. "I make no promises, sir."

"When I ask for promises"—the tones were silky soft—"you'll know it. At the moment I want nothing more than to talk with you."

Laura's gaze darted from the man's shadowed face to the corridor; she heard the muted strains of music and laughter from the house. War raged within her breast: She wanted to stay and talk with the stranger but knew propriety demanded she return to the ballroom. This conflict was a new feeling for Laura; never in her life had she been ruled by emotion—certainly not in the last nine years, not since George.

Although this indecisiveness, this urge to give in to a whim, was uncharacteristic of her, she was tempted to stay and talk. After all, this ball was very much the same as every other one held throughout the city. All the same people, the same conversation. She glanced at the elegant three-storied town house in the *Vieux Carré*, ablaze with light and festivity.

This aristocratic Creole society of New Orleans was her world. For no one, certainly not a stranger no matter how enticing his pleas, would she disobey its or her own strict rules of conduct. Once she had been ostracized from society through no fault of her own, but never again!

She stepped back and unfurled her fan, sweeping it elegantly in front of her face. "I really must return to

20

the ballroom. My escort went to fetch me a glass of punch." The last time she had seen Roussel he was in deep conversation with her father and Maurice. Refreshments were the furthest thing from his mind. Behind the fan she hid the grin that lurked at the corner of her lips. "I'm sure he must be wondering where I am."

The man lifted the cigar to his mouth, the tip casting a red glow across his visage. Laura wondered if indeed the Prince of Darkness had materialized; she wondered what color his eyes were. In the reflection of the cigar light they gleamed like gold. When he blew out the smoke, he asked, "Could it be that Miss Laura Talbot, the woman who single-handedly runs Ombres Azurées—one of the largest sugar cane plantations and sugar mills around New Orleans and who dares defy any man when her plantation is at stake—is afraid to talk with me?"

His mocking laughter wrapped around Laura's exposed nerves; she shivered and snapped the fan shut. She drew the stole even closer around her shoulders and neck, seeking protection more than warmth. Yes, she was frightened, more frightened than she had been in her entire life. At the same time, she was the most excited she had ever been. "How is it that you know so much about me, sir, when I know nothing of you?"

"You're a lovely woman, Miss Talbot. You must know without a stranger telling you. Bathed in moonlight, you look like a fragile butterfly." The smile deepened and the tones grew more sensuous; yet he seemed to be sincere. The eyes, shadowed by the darkness, glittered enigmatically. "I would imagine your name is on the lips of every eligible bachelor in town, who would do anything to win your hand in marriage."

"Ah, sir," Laura drawled, heady with excitement, quite forgetting that he had not answered her question. But she did not care; she had already forgotten it herself. "I can tell by your drawl that you're not a native of New Orleans. American, perhaps?"

"True, ma'am. I'm a Virginian by birth."

"Just passing through?"

"No, ma'am, I'm here to stay."

Laura could not account for the weakness that washed through her body. She could not remember a man ever having such an effect on her. While the feeling was exciting, it also frightened her. She prided herself on always being in control of her emotions, a lesson she had learned nine years previously.

"I—I really must return to the ball before I'm missed," she said. "Can you imagine the wagging tongues should it be discovered that I'm in the courtyard chatting endlessly with a stranger?"

"If that's your only concern, ma'am, I can remedy that easily and swiftly." He doffed his hat and swept it through the air as he bowed. The movement was fluid and graceful, an extension of the man himself. Yet the very ease with which he executed the flourish accented his virility. "In the absence of someone to introduce us, Miss Talbot, may I do the honors? I'm Clay Sutherland."

Laura smiled. "I'm glad to make your acquaintance, M'sieur Sutherland."

"And I to make yours, Miss Talbot."

Fascinated, she stared at him a moment before she extended her gloved hand. The tips of her fingers were caught in the warmth of his. His lips brushed over the hunter-green silk, lingering longer than propriety demanded to send a shiver of delight coursing through Laura's body.

"Since you're American, I assume you're one of M'sieur Dufaure's business associates?" Laura made no attempt to withdraw her hand.

A sardonic smile on his lips, Clay straightened and released her hand. "You might say that." He resettled the gray hat on thick black hair.

"Just—just what is your business?"

"I own the Golden Fleece."

"The Golden Fleece!" Laura's face went white in shocked horror. Clay Sutherland was nothing but a gambler! And he had taken his liberty in kissing her hand. "How dare you accost me like a common street wench." Without thinking, she moved closer and her hand flew through the air, the jade fan biting into his face. Even in the pale light that spilled from the windows, she saw the red line welt across his cheek.

Clay dropped the cigar to the ground and moved forward, his hands clamping around Laura's arms, his fingers crushing the delicate fabric of her sleeves. "That was a mistake, Miss Talbot. And if I'm treating you like a common street wench, it's because you're asking for it by being out here alone. But I'm not. If I were"—he hauled her fully against the length of his body—"this is what I'd be doing to you."

His intent obvious, his face lowered, but Laura twisted and turned her head. His hand loosened her arm but his fingers bit into her chin, causing tears to quicken her eyes. Dropping her fan, she cried out and began to fight him in earnest, her fists flaying his chest, her feet kicking against his boots. He laughed softly, and with so little effort it seemed, he totally disregarded her efforts and guided her face to meet his. Unable to stare into the unyielding face, Laura closed her eyes as his lips touched hers. Hard and relentless, his mouth settled firmly over hers as his arms embraced her.

Still, Laura would not open her mouth to the insistent thrust of his tongue. A novice at making love, she intuitively knew that once she opened her mouth, the kiss would become a caress rather than punishment. Urgency and some other emotion Laura could not define replaced his savagery. He pressed his hard body against the full length of hers. The shawl slipped from her shoulders.

Fire blazed through Laura's veins; she wedged her hands between their bodies and pushed, but Clay held her firmly. She tossed her head from side to side, yet could not escape the prison of his lips. Her flailing succeeded only in situating herself more firmly against the hard length of his body.

Beneath her palms she felt the strong thump of his heart, the rise and fall of his chest as he breathed. The warmth of his body penetrated the delicate barrier of silk and satin, caressing her skin itself; the scent of his cologne filled her nostrils. This was unlike all the chaste kisses she had shared with George—and they had been engaged. At the moment when she was losing control of her emotions, when all resistance was ebbing from her body and her mouth was relaxing, Clay lifted his head.

Through parted lips and dazed eyes Laura stared at him, at the steely face framed with thick and untamed black curls. His hat was gone, long since joining the shawl and fan on the ground. Quickly, she regained her aplomb and stepped back, her hand rubbing against her mouth in an effort to erase his touch. Her other hand, hanging to her side, curled into a fist. How she wished for her quirt! She'd show Clay Sutherland just what she thought of him.

His eyes moving from her fist to her face, Clay's

lips twisted into a sardonic smile. "I'm no horse to be whipped, Miss Talbot, and no boy to be played with."

"It's plain to see"—the words were a mere whisper—"you're no gentleman."

"No." He bent and retrieved his hat, swiping off the dust before he resettled it on his head. "I'm not, Miss Talbot. I'm a man."

"A lowly gambler," Laura snarled. "Taking advantage of the innocent in your den of iniquity."

Picking up her shawl, Clay laughed softly. "You've never been to the Golden Fleece. How can you describe it as a den of iniquity?"

"Judging from your behavior a moment ago—" Laura began, jumping away from him when he went to circle her neck with the scarf.

Clay shrugged and let the piece of cashmere drop haphazardly over one of her shoulders. "My behavior a moment ago has nothing to do with my gambling casino. I simply punished you for hitting me. Be glad I kissed you. I'd have killed a man for less."

Drawing up to her full five feet seven inches, Laura said, "I guess I must count myself among the fortunate that I'm a mere woman, else you and I would be dueling come morning."

He fished in his coat pocket for another cigar. "Miss Talbot, rest assured you'll never be accused of being a *mere* anything. *More* perhaps, but never *mere*. As to dueling, madam, we don't have to wait for morning; we've been engaging in that since the minute we first saw each other."

A lucifer grated against the stone statue, and the tip burst into a flame. The flickering light revealed a hard, indomitable countenance and mockery in the depth of golden-brown eyes that blatantly swept down her body.

"As to your being a woman—you look like one. But the gentlemen who frequent my establishment say you're not, Miss Talbot."

Furious, Laura's lips thinned; her eyes gleamed with hatred.

"They compare you to a block of ice," Clay continued. "Dufaure calls this his autumn ball, and folks about town say he gives it about the same time every year—a celebration of the coming winter. Since you're so frigid and cold, I wonder if perhaps this year it's given in your honor."

A muscle twitched in Laura's cheek; otherwise, her expression never changed. "As a matter of fact, it is given in my honor."

"Perhaps to convince New Orleans that you really are a woman."

"I don't have to convince anyone of that." Laura tilted her chin slightly. "I think the facts speak for themselves."

"They do indeed, ma'am. That's why you're going to have to convince me."

As quickly as it had come, Laura's fury dissipated to be replaced with pain. She hurt deeply and wanted to cry. Refusing to give in to such weakness, she drew back. Only then was she aware that her hat, knocked askew when Clay kissed her, dangled by a ribbon down her back. "I couldn't care less what men say about me, and I wouldn't go out of my way to convince you of anything. You're a lowlife who doesn't deserve the time of day, lurking out here in the shadows of the courtyard because you weren't good enough to be invited to the ball."

Before she lost her composure and made a complete fool of herself, Laura turned around and walked—she wanted to run, but pride forbade her to allow this man to know how much he had affected her aplomb—across the flagstones, through the hallway, and into the courtyard. The fringe of her stole rippled behind her. When she entered the house through the back door, she paused to stare at her reflection in the small wall mirror.

Her eyes still burning with tears, she hand-combed the curls that lay against her cheeks and set the hat atop her head as best she could. Angrily, she jabbed the pins through the hat, crying out when one of the points pricked her skin. When her breathing calmed and she was in command of her emotions, she walked down the corridor. She forced her stiff lips to smile.

Time to celebrate the coming of winter—*the season of ice and snow.*

But Laura had not always been so cold. She had been warm and loving. Eagerly, the seventeen-year-old had returned from Austria, where she visited with her great-aunt Sophia. She had patiently awaited her marriage to George Beckworth. But her mother had spoiled it all. When Beau had returned to England in the summer of 1804 and had demanded Charlotte accompany him to America, she had refused. Charlotte scandalized the entire family by demanding a divorce and openly admitting she had taken a lover—Randolph Carew, Lord Lythes—whom she wished to marry. Charlotte received her divorce but was disinherited by the family. Lord Lythes refused to marry her.

Laura had not escaped the scandal unscathed. Without preamble George had broken their engagement. Laura had cried and pleaded with him, but he had not changed his mind. Even now as she remembered her begging, embarrassment warmed her body. That was the last time Laura Elyse Talbot had begged. And that was the last time until tonight she had ever lost control of her emotions in front of anyone. She had promised herself the night George broke their engagement that she would never love again. Anger and hostility were fine emotions to feel. They acted like a protective shield. Not love. It left her open and vulnerable.

Numb with grief and shock, she allowed her father to bring her to America, but her sister, Judith, was left in England. Not because Beau did not love his younger daughter—he did. But he witnessed the child's uncontrollable anger and her lack of manners and felt that he was inadequate to handle her. A weak man, he did not know how to cope with a rebellious child. No matter what Charlotte had done, he thought Amelia Harrow would take her granddaughter under supervision and that Judith would be better off in England than in New Orleans with him.

Laura had been to wrapped up in her own grief to be concerned with Judith at the time. Later, when she could reason objectively about it, she wrote Judith and begged her to come to America. But Judith did not wish to do so. Through her letters she let Laura know she was happy in England.

And now Roussel Giraumont, the owner of the adjacent plantation, wanted to marry Laura. But Laura was not sure she wanted to marry Roussel, although the marriage would be one of convenience only. The combining of the two plantations would be an excellent move politically and economically. Yet Laura procrastinated. No matter how cold and calculating she may appear, she hesitated to commit her life to a man who was not stronger than she. Beau and his wife, Celeste, kept reminding her that she was not getting any younger, and she could do far worse than Roussel. So far Roussel had not pressed her for an answer, but he was growing weary.

Her composure regained, Laura pushed her ruminations aside and stepped into the ballroom from the rear entrance. At almost the same time, Clay Sutherland entered through the front French doors. Unlike Laura, he was not disheveled in the least. His hat gone, he stood beneath one of the chandeliers, the candlelight glimmering on thick black hair. Rugged and virile, he stood out in stark contrast to every other male in the room. Lucifer in all his magnificence could not have been more handsome, Laura thought.

When Clay saw her, he smiled, his right eyelid lowering in an audacious wink. Laura cast him a frosty glare, then straightened her shoulders and deliberately swept her gaze elsewhere in the room. But her smile, so carefully nurtured and developed through the years, did not erase the anger flashing in her green eyes. She closed her hand over the small jade phoenix that hung from a gold chain around her neck.

Papa had given her the necklace when she had first arrived in New Orleans. She reminded him of the phoenix. She, too, could rise from the ashes and begin her life anew. And she had!

Roussel Giraumont, a squat man of medium height, weaved through the crowd until he stood at Laura's side. "I've been looking all over for you." He ran his hands through thin and graying brown hair. "Where have you been?"

"Out in the courtyard for a breath of fresh air." Laura's gaze skimmed over Roussel's immaculate evening attire: the royal blue frock coat and tight-fitting breeches, silk stockings and pumps. Unconsciously, she looked from him to Clay, and for some reason which she did not understand she wished that Roussel were a little more rugged, more like the gambler. She much preferred the deep, resonant drawl to Roussel's petulant whine.

"It was getting rather stuffy in here," she continued. Her heart fluttered when out of the corner of her eye she saw Clay brushing through the crowd toward her.

"Ah, *chère* Laura, let me get you a glass of punch." Roussel moved away as he spoke.

"Yes, please," Laura murmured to his retreating figure. She turned to focus her attention on an elderly couple across the room and pretended to be unaware of Clay's approach, but she felt his presence the minute he reached her side.

"I found this in the courtyard," he whispered into her ear and unfolded the fan, holding it in front of him to study the intricate Oriental designs. "I wonder whose it could be."

The ostrich plume danced through the air when Laura's head jerked in his direction. She managed a tight smile and demanded in an icy undertone, "Give me my fan."

"How do I know it's yours?" Clay asked innocently, only now lifting and turning his head to look into her face.

Laura was positively fuming. "Give me my fan!"

"How about a please? No." He shrugged and tucked the fan into his pocket. "I'll just keep it, then."

"Please," Laura added grudgingly.

"After we dance." When she scowled, he cocked an eyebrow, wicked laughter gleaming in the depths of his golden-brown eyes, and drawled, "Create a scene, Miss Talbot, I'd like that. It'll come close to convincing me that you're human. Then we'll work on ways you can convince me you're a woman."

"I'm sure you'd love a scene, M'sieur Sutherland. That's a way of life for you. You like to live on the edge of danger and excitement. Well, I'm different." Laura's voice was frosty. "I'm civilized, M'sieur Sutherland. That's the basic difference between you and me."

Clay's eyes blatantly swept from the ostrich plume at the crown of her hat to the tips of her slippers that peeked from the hem of her gown. His gaze moved upward, lingering on the creamy swell of bosom revealed in the low décolletage. Her body burning with shame, Laura wanted to pull her shawl around her neck, but pride would not allow her. She would not let a man such as Clay Sutherland daunt her. She had outdone better than he.

"You may think what you wish, ma'am," the deep voice caressed, "but I must disagree with you. The basic difference between us is anatomy, a difference of which I definitely approve and one that promises to make our relationship interesting."

For the first time since she'd met Clay, Laura laughed. "Hardly anatomy, sir. Ice has none. And certainly don't entertain any ideas of a relationship between us, because we're not moving any further than tolerated acquaintance."

They dropped their guard and forgot the battle. Their eyes locked; their laughter mingled. Clay caught her hand and held it for the barest of moments before he led her to the dance floor.

"Perhaps I was wrong earlier, Miss Talbot. Maybe you're not really a block of ice but an ice maiden, a frightened woman lurking behind a sheet of ice. Maybe you're just waiting for the right man to come along to melt that veneer. Then without her mask we'll see what Laura Talbot really looks like."

Turning her head, Laura saw Roussel standing in the doorway, evidently looking for her, a cup of punch in each hand. She looked up to see Clay staring at the Frenchman also.

Clay lowered his head to gaze into her eyes. "Then we'll ask Miss Talbot if she's ready for a relationship with a *real* man."

"You've seen the only Laura Talbot that you're ever going to see, M'sieur Sutherland. And I've seen real men before; you don't begin to compare."

"Surely you know you can't judge goods by looking at the exterior of the package. Wait until you take off my wrapping."

Excitement skittered up Laura's spine. "That day shall never arrive, M'sieur Sutherland."

"I love challenges."

"That was a promise."

"Then it's one you're going to break."

Before Laura could retort, the orchestra began to play one of the new dances from Vienna. Pleased with herself because she had just recently learned the steps to the waltz, Laura turned to Clay and held her arms out. She hoped that he did not know them and would be embarrassed. As if he understood her secret desire, he smiled and winked and took her hand, remaining a decorous distance from her that none— not even the most critical eye—could fault.

"If I break something, M'sieur Sutherland," Laura said, her hand on his shoulder, her eyes glued to the rust-colored material that stretched over his shoulder, "it'll be the man, not the promise."

Clay threw back his head and laughed and swirled Laura around the room. "As I told you earlier, Miss Talbot, I'm no horse to be whipped . . . or broken. I'm a man." Without missing a step, his clasp tightened and he pulled Laura into his arms, holding her scandalously close. He grinned when she stiffened and drew back; he only leaned closer, his warm, whiskey-scented breath blowing against her face. His palm slid from Laura's shoulders to the small of her back.

Laura gasped as heat shot through her body to linger in her lower stomach. Although the sensation was quite unfamiliar to her, she found it pleasant. Her breathing accelerated; her heartbeat quickened, and she trembled slightly. Still, she refused to acknowledge her emotions. To do so was to admit that Clay Sutherland was influencing her, that his touch was not as repulsive as she wished it to be.

"Remove your hand from my waist," she demanded. Deeply affected by his touch, Laura felt a tremor of desire ripple through her body. While she despised that this man could elicit such emotional response from her, she was also enthralled by him. "You're . . . rumpling my dress." When Clay smiled, she knew he was aware of his effect on her. This angered her and made her want to wipe the smug arrogance from his face.

As if he could read her thoughts, his smile grew bolder. "In our short acquaintance, Miss Talbot, I've noticed that the word *please* is sadly lacking in your vocabulary. Do you always demand rather than ask?"

"I said, remove your hand," Laura repeated, her voice stronger this time. "People are going to stare at us."

Clay's fingers moved sensuously against the bunched-up material at her waist again to send excitement skittering through her body. "If I'm not mistaken, someone already is."

Her face flushed, her eyes filled with confusion, Laura turned to see her father's eyes glued to her. Ordinarily, Beau Talbot was a strikingly handsome man, tall and lean, with silvered hair. During the past nine years he had been a tender, loving father and had not been angry at her one time. It was as if he

33

were trying to make up to her for Charlotte's mistakes. Or perhaps he was making up for not having brought Judith to America with him. At the moment Laura saw disapproval stamped on his face.

"Do you think he's angry?" Laughter danced in the depth of Clay's eyes.

If Beau Talbot were not, Laura was! This man was pushing her to the sheer edge of discomposure for the second time in one evening. This was too much for her to endure.

"Turn me loose!"

Surprisingly, Clay did and Laura missed her step and stumbled. Clay caught her arm to balance her. "Let me return you to your anxious parents, Miss Talbot."

Throwing her shoulders back and lifting her chin, Laura jerked away from his clasp and moved to where her father stood. When she realized that Clay had followed her, she looked embarrassed. Finally, she stammered, "Father, may I present—"

"I already know M'sieur Sutherland," Beau interrupted, his lips a fine line of anger. As a servant passed with a tray of champagne, he captured one of the glasses. "I'm surprised that you do."

"Why, Mr. Talbot?" Clay asked smoothly. "I'm personally acquainted with many of New Orleans's finest citizens."

"And intimately acquainted with as many," Beau growled.

Before Clay could react, a petite Creole beauty in her late forties joined them. A headdress of feathers the same shade of pink as the appliquéd designs on her gown decorated a swirling chignon of black curls; long lashes framed chocolate eyes. "Not now, *mon cher*," she whispered in a heavy French accent, twining her hand around Beau's arm. "Laura's

34

dancing with M'sieur Sutherland is cause enough for tongue-wagging. Do not provide our friends with a display of your temper."

Beau drowned his anger with a swallow of whiskey.

"Hello, Mrs. Talbot." Clay smiled at Celeste, his face and eyes going soft. "How are you this evening?"

"Très bien, merci. And how is your evening, M'sieur Sutherland?" Her cheeks flushed with delicate color as Beau glared down at her.

Clay looked at Laura. "It has turned out to be most lovely, Mrs. Talbot. Most lovely."

"That is good," Celeste whispered, and her gaze dropped to the floor.

His arms extended, cups of punch in both hands, Roussel jostled through the crowd. When he reached Laura, he saw Clay for the first time. His face whitened. "M'sieur Sutherland, what a surprise to see you."

Black brows hiked above mocking eyes. "I'm sure it is, Mr. Giraumont, but it shouldn't be."

"I mean—I mean it is a surprise to see you here," Roussel stammered hurriedly, unable to meet Clay's steady gaze.

"Why should it be, Roussel? You of all people should know that some of the world's most important business is conducted at gala affairs such as this. Later you and I shall get together, Mr. Giraumont." Clay's tone was as steady as his gaze, his words authoritative and demanding. Then, dismissing Roussel as if he were of no more consequence than an annoying insect, Clay turned to Laura. "I'm so glad to have met you, Miss Talbot. Thank you for the dance. I wish I could stay to enjoy more with you, but I must greet our gracious host and thank him for a lovely evening."

The four of them watched Clay as he easily threaded his way through the crowd. Finally, Beau broke the uncomfortable silence. "What were you doing with him, Laura?"

Her eyes never left Clay. "I think it was evident that I was dancing with him, Papa."

"Don't you—"

"Lower your voice, Beau." Celeste tugged his arm as she cast a covert gaze around the room.

"I'm sure Laura was not aware who the man was." Roussel's tone was placating, but his eyes blazed angrily. His hands shook.

Laura took no notice of Roussel's anger. Her attention was centered on Clay Sutherland. She wondered how any woman could not be aware of him. He was the most handsome man in the room. He brought to mind her catechisms. Lucifer was reputed to be the most beautiful of all angels. And for a moment she wondered again if Clay Sutherland was indeed that fallen archangel. Was he indeed prince of hell?

"Here, take this!" Roussel jarred Laura out of her ruminations as he thrust a cup of punch into her hand. "I'm standing here holding these, looking like a fool. How did you meet Sutherland?" he demanded. He yanked a lace handkerchief from his pocket and mopped the perspiration from his face.

"He was in the courtyard," she confessed. Already she regretted her interlude with the gambler. Ignoring the glares she received from her parents and Roussel, she held the cup to her lips and let the cool liquid flow down her parched throat with relish.

Roussel laughed harshly. "I have never known you to be so indiscreet, Laura."

"I wasn't indiscreet." Laura's blood ran hot when she thought of Clay's kiss. "I was . . . merely being

36

gracious to one of Maurice's guests."

"Guest!" Roussel spat the word. "He's hardly a guest. He's a gambler."

Laura looked up to see Clay and Maurice standing together across the room. They were smiling at each other and talking. "He seems quite friendly with Maurice. I'm sure you must be mistaken, Roussel. Surely he received an invitation."

"*Certainement,*" Roussel murmured, his gaze going to the two men who stood on the far side of the room. "I'm sure Maurice must have invited him . . . one way or the other. With the coming of the Americans, gamblers are getting far too cocky to suit me. They're forgetting their place. Imagine his daring to come to Maurice Dufaure's home! You never know where you'll see him next."

"Beau," Celeste murmured, a hand going to her forehead. "I want to go home, *s'il vous plaît.* I'm . . . I'm not feeling well at all."

Immediately solicitous, Beau set his glass on one of the passing trays. "I'll send for the carriage, darling. We'll have you home in no time."

"Not the town house, *mon cher.* I want to go to Ombres Azurées, where Berthe can take care of me."

Concerned, Laura turned to look at her stepmother. The plantation was Celeste's refuge. Here she took flight when she had something in life she could not or did not wish to face. Evidently, her dancing with Clay had upset Celeste.

"You know I have to stay in town tonight." Beau's eyes darkened with concern. "Maurice and I must go over the books; we're having an inventory discrepancy. The port officials must have the report no later than tomorrow afternoon. Stay the night with me."

"No," Celeste mumbled, "I want to go home."

"I'm returning to the plantation tonight," Roussel said. "I'll be happy to see the women safely home, Beau."

Roussel's announcement settled the argument. Celeste waved her hand through the air. "Get my shawl, Laura dear. I left it in the study earlier when Beau and I were visiting with Maurice."

"I'll get it," Roussel answered. "I'm going that way."

When he was gone, Beau threaded through the crowd until he found Maurice. Laura observed the two of them talking, Maurice's gaze crossing the room to land on Celeste. He smiled and nodded his head.

"I do wonder what's keeping Roussel," Celeste murmured, her fingers gently massaging a temple.

"I'll go see," Laura said.

As she crossed the room, she looked for Clay, but he was nowhere to be found. Disappointed, she walked through the French doors down the long hallway, stopping when she reached Maurice's study. The door was slightly ajar, and before she knocked, she heard Roussel speak.

"You have no right!" he exclaimed.

"I had every right. You owe my establishment quite a bit of money. But perhaps you have something of equal value with which you might entice me."

"Meaning?"

Clay walked to the door. "I like your town house, Giraumont. I especially like the location—in the middle of the *Vieux Carré*. I think it'll cover the cost of your debt."

"You can't be serious!" Giraumont exclaimed incredulously.

"I have never been more so."

"My house is worth a hundred times the amount of my gambling debt."

"You must consider the interest, Mr. Giraumont." Clay laughed. "At the going rate, it won't be long before I have a claim to half of your plantation."

Roussel pointed a trembling finger. "Get out!"

"From the Creole gentlemen who frequent my casino, Mr. Giraumont, I've learned quite a lot about respectability and recognition. It's really not in the spelling of your name or the number of years you've resided in New Orleans. Respectability is wealth and material possessions, Mr. Giraumont. At the rate I'm going, I shall have a town house in a week. As you Creoles say, it's a *fait accompli*. Also following Creole custom, in a month or two perhaps I'll marry an heiress from one of the respectable Creole families. From her I'll inherit a plantation and a sugar mill. Yes, Mr. Giraumont, before long I shall have respectability, and my name will be the first and a must on each and every guest list that is sent out."

When Clay opened the door, Laura stared at him disbelievingly. He smiled and tipped his hat. "Good evening, Miss Talbot. How nice to see you again."

Laura pushed past him and strode across the room to stand in front of Roussel. Her stance was most protective. "You have audacity, m'sieur."

"Yes, ma'am, I do," Clay quietly admitted. His face was solemn, but his eyes twinkled. "While some claim it's a virtue, others say it's a fault. I have a feeling you think it's a fault."

Laura tensed; she refused to be beguiled by the beautiful golden-brown eyes. "Surely, m'sieur, you should know that you are out of your element."

Clay removed the cigar from his mouth and blew

39

out the smoke. His gaze lazily traveled Laura's slender form. "Since you seem to be an expert on me, ma'am, what is my element?"

The chin tilted haughtily. "You know better than I, m'sieur."

Clay chuckled. "Perhaps it's safer to remain in one's element, ma'am, but I guarantee you it's more exciting to venture out every once in a while . . . and certainly more lucrative. Now, if you'll excuse me, I'll be—"

Laura drew up and moved a step, placing herself directly in front of Clay. "M'sieur, I demand that you give Roussel an apology. He is a gentleman whom you have offended and affronted."

Clay looked beyond Laura to the red-faced and squirming man behind her. Then the eyes once again settled on her. "You, ma'am, are nothing but a hypocrite, and your sense of honor is strangely twisted." Laura gasped, but he continued without hesitation. "I'm the one who has been affronted. Roussel Giraumont wanted to gamble at the Golden Fleece, and I extended him credit. Now he's not making good on his debt to me."

Laura felt her face flush. "That . . . may be true, m'sieur, but you have no right to come to M'sieur Dufaure's ball to badger Roussel. That's not the way a gentleman would handle his business," she finished lamely.

"Certainly not," Roussel blustered, finally pushing past Laura. He tugged on the bottom of his waistcoat but still the satin material did not cover his paunch.

Clay's eyes flickered distastefully over Giraumont. His attention returned to Laura. "Perhaps not, Miss Talbot, but as I said before, I make no claim to being a gentleman. But, I will say this, gentleman or not, I

40

have a creed I live by. I believe a man's word is his integrity and honor."

Laura drew back, her face lifting again. "Are you inferring, m'sieur, that you're the only one in this room with honor?"

"I'll let you be the judge of that, Miss Talbot."

Chapter Two

The lanterns glowed brightly, illuminating the elegant interior of the carriage as it marked the distance between New Orleans and Ombres Azurées.

"I cannot believe the audacity of that ruffian," Roussel grumbled not for the first time since they had left the city. Slumping against the blue velvet cushion, he folded his hands across his stomach, the material of his waistcoat pulling over the paunch. "*Je ne sais pas!* That's what New Orleans is going to be full of now that we're a part of the United States. Uncivilized barbarians."

"Can he really be blamed?" Laura asked quietly, unable to escape memories of Clay Sutherland. "After all, Roussel, you are the one who ran up the debt."

"But, Laura," Celeste said, "gentlemen have always gambled. We must not judge Roussel so harshly."

Remembering Clay's blistering comments, Laura said, "But he is to blame for not paying his debts. Had he paid them, that odious man would not have been there."

Roussel waved her comment aside. "I will pay my

debt, my dear. I have always done so in the past. Even so, that man had no right barging in on Maurice's ball like that. He's setting a precedent for other sordid types like him. Americans!"

"Perhaps not." Bothered by her hat that she had not been able to anchor properly since she'd kissed Clay in the garden, she reached up to take it off. Tired of the argument, Laura leaned back against the cushions. "Depending on the outcome of the war, New Orleans could be under English rule next."

"Seems we really have no choice," Roussel confessed dismally but seemed to be relieved they had abandoned the subject of his gambling debt. "The one is about as bad as the other."

Tossing the hat on the seat beside her, Laura ran her fingers through the curls that framed her face. Still unable to get Clay's accusations off her mind, she said, "Have you ever thought about the hypocrisy of our society, Roussel? We don't want someone like Clay Sutherland socializing with us, but we don't mind gambling in his casino."

"Nothing hypocritical about it. We don't socialize with the man; we simply avail ourselves of the service which he offers. Everybody has a place in society; he should stay in his." He peered curiously at her. "Surely, Laura, you're not defending Sutherland's actions tonight."

"Good gracious no!" Visions of Clay Sutherland swam in Laura's mind. It seemed as if the brisk aroma of his cologne lingered in her nostrils. "But, you must admit, Roussel, he has audacity. Imagine coming to Maurice's house during the autumn ball to collect his debts."

"How could you, Laura!" Celeste nervously rolled her handkerchief in her hands. "I forgive you for dancing with the man. You couldn't have known

43

that he wasn't invited to the ball, but you don't have to praise his insensible behavior. People such as Clay Sutherland are dangerous. No telling what effect they're going to have on us."

"Sorry, *Maman.*" Concerned, Laura noted her stepmother's heightened color. "I didn't mean to upset you."

"Riffraff such as he proves we must break our alliance with the United States." Roussel jabbed his finger through the air.

"We have no alliance," Laura returned dryly, tired of the ceaseless talking about a new French empire, "but our connection with the United States may well be severed if England wins the war."

"No!" Roussel declared, and vehemently added, "We are not Englishmen; we are French. We shall build a new French empire—"

"You're forgetting, Roussel, I was born an Englishwoman."

"Ah, but, *chérie,*" he corrected her, "you are one of us. Is not Celeste your *maman* now? You have learned to speak French and have embraced our culture. *Oui,* you are one of us."

"No, Roussel, I am Laura Elyse Talbot."

In all other areas but politics Laura could accept the genteel French society of New Orleans, but as an Englishwoman she had difficulty accepting their blind allegiance to Napoleon Bonaparte. Yet she said nothing. During the past seven years, since her father had married Celeste, she had learned that to argue was fruitless. This was not the first time Laura had skirted the issue.

"Forgive me, *ma chère.* I did not mean to imply otherwise." Giraumont's soft voice dripped with sarcasm. He twisted in the seat, again fiddling with his waistcoat. "Beau told me you were considering

44

hiring an overseer. Have you given it any more thought?"

"Yes," Laura answered, "but I've decided that it's not a step I wish to take at present, Roussel. I enjoy managing Ombres Azurées."

"Hardly a woman's job!" He snorted his disdain. "Your production would increase twofold if you would—"

"I know," Laura interrupted, "if I had a good man to run the plantation. Well, I'm a good woman, Roussel. This year we're going to see a threefold increase."

Her gentle laughter mocked Roussel. He squirmed more firmly into his corner and glared through the flickering light at her.

"Oh, Laura," Celeste softly moaned, "my head is hurting so."

Laura scooted around on the seat and began gently to massage Celeste's temple. "We'll be home soon, *Maman*, and Berthe will have your medicines ready."

The coach swayed as it turned onto the oak-lined road that led to Ombres Azurées. Laura was glad when they came to a lurching stop in the carriageway at the side of the two-story house. Because the family was to have spent the weekend in town, no lawn lanterns glowed in welcome, and only a dim light shone through a window in the servants' wing at the rear of the house. By the time Roussel and Laura disembarked, the door flew open and servants filed out. A black man, shotgun in hand, led the way. Following him was a young woman who held a lantern high in her hand, the pale light flickering in a circle around the two of them.

"Maîtresse Laura." Saloman took the lantern from

Jeanette and moved closer to the carriage, "you're back early."

"Maîtresse Celeste wasn't feeling well," she answered, "so we decided to come home early. Where's Berthe?"

A heavyset black woman rushed out of the house. Her brightly colored wrapper billowed to the sides as she moved. From beneath the rolls of her night *tignon* wisped snow-white curls. Berthe brushed Laura and Roussel aside and whisked Celeste upstairs toward her bedroom.

Uninvited, Roussel walked into the small private parlor to pour himself a whiskey. While Saloman attended the room downstairs, Jeanette scampered to Laura's bedroom ahead of her mistress to light the lamp and build a small fire to ward off the chill. As she entered, Laura tossed her hat and shawl onto the nearest chair and slipped off the gloves.

"Turn down the bed and lay out my nightgown and wrapper," she ordered. "I shall be back shortly. I'm going to check on Maîtresse Celeste, then say good night to M'sieur Roussel."

"*Oui*, mam'selle." The girl quietly moved around the room.

When Laura entered Celeste's bedroom, she found her stepmother lying in the middle of the huge four-poster, a cool moist cloth against her forehead. On the mantel, candles flickered dimly and incense burned to fill the room with a thick, spicy odor. After Berthe withdrew to the kitchen to prepare Celeste's medicine, Laura pulled the folds of the thick curtains partially closed to cut out any draft, and sat down.

"Can I get you anything?" she asked.

"No, Berthe will take care of me." Celeste smiled weakly and added, "Return to the parlor and visit with Roussel. I'm sure you have things which you

46

wish to discuss."

Laura's lips twitched as they brushed Celeste's cheek in a good-night kiss. Celeste was a dear but could be trying. Tonight was a prime example. Celeste was determined that Laura would accept Roussel Giraumont's proposal of marriage immediately. Already Celeste was planning the next great celebrating in New Orleans—Laura's engagement ball.

"Is this a migraine of convenience?"

Celeste chuckled softly and lifted a hand to cup Laura's cheek. "No, little one, it is not. But with all my heart, I should love to see you married with a family of your own. I am a matchmaker, no?"

"You are a matchmaker, yes," Laura answered.

When Berthe returned, she had changed clothes. Now she wore a voluminous apron stiff with starch over her guinea-blue dress, and her head was swathed in a red, blue, and yellow *tignon*. She set the silver tray on the large washstand to the left of the bed and poured a cup of the herbal tea which she handed to Celeste; then she moved to the other side of the bed. She extracted a large candle and a handful of small objects which she set on the small table.

"I'll check on you before I retire for the night," Laura promised Celeste as she stood to move out of the black woman's way.

"No need, *ma chérie*," Celeste murmured, "I shall be fast asleep. The *tisane* will take effect very soon."

The words ended in a sigh as Berthe's big hands settled on either side of Celeste's face and began to massage her forehead. Softly the black woman sang, the low, husky words a blending of French and African. Although Beau hated Berthe's incantations, Laura saw no harm in them when they eased her stepmother's headaches. Walking out of the room

47

and down the hall, Laura slowly descended the stairs.

No matter that Roussel was eighteen years older than she, both Celeste and Beau favored such a marriage. Roussel was descended from a proud Creole family, one of New Orleans's oldest. A marriage between them would unite two of the largest plantations in the entire state.

But this is what you've wanted for the last nine years, a tiny voice nagged. *Why are you dragging your feet? When you were jilted by George, you declared that you'd never let another man touch your heart. While Roussel would like to have your heart, he's wise enough to settle for your body and Ombres Azurées.*

Therein was the conflict. Laura loved Ombres Azurées, or Blue Shadows, as she preferred to call the Devranche sugar cane plantation, and had ever since she had met Celeste Devranche eight years earlier. A year later, when Celeste and Beau married, Celeste welcomed Laura into her home and heart and accepted her as the child she could never have.

Celeste groomed Laura to be well received by the small and closed society of the city by tutoring her in the Creole language and customs. Celeste also taught an eager Laura the duties and responsibilities of a plantation maîtresse. Laura loved being a member of the Creole aristocracy and mistress of the largest sugar cane plantation in Louisiana. She thoroughly enjoyed being feminine, having and wearing the latest clothes in vogue. But she could not tolerate spending endless days on the veranda, sipping mint juleps and embroidering.

Being an avaricious learner as well as an ambitious woman, Laura wanted to do more than gossip on the front porch and visit the slaves and tenant farmers and tend the sick; she wanted to be *the mistress* of the

48

entire plantation and sugar mill, to plan and oversee the planting and harvesting of crops and to experiment. In short, she wanted to be a gentleman farmer.

Beau, primarily interested in the Talbot Shipping Line, had been quite willing for this responsibility to fall on Laura's capable shoulders. And Celeste was most agreeable too; she found the job of managing the plantation disgusting and time-consuming. Laura's taking over allowed her more time to play hostess and to socialize with the plantation's many and frequent guests, the most frequent being Roussel Giraumont.

Oh, yes, marriage was in the workings, and for all the advantages of such an alliance, Laura shied away from the commitment. Marriage to Roussel Giraumont would mean her total acceptance into New Orleans society because she would then bear a French surname. And while she enjoyed being a member of the elite few, she also enjoyed having her own identity. And she was proud of her English heritage.

Marriage to Roussel would bring unwanted changes in her life. She knew he frowned on her great interest in agriculture technology, and she feared that once he became her husband he would demand she give up her managerial and administrative position. Already he was in conspiracy with Beau to hire a new overseer for Ombres Azurées. So far Laura had won. But there was always another day!

She entered the parlor, where Roussel lounged in front of the mantel, gazing into the fire and drinking his glass of whiskey.

"How is she?" he asked absently, not really caring.

"She'll be fine in a little while. Berthe is with her."

Roussel's face screwed into a grimace. "You know how Beau feels about that woman practicing her voodoo on Celeste."

49

"Berthe doesn't practice voodoo," Laura snapped, "and I wish you wouldn't accuse her of it."

Setting the glass on the mantel, Roussel turned and walked to where Laura stood in front of the love seat. He caught her hands in his and tugged. "Not tonight, Laura. Let's not quarrel over a slave or anything. I want us to talk about ourselves and our future."

"Roussel, please—" Laura pulled her hands free from his clasp. How smooth and soft his hands were in comparison to Clay Sutherland's. Clammy rather than warm. Greedy and grasping rather than firm and demanding. "It's late and I'm extremely tired. Let's talk about this another time."

"I want to talk about it now," Roussel exclaimed, barely able to keep a civil tongue. He jerked on the hem of his waistcoat. "I've asked you to marry me, Laura, and I want an answer. Neither of us is getting any younger, and I want a son to carry on my name."

But even more, you want a son so that he can inherit Ombres Azurées. Laura walked to the round reading table in the center of the room and posed behind one of the high-backed chairs.

Roussel followed. "I know I'm old enough to be your father, but I'll be a good husband to you, Laura. You'll have no cause to complain. Once our plantations are combined, we'll be the most powerful land owners in this entire state. We—"

"Roussel," Laura interrupted, gently pulling her nails over the damask upholstery. "I appreciate your proposal, but I want more time to think about this. I'm . . . not ready for . . . marriage."

Laura knew her father and Celeste were disappointed with her. They expected her to be grateful that someone like Roussel was proposing marriage

50

to her. How frequently they had pointed out to her that she was indeed fortunate that her grandmother was a countess; otherwise, the marriage would have been more difficult to arrange. Yet, Laura refused to think seriously about his proposal. If she ignored him long enough, she thought, perhaps he would go away.

"My God, Laura," Roussel exclaimed, "you're twenty-six years old, well past your prime. How much longer are you going to wait before you're ready?"

"Until I'm ready. Besides, Roussel, I'm worried about your gambling."

Roussel's hand balled into a fist. "That damned man," he muttered. "He had no right to do this to me."

"You did this to yourself, Roussel."

From the doorway Berthe announced, "Maîtresse Celeste is asleep, Miss Laura. And Jeanette has your bed ready and your nightclothes laid out."

"Don't you know better than to sneak into a room?" Roussel whirled around and shouted. His words were a snarl of hatred. "You ought to be beaten."

"Roussel! You may speak to your servants any way you choose, but you will not speak to mine in that tone of voice. Please go now. It's quite late. We'll continue our discussion another time. Saloman!" The servant materialized in the doorway. "M'sieur Giraumont is leaving."

Roussel opened his mouth, then looked at Berthe, who stood beside Saloman, her hands clasped in front. Her facial expression had not changed a jot since she first appeared in the door.

"All right, Laura. Another time." His wedge-heeled pumps clapped across the floor, and he yanked his hat from the black man.

Wearing a white organdy morning dress, Laura sat at the table in the small dining room and read her latest letter from Judith. The snow had already begun falling, her sister wrote, and the fields were covered in white. At the moment she was sitting in Charlotte's room in front of a blazing fire; her mother was sleeping. Sighing, Laura imagined an English winter—a winter she had not seen in nine years. Their mother, Judith went on to say, was increasingly dependent on pain-easing drugs, and not long ago she had broken the antique Chinese vase.

Laura lowered the letter and looked at a twin vase sitting on the mantel. Tears burned her eyes and blurred the beautiful piece of translucent porcelain with its delicate paintings. When she had left England with her father, she had taken one of the vases. The other she had left for Judith. She had always felt as if this had created a bond between them. Now Judith did not even have that.

Assailed with a homesickness such as she had not suffered since she left England, Laura refolded the letter and slid it into the envelope. Perhaps it was time for her to consider a holiday. Still, Laura hesitated. While Judith's letters to her were regular and newsy, their tone was polite rather than sisterly. Judith never asked about Beau, nor did she invite Laura for a visit. Nor did *Grandmère*. The old woman had never forgiven Laura for sailing to America with Beau.

Laura sighed and slipped the letter into her pocket. She poured a second cup of coffee and began to read the newspaper, looking up only when she heard the soft knock on the door. "Yes?"

"A M'sieur Clay Sutherland is here to see Maîtresse Celeste, mam'selle," said Saloman.

Clay Sutherland! Laura's heart skipped a beat and she lowered the paper to the table. Strange that he wanted to see Celeste. She wondered if her stepmother had run up a gambling debt with the man. "Did he say what he wanted?"

"No, ma'am."

Laura lifted the paper again, but the black print danced before her eyes. "Tell M'sieur Sutherland that Maîtresse Celeste is resting and is not to be disturbed. He may leave her a message if he wishes. I'll see that she receives it."

"Yes, ma'am."

Laura was so nervous, her insides were fluttering. Laying the paper aside, she walked to the window and stared at the back gardens, which were as lovely as the front, although much smaller. Knowing Clay Sutherland was here in the house disturbed her greatly. All too quickly she remembered the feel of his body pressed against hers, the rough sweetness of his lips.

Saloman returned. "Mam'selle, since M'sieur Sutherland cannot see Maîtresse Celeste, he would like to see you."

Laura lifted a finger and ran it down the cool pane. "Inform M'sieur Sutherland that I'm much too busy to receive visitors this morning."

"*Oui*, mam'selle." His expression never changing, the servant disappeared down the hall.

A moment later from the doorway she heard the deep resonant tones, "When would be a good time for me to come see you, Miss Talbot?"

Laura gasped and spun around to see Clay lounging indolently in the doorway, elegantly dressed, as he had been last evening when she first saw him in Dufaure's courtyard. So quiet was his appearance she could almost believe he materialized and disappeared at will. Today a black coat contrasted with gray trousers. He held his hat in his hand, riotous black curls framing a devilishly handsome face.

"You have audacity, M'sieur Sutherland." She composed her voice with greater ease than she did her nerves.

"I thought we were agreed on that last night," he mocked, brown eyes alight with laughter.

He leaned more fully against the door frame and stared at Laura, who was bathed in the fragile glow of morning light. Last night she had been lovely; today she was beautiful. The sun set her auburn hair on fire, and her green eyes, framed with long, dark lashes, sparkled with life and vitality.

"May I come in and talk with you a minute?"

"I run a sugar plantation, M'sieur Sutherland, and am extremely busy. I have no time for frivolous conversations, and since I have never gambled in your establishment, I know you're not here on business . . . if you know what I mean."

Clay reached into his pocket and extracted her fan. "I have to admit my business is more frivolity than business. I wanted to return this to you. Somehow, last night we forgot about it."

Laura was puzzled. "If you came to return this to me, why did you ask for my stepmother?"

The firm lips lifted in a dazzling smile. "Last night you seemed to be distressed because I was no gentleman. Today I wanted to prove to you that

54

although I'm not, I have manners."

Laura stepped forward to take her fan. "Thank you, M'sieur Sutherland. Now, if you'll excuse me. I must be going. Saloman, please order my gig to be hitched," she called.

Following the servant's faint *oui*, Clay asked, "Where are you going?"

Laura moved from behind the chair and gave Clay a cold glare. "That is absolutely none of your business."

Clay looked first at Laura's morning dress, sunlight gleaming in the window to silhouette her shapely legs through the thin material, then at her house slippers. He glanced at the newspaper on the table, and while his countenance was serious, his voice was underscored with gentle amusement.

"Are you going out attired in your morning dress?"

Laura glowered at him, despising the smile that tugged at his lips. "How I dress is also none of your business, m'sieur."

"I must disagree with you, mam'selle. Let me drive you, and we shall discuss the point at length. My gig is hitched and waiting."

Laura hesitated only momentarily, then said, "I'll be gone all morning, M'sieur Sutherland. I certainly don't intend to argue with you, and as we don't have any interests in common, I'm sure we don't have that much to talk about. And I wouldn't want to impose on you."

"You might be surprised to find out that we have many interests in common, Miss Talbot." He stepped fully into the room, his boots clicking against the hardwood floor as he moved to stand in front of the fireplace. "My gig and I are at

55

your disposal."

"M'sieur Sutherland—" Laura straightened her back and stepped away from the window, careful to keep the table between her and Clay. "I don't want either you or your gig. First, I own one of the newest and latest models of the English Stanhope gig, imported directly from the Continent. Second, when I want an escort, I shall find one who is worthy of me and my station in life. Now, if you'll excuse me, I have work to do."

On shaking legs Laura turned to walk out of the room, but Clay's long strides covered the distance to block her exit. Standing directly in front of her, his brown eyes smoldering with anger, he glared into her face. He stood so close, his breath splayed against her skin.

"I don't pretend to be a gentleman, Miss Talbot, and certainly I'm not one of your Creole aristocrats, but I am a person and as such I demand respect. You can stick your pretty little nose up in the air as much as you like and pretend that I don't exist, but deep down both of us know I do. We know that I affect you in exactly the same way that you affect me."

"If that's true—" Laura took courage in her anger. "Then you abhor me, M'sieur Sutherland. You take advantage of the innocent, luring them into your—"

"Ah, yes," Clay drawled, moving a step closer to her, drinking the sweet scent of her clean body. "I'm the devil, am I? Luring the innocent into my 'den of iniquity.' I believe that's the way you described the Golden Fleece. Did you bother to learn from the city officials that my casino is one of the most reputable in New Orleans? Do you know that I don't use rigged tables or loaded dice or marked cards? Do you know that I hire security personnel to police my establish-

56

ment and to protect my customers?"

Mesmerized, Laura stared into the indomitable face.

"No, Miss Talbot, you don't know any of these things; yet you point an accusing finger at me. You call me a lowlife without knowing anything about my life."

"M'sieur Sutherland," Laura said, extremely uncomfortable under the heat of his accusations, "leave now. You and I have nothing to say to each other."

"You may think you have nothing to say to me," Clay said, "but one of these days you'll realize you do. I knew the minute I saw you last night in Maurice Dufaure's courtyard that fate had put us together."

"I think greed more than fate is the reason you were at Maurice Dufaure's," Laura said mockingly.

"I was speaking of our meeting, Miss Talbot," Clay returned, "not my reason for having been at Dufaure's home. I know why I was there, and let me assure you, greed had nothing to do with it."

"No?" Laura questioned, feeling herself on firmer ground now. "You didn't threaten to take Roussel's home?"

"I never make threats. I came to collect money owed me. I was always taught that paying one's debts is good business. If one gambles and loses, one must be prepared to pay the consequences."

In the distance Laura heard a bell tinkle and knew Celeste had awakened and was calling for breakfast. "Thank you again for returning my fan," she said. "Now, I really have work to do, M'sieur Sutherland. Good day."

"Before I say good day, Miss Talbot," he murmured, his eyes lingering on the fiery curls that framed her face, "I would like to apologize for

57

last night."

Laura felt heat rush to her face. His nearness, coupled with the memory of their kiss, unsettled her. As they had done last night, her heartbeat accelerated and the blood rushed through her body quickly to make her head roar. "There's . . . really . . . there's no need."

"Oh, yes," he insisted, "there is." Without her being aware of the movement, Clay hooked his hat over the back of a nearby chair and moved closer to her. "Last night I left you with a bitter taste in your mouth. I kissed you merely to punish you for slapping me."

His fingers tweaked one of the silky curls, the callused tips brushing against the inflamed flesh at her temples. Laura wanted to dodge the touch; she knew she should but somehow her body, running truant, trembled beneath the caress. When Clay took another step, she backed up but found herself wedged between him and the table.

"I accept your apology," she said in a breathy little voice, her gaze irresistibly drawn to his mouth. Slightly parted, his lips were firm and generous, turning up at the corners in a perpetual smile. Visually tracing the shape of his mouth with her gaze and remembering it against hers, she wondered what it would feel like beneath her fingertips. Unconsciously, her tongue darted out to moisten her lips. He had not touched her, but already desire raged through her.

Clay moved that imperceptible few inches that brought their bodies together. He caught Laura into his arms to clamp her hands between them. His grip was strong enough to dissuade any resistance but gentle enough to send her senses whirling, sensual enough to set her afire with desire.

"Today I want to leave you with a sweet taste. I want to show you what a kiss of pleasure can be."

"No!" Laura twisted her head from side to side, dodging his face.

"I must, Laura." A hand fastened on her chin to hold her face still. "I can't have you entertain such lowly thoughts of me."

Soft laughter flowed over Laura as firm masculine lips tentatively touched hers. Had the kiss been as savage and brutal as the one the previous evening, she would have fought for honor and integrity. But his gentleness was her undoing. After a night of tossing and turning, of wondering what really being kissed by Clay Sutherland would be like, she abandoned all thoughts of honor and integrity and gave herself to the wonder of discovery. Again and again his mouth brushed lightly across hers.

Laura had often imagined what went on between a man and a woman, but she was totally unprepared for these feelings that Clay was stirring in her. Reason abandoned her; desire and instinct guided her actions now. She pressed herself closer to him, feeling his hardness through the thin layer of organdy. Her hands slid up his chest.

When Clay braced his neck, pulled his head back, and did not immediately meet her lips with his own, Laura's hands twined around the base of his head. Silently begging and unashamed of doing so, she pressed his lips closer to hers.

"Ah, yes, sweet," Clay murmured. "This is the way it should be between a man and a woman."

The last vestige of Laura's resistance fled when Clay's mouth captured hers, his firm touch sending a flash of heat through her body. Though still gentle and inquisitive, his kiss was steadily becoming demanding and proprietary and urgent. His mouth moved back and forth on her supple lips, the insistent tip of his tongue pressing along the indentation that marked the entrance into her mouth.

"This is wonderful," Clay mumbled, his lips moving against hers without releasing her, "but it can be so much more wonderful, Laura Elyse." His warm mouth glided up her cheek, his lips kissing her eyes shut.

"Please, Clay," Laura begged.

Clay bent to claim Laura's parted lips before she could close them on his name. His tongue penetrated the sweet moistness of her mouth to fill it with the essence of his kiss. Laura's lips opened beneath his as she fully received the caresses of his tongue. Freely she allowed herself to be carried into the wild, wonderful world that Clay Sutherland's touch created.

Laura moved her hips restlessly and moaned. Each movement of his tongue inside her mouth nudged and tugged at that secret place in her lower body. Caught up in desire, she responded intuitively. Her tongue tentatively touched his.

"So sweet," Clay murmured. His lips traveled over her cheek to her neck to leave a trail of hot kisses in their wake.

Though his lips on her neck were sending exquisite shivers over her body, she wanted his mouth on hers, his tongue touching hers. Laura moaned softly and arched against Clay. Turning her head, her mouth sought his.

Clay's hands banded around Laura's upper arms, and he set her away from him. She opened her eyes and blinked uncomprehendingly at him. Breathing deeply, he stared into the green passion-glazed eyes. Involuntarily, Laura swayed toward him.

"If we don't stop now," he murmured, "I won't be responsible for what happens next. I may not be a gentleman, but I'm not a seducer of the innocent. Neither do I intend to be seduced."

The words were like a splash of cold water in the face. Laura gasped and stumbled back from Clay. Last night had been excusable; this was not. She had allowed this man to walk into her home, into the intimacy of the family dining room, to take advantage of her. Humiliation raged through her. She lifted her hands to her swollen lips.

"Get out," she whispered, "before I have you whipped for the dog you are."

"If I'm a dog, Laura," Clay said with total disregard for her title and position, "what does that make you? A bitch?"

Laura's hand flashed out, but Clay caught it. "You slapped me once. Not again."

"Get out of my house, and don't ever darken my door again," Laura spat out. "I never want to see you again."

Clay stepped back and picked up his hat, settling it on his head as he walked away. When he reached the door, he stopped. His back to her, he said, "I owe you another apology, Laura. Last night I accused you of being an iceberg. You're not." He turned. "Underneath the icy trappings is a fiery woman begging for release. I would love to be the man to free her."

"Get out!" Laura clasped her hands together, barely hanging on to her composure.

After Clay left, Laura stood in a rage of anger and humiliation. Never had she been so used by a man before, so degraded. Not even George had done this to her. Bitter tears stung her eyes, and her hands shook. Never had she felt so empty and alone as she did when he stopped kissing her. The man would not be satisfied until he had totally destroyed her.

Laura raced through the house, wiping the tears from her cheeks as she ran. Standing in the window behind the gauzy curtains, she watched him climb into his gig and drive down the oak-lined avenue, leaving a cloud of dust in his wake.

Slowly, Laura turned and walked up the stairs to Celeste's room. The drapes were drawn, and sunlight streamed into the room. All the incense and candles were removed.

"Bonjour," she greeted Laura, lifting a cup of *café au lait.* "Come join me."

"No, thanks," Laura said, moving to the window on the other side of the room. "I just finished breakfast myself. How's your head?"

"Fine. I think I shall be up and about in a few hours. What are you planning to do today?"

"Mandy's grandson fell and hurt his leg yesterday. I'm going to see how he's doing."

"Laura, will you not consider the idea of an overseer?" Celeste set her tray aside and slipped out of bed, pulling her wrapper on.

Laura sighed and arched a brow. "You know how I feel about the running of Ombres Azurées."

"When, Laura, are you going to learn that there are certain privileges to being a woman?" Celeste waved her hand through the air. "You do not have to get out in the sun and work the plantation like a field slave."

"I like earning my privileges because I'm a person, not a woman. I like working the plantation. And I don't like Papa and Roussel conspiring behind my back to hire me an overseer."

"They have not conspired, *ma petite*. Roussel has recommended this M'sieur Donaldson, and your papa has asked that you consider him."

"I did. His previous employers spoke highly of him, and his qualifications were excellent, but I don't want to hire him at the present time."

Celeste threw her hands up in exasperation. "Oh, Laura, what are we going to do with you! You are such a stubborn child, determined to make yourself a place in a man's world. Running a plantation. Practicing with swords in Exchange Alley. Why could you not be content to embroider? It is so much more genteel and ladylike." After a moment she added, "I suppose you'll be going to practice your swords tonight?"

Laura laughed at her stepmother's turn of phrase. "Yes, if all goes well today, I will fence tonight."

"And I suppose that means you'll be spending the night in town?"

"If I should finish before the curfew, I'll return to Ombres Azurées. Otherwise, I'll stay at the town house." Laura leaned against the window casement and stared in the direction of the fields. After a few minutes in which Celeste fussed with her toilet, Laura said, "Today's going to be a long day. We start the planting."

"And soon the grinding."

"Soon the grinding." Laura warmed to her favorite subject. "I figure this year, Celeste, our grinding will last two months and will produce two hundred fifty thousand pounds of sugar."

"Very good," came the absent reply. The running of the plantation was not Celeste's favorite subject, and she spared it little thought and attention. Using two fingers, she gently massaged the muscles at the corners of her eyes. "Deeding the plantation to your father and turning its supervision over to you were two of my best decisions, I think. Because of you we have more than doubled our production."

"Tripled," Laura corrected her.

"You need not be so arrogant, *chère* Laura," Celeste chided gently.

"Not arrogant," Laura returned. "Just proud."

"And well you might be. Did I hear you talking with someone earlier?"

"Yes."

"Must I guess whom?" Celeste lifted the lid off the ivory powder box.

"Clay Sutherland," Laura muttered.

The large puff suspended in midair, Celeste's brows lifted in surprise. "What was he doing here?"

"He returned my fan. He found it in the courtyard, where I dropped it last night."

"M'sieur Sutherland is sweet on you, *chérie*, yes?" Celeste discreetly dabbed the powder on her face and laughed.

"It's not funny," Laura snapped.

"Of course not, but it is romantic, *oui?*"

Turning, Laura grinned. "You're an incurable romantic, Celeste."

"I am."

"I didn't think you liked Clay Sutherland. After all, he's an American and a gambler."

"He's an American, but in case you haven't noticed, *chérie*, I'm quite intrigued by foreigners. I married one. And I love gambling."

Laura laughed. "Clay Sutherland is nothing like Papa. He's contemptible."

"Perhaps you think so at the moment. But I'm not so sure. He has a good reputation. People like him."

"Not me. I hate him."

Celeste brushed the curls around her face for a few minutes, then said, "That is a dangerous sign, Laura. It sounds to me as if you might be falling in love with the man."

Laura spun around to gaze in puzzlement at her stepmother. "Whatever do you mean?"

"Clay Sutherland reminds me very much of your father when I first met him. Rather a rogue. A very attractive rogue. Perhaps like Beau, Clay is nursing a great loss." Celeste laid the brush down and stared unseeing into the mirror. "I don't know what I would have done, *chérie,* had I not met your papa." She hesitated briefly. "Had he not come along, everything I had would have been lost. He has been so good to me."

"You've been good for him," Laura said softly.

Celeste turned around and large tears rolled down her cheeks. "But I do not know if your father has gotten over his love for your mother or not. Always I am plagued by doubt. Because they are divorced, he and I are not married in the eyes of the church. Always I wonder if one day he will return to England to her. She is so beautiful."

Laura rushed across the room and took Celeste into her arms. "Papa loves you," she said. "You're the only woman in his life. He and Charlotte were not in love with each other; their marriage was arranged. He never loved until he met you."

"At first we did not love," Celeste said. "We married for convenience. Both of us wanted Ombres Azurées. He was willing to pay my debts, and I was willing to marry out of the church."

"But you love each other now."

"I love him." Celeste hugged her stepdaughter tightly. Then she pushed away and wiped the tears from her eyes. "Be careful, *chère* Laura. You and I are both victims of the society we embrace. As long as you are discreet, you may have your lovers, but you must make a good marriage. You must marry Roussel Giraumont, *oui?*"

Berthe knocked on the door. "Maîtresse Celeste, you rang for me."

"Yes." Celeste stared at Laura. "I'm ready to get dressed." In a lower voice she repeated, *"Oui?"*

Closing her eyes, Laura recalled Clay Sutherland's soft, mocking laughter and the feel of his hard body pressed against hers.

Chapter Three

Laura and a young black man in his mid-twenties stood beneath the shade of a huge oak tree. Tall and slender, the man's body was sheer whipcord. Their gazes swept over the field in front of them. It was plowed into six-foot-wide rows. Oversize flatbed wagons loaded with planting stalks stood at intervals along the borders.

The afternoon breeze caught Laura's veil and blew it across her face. She tucked it into the band of the straw hat. She was pleased because the production of her workers had tripled since she implemented the three-quarter watches—a nautical expression she had learned from Beau. Every six hours the watches relieved each other. Quickly, Ombres Azurées had gained the reputation of being the most productive sugar cane plantation around New Orleans.

"How is the planting, Joshua?"

The young man pulled his hat lower to shield his face from the glare of the sun. "We have three crops of cane to harvest, Maîtresse, and two to plant—one in cover crop, the other in cane."

Laura was thrilled. "Barely enough time to get the new cane planted before we start grinding."

"But we can do it, Maîtresse. I promise you."

Laura smiled. "I know all of you can, Joshua."

Joshua moved slightly, his gaze running down the lines of workers in the field. "M'sieur Talbot said you were thinking about hiring an overseer, Maîtresse."

Laura sensed the slave's uneasiness and understood it. Overseers had a reputation of being cruel and inhuman. "No," she assured him, "I'm not. I'm quite happy with the way you're supervising the field workers. And I'm not ready to give up my overseeing position." She reached up to lower the veil over her face once again. "Now, let's get to work. We have a lot to do before the day is over."

The elegant carriage stopped in front of one of the many three-story buildings along Exchange Alley. A young footman clad in the tan livery of Ombres Azurées, leapt from the back of the carriage, raced to the door, and dropped the stepping stool in place.

"*La salle d'armes de* Maître Herbert Fortier," he sang out, and swung open the door.

The hood of the thick velvet cape shielded Laura's face as she disembarked. From open windows she heard the rasping of the swords and impassioned cries of the spectators—a group of dandies who lounged in the salons, sipping coffee and liqueurs and hissing or applauding the youngbloods.

The day had been long, and Laura was exhausted. But the very atmosphere of the salon revived her. Her blood began to race through her veins; her heart pounded quickly with excitement. She enjoyed fencing because it was a game of control and skill, one at which she excelled.

Jeanette, a portmanteau in one hand, followed her mistress into the house and up the dim stairs into one of the rooms, adjoining the large *salle*. "Oh, Maîtresse," she murmured when they were closeted in the small dressing area, "could you not have found another sport to teach you grace and keep you agile? One that is not so bloody."

"*Oui*." The hunter-green cape rippled through the air as Laura hung it on the nearest rack. "But none that I enjoy more. And none in which I can better a man. Do you notice how many spectators are here tonight?"

"Oh, Maîtresse," Jeanette scoffed, "that is not for you to be proud of. Every Friday night the crowd and the wagers grow. Men coming to see a woman fence, and they see you in this—this white jacket and breeches that only men wear. Why, they show every line of your figure." She yanked the white canvas garments out of the portmanteau and shook them in the air.

"They can see women anytime they wish," Laura answered pensively, moving so that she could study her reflection in the full-length mirror standing against the wall. She coiled her hair and pinned it atop her head. "New Orleans has more than its share of beautiful women. But when people come here to the *salle d'armes*, Jeanette, they don't come to see a woman, they come to see my skills as a swordsman."

"*Mais non*, Maîtresse, *mais non*." Jeanette shook her head vigorously. "They come to see the man who can whip you. They wait for the day when you must grovel at some man's feet. Then they will laugh."

"Perhaps you're right," Laura conceded. "So I'll just have to practice harder to make sure that day doesn't arrive, won't I?"

"With your attitude, you're going to find yourself fighting a real duel one of these days. And that will be quite nasty, Maîtresse."

Laura laughed. "Probably so."

"Oh, Maîtresse, you take me too lightly!" Jeanette shook her head helplessly.

Minutes later Laura, clad in the white canvas uniform and pulling a chamois gauntlet onto her left hand, walked out of the dressing area into the *salle*. When she heard the round of applause that drowned out the hisses and boos, she smiled and her adrenaline flowed. Taking her mask from Jeanette, she tucked it under her right arm and held her foil loosely but firmly in her left hand. Although Maître Fortier was nowhere to be seen, the judge, speaking in French, called her to the *piste* and she took her place to the left of him.

The applause dribbled into silence that was immediately followed by a rush of whispers. Stunned speechless, Laura watched Clay Sutherland step behind the vacant guard line. She was only vaguely aware of the seconds who positioned themselves on either side of her and Clay.

"We meet again, Mademoiselle Talbot," Clay murmured.

"Where is Maître Fortier?" Laura rubbed a clammy palm down the side of her breeches. Suddenly, the heavily padded outfit she wore was suffocating.

"Unavoidably detained," Clay returned smoothly. "He asked me to stand in for him."

"No," Laura whispered, "I shan't fence with you."

Clay shrugged. "Whatever you say, ma'am."

"You're not my *maître d'armes*."

"Absolutely not."

"I don't have to fence with you."

Clay laughed softly and shook his head. "Of course not."

Laura's eyes swept over the crowd pressing closer.

70

Their faces were flushed with eager anticipation; money flying through the air as new—higher— wagers were laid.

"Don't worry about them, ma'am," Clay softly admonished. "Whatever you wish is my wish."

"You're lying!" Laura seethed between clenched teeth. "You did this deliberately."

"I'm not lying, and yes, I did do this deliberately. I wanted to see you again. I've sent you note after note during the past three weeks, and you've returned all of them unopened."

"Evidently, you don't take no for an answer, M'sieur Sutherland."

"I could take no as an answer, Miss Talbot, but I absolutely refuse to be ignored."

The judge asked briskly in heavily accented English, "Are you fencing tonight, M'sieur Sutherland?"

"I am, sir. I don't know about the lady."

Laura glared into the laughing brown eyes for a long while before she answered in French, her voice loud and clear, "*Oui*, M'sieur, I am fencing."

Pointedly ignoring Laura, the judge again addressed himself to Clay. "Four touches, since you are fencing with mam'selle, m'sieur?"

"Five touches, since I am fencing with m'sieur," Laura returned in French, fiery anger running through her when Clay's lips twitched sardonic laughter.

The judge looked from Laura to Clay.

"If that's what mam'selle wants." Clay's gaze moved to the swell of her breasts beneath the padded white canvas vest. "The more touches I can get, the better I like the game."

As if he had touched her flesh, Laura trembled. She wanted to run. Everything in her screamed for her to

71

get away from this man. Her eyes darted toward the dressing room door; Clay followed her gaze.

"I would only come after you," he said, the words loud enough for her ears alone. "The world isn't big enough for you to escape me, Laura Elyse Talbot. Wherever you go, I'll find you."

"Why me?" Laura asked.

"You're a challenge," Clay answered.

"Nothing more?" Laura was surprised to hear herself ask. She was even more surprised to find that she was eagerly awaiting his answer.

"Not now—" The tip of his tongue moistened the full, firm lips, and his eyes, sultry brown lust, moved down, then up the length of her body. His gaze lingered on her breasts. "But later you will be. I promise."

"You shouldn't make promises you're unable to keep," Laura snapped, her reply short and breathless. Her heart was beating so loudly she wondered if everyone in the *salle* could hear it.

"As I told you before, Miss Talbot, I don't. I'm a man of my word."

Impatiently, the judge's head swung from one to the other. "Five touches."

"*Oui*," Clay answered, "five touches . . . for now."

Laura snapped to attention, flexing her left arm at the elbow and bringing the bell of the foil to her mouth. Her eyes ablaze with anger, she honored her second, the judge, then Clay Sutherland. In salute the foil sang through the air and snapped. The judge's foil dipped into the center between them.

Slipping the foil underneath her right arm, Laura caught the bib of her helmet with her thumb and slipped it over her face, the tongue to the back. Masked, she and Clay crossed foils over the judge's foil. Then she was staring through the cage of silver

72

mesh into dark, sultry eyes.

"En garde."

As Laura dropped into position, the judge's words echoed the cry of her heart. Although it was a cool day in early October, she felt sweat course down the indentation of her spine. The ping of metal sounded through the hall as foil hit foil. Laura lunged, lifting and kicking out the forward foot and simultaneously straightening the rear leg. At the same time that both legs moved, she flung her right arm backward and adduced.

Surprised at her strength and grace, Clay retreated from the attack. Laura recovered forward, the bell of her foil right over her heart. Even through the mesh Laura could see Clay's crooked smile as he deftly rolled the bell and parried her attack.

Clay feinted. Laura parried. She should not have. She had exposed her heart. Clay evaded the blade and disengaged to an open line. He extended his foil arm toward her chest and lunged. Through the thickness of the padded material that covered her chest, Laura felt the point.

She stepped back into position. *"Touché."* She saluted and dropped her point.

Six minutes stretched into fifteen, Laura and Clay each having four hits. He admired her ability to fence. She was skillful and composed . . . and composed won in fencing.

Attack. Parry. Riposte. The clashing of metal rang through the *salle;* the dandies held their breath, speaking only to raise their wagers and then softly so as not to break the spell that bound the fencers.

Laura's left arm ached; the muscles in her thighs burned and quivered. The bib was suffocating around her throat. Perspiration drenched her hair and ran down her neck.

73

Yet she found her tiredness to be an advantage. The more exhausted she became, the more controlled her motions, because she did not want to overextend. She had nothing with which to overextend. Her parries became more controlled, smaller, more subtle.

Always her thigh muscles burned!

Then she had an adrenaline rush. She took a deep breath, the intoxication going to her brain. All of a sudden everything was working smoothly. She was so fluid, so powerful, so correct. Confidence surged through Laura, and she knew no one could beat her. The foil sang through the air, the point landing on Clay's chest.

"*Touché*. You win, Miss Talbot." Laughter underlined his words. "You've hit me directly in the heart."

The applause was deafening, lingering, but Laura did not hear it. She was drunk on her victory. Pulling off her mask, she stared through the silvery mesh that covered Clay's face into golden-brown eyes and smiled. "No, M'sieur Sutherland, I've hit you where your heart would be, had you one. Now I must bid you *adieu*." She turned, and head held high, she marched into the dressing room.

Laura lifted her face and welcomed the cold water that Jeanette sluiced over her head and shoulders. Stepping out the tub when she had finished bathing, she hurriedly dried off and redressed. When at last she had covered herself in the swirling fold of the cape, she and Jeanette slipped through the crowd, down the narrow stairs, into the street. In the distance she heard the muted chanting and saw the arch of a large bonfire in the blackened sky.

"May I drive you home, Miss Talbot?"

Laura saw the lucifer flame into life seconds before Clay pushed away from the building. Illuminated in the brilliant burst of light was the bottom part of his face; the brim of his hat shaded the upper.

"No, thank you, M'sieur Sutherland," she returned. Her head moved imperceptibly beneath the billowing hood as she looked for her carriage. Out of the corner of her eye she saw Jeanette glowering her disapproval. "I always see to my own transportation."

"Roussel Giraumont?" Clay asked.

"No," Laura returned a little more curtly than she intended. "M'sieur Giraumont had an important business meeting tonight. That's why he didn't accompany me to my fencing lesson."

"M'sieur Giraumont is a busy man," Clay said dryly.

Not liking Clay's insinuation, Laura lifted her chin and turned her face away from him.

"If I were engaged to a woman like you, Laura Elyse, I wouldn't let you run up and down the back streets of New Orleans unescorted." He moved closer to her, his voice lowering to a seductive murmur. "I would find every excuse I could to be by your side day . . . and night."

"M'sieur Sutherland"—Laura stepped away, the velvet cape brushing against Clay's boots—"although it is none of your business, I am not yet engaged to Roussel."

Clay hiked a mocking brow. "That's not what M'sieur Giraumont is saying."

"Then, M'sieur Sutherland, you must decide which one of us you believe."

"That's no choice. I always choose to believe the woman."

"Then you should know that I am my own woman; I don't need a keeper. I go where I please when I please. As you acknowledged the night of

M'sieur Dufaure's autumn ball, I oversee my own plantation, sir."

"But according to rumor, even that is changing, Miss Talbot. I hear that you're considering Leroy Donaldson as the next overseer for Ombres Azurées."

Laura bristled. "This is rumor, M'sieur Sutherland, and nothing more. But I would like to know who told you?"

Clay shrugged. "So many come and go in the Golden Fleece, it's difficult to say."

A carriage rattled down the street, and three women, broad smiles curving their painted faces, waved through the windows. One of them called, "Clay, *mon chère*, come to Bayou Saint-Jean. We will have fun tonight, *non?* Jena Benoit, she will be there."

When Clay smiled and waved at the woman, Laura felt a slight tinge of jealousy. "You attend the voodoo rituals on Bayou St. John?" Her voice lifted in condemnation.

Returning his attention to Laura, Clay grinned. "Not regularly. I've been a time or two. Have you ever seen one?"

"They're of the devil!" Laura spat the words.

The tip of Clay's cigar glowed against his sun-browned skin. He blew the smoke out. "Have you ever seen one?"

"No." Her palms were clammy with fear.

"I've noticed, Laura"—he reverted to the familiar use of her given name—"that you have a tendency to condemn and judge."

Laura drew herself up. "I have the right to my own opinion, *M'sieur Sutherland.*"

"You do, but don't you think it would be wise of you to gather facts and study them before you shout your conclusion to the world."

"You're referring to my opinion of voodoo rituals?" Laura parried.

"That, and to your condemning me and my establishment before you knew anything about me or it. You referred to me as a devil, it as the den of iniquity."

Laura saw her carriage turn onto Exchange Alley. "Perhaps one night I shall go to the Golden Fleece, M'sieur Sutherland, and give you the opportunity to change my mind."

Jeanette moved closer to Laura. "Come, Maîtresse," she said. "It is time for us to be leaving. Maîtresse Celeste will be expecting us."

"I don't know that you really want to come to my place." Clay looked over the servant's head. "You stand a chance of melting and becoming a woman if you do."

"I am one already," Laura quietly replied, "and I don't have to prove it to you or to anyone. Your conceit in your ability to arouse my emotions doesn't provoke my interest in you at all. I'm totally immune to your virility and charm, M'sieur Sutherland."

Jeanette gasped in dismay and tugged on Laura's arm all the harder. She raced to the carriage as soon as the footman opened the door. But Laura did not move; her gaze was riveted to Clay.

He laughed, the sound low and rich, the tones wrapping themselves around Laura. "If you're totally immune to my . . . er *virility and charm,* Miss Talbot, why not spend the evening with me? Why not come back to the Golden Fleece and see firsthand what a den of iniquity looks like? Come see Lucifer in his true surroundings."

His laughter and softness drew Laura to him. Briefly, she considered his request . . . then she drew back. Giraumont frequented the Golden Fleece; she

77

had no desire to see him. She wanted no impassioned promises from him once she discovered him with his mistress. At the moment it suited her for Roussel's sexual appetites to be filled elsewhere. Nor did Laura wish any of her acquaintances to see her with Clay Sutherland at his gambling casino.

"No," she said, surprised and angry at the soft, breathless tone. She took a step toward the carriage.

"Are you frightened?" Clay followed her.

Eventually, she said, "I'm . . . not dressed to go out. My hair is wet."

A large, callused hand closed around the drawstrings at her neck and gently tugged her closer. "You're well hidden."

Laura's heart pounded against her rib cage. His breath was a blending of tobacco and whiskey, a warmth oozing over her face and neck. Through the thickness of her cape she felt the pressure of his hand on her chest, his arm grazing the tips of her breasts. In the very pit of her stomach she felt the stirring of desire—exciting and wonderful but frightening and dangerous.

"But you're afraid to go, are you not? Of me and of the voodoo?"

"Surely by now, M'sieur Sutherland, you should know that I am not so easily frightened."

Laura was more than frightened; she was terrified. But this was an opportunity she would not let pass her by. Because she had been bored and needed excitement in her life, she had taken up fencing— much against her parents' approval. Now she had met a man who stirred up emotions in the core of her being, a man whose proximity sent her blood soaring. She would not let him go. She would prove to Clay Sutherland before this night was over that he had underestimated his adversary.

78

"I'd like to spend the evening with you, m'sieur."

Jeanette gasped. "Maîtresse Laura," the maid pleaded, "please, let's return to Ombres Azurées."

A sardonic smile lifted the corners of Clay's mouth. "I'm going to Bayou St. John."

"I figured you were when your . . . friends extended their invitation. May I come with you?" she asked.

"*Mon Dieu!*" Jeanette gasped. Maître Talbot would have her beaten if she allowed Laura to go to Bayou St. John. She scampered out of the carriage. "You can't, Maîtresse. You can't."

Curious, Clay returned to where Laura stood. He reached up and flipped the hood from her head and stared into her upturned face. "You won't come to the Golden Fleece with me but you'll go to a voodoo ritual?"

Exhilaration running through her veins, Laura nodded her head. "I've never been," she explained. "I've lived here for nine years, and I've never seen a voodoo ritual."

"They can be frightening."

"Are you afraid?" she asked.

"No, but I don't take it lightly either."

"I'm not afraid." Laura shook off Jeanette's tugging hand. "Return to the carriage and wait for me." Reluctantly, the girl departed.

"I know." Clay stroked her hair away from her cheeks. "That concerns me."

"Because I'm a woman and you're a man."

"No"—he laid his palm against her cheek—"that pleases me."

"Take me with you," Laura begged. "I want to see it myself."

"The Golden Fleece is safer," he argued.

"I don't want safety," Laura returned, not the least

79

perturbed at her temporary loss of propriety. Sanity, she thought, was much like her fencing mask—it could be put on and taken off when needed. For the first time in her life she was rebelling against the shackles of society; sweet and heady were the results.

Clay leaned down and touched his lips to Laura's. When her mouth moved beneath his, he lifted his head and breathed in deeply. "You'd better go home, Miss Talbot. I allowed you to win the bout, but—"

"You *allowed* me to win the bout!"

"I allowed you to save face in front of your Creole dandies," he continued, totally ignoring her outburst, "but I won't be so chivalrous again. If you go with me to Bayou St. John, you're responsible for the consequences."

As surely as if he'd slapped her face, Clay Sutherland had issued Laura a challenge, one she would not refuse. "No matter what you say, M'sieur Sutherland, I won the bout. I have no worries about accompanying you to Bayou St. John. When the evening is over, I shall return home with Telfour and Jeanette. The sooner you learn that you are of no consequence to me, the better it will be for all concerned."

Chapter Four

The bright orange flames of the bonfire leapt into the night-darkened sky to silhouette a sleek black male dancer. Clad only in cut-off trousers, his thickly muscular body moved in rhythm to the frenzied beat of the drums. A red satin sash tied about his waist swirled through the air. He threw back his head and chanted in an African dialect; the veins on his neck strutted. Rivulets of perspiration ran down his cheeks, down the powerful neck onto the broad, muscle-corded chest. A mulatto stood on the sidelines, a smile on her beautiful face. Her golden-brown skin glimmered in the golden light of the fire, and a huge snake coiled around her upper body.

The crowd, caught up in the music and almost in a trance themselves, hummed low and pressed closer in on Clay and Laura as they tightened the circle around the ritual dancers.

Clay heard Laura humming and looked down to see her eyes closed, her head thrown back. His hand tightened around her wrist and he tugged her closer to his side. Priests and priestesses moved through the crowd, plying the spectators with plenty of taffia. Those who were not mesmerized were drunk.

Thoroughly enthralled with the spectacle, Laura freely imbibed the brew.

The drum stopped; the humming changed into words. Feet were tapping on the hardened earth. Then from a dark corner there came suddenly the soft throbbing of another drum, a different tone, a different rhythm. Boom. Boom . . . boom . . . boom . . . Boom. Boom . . . boom . . . boom . . . The effect was hypnotic. The humming became louder, more pronounced but wordless again.

"Would you care for another, mam'selle?" a young woman asked, reaching out to lay a gentle hand on Laura's shoulder.

Laura's eyes flew open and she stared into the face of the priestess. The black woman would have been pretty had it not been for the deep smallpox scars on her face; she wore a blue wrapper and was barefoot; a white cloth was tied around her head.

"One more." Laura said as she held her cup toward the gourd dipper.

"You've had enough." Clay's hand clamped around her wrist and he emptied the taffia on the ground. "You'll soon be drunk."

"What better way to get drunk"—Laura giggled, snatching a container of taffia from yet another set of hands—"than on sugar cane juice and rum. I must see that my product has a market."

Clay grabbed the gourd and tossed it to the ground. "I mean it, Laura. Don't drink any more of this stuff."

"No one tells me what I can or can't do!" Laura pulled away from him and backed up. She pushed the hood off her face and her eyes sparkled defiantly. "If I want to drink taffia, I will."

"It's high time someone took you in hand." Clay caught her wrist again in a viselike grip and hauled her to his side. "Don't you dare move."

The mulatto who had been standing in the shadows stood and walked closer to the circle of light. The crowd went wild with adulation. A red calico dress covered her tall, slender form to accent round breasts and supple, firm buttocks. Gleaming black hair was pulled into a chignon atop her head. Large gold hoop earrings brushed against her cheeks. Cosmetics enhanced the natural beauty of her face. She was one of the most exotic women Laura had ever seen.

"Who is she?" Laura whispered.

"Jena Benoit."

"The voodoo queen?"

"Yes."

The male dancer's chest heaved as he dragged air into his lungs and collapsed to the ground at Jena's feet. He crawled closer and kissed the tips of her toes; then he looked up into her face. The drums lulled into a softened beat, and Jena gazed down at him. She ran her tongue around her parted lips. A murmur of excitement ran through the crowd. Then Jena turned her head to gaze through the crowd. Lifting a hand, she beckoned. Two men pushed into the center of the circle to cast a frightened girl about seventeen at Jena's feet. The voodoo queen stared at her for a few minutes before she turned and walked to the edge of the crowd. When she nodded her head, the drums began their frenzied beating again.

A hush fell upon the throng, and like the waters of the Red Sea, they fell aside to allow a tall black man passageway. A red satin cape billowed around him. When he stood over the girl, she cowered from him. He flashed her a brilliant smile and unfastened his cape, the material richly swirling through the air. In fluid motion he bent down and clasped the girl's hands in his, pulling her to her feet. She tried to pull away from him, but he held her fast, forcing her to look into his eyes. He talked to her, and finally her lips began to move in answer. The tempo of the music increased as other instruments joined the drums.

A smile suddenly exploded on the girl's face, and she pulled away from the male dancer. She tossed her head, a mane of black hair cascading down her back, and cupped the swell of her breasts with her hands. Smooth cinnamon flesh mounded above the low-necked blouse. Her palms glided down her midriff to her waist . . . to her hips. Her fears were gone now; her eyes were wide and glazed. She was one with the man, both an integral part of the ritual. Dancing around her, he unbuttoned his shirt, tugged it free of his trousers, and shrugged out of it.

The white material floated to his feet, and soon both he and the girl were stamping it into the dirt. He caught her in his arms and twirled her around, their bodies coming so close yet never touching. They dipped and swayed; they twirled through the air. Their arms and legs moved in synchronized beauty.

She slipped to the ground, and he backed away from her. Long slender fingers went to the buttons on his trouser placket; soon the gray broadcloth fell down his legs. He was clothed only in tight short trousers, and a red handkerchief was tied around his neck. The tempo of the drums intensified; loud chanting filled the air. Caught up in the frenzy of worship, the young female moved closer to him, her mouth parting seductively. She moistened her lips with her tongue and arched her back to thrust out her swollen and strutted breasts. Nimble fingers unfastened her blouse and threw it aside; they unbuttoned her chemise to reveal full golden-brown breasts. The crowd gasped its pleasure.

"Oh, my God," Laura murmured. She had never witnessed anything so animalistic, so primeval, in her entire life.

"Let's get out of here." Clay's hand tightened around Laura's waist as he turned and pushed aside the ranks of suffocating humanity.

"No, I don't want to leave." Laura clawed at Clay's hand, and, freeing herself, darted back into the crowd.

Clay pursued, but the people closed around Laura quicker than he could follow. When he finally reached her, she was drinking yet another container of taffia and staring at the black couple in the center of the circle.

As Jena Benoit moved toward the male dancer, he backed away, clapping his hands and chanting. His naked, sweat-moistened flesh gleamed in the firelight. Closer and closer Jena came to the girl. Finally, she draped the snake around her shoulders. Rudely jarred from her trance, the girl's face whitened visibly. She staggered backward. As the serpent hissed and wrapped itself around her, she fainted and fell to the ground. Jena bent to retrieve her snake while a priestess threw a bucket of cold water on the girl. When she regained consciousness, she was handed a cup of potion from the boiling cauldron on the fire.

"No!" The girl shoved the container aside, some of the blackish liquid spilling to the ground.

"You will drink." Jena Benoit's voice was low and sultry.

Clay's fingers bit through the cape into Laura's shoulder. "For God's sake, let's get out of here, Laura. Your father's going to be turning New Orleans upside down to find you."

Laughing, Laura tossed the empty gourd to the ground, then shoved the hood from her head. Firelight glinted off tight auburn curls that wisped around her face. "Beau Talbot is more concerned about my reputation than about me," she slurred, "but he won't be turning New Orleans upside down hunting me. He's at the town house working on his figures for Talbot Shipping Line." Laura pressed her index finger against Clay's chest. "That's Beau Talbot's love."

"Laura, let's go."

Laura turned into Clay's arms and rested her cheek against his chest. She listened to the regular cadence of his heartbeat. "What's your love, Clay?" she finally asked, then said before he could speak, "You don't have a love, do you?"

"This isn't the time or place to be talking about love."

Again Laura laughed. "What about lust, M'sieur Clay Sutherland? I'll wager you've lusted after many women in your life, haven't you?"

"This time I give you warning." Jena Benoit's sultry voice quieted the crowd, and she moved closer to Clay. Although she spoke to the naked girl who sprawled on the ground, the mulatto's eyes blazed at Laura. "Never touch a man that Jena Benoit has claimed as her own. The next time I shall not save you."

Inebriation dulled Laura's senses but did not keep her from knowing that the woman was talking directly to her about Clay. A shiver slid down her spine, and she wanted to snuggle more closely to Clay. But she had never cowered behind another human being; she was not going to start now. She pushed away from Clay, her green eyes staring unflinchingly into the black ones.

86

"Come on." Clay swung Laura into his arms. "Let's go home."

"Yes," Laura whispered, and pressed her cheek against his chest. She closed her eyes. Clay made her feel safe. "Let's go home."

Laura yawned and stretched, her slippers brushing against the satin sheets. When she realized she was fully clothed and in a strange room . . . in a strange bed . . . she opened her eyes to gaze at the canopied top. For a moment she wondered where she was, then she turned her face to see the thick brushes on the dresser. A green cravat lay in a tumbled heap next to several tall bottles of hair tonic and perfume.

She remembered and smiled and stretched. The room was warm and inviting. A fire had been laid in the hearth; golden shadows danced around the strange room. The furniture was bold and masculine. On the back of one chair hung her cloak. On another hung a wine-colored robe; slippers rested beneath it. On the nearby table was a japanned cigar box. Laura saw the lucifers and remembered Clay. Her head turned so that her gaze fastened on the blazing fire.

If he were indeed Lucifer, this was hell—his domain. If this were hell, it was warm and beautiful. Then, weary of thinking, she closed her eyes. Her senses still numbed from alcohol, she curled into the comfort of the mattress and sought refuge in the oblivion of sleep. She cared not that she had not undressed for the night or that she was not home safely tucked into bed. Minutes later she awakened, previous thoughts forgotten, disoriented all over again.

In a remote part of her brain she knew something was wrong, but her thinking was too fuzzy for her to be concerned with it at the moment. She was exhausted—she had won a bout against . . . against . . . She yawned; she was so sleepy. She sniffed the coffee and sighed. Berthe made the best coffee in all of Louisiana.

Minutes passed—perhaps years—before Laura heard the door open. China dishes rattled on a metal tray. Coffee—she knew it was coffee because she could smell it—splashed into a cup. Firm steps crossed over the Oriental rugs.

"Are you awake?" From far away Laura heard a man's voice.

Lucifer! Lord of hell. Was he offering her pomegranate to lure her into his world forever?

"Laura, are you awake?"

She smiled and nodded her head, her cheek brushing against the satin pillowcase. She liked Clay Sutherland; she should not but did. His presence caused a peculiar feeling in her—a tightening in the chest, a warmth when he smiled or spoke to her, a hurting in the very pit of her stomach.

"Then, ma'am—" Amusement laced his voice. A knee pushed into the mattress, and strong hands caught her shoulders and whisked her up, plopping pillows behind her back. "It's time for you to be up. How about a cup of strong black coffee?"

Not a pomegranate. Simply coffee.

Disappointed, Laura blinked into Clay's face. He was so close to her that she could smell that familiar herbal cologne he wore. His touch was a fire starter that ignited a blaze of desire through her entire body. She was aflame with wanting and yearning. Her gaze lowered, and she saw the crisp dark hair in the open neck of his shirt. Her cheeks flushing, she quickly averted her eyes. She wanted to stare longer, to drink her fill of his masculinity, but to stare at his nakedness was most unladylike. To keep from reaching out to touch him, she dug her fingers into the sheet.

"Sugar, please."

Riotous auburn curls tangled around Laura's face; her eyes were crystal-green pools of seduction. Clay moved his hands from her shoulders and pushed himself off the bed.

"Black." Clay moved to the tray.

When he handed her the cup, their fingers touched and for a moment the world stood still around them. Huge green eyes gazed spellbound into warm brown ones. Sweeping her conscience out of the way, Laura laid her hand over his. She wanted Clay Sutherland, and she was going to have him. Gazing at him with those wide, innocent eyes, she asked, "What if I want more than coffee, Clay?"

His eyes darkened and he breathed deeply as he pulled his hand from beneath hers. "Drink the coffee, Laura. You're drunk and don't know what you're saying."

Laura set the cup on the night table and crawled to the edge of the bed, pushing up on her knees. "I'm drunk, and I know what I'm saying. I want you to make love to me, Clay."

"For God's sake, Laura"—his voice was gruff—"drink the coffee and sober up so I can take you home."

He turned and walked to the huge dresser across the room, where he picked up a cigar and lit it. Smoke swirled around him as he looked into the mirror to see Laura slip off the bed. Above the low, scooping neckline, he saw the gold-shot jade phoenix cradled in the swell of creamy satin breasts. A lamp to her back reflected through the thin muslin

89

dress she wore. The gauzy material hinted at long shapely legs and rounded hips; it hinted at the beauty and warmth at the juncture of her thighs and hips.

A woman can have a lover as long as she's discreet, Laura thought hazily, her goal stated, her resolve firm. Celeste had told her so. Laura wanted Clay Sutherland as her lover. She had been attracted to men before and had wondered what it would be like to make love to them. But no man had ever stirred her body and soul like Clay Sutherland had done . . . was doing. Even though she knew his touch would brand her for life, even though she knew she would be scarred for time immemorial, Laura wanted to go no longer without knowing his most intimate touch. She would risk the future for the pleasure of the moment.

She wanted to be one with this god of the underworld.

"Is this your home?" she asked.

"Yes." He laid both hands, palms down, on the dresser and braced himself.

"We're above the Golden Fleece?" Laura asked.

Clay lifted his head and nodded, their gaze meeting in the mirror. Time in abeyance, they stared at each other. As if he read the message in her eyes, Clay whirled around. He stuck the cigar into the corner of his mouth and strode across the room, picking up her cape from a nearby chair as he passed. When he stood behind her, he slung the green velvet around her.

"Time for you to go home," he announced, his voice thick and husky. Yet his hands lingered on her shoulders.

Laura felt him tremble. "I think not," she whispered. She turned her face and brushed a kiss over the tops of his fingers, her lips fluttering over each knuckle. Then she leaned back to press her body

90

against the lean, hard length of his. He breathed in sharply; she smiled. By choice Laura had entered a man's world when she decided to be the acting manager of Ombres Azurées, but that did not mean she could not enjoy the pleasures of being a woman. She would have the best of both worlds. A man had a mistress. What was to keep her from having a . . . a . . . lover? Celeste had told her it was all right . . .

"Do you really want me to go home?" she asked.

Clay stiffened, his eyes narrowed to mere slits. "Do you know what you're saying?"

"I know." Laura's voice was steady and calm. She trembled in anticipation. "I'm drunk but fully aware of what I'm doing . . . and saying . . . and wanting."

"Then, ma'am,"—he lay his cigar down—"be it far from me to displease the lady."

He caught the cape and pulled it off her shoulders, the material pooling to the floor around their feet. As his hands slowly slid down her shoulders to her arms . . . to her wrists, pleasure rippled through Laura. Trembling in part from anticipation, in part from fear, she turned to face Clay. Her body remembered his kisses and wanted more. His hands lightly clasped her waist, and he leaned forward to brush his lips against her forehead. His head lowered and his lips hovered near hers in excruciating pleasure.

Eyelids closed over green eyes, and Laura lifted her face, her lips coming up to touch his, tentatively at first, then more firmly. Giving herself to him might bring regrets with the coming of the dawn, but right now she wanted the touch of his lips on hers again.

Clay allowed her mouth to play with his, but he did not deepen the kiss. Finally, he drew his head back and stared into her flushed face. Drawing in a

91

deep, wobbly breath, Laura lifted her hands and placed them on his chest. Beneath her fingers was the steady beat of his heart. The tempo quickened her breath. She stared at his thick, muscular neck, at his firm chin and partly open lips. At last she stared into those sultry brown eyes.

"Be sure, Laura," he whispered. "There's going to be no turning back."

"I'm sure." Her hands slid up his shoulders.

Persuasive lips touched hers and a warmth coursed through her that had nothing to do with the blaze in the fireplace. With her fingers entwined in the thick hair that met the collar of his shirt, she responded to his kiss, hesitantly at first, but then gradually her lips moved against his and she gave in to the wondrous urges that flowed through her.

Her lips parted to welcome the thrust of his tongue, and she fell deeper under his spell, welcoming his sweet invasion. Laura held him tightly to her. She marveled at the strength of him and trembled in amazement. The mysteries of sensual pleasure that she had long ago accepted as fact but not yet felt were unfolding beneath Clay's kiss. The reality of that pleasure mixed with desire was far more powerful than her imaginings had ever been.

Insistently, Clay stroked her back as his kiss deepened. She thrilled at his touch, and when one hand moved around to caress her breast, she arched and offered herself more easily to him. His body tightened. He pulled away, but only to pick her up in his arms. With her head nestled against his shoulder, he strode across the room to lay her on the bed, climbing in and stretching out beside her. He propped himself on one elbow and leaned over to stroke her hair, her face, her throat down to the edge of the scoop neckline.

His touch was equal parts of agony and pleasure. A hot, hungry passion curled within her. She freed her hands from their imprisonment against his chest and wrapped her arms around his neck. She drew him closer until her lips burned against his.

He cradled her tightly, the full length of his body against hers. She felt the pressure of his arousal between her legs. Desire obliterated thought. With no experience to guide her, she did what seemed natural and settled deeper into his embrace. His response was a low moan. His arms tightened around her, his lips bruising hers with the intensity of their kiss.

A warm longing effused Laura to displace any fears or inhibitions she might have had. If it were possible, she pressed herself tightly against the muscled walls of his chest. After a long, sweet moment Clay pulled away.

"Shall I stop?" Velvet-brown eyes, hot with desire, gazed into Laura's flushed face.

"No." Her voice was little more than a whisper.

Clay pulled her back into his arms and covered her face and throat with hungry, relentless kisses. When their lips met at last, Laura's world slowly melted away. She willingly accepted Clay's. She was powerless to resist and entertained no thought of doing so. The warmth she had felt at his first light kiss became a raging fire. Whatever reasons she had given herself for surrender to his will were lost in its flames. Under the spell of his hot kisses she wanted him in a primal way that had nothing to do with thought . . . or reason . . . or justification.

Instinct guided Laura. Her hands rubbed against him. Beneath the fabric of the shirt she felt his muscles tense. She felt him tremble. Then he pulled away, and for a moment she was bereft. Her hands searched for and found his face.

Clay's eyes roved over her face as his lips had. Pulling the pins from her hair, he watched the long auburn curls tumble around her shoulders. His hands moved down the wide neckline, his fingers brushing against the satin-smooth skin of her half-exposed breasts. One by one he undid the row of tiny buttons; deftly, he released the tie at her waist. Laura gave only a passing thought to the skill and smoothness with which he worked, marveled little that he knew so easily the mechanics of a woman's gown.

He slipped the dress from her shoulders. All the while his eyes burned into hers, dropping only when the gown had been brushed aside. He gazed at the white shoulders and creamy breasts. His eyes caressed her like velvet.

When she lay naked before him, a shyness unlike anything Laura had experienced overcame her, and she grabbed for the coverlet. Clay caught her hands in his and pulled her arms aside.

"You're a beautiful woman, Laura Elyse Talbot, made to look at . . . made to love."

His eyes left her face and moved to the phoenix, to the fullness of her high-tipped young breasts, to the gentle curve of her hips, to the fiery down between her thighs. His gaze lingered, then trailed the length of her slender legs before returning to her face.

"You are indeed a woman, Laura, and a beautiful one."

"An ice maiden," she murmured.

"A hot-blooded woman made to love." His lips gently kissed around the phoenix. "Is this a special piece of jewelry?"

"Yes. Papa gave it to me when we came to New Orleans."

94

"A new beginning," he said, and smiled. "I know the myth well."

"Yes." She reached up to touch his lips with the tips of her fingers. "Please, no more talking."

Clay drew her into his embrace, his hands stroking where his eyes had been. He held her for a long moment. His breath quickened and his lips pressed against her hair. Whatever Laura had expected, it was not this gentle loving, this slow, inexorable movement in the mist of passion. The pleasure his touch gave was like nothing she had felt before.

She felt like a fragile treasure in his arms, but somehow knew the next step was hers. She must follow the example he had so smoothly set. By the time her nervous fingers had managed to unfasten the first few buttons of his shirt, Clay was grinning down at her.

"Let me," he said.

Shyly, Laura smiled. Clay lowered his head and took her lips in a deep, passionate kiss. He seemed to draw her within him, and again she let him take control. Her bare skin against the roughness of his clothing had an electrifying effect on her.

His arms encircled her and his fingers dug lightly into her spine as they journeyed downward. They paused at the small of her back and traced little circles in the hollows above the flare in her buttocks. Then they moved lower to cup her firmly against him. Clay's muscled strength, she discovered, extended the full length of him. Long, drugged minutes later she burned from the sweet torture of his touch.

Clay rolled off the bed and shed his breeches. His movements were quick and graceful and powerful. Laura gazed at him unashamedly, and when he stood before her in his unleashed magnificence she was reminded of idealized manhood in the classical paintings she had studied.

Only Clay was not painted on canvas. He was hot, demanding flesh, and beneath a fine layer of dark hair the skin of his arms and legs was tight and smooth. He knelt, one knee on the bed beside her, his hand on her white breast a startling brown.

He bent to take her breast into his mouth, and the banked fires of Laura's desire flamed anew. His fingers moved slowly down her body, gently caressing a path down to her parting thighs. He stroked the inside of the thigh to the warm, damp secret of her body. Laura shuddered as his fingers slid through her silken hair to part her body even more. They touched the tiny bud of pleasure at the very core of her. He caressed her with gentle thoroughness to send passion urgently coursing through her. She clutched the taut sinews of his arms and writhed beneath his touch.

"Clay." She little realized what she begged for; she knew only she must have more.

His hand parted her legs wider and he laid his body on top of hers, pressing her down into the soft bed with his weight. Slowly, with tender expertise, he eased himself into her warm moistness. He felt the thin membrane. Laura tensed. He held her more tightly. His mouth covered hers in a deep kiss as he pressed fully into her. He swallowed her cry of pain.

Pleasure totally obliterated Laura's pain. Caught up in desire, she began to move her hips and thighs in accordance with his rhythmic thrusts. Their breathing quickened, and they gasped as they exploded into ecstasy.

"Clay." Her cry mingled with his, and she held him tightly as if he would disappear if she did not.

How wonderful it was to lie with him and to let him hold her in the aftermath of their lovemaking.

He was so strong, his embrace so protective and reassuring. How easy it would be for Laura to let Clay Sutherland become an integral part of her life.

Beautiful thoughts drifted through her mind as she closed her eyes and slept. Sometime during the night she awakened and rolled over. Clay turned also and molded his body to hers. He laid an arm over her. Breathing deeply, Laura smiled and closed her eyes, sleeping once again.

The morning was still dark when Laura awakened, her mouth thick and fuzzy from too much drink. She pushed up on the bed, the coverlet slipping down to expose the creamy swell of her breasts. Her clothes had been neatly folded and laid over the back of a chair. Clay stood in front of the darkened fireplace, gazing intently at her.

"Good morning," he murmured, a slight smile pulling his lips. His eyes were warm and friendly. "I see that you're finally awake."

"Good morning," Laura returned stiffly, averting her eyes as memory returned full force. The impact was most painful, and her entire body suffused with the heat of embarrassment.

He neared the bed. "How are you feeling this morning?"

Laura looked down to discover her breasts were uncovered; she clawed frantically at the cover, pulling it beneath her chin. "I . . . feel fine, thank you." To cover her embarrassment, she added, "Should I feel otherwise?"

"No," Clay returned slowly, "I guess not." He seemed to be baffled.

Pretending a nonchalance she was far from feeling, Laura wrapped a sheet around herself and

97

moved to the chair over which her clothes had been draped. Grabbing the undergarments, her gaze swept the room as she sought a dressing screen.

"I'll leave," Clay said in a flat tone, and walked out of the room.

Relieved to be alone, Laura moved to the hearth and hurriedly put on her clothes. By the time Clay returned with a tray, she was sitting in the high-backed chair in front of the fireplace.

"Breakfast will soon be ready. Are you hungry?" he asked.

"No," Laura answered rather primly, her hands crossed on her knees, her gaze straight ahead. "A cup of coffee will do just fine. I'll eat when I get home."

The dishes clattered as Clay set the silver pot on the tray and walked to stand in front of her. "You're not leaving without our talking." He caught her hands in his and dropped to his knees in front of her.

"We don't have anything to talk about," she replied, her gaze pinned to the dancing flames.

"Laura," he said, "ignoring what happened last night isn't going to erase it. You have nothing to be ashamed of."

Clay's words touched a tender cord in Laura's heart, but she refused to acknowledge it. In the light of day she pushed aside the emotions that had gripped her last night and had taken control away from her. She knew what she must do, and she would do it. She pulled her hands from Clay's.

"And nothing to be proud of," she replied, standing so abruptly he tumbled to the floor. She moved to the table and poured herself a cup of coffee. She had to; her nerves were frayed and she was going to lose control . . . again. Dear God, not again! The spoon clinked against the china as she stirred in the sugar. She took several swallows. "I'm not ignoring it, but I'm not going to make more of it than it was."

"Laura, I'm not going to lie to you and say—"

"You don't have to. I understand the facts of life quite well. After all, I'm twenty-six years old."

"Laura, I want you to marry me."

Laura forced herself to take another swallow of coffee, but the beverage tasted like bile. "I'm sure you do."

Clay looked at her curiously.

Her eyes, now on him, were frosty. "You forget, I was outside M'sieur Dufaure's office at the autumn ball when you told Roussel about your plans. In a month or two you planned to marry an heiress from one of the respectable Creole families and from her you would inherit a plantation and a sugar mill."

Clay looked at her in stunned silence for a moment. "Laura, I want to marry you because—"

"You want respectability and recognition, M'sieur Sutherland, and marriage to me would guarantee that, would it not?"

Clay sighed. "Last night you told me I could believe you or Giraumont about your marriage plans. Now I'm saying the same to you. I'm asking you to marry me because I have—" He broke off and paused. As if struggling with himself, he finally said, "I've taken your virginity."

His words touched Laura, but she brushed sentiment aside. She had wallowed in that enough for one night. She hid her vulnerability behind bitter laughter. "I'm surprised at you, M'sieur Sutherland. You're making more out of the situation than it warrants."

Clay's expression hardened, as did his voice. "If I were a fancy Creole gentleman, you would expect this kind of behavior, Miss Talbot. Why is it so different when I react with honor?"

99

"Because, m'sieur, you are not a gentleman, and your proposal is fraught with underlying motivations. I do not intend to marry every man with whom . . . I am intimate." With more aplomb than she felt, Laura uttered the words that sounded so foreign and stilted to her ears. "I'm not the woman who will guarantee that your name will be the first on every guest list sent out by the established Creole families."

Clay tossed the cigar into the fireplace and strode to her. Taking the cup from her hands, he set it on the tray and caught her in a tight embrace. "Don't talk such nonsense to me. You're not the kind of woman who is promiscuous, and you can't possibly marry a man like Roussel Giraumont . . . or any man . . . when you respond to me the way you do."

"I'm that very kind of woman." Fearing the vulnerability this man aroused in her, Laura retreated behind a mask of cold indifference, of calculated unconcern. "If you didn't know that last night when I seduced you, you know it now. Consider yourself outdone at fencing and at . . . lust, Clay Sutherland."

Clay stared at her, unidentifiable expressions flitting across his face. "Yes, Laura Talbot, you seduced me all right. A first for me, I might add." He bent and picked up the silver pot to pour himself a cup of coffee. Then he moved to the fireplace and hiked an arm on the mantel. "While for me the experience was simply a passing pleasure, it was more for you."

Laura could not deny the truth of his words. Mortification rushed through her veins; yet her demeanor never changed.

"You see, Laura, there's a special feeling that goes with that first seduction. A person has a tendency to

100

fall in love with the first person with whom they make love."

Her back to Clay, Laura carefully set her cup on the tray and ran her finger around the rim. "Perhaps I will fall in love with the first man with whom I make love. You and I, M'sieur Sutherland, enjoyed a night of desire, nothing more."

Clay's eyes were pure flint. "You can't just walk away from what we shared last night," he taunted. "Now that your body is awakened to the touch of a man, now that you've experienced the pleasures of lovemaking, you're going to want more . . . and more."

Laura smiled and turned to face him. "And we can have more . . . and more."

Clay drew back and stared at her curiously.

"Men have their mistresses." She spoke so coolly she surprised herself. "I see no reason why I can't have a . . . a . . ."

His lips parted and harsh laughter filled the room. Long steps carried him to her, and his hands grasped her arms. "Go ahead and say it, Laura. If you're going to have one, you might as well learn to say the word. You want a stud. Say it, Laura. I want to hear you say it."

"Let me go," she whispered.

"Say it, Laura." He was so angry he shook her, the auburn hair tumbling about her face.

The word was so vile, Laura could hardly utter it, but her anger gave her strength and resolve. With it came control. "Stud!" she shouted. "Stud, Clay Sutherland! I want you to be my stud!"

Repulsed, he slung her from him and strode out of the room. Clasping the arm of the chair, Laura picked herself up and walked out of the bedroom into a large parlor. She saw her cape lying on the divan.

101

Picking it up, she slung it over her shoulders and moved to the door, down the stairs. The hood she drew over her face. She slipped through the empty casino and out into the street, already crowded with wagons, creaking under the weight of their loads.

In the grayness of early morning a lucifer burst into flame to outline the contours of Clay's face. Once the cigar was lit, he poured a cup of coffee. Then he picked up the flask and poured a healthy measure of whiskey.

Sitting down in the high-backed chair in front of the hearth, he stretched his feet to the fire and smiled. Laura Elyse Talbot was an enigma to him. Concerned about the effect her loss of virginity would have upon her, he reckoned he would be presented with tearful grief and angry recriminations on her awakening. Instead, she was in total command of the situation; she orchestrated every move.

Imagine her asking him to be her lover! He laughed aloud—the sound totally devoid of mirth. At least their relationship would be far from dull. Laura Elyse promised to be a delightful vixen.

But a part of Clay was angry and disappointed. He wanted more than a clandestine affair with Laura. He desired more than shady meetings in out-of-the-way places. He desired more than lust. He did not profess to love her, but he readily admitted that their attraction was more than mere desire.

He drained the last dregs of coffee and whiskey out of the cup. Then he rose and walked to the desk across the room, where he sat down and wrote a short note. When he was through, he pushed back in the chair. "Churnbarker."

"You called, sir?" the stooped-shouldered little

man asked from the doorway.

"Yes." A mischievous grin on his lips, Clay stood at the dresser. He thumped the cork into the neck of his after-shave cologne. Walking toward the servant, he waved an envelope through the air. "I want this note delivered to Miss Laura Talbot today."

Arthritic hands reached for the paper. "Yes, Mr. Sutherland. Shall I have the messenger wait for an answer?"

"Yes . . . and, Churnbarker. I want to send her a box of bonbons. See to that, will you?"

"Yes, sir. What message shall I send with them, sir?"

"Give her this card," Clay answered.

Churnbarker took the card and stared curiously at the fencing mask Clay had drawn. "Yes, sir." He turned to walk out of the room. That his employer was acting strange bothered him not one whit. He was paid to run Clay's household and to keep the other servants in line. That is what he did and did well.

But even Thompson Clovis Churnbarker thought it rather strange of Mr. Sutherland to send a perfumed letter to a woman. That was most untypical behavior for him.

Chapter Five

"Is there anything else I can do for you, Maîtresse Laura?" Jeanette asked.

Laura sank into the chair in front of the fireplace in her bedroom. "No. I want to be by myself for a few minutes. And . . . Jeanette, I don't want you discussing last night with anyone."

"*Oui.*" The maid paused at the door and added softly, "I would not tell even if you had not given the order, mam'selle. I do not judge as harshly as others do."

"Thank you, Jeanette," Laura whispered.

When the door closed behind the servant, Laura leaned over to the small table beside her chair and poured a mug of hot chocolate. Oblivious to the storm that raged outside, she pulled her thick robe closer around herself.

Never before had she been tangled in such a web of deceit . . . even to the point of enlisting her maid's service and silence. What a fool she had been to go to Bayou St. John with Clay Sutherland last night! An even bigger fool to have made love with him. In throwing caution aside, in tasting the forbidden fruit, she was indeed a part of Clay Sutherland's world. Only a few hours had passed since she left him, but it seemed like years. Tears burned her eyes.

From the beginning she had insisted on making love to him; resistance was not included in her game plan. But she had intended to have total control over the situation. From the minute his hands and mouth began to work their magic on her, she lost self, she lost control. She had given Clay Sutherland her virginity, but he had stolen her self and her control. Pleasure surged through her body as she thought about Clay's caresses; a fiery blush colored her cheeks at the memory of her responses.

He really was Lucifer and she had walked through hell with him. Her hand curled around the phoenix. She should hate him, but, oddly, she did not. She hated herself because she had allowed him to take her mind and intellect. But she would not let him reduce her to ashes. She would rise above them. She had put George behind her. She could do the same with Clay.

How easily the thoughts came to mind; how quickly the body disagreed. As if it were an everyday occurrence in her life, she had asked him to be her lover. Her heart ached; her body ached. She was only beginning to understand the hold Clay Sutherland had over her.

"Maîtresse Laura, the mail has arrived," Jeanette called as she knocked on the door.

"Bring it in."

The door opened, and the servant entered. "Look," she exclaimed, holding a large box in the air, "someone sent you bonbons, mam'selle. Two letters. This one," she murmured, sniffing the envelope, "but it smells good and, oh, so masculine."

The faint, familiar odor of herbal cologne permeated the room.

"Ah, mam'selle," Jeanette gurgled, a conspirator's

smile on her lips, "you have never before received bonbons and a perfumed letter. Someone is indeed *sweet* on you." She laid the letters on the tray behind the chocolate pot and handed the candy to Laura, watching curiously as her mistress extracted the card from beneath the ribbon.

Laura's fingers trembled as she held the card up and looked at the fencing mask. She read the words beneath: *Be kind to the vanquished.*

Jeanette clapped her hands together. "Ah, you have a secret admirer. Now I will leave so you can read your letter and eat your goodies." The large black eyes settled on the box of candy.

Laura laughed. "Have a bonbon, Jeanette. Have as many as you wish."

"Thank you, mam'selle," the girl gushed, opening the box and taking two of the chocolate treats. The one she crammed into her mouth, chewed, and sucked in her breath. "Ah, Maîtresse Laura, they are marvelous. Simply marvelous."

When Laura was alone once again, she opened Clay's letter to read: *When may I see you again? Give me a specific time, or I shall be forced to come to Ombres Azurées. I know this sounds cruel, sweet Laura, but I find that you are in my blood. Thoughts of you fill my waking hours; dreams of you fill my long nights. My man will return at three this afternoon for an answer; I shall see you soon.*

Livid with anger, Laura leapt to her feet and paced the floor. How dare Clay Sutherland do this to her! She could hear his soft, mocking laughter as he made fun of her. Bonbons! She kicked the box of candy off the divan, chocolates sailing across the room. Perfumed letters! Playing his role to the hilt! His man coming to her home for an answer to Clay's note of assignation.

106

This was too much for her to take . . . absolutely. She lifted her hand to her temple and gently massaged. She had the beginnings of a headache. Looking down at the tray, she saw the other letter. Immediately, she recognized the delicate hand-writing and the postmark. She tore through the envelope and unfolded the sheet of paper to read her sister's letter.

"*Chère* Laura," Celeste called as she opened the door and peeked in, "you chose to stay in town last night?"

"Er . . . yes," Laura faltered. Her body grew warm as she recalled her night in Clay's bed, in his arms.

"Jeanette said you were exhausted."

Laura's cheeks flamed with embarrassment. Rather sheepishly, she said, "Yes, I was."

The matter forgotten with a wave of her hand, Celeste stared at the candy strewn across the room and smiled. "Also Jeanette tells me that you have a secret admirer who sent you a box of bonbons." Inside the bedroom now, she looked up to encounter Laura's stricken face. "*Mon Dieu!* What has happened?"

"Charlotte." Laura lifted her head and stared at her stepmother. "She's gravely ill."

"*Non!*" Celeste ran to take Laura into her arms. "*Non.* Oh, I'm so sorry."

"Judith doesn't ask that I come, but I must go to her, Celeste."

"I can understand your wanting to be with your *maman*," Celeste said, "but you are forgetting we are at war with England. Travel on the seas is danger-ous."

The letter fell from Laura's hand to flutter to the floor. "I'm not going because of Charlotte. I'm going because of Judith. She needs me. I must get to

107

England as quickly as possible."

Celeste wrung her hands. "Your papa will not like this, Laura."

"No," Laura agreed quietly, "he won't. Facing your past requires courage. Perhaps more courage than either of us has."

Celeste crossed the room and laid a gentle hand on Laura's arm. "Always you assign the wrong motives to your papa. He will not want you to go because he fears for your safety. He could not bear to lose you. Nor could I. You have become like a daughter to me."

Laura looked down into her stepmother's face and said in a teary voice, "You're like a mother to me. But I must go. I want to go."

"Yes, of course you must. But what about the plantation, *ma petite?*"

Laura unconsciously lifted a hand and rubbed her temple. "I can't leave it under Joshua's supervision. He's much too inexperienced."

"Perhaps you might think about that . . . about that—"

Laura's face brightened. "M'sieur Donaldson. Yes, I shall do that. His letters of recommendation were excellent."

Celeste stepped back, her gaze following the pieces of candy strewn across the room. "I will send Louis into town to tell your father so he can arrange for your transport. Jeanette will start packing at once." As she walked to the bellpull, she stepped around the candy. "The bonbons were not to your liking, *ma chère?*"

"The suitor was not to my liking." Laura refused to look at the candy.

Celeste picked up the chocolates and replaced them in the box. "Perhaps, *chère* Laura, you're going to find M'sieur Sutherland more than you bargained for. Always it pays for a woman to find a lover who is weaker than she is. Weaker men can be handled; stronger men prefer to handle."

Laura smiled. "Thank you for the advice, Celeste, but I know what I'm doing. I can handle M'sieur Sutherland quite well. Of the two, I'm much the stronger."

"You are a strong woman, *oui*," Celeste agreed as she lifted a napkin from the tray and wiped traces of chocolate from her hands, "but you must realize he is an equally strong man. Estimate your adversaries well, Laura. Else you're going to be in trouble."

The door opened and Jeanette entered the room. "You rang, Maîtresse?"

"Maîtresse Laura is going to England. Send Henri to get the trunks and start packing at once. Also pack your things, Jeanette. You'll be traveling with your mistress."

"*Oui*, madame." Her lips curled into a full smile, her eyes sparkling, Jeanette scurried out of the room.

Laura lost all sense of time as the household rushed around getting her trunks packed. Accustomed to the mild weather in Louisiana, her wardrobe was hardly suitable for the severe English winter. Despite the norther that blew in, she and Celeste traveled into town.

Before they did their shopping for Laura's clothes, they stopped by the Talbot Shipping Line office. When Celeste walked into his office, Beau was hunched over his desk adding a column of figures. He was haggard, his hair tousled. He smiled and rose, taking his wife into his arms and kissing her.

"And to what do I owe this pleasant surprise?" His gaze raked across Celeste's head to Laura, who stood in the doorway. He read her expression correctly. "Or

109

is it not such a pleasant visit?"

"I'll let you determine that, Papa." Laura opened her reticule as she walked into the office and withdrew Judith's letter.

"I will wait in the outer office." Celeste withdrew from his embrace.

"You don't need to go." Beau caught her hand and pulled her to his side. He slipped an arm around her waist. "Surely you know that anything Laura and I have to say to each other can be said in front of you."

"I know that, love." Celeste stood on tiptoe and kissed Beau lightly on the lips. "But this is quite personal. It is something the two of you need to discuss alone."

Beau's puzzled glance went from his wife to Laura. As Celeste slipped out of the room and closed the door, he ran his fingers through his hair as if he were not eager to take the letter Laura held out to him. Eventually, he did. When he finished reading it, he dropped it on top of the desk. Bending, he opened the bottom drawer of the desk and pulled out a bottle of brandy. He poured himself a drink.

"I take it you have a burning desire to go to England?"

"Yes." The brazier full of burning coals was not enough to dispel the chill in the air. Laura pulled her cape closer around her shoulders.

Beau shook his head. "I'm not going to let you go."

"Why?" Laura's question was calm.

"My God, Laura, we're at war with England. The high seas is one of the most dangerous places to be."

"Merchant ships can get through."

Beau raked his hand through his hair. "Some of them do. Some do not. Have you any idea what men, both English and Americans, are doing in the name of patriotism? All this war has done is legalize piracy."

"Judith needs us, Papa. We have to go to her."

Beau stopped his pacing and stared at Laura. "I can't go to England, Laura. It's absolutely out of the question."

"Not really."

Beau flung his hand out in exasperation. "Someone has to stay here to supervise the lines, Laura. And that someone is me."

"You have M'sieur Dufaure," she countered.

"I can't leave all this on his shoulders." He sighed. "Dear God, we not only have the English to worry about, but Napoleon as well. Just this morning Dufaure and I were talking about the Bonapartist movement."

"I suppose M'sieur Dufaure is all for New Orleans giving Napoleon sanctuary." Laura then added sarcastically, "He might even persuade you to send one of our ships to get him."

"Don't be silly," Beau snapped. "Whatever else Maurice might be, he has a business acumen that I envy. His loyalty and love belong to his business. He's not about to get caught up in any of these political machinations. He's too shrewd for that."

"Then you should have no qualms about leaving the shipping lines under his supervision, Papa."

Beau took another swallow of whiskey. "Besides the shipping lines, we have Ombres Azurées to worry about."

Laura was prepared for this. "The plantation is not a worry, Papa. I will hire an overseer. I have already sent word to Roussel that I would like to interview M'sieur Donaldson."

Beau nodded his head. "Excellent. Roussel said Donaldson was one of the best overseers in

111

these parts."

Laura moved closer to her father's desk and laid her gloved hand on his lower arm. "Believe me, Papa. With Joshua to help him, M'sieur Donaldson can handle the plantation while we're gone."

Beau caught the nape of his neck in his hand and massaged gently. "Laura, I have the feeling that in your mind you've already hired this overseer and that you're going to England whether I approve or not."

"I am. Please come with me, Papa."

"I have no desire to see your mother again, and I would think after all she did to you, you wouldn't either."

"I'm not going back because of Charlotte," Laura answered for the second time that day. "I'm going back because of Judith. Have you given any thought to her?" Beau turned his back to Laura. "She needs us, Papa."

"I can't go, Laura. I've already told you. I'm needed here. I've explained all the things we're up against at the moment. In all good conscience, I can't let Dufaure handle this by himself. Besides, someone needs to be here to train Donaldson."

"But in all good conscience you can neglect Judith a second time." Her voice was thick with emotion.

Beau spun around, his hands outstretched. "Don't make this any harder than it is, Laura. Surely you can understand my responsibility."

She stared at him through tear-blurred eyes. "I understand, Papa. More than you think."

"I know this doesn't give you much time to prepare, but I have a ship setting sail for England this evening. The *Laurel*. You can travel on her," Beau said.

"I can't leave that soon. I have to interview Donaldson," Laura returned.

"I'll do that for you." Beau walked up to Laura and took her into his arms. "That is, if you trust my judgment."

Laura smiled weakly. "I do."

Saddened by her father's refusal to accompany her to England, Laura was barely conscious of his following her out of his office and saying good-bye. He promised he would be at the town house in time to escort her to the docks. He and Celeste would see her off.

Laura was unusually quiet the remainder of the day. The shopping venture that should have been a pleasure became a chore. By the time she and Celeste returned to the town house that afternoon, Celeste was exhausted. Willingly, she shed her cape and changed clothes. Later, clad in her dressing gown, she stretched out on the chaise longue in the drawing room.

"Ah, thank you," she murmured when Laura draped a cashmere shawl over her legs and feet. "I was indeed wet to the bone. But you have some beautiful new clothes for your visit, *oui?*"

Laura stood in front of the window and gazed into the busy thoroughfare below. Despite the rain, carriages rattled back and forth. Wagons piled high with their goods creaked by. Drivers shouted and beat their horses. Whips cracked. Two nuns wearing dull blue robes and stiff white headdresses walked slowly along with their heads bowed. A young Negro man passed, bearing upon his head a flat basket filled with brightly colored flowers; the basket bobbed in the air above the crowd, and as he passed by, he whistled a trill of clear, liquid notes.

"The blue one," Celeste said, "that was not for you, *chère* Laura?"

"The blue one?" Laura asked.

113

"The blue gown."

"No," Laura answered, "I bought that one for Judith. It made me think of her."

Leaning her forehead against the chilled pane, Laura's lids closed, and as clearly as if Judith were standing in front of her, she saw her. Judith's eyes were beautiful sapphire-blue eyes—eyes just like Beau's. The years whirled backward, and Laura remembered the defiant little girl with the mop of riotous red curls who wore a lovely blue dress with lots of Irish lace; around her neck hung a sapphire pendant.

Daydreams and fantasies, Laura told herself, *none of it true.* She felt tears thicken on her lashes. She did not know what her baby sister looked like. Judith had never sent them a portrait of herself. If only she and Papa had brought Judith with them . . . If only Papa were going to England with her . . .

A servant quietly slipped into the room to set a tray on the table next to the chaise longue. "You are not to worry." Celeste poured the coffee. "Your mother is young, much too young to die."

"Yes, she is," Laura murmured. *Charlotte is too young to die.* Visions of the petite beauty floated through Laura's mind. Blond hair that glistened like gold; eyes the color of jade. Unconsciously, Laura's hand lifted, and her fingers clutched the small phoenix that hung around her neck.

"Oddly," Laura said, "I'm not worried about Charlotte. I'm worried about Judith."

"You are also upset because Beau isn't going with you, *oui?*"

Just as a carriage stopped across the street in front of their town house and a man covered in a heavy raincoat disembarked, Laura turned. "I don't want him to go because of Charlotte or because of me. I

114

want him to go because of Judith. He owes that to her. He . . . we all but deserted her nine years ago. We can't do that again."

"You are angry at me because I am not insisting that he go?"

Laura was silent.

"This is a decision your papa must make himself, *ma chère*. I am not keeping him from his daughter; never would I do that—no matter what I may think of your *maman*." She lifted the delicate china cup to her lips and sipped the coffee. "In many ways, *chère* Laura, your father is a little boy. He wants to be an adult without having the responsibilities. When Beau was having troubles in England both with his business and with his marriage, he chose to run rather than face them."

"Believing this, you married him?" Laura's voice lifted with incredulity.

"I needed him at first," Celeste said simply. "Now I love and accept all that is Beau Talbot."

"You think Beau weak?"

"No. He has his weaknesses, but he is not weak. He also has his fears. And one of those fears is being rejected again. First by your mama, and now by your sister. Compound the anguish you are suffering because you left Judith in England nine years ago; then you will know Beau Talbot's pain."

"If only we had brought Judith with us when we left," Laura cried. "How different it all would be."

"You didn't," Celeste returned firmly. "The past cannot be changed by worry or guilt; therefore, both are useless."

"Do you think I ran?" Laura asked.

"Um-hum. You may have the green eyes like your *maman*, but you have many characteristics like your papa. You left England rather than stay and face the scandal of your parents' divorce."

"I could have faced the divorce," Laura answered tightly, tracing a rivulet of rain on the pane with the tip of her finger. "But the divorce coupled with Mama's affair with Randolph Carew ruined my life. The Beckworths demanded that the engagement be broken."

"Had George really loved you," Celeste said, "he would have married you no matter."

"Not really," Laura murmured. "The *ton* would never have accepted that."

"*Ma chère,* do not speak to me of such nonsense. Society is the same whether English, French, or Creole. One uses it as a guideline; never should it become a cage. George was not the man for you."

"I loved him," said Laura in a small voice.

"*Non—*" Celeste waved Laura's declaration aside. "Had you really loved George Beckworth, you would have stayed in England and fought for him. To prove my point, be sure to visit your viscount while you're in England." Celeste's husky laughter wafted through the room. "You'll be surprised."

"It seems odd to think I'll be spending Christmas on a ship on the way to England," Laura said.

Celeste lifted a delicate hand and touched a lace handkerchief to the corner of her eyes. "But you will have fun, *ma chère.* Once you arrive in England, you will enjoy being with your *maman* and sister."

Her eyes burning with tears, Laura turned and crossed the room to throw herself into Celeste's arms. "But I'm going to miss you, *Maman,* and Papa and New Orleans."

Celeste rubbed her hand down the back of Laura's head. "We are going to miss you, *ma chou.*"

Laura lifted her head. "I love you, *Maman.*"

"*Je t'aime.*"

116

A servant entered the room. "M'sieur Giraumont is here to see you, Maîtresse Celeste."

Laura pushed away and rose while Celeste wiped the tears from her cheeks. "Send him in."

His raincoat discarded, his hair slightly damp, Roussel walked to the lounge and took Celeste's hand. "Madame Talbot, how are you feeling today?"

"Tired but content," Celeste answered. "Laura and I spent the entire morning shopping. But, of course, you know she's going to England to visit with her family."

"Ah, yes, that is why I am here." Roussel clasped his hands behind his back. "I have spoken with M'sieur Donaldson. He is to go to the shipping office in the morning to interview with Beau."

"Do sit down and join us for a cup of coffee, Roussel," Celeste said. "Beau will be here shortly to drive us to the docks."

Roussel lifted his chin and ran his finger around his collar. Clearing his throat, he said, "Er . . . Beau is not coming, madame. He . . . er . . . asked me to drive Laura to the dock."

Laura whirled around and glared at him. "Why?"

Roussel was most uncomfortable. Again he cleared his throat and looked from Laura to Celeste and back to Laura. "Because of the rain, several of our wagons have been unable to get into town. He and a crew of our workers are out there transferring the goods from wagon to barge."

"Oh, yes—" Laura's smile was brittle. "That's my father. Talbot Shipping Line has always taken precedence over everything else. His daughters included."

Wearing a harvest-yellow satin gown, Laura stood

117

at the porthole, gazing at the blackened night. The storm was coming in full force. Rain fell incessantly; thunder cracked and jagged rays of lightning pierced the sky. At times she felt as if the talons of electricity were clawing for her. The wind was so strong, the *Laurel*, Beau's merchant ship named after Laura, swayed in the water.

The door swung open and Clay strode into the room. Laura gasped in surprise and her hand went to her cheek. She had not expected to see him before her ship departed. Water dripped off the brim of Clay's hat. His countenance was as black and thunderous as the outside sky. His mouth was set in a grim line. He whipped his hand out of his coat pocket and waved a piece of paper through the air.

"What the hell do you mean, you don't want to see me again?"

"For God's sake, quit shouting." Laura had regained her composure. She looked down the companionway over Clay's shoulder to see if anyone was observing.

Clay brushed past her to shut and lock the door. Then he leaned against the wall and crossed his arms over his chest. "Now for an explanation."

"Don't be absurd." Laura withered him with a stare.

"When you left my apartment this morning, you informed me that we were lovers. As your lover, I have a right to know why you suddenly decided you didn't want to see me again."

"As my lover you have no right to make demands," Laura barked. She swallowed the embarrassment that knotted in her throat. She had never discussed such intimacies with a woman before, much less a man.

"I have the right to an explanation."

118

"No rights whatsoever, M'sieur Sutherland. But since you are here, I might as well inform you that I was mistaken earlier today. I do not want you for my lover at all."

"Forever changing your mind, Laura?" Clay's gaze swept over the trunks that cluttered the floor at the foot of the bed. "Are you running away from me or running away with him?"

"Him?" Laura lifted an eyebrow.

"Giraumont."

Affronted, Laura drew back. "I'm doing neither! I'm going to England to visit my sister."

"In this kind of weather?" Clay taunted as he pushed away from the door and walked more fully into the stateroom.

"It's an emergency. My—my mother is quite ill, and my sister needs me." The impact of his question hit her, and she laughed scornfully. "You really have an exalted opinion of yourself if you think I'm running from you. And what are you doing here, m'sieur? Trying to collect another gambling debt from Roussel?"

"No, he's already paid me. But I learned my lesson. Roussel Giraumont will receive no more credit from the Golden Fleece." Clay shed the raincoat, hanging it on a nearby wall rack.

"What are you doing?"

"I thought I'd see you off."

"You can't do this," Laura said. "The ship will be sailing immediately."

"Not for another couple of hours," Clay informed her. "I overheard M'sieur Dufaure telling the captain that he must wait for some last-minute cargo that's been detained by the storm. Must be mighty important to hold the ship up a couple of hours. I wasn't surprised to see Giraumont here to see you off, but I am surprised that your parents aren't here."

"Oh . . . oh, yes. Celeste was exhausted after all the shopping we did today, and as fragile as her health is, she doesn't need to be out in this kind of weather. And my—my father had some business to attend to," Laura said.

Unconsciously, she wrung her hands together. Still ringing in her ears were the flimsy excuses he gave for not going to England. Perhaps she could forgive Beau for not insisting that Judith come to America with them, but she could not forgive him for not accompanying her to England now. Laura looked around in time to see Clay shed his jacket.

"Why are you doing that?"

Rummaging through the pockets, Clay extracted a bottle of champagne. "Could I have wished you a *bon voyage* without this?" Grinning, he pulled from the other pocket a small glass. "You didn't think I was going to let my woman leave without a proper farewell, did you?"

"I'm not your woman," Laura snapped. "Now, get out. *Tout de suite*. Roussel will be returning any minute now."

Clay laughed and shook his head. "Not true, dear lady. He's going to be unavoidably detained."

Laura's eyes narrowed suspiciously. "What have you done to him?"

He shrugged. "When he was on his way to the office to deposit his documents with the ship's officer, his attaché fell into the river. Alas, it came unfastened and all his papers were ruined. They must be drawn up again. He's now waiting in Dufaure's office for the scrivener and the attorney to arrive. The mere writing of the documents will take quite a while, my dear. Even longer if he must compose them again."

120

"Even so." Laura drew up to her full height. She felt her control slipping. "Jeanette is nearby; she'll be joining me shortly."

Clay shook his head. "No, she's having quite a time with her friends below. Seems that someone was thoughtful enough to share several bottles of champagne with them."

"How kind," Laura retorted.

"Yes, it was kind, but the deed was done out of necessity rather than kindness," he admitted. "I had to lure your guard dog away so I could talk with you." He filled the glass with the sparkling wine and moved to where she stood. He handed her the glass and said, "Sorry, with several bottles of champagne, I could manage only one glass. To a safe journey."

She sipped the wine. "To a safe journey."

Clay caught her hand in his and brought the glass to his mouth, touching his lips over the spot where hers had rested. He took a swallow, then murmured, "I didn't know you had a sister. Is she anything like you?"

"Papa says we're as different as ice and fire."

"You're the ice and she's the fire?"

"So Papa says."

"Why is she in England?"

Laura pulled her hand from his and moved away. "My parents are divorced. I chose to come to America to live with my father. Judith Claire—my sister—she was only nine years old—she stayed with my mother."

"This isn't the best time of the year to be traveling."

"No." She set the glass down.

"How long are you going to be gone?"

"I don't know."

Clay walked to stand behind her. His voice soft-

121

ened. "I'm going to miss you, Laura Elyse."

"Not really." Her voice was thick with tears. "We don't really know each other."

His hands curled around her shoulders; his fingers gently kneaded the tender flesh. "How much better can we know each other?"

Laura felt her resolve evaporating. His touch, his very presence, set her aflame with desire; it completely obliterated thought and reason. But Laura had sworn that she would never give in to base emotions again. Drawing a deep breath, she remembered her promise to herself. The previous night she was drunk and entranced by the voodoo; that's why she lost control. Today she was in absolute control of her life and her feelings.

"I take full responsibility for last night, Clay—"

He laughed. "Don't be so presumptuous."

She ignored him altogether. "And I apologize for it." Her voice wavered slightly but grew more firm as she spoke. "I was wrong in allowing it to happen."

"That may be," he replied, his fingertips sliding farther down the front of her dress, "but it did happen."

"It's over," Laura insisted. "I don't want it to happen again."

Clay bent his head and breathed hotly against the curve of her neck as his lips nibbled her earlobe. "But it will happen, Laura, again and again."

"Not if you stay away from me," she murmured, lowering her head, exposing more of her slender neck to his gentle plunder.

"I promise I'm not going to stay away." He turned her around to catch her in an embrace. His velvet eyes caressed her face, her throat, the ivory softness of her breasts above the scooped neckline of her gown. "A man doesn't willingly give up manna for slop. For just one touch of your lips I'd walk through hell."

Surely Clay Sutherland is the devil, Laura thought as she fought the compelling sensations he aroused within her.

On her cheeks she felt the warmth of Clay's breath; she smelled the faint odor of champagne mixed with the expensive blend of aromatic tobacco. He lowered his dark head and pressed his lips against hers most tenderly. Liquid fire burned all the way down Laura's body, melting her bones. She opened her mouth to make another protest, but none would come.

Clay took advantage of her confusion to kiss her again, this time his lips more ardent, more demanding. Laura's mouth opened wider beneath his. She swayed, pressing her swollen breasts against the solid wall of his chest. Clay's blood boiled. His arms tightened to draw her closer, and the kiss deepened.

Even after last night Laura found his kiss to be erotic. Clay nibbled the fullness of her lips; he nibbled at each corner. As their mouths touched again, as his lips and tongue moved intimately against, then within, her own, a thrill ran through her—a charged thrill that encompassed every fiber of her being. With the tip of his tongue he traced the line of her lips, then surged between them to savor the velvet flower of her inner mouth in a way that made her knees grow weak and her heart thunder. Eventually, his lips left her mouth to taste her chin, trace her jawline, and linger on the throbbing pulse at the base of her neck.

"Tell me to go away," Clay whispered, brushing his lips up her cheeks to her ears, "and I will. Tell me, Laura." He dragged his head back and stared into her face.

"I want you," she whispered, despising herself

123

because she was so weak where Clay Sutherland was concerned. She closed her eyes when he kissed the corner of her mouth. Then he kissed each eye and a soft moan escaped her lips.

Her hands slid up his chest and locked around his neck. Her fingers twined through his thick, damp hair. She pulled him close. Each breath dragged through her like fire. Each part of her burned for his touch, for the melding of their bodies.

"I'm going to make love to you, Laura."

"Yes," she whispered fervently. Roussel . . . everything was forgotten in the flow of their desire. "Oh, yes."

They parted only to undress, their clothes falling into a careless heap at the foot of the bed. Then they embraced. His hungry lips claimed Laura's. The tip of his tongue grazed hers, then claimed the moist interior of her mouth. Hot hands stroked her shoulders and worked down to play at the tips of her breasts.

Laura began her own eager assault as her hands moved down his strong chest, fingers massaging as they moved, circling in the coarse hair. His response was a mightly shudder. The feel of his rugged strength brought to tremors under her touch was a thrill unlike any she had ever known. His hands on her breasts brought those same tremors rippling through her own body. They seemed to be moving together in their growing passion. It was a harmony that made her feel they were one.

Clay picked her up and laid her gently on the bed and knelt beside her. Her fingers trailed down his chest, over the flat plane of his tight stomach to the powerful manhood that sprang from the nest of black hair. Clay's lips moved slowly up her abdomen to kiss each breast—a long, teasing play of a kiss—

124

then to the pulse point at her throat.

By the time he stretched his full length beside her on the bed, Laura was mindless with desire. Again her sure hands stroked his chest, moving around to his back, drifting down to taut buttocks and thighs. His body pressed against hers. He was hot and hard and ready.

Her legs parted and she enfolded him within her. Her soft, moist flesh welcomed him. The reality of Laura, her body coupled with his, was far more enrapturing than anything he had imagined during his life, far more exciting than their first uniting. She was soft and yielding, yet demanding at the same time. Her body, moving with incredible sweetness beneath him, claimed a pleasure of its own even while it drove him to the edge of madness.

Their rhythms quickened, their hearts a primal drumbeat to their need. Each existed only for the other, giving and taking in a union that was born of more than just the bright flame of carnal need.

A violent tremor shook them. Still they clung to each other, arms and legs entwined, lips pressed tight, as though if they loosened their hold the other might slip away forever. For a long, sweetly spinning moment their rapture was complete.

The world seemed gradually to settle into place around them, and Clay stirred. He reached for the champagne bottle on the night table and filled the glass. Tipping it to his lips, he said, "To lovers, Laura Elyse."

Bitter tears burned Laura's eyes. "To lovers," she whispered in a husky voice and grabbed the glass from him to quaff the wine. Then she stood, her slender body sculpted silver by a flash of lightning. She retrieved her clothes and slowly began to dress.

When she stood in front of the small mirror and

combed her hair, she announced quietly, "It's time for you to leave."

"Yes, it is." Clay set the glass on the table and slipped out of bed.

Unashamedly, Laura looked at his nakedness, the pull of sinew and muscle as he slipped into his gray trousers and white shirt. He joined her at the mirror and deftly tied the gray and yellow striped cravat around his neck. They gazed at each other's reflection. He smiled and moved away to slip into his black tailcoat.

"I'll be waiting for you when you return from England." He reached out and tucked an auburn curl behind her ear. "I know a part of you hates me, Laura, and is saying you won't see me again. But you and I both know differently." He leaned down to press his lips lightly against her forehead. "Mark my words, you'll come looking for me when you return from England. You wanted me tonight in a way that spoke of repeated nights of passion."

He slid into the heavy raincoat and buttoned it down the front. Then he picked up his hat and moved to the door. He slid the bolt before he turned to look at her. "You may be the mistress of Ombres Azurées, but you're not mistress of your emotions any longer, Laura Elyse. Whether you'll admit it or not, you belong to me. Tonight I made you mine."

He opened the door to stare into the ashen face of Roussel Giraumont. Clay's mouth thinned in anger, and Laura gasped. Roussel's gaze swept over Laura, who seemed to be composed. His eyes flamed with anger. He balled his hands into fists at his sides.

"I did not know you were expecting company, *ma chère.*"

"It was none of your business."

"Business, I presume," he said sarcastically. When

126

Laura said nothing, his tone changed. "I'm sorry to have interrupted. Perhaps you would prefer that I come back later?"

Snorting his disgust of the man, Clay looked first at Laura, then at Giraumont. "There's no need for you to come back later, *Mr*. Giraumont. You've interrupted nothing. Miss Talbot and I are through with our visit. I'm leaving." He shoved through the door, pushing the Creole planter against the wall. Clay's footfalls echoed through the silent chamber.

"Laura, I did not mean to be gone so long." Roussel's voice carried down the companionway.

Because the cabin was stifling hot and humid, Laura turned and walked to the porthole which she opened. She stood there, letting the wind blow against her heated flesh. She listened to Roussel explain the reason for his long absence, but her thoughts were on Clay. He had promised to wait for her return, and she knew she would return to him.

Roussel laid his cold, clammy fingers on her arm. Laura jumped, and he quickly withdrew his hand. "Laura, I know you are much younger than I and have not seen as much of life as I have. Therefore, I am an understanding man. Yes, my dear, I am a very understanding man and am willing to forgive your indiscretions . . . as long as they don't interfere with our marriage. I for one am for each of us living his own life after we're married."

Turning, Laura glared at Roussel with contempt. Unaware that her voice carried through the opening, she said, "Your audacity appalls me, Roussel. I have committed no indiscretions of which you have any knowledge. And even if I have, they are of no concern to you. You have asked me to marry you, Roussel, but I have always declined. Until I say yes, do not presume otherwise. When I need forgiveness, I'll ask for it."

Roussel backed to the door, his hand moving to the handle. His voice was softly ominous. "I forgive youth its brashness, Laura. You'll need me one of these days, and I'll be here waiting. It is destined that you and I shall marry."

When the door closed behind Roussel, Laura ran across the room and pushed the lock into place. At that moment she knew the difference between honor and dishonor. She knew which man was the most honorable but could not bring herself to admit it. She could not forgive Clay Sutherland for having touched her soul and for having made it an integral part of his.

"I despise you for what you're doing to me, Clay Sutherland," she muttered, hot, angry tears coursing down her cheeks.

Chapter Six

Keeping to the narrow brick sidewalks that clung close to the facades of the buildings and were protected by overhanging balconies railed with wrought iron, Clay slowly walked back to the casino. He had never liked Roussel Giraumont, and after overhearing his conversation with Laura, he liked him even less. That he had been eavesdropping on their conversation did not bother Clay in the least. The porthole was open, and he happened to be walking past in time to hear them. He found the information invaluable.

Giraumont was absolutely spineless. Knowing that Laura was possibly making love to other men, he still wanted to marry her. Indeed, he groveled at her feet. Clay wondered why. Roussel certainly did not need the money or the plantation. If he were interested only in an heir, there were plenty of other women available. But it was Laura Roussel he wanted.

Clay would have enjoyed calling Giraumont out.

Slipping his hand under the coat, Clay felt for a cigar. Finding none, he stopped and scanned the stores on both sides of the street. He spied a tobacco shop. Careful to balance on the planks that someone had thrown from sidewalk to sidewalk, he crossed the muddy thoroughfare. No longer protected by a portico, he lowered his head against the heavy pelt of rain and hurried to the shop in the middle of the block.

He swung the door open, the bottom grating against the floor. The interior, despite the small pools of light that sputtered from candles placed at regular intervals along the wall, was dim and dingy. A small, nondescript man bustled from behind the counter at the rear of the store.

"Sorry, I'm just closing," he said, pulling a watch out of his vest pocket and peering at it through wire-rimmed spectacles. Candlelight reflected off the lenses to give him an owlish look. "Eight o'clock, you know."

"The cannon hasn't sounded yet," Clay reminded him.

"Can't go by the cannon. It's always late. Always," the man chirruped. He tucked the watch into his pocket and hurried to the front of the shop.

"I won't take a minute," Clay called over his shoulder. "I'd like to buy some cigars."

"On the counter." The man pointed, then turned to lower the shades over the front windows. "Those in the red and yellow box are special from Havana. The ones in the red and white box are from North Carolina."

Clay studied the line of boxes on the counter in front of him. All were gray with a thick coating of dust; he wondered how he was to know the red and yellow box from all the others. Finally, he ran his index finger across the top of all of them. Blue. White. Green. Red and yellow. He opened the lid and extracted two cigars. They, too, were covered in dust. With a disgusted shake of his head, he threw them

130

back, turned, and walked out.

"Didn't find what you wanted?" the man asked.

"No, you don't carry my brand," Clay opened the door and walked out, wondering that the man sold anything in such a filthy place.

No sooner did Clay step into the street than the lock clicked into place and the municipal cannon sounded eight o'clock. Shades were drawn and doors locked as businesses closed for the night. The streets were deserted. Here and there oil lamps, hanging at intersections and protected from the heavy rain, glimmered weakly, casting the muddy streets and sidewalks in a blue haze.

Clay walked faster to escape the biting cold. When he finally reached the Golden Fleece, he skirted the front entrance. He much preferred solitude to the boisterous crowd that frequented his place of business. He wanted dry clothes, warmth, a cigar, and a bottle of whiskey. He wanted to forget Laura Elyse Talbot.

Entering through the side gate, he hastened down the narrow passageway, lit by a lantern that hung from the heavy beams above. Through the arches he entered the court that was paved with blue flagstones, their color barely discernible in the flicker of dim light. Clay took pride in his garden and had spared no expense on its decorations. Palms, reaching for the sun, grew high. An imported iron fountain trickled. Beside the flower beds were wrought-iron benches and tables. High up was the top of the courtyard wall, iron spiked, and beyond the black gables of other houses, the darkened sky.

But tonight he took no notice. He rushed to an arch that had been glassed in, and behind which the stairs rose, a graceful curve from the courtyard to the roof. His boots hit the bottom stair, and his hand curled around the mahogany rail. Three steps up he stopped. He thought he saw something move. He listened, hearing nothing but rain splattering against the flagstones and the ominous roll of thunder.

Backing down, he ducked his head and gazed through the water-drenched sky. He swung the lantern from the hook and advanced slowly, moving around the huge potted plants and curbed gardens, his eyes searching out the corners. Finally, when he assured himself no one was there, he returned the lantern to the hook and hurried up the stairs.

"Thank God you're home, sir. I despaired of your returning," Churnbarker exclaimed when Clay entered the apartment.

The receiving room was the keystone of the entire house. Across the side facing the court were three large fanlight windows, shuttered against the winter storm. The room was nearly all doors, double glass doors opening to the inner rooms. The stairs passed through this room in a gentle curve to disappear into the shadows of the floor above. The walls were of plain white plaster with a wide cornice. In the center of the room hung a large and ornate chandelier. A few pieces of furniture stood about—a sofa, two armchairs, a table. Plants abounded in large jars. Ferns hung in baskets in the windows.

Churnbarker took one look at the muddy boots. "Either take them off, sir, or don't move until I clean them. I'll not be mopping the floors at this late hour."

Clay laughed as he flipped his hat onto the rack and slipped out of his raincoat. "I always find my way back home, Churnbarker. Don't you know that by now?"

"Have you had dinner, sir?"

"Don't want any." Clay shed his tailcoat. "I want a fire laid in my bedroom, a bath drawn, and several bottles of whiskey. You may do whatever you wish, Churnbarker. I'll have no need for you the remainder of the night."

Churnbarker hung the dripping coat on the rack next to Clay's hat. "Yes, sir, I shall do all you ask. Now, sir, let me clean your boots." The servant disappeared, only to return shortly with a basin of water, several towels, and a newspaper which he set on the floor in front of Clay. Kneeling in front of his employer, he spread the paper and pulled a pocket knife out of his pocket. "Before you bathe, sir, you have a visitor in the parlor."

Clay frowned and lifted a thick black brow in question.

"I told her you were out, sir, but she insisted on waiting. She said you had to come in sooner or later."

Clay's brow immediately cleared when he heard a "she" was waiting for him. "She?"

"Yes, sir." Churnbarker scraped the last of the mud onto the newspaper and began to wipe the leather with a wet rag. "Madame—"

"M'sieur Sutherland." A soft feminine voice echoed across the room.

Clay looked up to see one of the double glass doors open. A frown pulled his forehead. "Madame Talbot!"

Celeste, a vision of loveliness in pink and gray velvet, moved toward him. She laughed quietly. "My being here should not come as a surprise, *non*. My reason for being here is."

"There you are, sir," Churnbarker said, standing.

As soon as Churnbarker disappeared into another part of the house, Celeste said, "Don't worry, m'sieur, I haven't come to gamble tonight. I have

133

come tonight to talk with you. Shall we retire to a more private place?"

She wrapped her tiny, gloved hand around Clay's arm and allowed him to guide her into the drawing room—a rectangular apartment—about thirty-five feet long and more than half as wide. A fire burned invitingly in the hearth, and fifty candles twinkled from the huge crystal chandelier that hung in the center of the room. Clay led Celeste to the rosewood chair that sat in front of the fireplace.

"Does M'sieur Talbot know you're here?" he asked.

"Of course not." Celeste smiled. "Do you think I would be so foolish?"

When they were seated in matching chairs in front of the fire, Celeste rested her hands in her lap. Curious, Clay stretched his feet to the fire and lounged back to watch her.

Eventually, she said, "I've come about my stepdaughter."

Immediately, Clay rose and moved to an exquisitely carved table against the front wall. He pushed the lacquered tray aside that held the crystal decanter and glasses, reaching instead for a small tobacco box. Extracting a cigar, he gave it special attention.

"You are infatuated with her, no?" Celeste's husky voice drifted over to him.

Clay scratched the lucifer on the bottom of his boot and lifted it to his face. "She's a beautiful woman."

"You are infatuated with her, m'sieur, and she with you."

Clay blew smoke into the air. "Is this an assumption on your part or has she confided this to you?"

"I am not blind," Celeste answered curtly. "I want

134

you to leave her alone, m'sieur."

"Is that not for the lady to say, madame?"

Celeste rose and walked to where he stood. She tilted her head to look into his face. "I'm begging you, M'sieur Sutherland, please don't ruin her life. She has already had one great disappointment, one embarrassment in her short life. Don't add to that." Brown eyes, framed in long, curling lashes, gazed beseechingly at him.

Clay's expression never changed, but his voice became ominously quiet. "Why do you come to make such a request, Madame Talbot? Your stepdaughter has already departed for England."

"She will not be gone forever, m'sieur."

"By the time she returns, perhaps she will have forgotten all about me."

"No, m'sieur, you are not the kind of man a woman easily forgets."

"Nor am I the kind of man a lady like Laura Elyse Talbot marries."

Celeste gazed at him for a long time before she said softly, "No, m'sieur, you are not." She paused. "I'm sorry to say . . . honor does not permit. She must marry Roussel Giraumont. Now I must go."

"Pardon me, madam, if I have little respect for honor," Clay said firmly. "I think it's only a euphemism for double standard and hypocrisy."

"Truly I wish society were different, m'sieur," she murmured sincerely, and reached out to touch his arm.

"I keep forgetting," he replied flatly, "that Laura is very much a part of Creole society."

"She is." Celeste removed her hand from Clay's arm and stepped back. "But where you are concerned, M'sieur Sutherland, Laura would bolt the braces of society. That is why I have come to you."

135

After a long period of silence Clay said, "I'll send someone with you."

"That is not necessary. My servant is waiting for me downstairs. I'm spending the night in town."

Long after Celeste was gone, long after he had bathed and emptied half a bottle of whiskey, Clay sat in front of the fire in his bedroom. He thought of Celeste's visit and wondered if perhaps Laura's feelings for him were more than mere passion. If they were, of what value would it be to him? As he had told Celeste earlier tonight, Laura was a product of her environment. That was evident the night of the autumn ball, when she defended Roussel Giraumont.

Still Clay could not dismiss Laura so easily. Visions of the tall, slender beauty swam before his eyes. He had wanted women before, wanted some of them pretty damned badly, but being this obsessed with a woman was a new experience for him.

Like an adolescent in love for the first time, he had chased her to the docks and watched her and Roussel Giraumont board the ship. Just the thought caused his gut to knot. In the pouring rain he had waited and waited. Then Giraumont left, and he had charged into Laura's cabin. Angry that Laura had so easily pushed him—Clay Sutherland—out of her life, angry because it mattered so much to him, he determined to get her out of his system once and for all. But he had not. Not even Celeste's visit had fazed him. He wanted Laura Elyse Talbot now more than ever.

He heard the soft knock on the door but did not answer. He drained the glass of whiskey, then refilled it.

"A Mr. Graham Bradford is here to see you, sir," Churnbarker called. "Says it's urgent."

"Graham Bradford." Clay straightened up and set the glass on the nearby table. "Send him in."

A blond, blue-eyed giant walked through the door. "Hello, Clay."

"Graham! Graham Bradford!" Their arms outstretched, they rushed across the room. They hugged and slapped each other on the back.

"Can I get you something to eat. No. To drink?"

"Glass of that." Graham eyed the whiskey bottle. He walked to the fireplace and spread his hands over the blaze. "Mighty cold out there."

"Your business must be important to bring you here this time of night and out in this kind of weather." Liquor splashed into the glass.

"Urgent describes it better than *important."*

"I take it you didn't come all the way from Virginia to see me."

"Wrong." Graham took the glass and greedily downed the whiskey. "I am here just to see you. In fact, I came earlier but you were gone."

Clay looked at him in surprise. "Churnbarker didn't tell me."

Graham grinned. "I let myself in."

Clay shook his head. "Up to your old tricks again?" Then he remembered the shadow he had seen in the courtyard earlier. "Does anyone know you're here?"

"No."

"Can you tell me?" Clay asked.

"As you've already guessed, I'm on assignment."

Clay sat down and crossed his legs. "Ah, yes," he drawled, "we're at war with England, and New Orleans is one of our major ports."

"That's true," Graham replied, "but there's more."

"Always is when you're dealing with spies."

137

"We have reason to believe this Napoleon is about to shift his base of operation from Europe to New Orleans."

"Is your reason to believe based on assumption or fact?"

"We apprehended one of his agents in New York. He was making his way here."

"You believe him."

"One of our English agents recognized him and knew he was one of Napoleon's key men. He died before he could say anything to us. When we searched his apartment, we found certain documents sewed into the lining of his coat. From them we learned that another of Napoleon's emissaries was coming directly to New Orleans to meet with the Bonapartist Creoles."

"And you've come to arrest them or him or all?"

Graham laughed without humor. "I wish it were that easy. It's not. Great precaution was taken; none of the men were mentioned by name, and the agent's contact and the emissary are referred to by code names. I'm here to find the emissary."

"By yourself?"

"Not if you'll help me."

"I left espionage behind, Graham, when I left Virginia," Clay answered. "Life is short enough as it is. I have more important things to do than run around sticking my nose in other people's business, always wondering if this will be my last breath. Never knowing what my name is. Never knowing who my friend or foe is."

"Clay, I need you. You've been here for the past four years running this casino. You know this city like the back of your hand; you know the people. You have sources I could never have."

"And you have sources down here that I'll never

know about."

Graham's blue eyes twinkled. "As you say, New Orleans is one of our major ports. We wouldn't sit by and let the British take it, now, would we? Or the French? Will you help me?"

"I'll think about it," Clay answered.

"How about a contact who knows all the wealthy Creole families? Someone who would know which ones are loyal to Bonaparte?"

Clay shrugged. "I said I'll think about it. Now, where are you staying?"

"Thought I'd stay here," Graham replied. "From what I understand, you lost one of your dealers tonight."

Clay's right brow hiked. "I did?"

"Sure did." Graham pulled a brand new pack of cards from his pocket. "He suddenly decided he didn't like the weather in New Orleans. Landed himself a job making bigger bucks and headed upriver."

Clay grinned. "I take it I now have a new dealer."

Graham sat down at the table and shuffled. "How about a game of cards?"

"Not tonight," Clay answered.

"What's preoccupying your mind, my friend? Or, rather, shall I say who? Laura Elyse Talbot, spinster daughter of Beau Talbot."

Clay's head jerked around.

"I saw her leaving your place this morning. She's pretty." Graham spread the cards on the table and prepared for a game of solitaire. "What does she mean to you?"

Clay watched nimble fingers flick the cards into line. "I may need a dealer, Graham, but I don't need a father confessor. You can stay here, and I'll help you all I can, but you keep your damned nose out of

139

my business.''

A grin lurking in the depth of his bright blue eyes, Graham raised his head. "Yes, sir, Mr. Sutherland," he drawled. "Yes, sir." He laid more cards down, then said, "Laura's stepmother is a Creole, is she not?"

Clay did not dignify Graham's question with an answer. He walked to the window and stared at the street below. All he saw was a vision of loveliness: a tall, slender woman with hair the color of fine beaujolais, eyes the color of jade, and skin pure as ivory.

Before tonight *lonely* had been only a word to Clay; now it was a feeling.

Chapter Seven

The room had been aired earlier—as it was every day—yet it stank. It reeked of death. Although a fire blazed in the fireplace, the room was chilled. Outside, a cold January wind blew. Her shawl pulled closely about her shoulders, Laura dozed in one of the twin wing chairs. A dim circle of light fell on the cluttered nightstand as the lone candle fought for space. An empty Waterford pitcher sat next to the basin, a damp washcloth hung precariously over the rim. Clustered together were spoons, glasses, and several bottles of medicine. Diagonally in the room between two windows sat a chaise longue, a brightly colored blanket draped across it.

"Judith, where are you?" Charlotte's cry was ragged.

Asleep in the chair in front of the hearth, Laura opened her eyes and stared blankly into the fire but could not immediately orient herself.

"Judith!" The raspy cry turned to desperation.

"Coming!" Laura leapt from the chair and rushed to the bed to lean over her mother. She reached for a hand, but Charlotte snatched it away and tucked it under the coverlet. "Don't be frightened," Laura said. "I'm here."

Charlotte's green eyes were large and haunted. They flicked dully over Laura's countenance but showed no signs of recognition. Cowering away, she pressed her thin frame into the stack of fluffy pillows. "Who are you?" she asked, then whimpered pitifully, "Where's Judith? I want Judith."

"It's me, Mama. Laura. Don't you remember? I've been here since early this afternoon."

The green eyes again flicked over Laura's face and fell back to the cover. "Where's Judith?" Charlotte mumbled.

"She was gone when I arrived," Laura explained. "Morris said she's gone to see Uncle Harry. She'll be back soon."

"Harry? My brother Harry? Do you suppose they'll let me return to Harrestone? I do hope so. I want to be in my own bedroom." Charlotte's voice was suddenly animated. For an instant her eyes flared to life. As quickly the spark was replaced with suspicion. "No, that can't be. Why has Judith gone to see Harry?"

Laura smiled and brushed a strand of hair out of her mother's face. "She thought it would be a good idea for you to return home."

"Home." Charlotte sighed and relaxed against the pillows again. Once more something flickered in the depth of her eyes, and a sad smile slowly curled her thin, pasty lips. In a dreamy voice she said, "Yes, I'd like to go home. I've missed Harrestone. Where is Morris? Has he begun to pack yet?"

"No, I sent him and Cook to bed," Laura answered. The Morrises had been bone tired when she arrived midafternoon to learn that Judith was in London visiting with their uncle. "We'll begin the packing first thing in the morning."

Two large tears rolled down the hollow cheeks.

"I'm not really going home, am I? Harry will make me stay here the rest of my life, won't he? He'll never forgive me! He won't. I know he won't." How quickly her emotions vacillated. She cried softly for a moment; then she tensed and stared at Laura through narrowed eyes. She bunched the covers in her fists. "You've lied to me. Judith's left me. She's left me all alone. Where's Morris? Where's Cook?"

"They're asleep, Mama, and you're not alone. I'm here with you." Carefully Laura sat down on the mattress to keep from jarring her mother's broken hip. She pried her mother's fingers loose and held the bony hand in hers, rubbing the cold skin. "It's me, Laura, and I'm right here."

"Laura?" Charlotte lifted her head to peer more closely. "Yes," said the raspy voice, and a thin hand rose, bony fingers tracing the contour of Laura's face, "you are Laura." For a length of time she was content merely to touch her daughter, to convince herself that she was real and that she was there. Then the spidery hand retracted and dodged beneath the covers; suspicious green eyes settled on Laura's face. "You can't be Laura. She's in America with Beau."

"I was in America." Once again Laura sought the hand, found it, and clasped it within the warmth of hers. "Now I'm here . . . with you."

"Oh, Laura," Charlotte whispered. "I'm so glad you've come home."

"I am too." Laura blinked against hot tears. Gone were the bitterness and loneliness she had felt at spending Christmas alone. The long, tiring weeks on the sea had been a small price to pay to see her mother once again. The new year was bringing her a peace that she had not felt in years, not since she left England.

Charlotte breathed in deeply and exhaled, the

143

tension slowly leaving her body. Her eyes closed, her dark lashes lying in stark contrast on her jaundiced flesh. The skin was prematurely wrinkled and mottled with liver spots, the veins purple and strutted. Her fingernails rasped over the lace coverlet. "Are you married, Laura?"

"No." Laura dipped the cloth into the basin of scented water and wrung it out, placing it on her mother's forehead.

Tears slipped from the corners of Charlotte's eyes to drip down the sides of her face and dampened the cream linen pillowcase. "Will you forgive me?"

"I . . . forgave you a long time ago," Laura answered, reluctantly giving voice to the lie.

"No." Charlotte's lids opened and she settled faded eyes on her elder daughter. "You haven't forgiven me. You've forgiven the sick woman you see lying here, but you haven't forgiven me."

Charlotte's gaze swung to the large portrait that hung over the fireplace. Youth was always beautiful. So vital and alive she had been when her father had commissioned the painting. She was wearing the green riding habit that Papa had bought for her eighteenth birthday. The same shade of green as her eyes. A gauzy white veil furled sensuously from the top hat. The world and the *ton* had been at her feet that season. Not anymore . . .

"You hate me, don't you, Laura? Like Mama. Like Harry and Cybil and Judith and the rest of the family."

"I don't hate you," Laura said. "Neither does Judith."

"Yes, she does," came the weary words. "Judith takes care of me, but she hates me too."

The small clock on the mantel chimed the half hour and Laura, remembering Cook's instructions,

144

leaned toward the nightstand, her hand searching through the clutter to circle the squat brown bottle.

"Time for your medicine." Laura laid the cork next to the basin and poured a spoonful of the thick, smelly liquid into a glass full of water. Holding the medicine in one hand, she slipped the other behind her mother's back. "Here," she said, gently lifting Charlotte. "Drink this down."

Charlotte twisted away from Laura and slapped her hand, knocking the glass to the floor and splattering black liquid all over Laura's new ecru velvet gown. Horrified, Charlotte watched the darkened circles grow larger and larger. Her eyes darted from the gown to Laura's face, back to the gown.

Laura sighed, refusing to think about the damage to the dress. She remembered another time—so long ago—when another of her new dresses had been ruined. How childishly she had behaved. Not this time! After all, it was only a gown and could be replaced. She knelt to pick up the splinters of glass and toss them into the nearby wastebasket. Using the damp washcloth, she mopped up the spilled liquid.

When Charlotte realized that Laura was not going to explode into a furious tirade, she whined, "I don't like that medicine. It doesn't make me feel better."

"You're going to take it." Laura's steady hands found a second glass, which she half filled with water. She measured another spoonful of the black medicine. She stirred the mixture together.

"I don't want medicine," Charlotte shouted, then lowered her voice to a whine. "I want a drink of brandy, Laura. Just one swallow. Judith won't know. I won't tell her if you won't." The long, bony fingers clamped around Laura's wrist and bit into the tender flesh, pushing the glass away. "Please, just one swallow."

"I can't." Laura was surprised at her mother's strength.

Charlotte wilted against the mattress. She hid her face in the down pillow, refusing Laura access to her mouth. "I won't take it," came the muffled cry.

Unaccustomed to dealing with her mother and not wanting to awaken the Morrises, who needed their rest, Laura set the glass down. Charlotte heard the thud and turned slightly. She peered out of the corner of her eye.

"What's one drink going to matter in the scheme of things?" she whispered. "What's one drink to a woman who's dying?"

"All right," Laura said, "we'll compromise."

Charlotte pulled the quilt under her chin, only her face and fists showing. Thin, brittle gray hair tangled around her face. Her eyes flicked from Laura to the glass on the nightstand.

Bowing her head, Laura stared at the dark spots on her skirt. *What indeed did it matter?* "Take your medicine, and I'll get you some brandy."

Charlotte peered suspiciously. "Promise?"

"I promise."

She cackled and dug her fingers into the covers. "Judith won't like this."

Laura smiled and patted her mother's hand. "This will be our secret."

After Charlotte swallowed the bitter liquid, Laura walked out of the room, returning shortly with a small glass of brandy. Greedily, her mother gulped down the liquor and wiped her mouth with the back of her hand. Looking up at Laura with pleading eyes, she held the glass out.

"No more," Laura answered. "You need to get some rest now."

Charlotte threw the glass across the room. It

146

shattered against the fireplace. "I don't want to sleep," she screamed.

Laura sat on the side of the bed and embraced her mother's frail form. Thin limbs wrapped around Laura, and Charlotte clung, sobbing. Her fingernails dug into Laura's shoulders.

"Every time I go to sleep, I'm afraid I'll never wake up again. I want to stay awake," she cried, tears flowing down her cheeks. "I want to stay awake. I want to live, Laura. I want to live. Let me live. Please, let me live."

Laura held her mother close and soothed her as the impassioned tirade turned into tears, then into hiccups. When Charlotte was spent, Laura eased her down on the bed and brushed the wisps of gray hair out of her eyes. She wished she had the power to grant life, even to turn the hands of the clock backward, but she did not. At the moment she felt helpless . . . utterly helpless. How had Judith coped with this for so many years?

But at the same time that she felt sorry for her sister, Laura was angry. Why had Judith not informed her of Charlotte's failing health? It had taken more than a few months or a year for the woman to become this ill. Laura was wondering if all those chatty letters Judith had written were lies. Charlotte and Judith lived in the gamekeeper's cottage like peasants!

Laura's hands worked their magic on Charlotte, and she was soon asleep. Her soft snores echoed through the room. Laura rose and walked to the window. Pulling the lace inner curtain aside, she stared into the moonlit night. Against the blue-white snow that thickly covered the ground, the trees and bushes were black skeletons, their spindly arms lifted in a ritual of death. Downstairs the clock sounded the midnight hour, the ominous tones echoing through the entire house.

Laura was worried. Judith should have been back hours ago. Chilled, she returned to the hearth, where she picked up the shards of yet another glass, then put more coal on the fire. She picked up the cashmere stole—a going-away gift from Celeste—and wrapped it around her shoulders; then she sat in the large wing chair, stretching her feet to the blaze. She looked at the portrait of her mother above the mantel.

Charlotte was indeed the most beautiful woman Laura had ever seen. Her crowning glory was the thick blond hair. Her lips were sensual and full, an enigmatic smile clinging to them; her green eyes danced with mischief; they sparkled with a mysticism that lured men to her side. Laura almost heard the gentle laughter that made fools of so many—even after Charlotte married Beau.

Lost in faraway thoughts, she was unaware of the back door opening or the soft steps on the stairs.

"Laura?"

The tentative tones startled Laura. She turned to see the shadowy form standing in the door. "Judith?" She rose; Judith stepped into the room. Both of them stared at each other.

Could this woman be the child-sister whom she'd left nine years earlier, Laura wondered. Having received no portrait of Judith, she could only assume it was. She had been prepared for the obnoxious little girl, not for a woman.

"Judith Claire, is this really you?" Laura's anger quickly melted away.

A shapeless gray cape hung from gaunt shoulders. Hands lifted, and long, slender fingers pushed the hood from her head. Red curls, glinting in the firelight, escaped the severity of the chignon into which they had been coiled. Underweight, Judith

148

was worn and haggard; she looked old. Dark circles of fatigue hid the beauty of sapphire-blue eyes.

"Oh, Judith!" Laura cried.

Judith rushed into her sister's outstretched arms. "I'm so glad you came," she sobbed. "I didn't know if you would. In my heart I never believed I would see you again."

They hugged each other tightly, both crying and laughing at once.

"Papa—" Judith said, "he—he didn't—"

"He couldn't come," Laura said as Judith pulled away from her. "He wanted to, but the business . . ." Laura's voice trailed into silence; the excuse sounded lame even to her. She saw some of the sparkle die in Judith's eyes.

"Yes." Judith recovered her composure. "I know all about the business. How is Celeste?"

"She wasn't feeling too well when I left," Laura answered. All warmth seemed to have evaporated from the room and from the sisters. Both had retreated behind cool formality. "She suffers from migraine headaches."

Judith arched her brows. "How convenient!"

"It's not like that at all, Judith," Laura said defensively, not liking the sarcasm in her sister's voice.

"The pampered rich," Judith retorted.

"I said she's not that kind of person," Laura said. "She's a wonderful woman. You'll—really like her."

Judith's beautiful lips curved into a smile that was devoid of humor. "Everything that Laura Elyse Talbot-Harrow admires in a woman, you mean. Celeste Devranche Talbot is a wealthy Creole aristocrat from one of the old founding families of New Orleans—I believe those were the words you used to describe her to me in one of your letters."

149

"Speaking of letters," Laura said. "I would like an explanation of this."

Judith's cloak swirled through the air as she took it from her shoulders and hung it on the rack by the door. She neared the fire and spread her hands over the leaping flames. "Explanation of what exactly?"

"Mama's illness. Your living here in the game-keeper's cottage like paupers."

After a long pause Judith said, "After you left, Mama became more and more involved with Lord Lythes, and he used her until she was used up. Then, when she was an alcoholic, he abandoned her. Her health has gotten increasingly worse through the years. She fell and broke her hip several weeks ago."

"What about you?"

Without answering, Judith stood a moment longer, savoring the warmth from the fire; then she walked to her mother's bedside. Automatically, she straightened the clutter. She corked the bottles and lined them up. Dropping the spoon into the glass, she set them on the small tray to be taken to the kitchen. She pushed the candle closer to the bed and stared at her mother.

As if Laura had just spoken, Judith said, "I stayed at Harrestone for a while."

"Why on earth did you leave, Judith? *Grandmère* would have taken care of you."

"She would have taken care of me, Laura, but she would never love me."

"That's not true."

Judith smiled dully at her sister. "Did you not know, Laura dear, that I'm a failed experiment. Charlotte deliberately became pregnant with me in order to provide the Harrows with a male heir. When I was born, Charlotte lost all interest in me. Papa was in New Orleans with his shipping lines, and you

150

spent all your time with *Grandmère*."

Judith turned now and looked at Laura. "No thanks to *Grandmère*, Uncle Harry allowed Charlotte and me to move into the cottage, which was a godsend, seeing that we had only Papa's allowance."

"Why didn't you tell me, Judith?"

"Not now, Laura. Please, not now." Judith lowered her head and gazed at her mother. "She's sleeping peacefully, isn't she?"

"Yes."

"She's smiling as if she has a secret."

"She does." Laura tipped the shuttle, coal lumps falling into the glowing ashes. "I gave her some brandy."

A smile briefly fluttered on Judith's lips. "It doesn't matter anymore, does it?" Dully, she turned and moved to one of the chairs in front of the fireplace. Sitting down, she leaned her head against the cushioned back and stretched her feet to the fire. "If it makes her feel better, I let her have it. Now that she's bedridden, I don't have to worry about her getting it."

Laura settled in the chair next to Judith, her beautiful hands unconsciously smoothing the wrinkles out of her skirt. Surreptitiously, Judith watched her sister. Ivory combs swept Laura's auburn hair into a mass of curls atop her head. She wore a brown velvet spencer with the high collar and long tight sleeves. The satin ecru gown was covered with velvet appliqués. From beneath the hem of the skirt peeped brown kid slippers. After having nursed their mother all afternoon and most of the night, Judith thought, her clothes were virtually unwrinkled. Even the stains on her skirt did not distract from her immaculate appearance.

"When did you arrive?" Judith asked.

151

"Early this afternoon," Laura replied. "Not long after you'd left for Harrestone. Did you accomplish what you set out to do?"

Laura's eyes moved over Judith's dress, making her aware of its drabness. She could almost imagine what her beautiful sister was thinking. *How could anyone go to Harrestone to meet with the Earl dressed like a beggar . . . except you, Judith!* Judith repressed her laughter. How little her sister had changed through the years. Had she changed so little, she wondered.

"Well?" Laura asked impatiently when Judith made no reply, "did you get to talk with Uncle Harry?"

"Morris told you?" Judith said without opening her eyes. "My faithful servant is getting to be quite a gossip in his old age. No wonder *Grandmère* threw him and Cook out years ago."

"Judith," Laura snapped, "for God's sake, stop the silly prattle. Did you get to talk to Uncle Harry about bringing Mother home?"

"No."

"Then what took you so long to get home?"

"I talked with *Grandmère*." Judith was not about to confess that she had spent hours begging for money to buy Charlotte's laudanum. Having lived through it was humiliating enough.

"Did you convince her to talk with Uncle Harry?"

"Yes." A smile curled her lips. "Surely in the finer circles of society, Laura, a glass of golden white wine would be in order to toast my first conquest with the great dame of Harrestone, but since I can't abide either social circles or spirit, we'll just enjoy the golden warmth of the fire." She laced her hands together and rested them on her stomach. "I should feel happy that I persuaded her to allow Charlotte to come home, but somehow I don't. All the way home I wondered what self-serving motive she might have had."

"I'm sure there is none." Again Laura's eyes ran over Judith's drab wool dress to the scuffed shoes protruding from beneath the hem. "You never wanted to understand *Grandmère* and have always made it a point to irritate and rub her the wrong way."

"And you, sister dear," Judith said dryly, "have not changed one whit. When you left nine years ago, you were scolding me, and you haven't been back on English soil more than a few days and you're scolding me again."

Laura grinned. "Have you eaten? Perhaps you would like something hot to drink?"

Judith returned the grin. "No. Yes."

They laughed together. "Let me get you something," Laura said.

"Let me." Judith rose. "After all, I'm the host and you're my guest. Also, I'm more familiar with the kitchen than you are." Her eyes landed on Laura's beautifully manicured hands, and her expression clearly said *you're not familiar with a kitchen at all.* "I'm surprised you didn't stay with *Grandmère*."

"I've already written her a note telling her I'll be coming up to visit her," Laura answered, "but I came to be with you and Charlotte."

"Don't leave me!" Charlotte screamed and bolted up in the bed, tears streaming down her cheeks. "Come back. Don't leave. How could you? After I've given up everything for you."

Laura and Judith rushed across the room, but Judith was the one who caught her mother's shoulders and gently shoved her down. "It's all right," she said. "I'm here."

153

"Where's Randolph?" Charlotte cried, her eyes wildly searching the room. "You're keeping him from me. I want to see him."

Randolph Carew, Lord Lythes! Laura stumbled back to the chair. All these years and her mother was still crying for him. Laura hated the man, absolutely hated him. She thought the past was behind her but quickly discovered it was here waiting for her. All the bitterness and hatred quickly surfaced. Ghosts suddenly became flesh and bone. She grasped the poker and banked the fire, watching the flames as they danced into the air and disappeared into the chimney.

"You know he couldn't stay here. The cottage is too small," Judith explained. "He's staying at the inn."

"He's coming back, isn't he?" Her wild eyes locked on Judith's face; her hands grabbed a fistful of Judith's dress. "When is he coming back?"

"Later," Judith answered. "He'll be back later."

"My hip!" Charlotte screamed in agonizing pain. "My hip, Judith. I can't stand the pain. My medicine. I need my medicine. You—you have my medicine?" Her tongue darted out to moisten dry, cracked lips. "Judith, you have my medicine, don't you?"

"Yes." Judith sighed. "I got it."

"Good. I can rest now."

Judith reached into her pocket and pulled out the small package. A couple of drops from the bottle no larger than the first joint of a little finger mixed with water eased the terrible pain.

"My hair," Charlotte said not long after she drank the laudanum. Her voice was dream-soft now, and calm. "Comb my hair, Judith, and plait it. Beau always loved it when it hung down my back in the single braid. Bring me my riding habit. I'm sure we'll

154

go riding when he comes home. We are going home to Harrestone, are we not, Judith?"

"Yes," she murmured.

"Good. I must look my best when I return home." Charlotte's lids closed, and she breathed deeply. Her body relaxed in sleep once again.

Judith stood at the bed and stared down at her mother. Laura remained in front of the fire.

"She's still in love with Lythes," Laura said.

"No," Judith answered dully, "not really. She's in love with her memory of Lythes."

"How long has she been on laudanum?"

"For over a year. The dosage has increased since Lythes came to see her a few weeks ago." Judith lifted her hands and brushed loose strands of hair into her chignon. "He couldn't stand the sight of her and couldn't be away from her quick enough. She broke her hip trying to get to him. It isn't healing and the physician recommended double dosing for the pain. It's about all that helps."

"Oh, Judith!" Laura crossed the room and embraced her sister.

"I'm so glad you're here." Judith clung to Laura. "I'm so frightened. The other night when . . . when Lythes came to visit Charlotte." The mere thought of Randolph Carew sent a shiver of apprehension down Judith's spine, and Laura held her even tighter. "He—he tried to—tried to—"

"I know," Laura soothed. "I know what kind of person he was, Judith, and men like him do not change."

"When he discovered Charlotte was of no use to him, he wanted me. Oh, Laura, it was horrible. I had to fight him off."

"He's not a man to give up when he wants something," Laura said. "And my guess is that Lord

155

Lythes wants you, Judith. But I'm here now."

"Yes," Judith murmured, "you are, and I feel so much better. Safer."

"You are," Laura promised, tears coursing down her cheeks.

Finally, Judith pushed away from Laura as if embarrassed by her show of emotionalism. She turned from Laura and pressed a handkerchief to her face. Walking out of the room, she said in a thick, husky voice, "I'm rather hungry. I think I'll get a bite to eat while Charlotte's sleeping."

"Miss Judith—" Holding a candle above her head, Mrs. Morris stood at the bottom of the landing and peered up the stairs. "Is that you?"

"It's me, Cook." Judith blew her nose and returned the handkerchief to her dress pocket.

"It's thankful to God I be," the old woman mumbled. "What with that snowstorm coming. Me and Miss Laura, why we've been worried sick about you, child."

Judith laughed and dropped an arm around the stooped shoulders. "You should know better than to worry about me, Cook. I'm a big girl, quite capable of taking care of myself."

Not wanting to leave Charlotte alone, Laura remained in the bedroom. She, too, was glad to be alone for a few minutes in order to regain her composure. Her decision to come had been a wise one. Judith was happy to see her. Laura smiled; she was sure the two of them were going to grow closer during the coming days.

When Judith came up later, she brought a tray laden with sandwiches and a pot of hot tea, which they shared. Barely had they finished eating when the clock chimed the early morning hour. Judith yawned and stretched.

156

"Go on to bed," she said. "I'll sit up with Charlotte."

Laura shook her head. The circles of exhaustion around Judith's eyes were a dark contrast to her pale cheeks. "Let me, please. I'm not tired. The three of you need some rest."

Exhausted physically and emotionally, Judith offered no argument. "If you need me, call."

"I will," Laura promised.

Judith wandered to the bed to have a last look at Charlotte. She brushed a strand of hair from her cheek. "Good night," she whispered. "I'll see you in the morning."

After Judith went to bed, Laura read awhile, but the novel was dull and did not hold her interest. Chilled, she built the fire and drew her stole closer around her shoulders. Walking to the window, she gazed outside. The wind howled around the house to rattle shutters and doors; snowflakes splat against the windowpane, melting and sliding down, leaving a teary trail in their wake. Finally, Laura turned from the forlorn scene and moved to the chaise longue.

Tossing the quilt over her legs, she leaned her head against the tapestry pillows and closed her eyes. Exhaustion quickly caught up with her, and she fell into a fitful sleep. Her dreams were chaotic and restless. She was in a gambling casino; Beau and Celeste and Clay circled her. Each begged her to come with them. Beau and Celeste were pulling her in one direction, Clay in the other. And then Roussel, like a vulture, swooped out of the sky, flying directly toward her. She heard his maniacal laughter. When she felt his taloned hands cutting into her body, she screamed . . . she awakened.

She shifted position and shook the life back into her arm. Coals glimmered in the hearth but no fire blazed. The room was quiet and cold. The storm was over; the wind no longer blowing. Loathe to move from her warm cocoon, Laura snuggled under the quilt and closed her eyes again. Then the quietness enveloped her. She bolted up and listened. She could not hear Charlotte breathing.

"No!" She threw the cover aside and rushed to the bed. She fell to her knees, laying her head on her mother's chest and praying for a heartbeat. "Mother—" she caught the bony shoulders in both hands. "Wake up. Please, wake up."

Laura sat in the drawing room of Harrestone, where she drank a cup of tea with her grandmother. Even in mourning she was elegantly beautiful and gave new meaning to the simple lines of her mourning gown.

"The funeral went well, don't you think?" Amelia Harrow said. "I'm quite surprised after all these years that so many came."

"I don't think you should be surprised, *Grand-mère*," Laura returned coolly, returning her cup to the silver tray. "You know as well as I do that people came out of curiosity. They wanted to view the daughter of the *ton* who had disgraced her family; they wanted to view the granddaughters—to see if they favored Beau Talbot in the least—to see if they had taken after their mother." Laura shuddered. "Dear God, what an ordeal."

"Well, Judith didn't help matters," Amelia grumbled and leaned forward to refill her cup. "That girl goes out of her way to be ugly. Slicking her hair into that knot on the back of her neck and wearing those drab, shapeless wool dresses. To appear in that fashion for a funeral. People stared and nudged each

158

other. Fortunately, we can put it all behind us."

Yes, that's behind us now. Charlotte is dead; Judith and I are alive and are literally an ocean apart. Where do we go from here?

As if she had read Laura's mind, Amelia said, "Now is the time for you to move back to London, Laura. I noticed that George was quite smitten with you at the funeral. Now that the scandal is laid to rest, you two can be married."

Laura's laughter rang hollow. "To George Beckworth, *Grandmère?* The man who broke our engagement nine years ago?"

"To the Viscount Chichester," Amelia said. "He is not to blame for what happened. He wasn't at fault. He did what he had to do under the circumstances."

Laura repeated the words Celeste had spoken to her only weeks prior. "Perhaps I don't blame him for what happened, *Grandmère,* but I do blame him for not loving me enough to fight for me."

"Nonsense!" An arthritic hand waved through the air. "Who cares a fig about love? I want to see you married and married well, girl. At your age you will not have a better chance."

Unbidden thoughts of Clay Sutherland filled Laura's mind. An ocean lay between them, yet, unbidden, thoughts of him crept into her mind. He had created a hunger in her that no one but he could assuage. Laura's hand curled into a fist. Never had she been so torn. Never had her emotions vacillated so erratically. Until she had met Clay, ambivalence had never been one of her weaknesses; now it was her one consistent characteristic. She desired Clay Sutherland; she wanted to experience all those wonderful things he could do with and to her body. Yet she hated him; she despised herself for being so weak that she was allowing herself to be enslaved by this man's passion.

"You don't have to return to New Orleans," Laura heard Amelia say. "Write your father to let him know you're staying and that you'll be marrying Beckworth."

Laura set her cup down. "I shall surely be returning to New Orleans, *Grandmère*. First, I am the mistress of one of the largest plantations in the state of Louisiana, and second, you're being quite presumptuous in thinking George would still want to marry me after all these years."

"Harumph!" Amelia reached for her ebony and silver laced cane. "At my age I dare to be anything I want, and it's not presumptuousness that has me thinking George Beckworth is willing to marry you. I know what my own eyes tell me. Now, I have things I must do." Her arthritic legs stiff, Amelia rose, leaning heavily on the cane. "I'm going to send Huddles to get your luggage. Now that Charlotte is dead, I'm sure you won't wish to stay at the cottage. Your courtship will be much smoother carried on from here."

"As long as Judith considers the cottage her home, I'll be staying," Laura answered.

Amelia angrily tapped her cane on the floor. The jade-green eyes scanned her granddaughter's face. "You are not going back to that hunting lodge, Laura. It's not fit for a lady."

"Yet it's housed two ladies for all these years." Laura's eyes, the same shade of green as her grandmother's, never wavered from the piercing stare; they refused to be intimidated. "And no one saw fit to have them removed."

With a snort of disapproval Amelia hobbled out of the room, leaving Laura alone. Grinning, Laura picked up the newspaper and began to read—a horrible habit for a woman, and *Grandmère* deplored it. An hour later a servant quietly entered the room, a silver tray in hand.

"For you, Miss Laura."

The second she saw the bold script, the note had Laura's full attention. Even if the handwriting were not immediately telling, the coat of arms would have been. How many pieces of linen had she embroidered for her hope chest with the same insignia?

Dear Laura, the note read, *I was delighted to see you again, although I wish it could have been under different circumstances. Perhaps before you return to America you will be so kind as to see me. With all my heart I hope so, Laura. I have so much to tell you, so much to apologize for. I await your answer.*

Laura refolded the paper and slipped it into her pocket. A small smile played at the corners of her mouth. Perhaps *Grandmère* was correct: George did want to marry her. She found the thought—no matter what the reason—satisfying.

"Are you going to be wanting to send an answer, mum?"

"No," Laura said quietly, "it doesn't require an immediate answer."

Interlude I

Although a fire burned in the grate, the library draped in mourning black, was cold and depressing. Outside the room, heavy thuds and footfalls could be heard as servants moved up and down the narrow stairs cleaning out Charlotte's room.

"You have to come to New Orleans," Laura insisted not for the first time since her mother's funeral. "With Charlotte gone you have no reason to stay in England by yourself."

Judith lifted her head proudly, her thin shoulders straightening beneath the paisley shawl she wore. She stared beyond Laura. "I am an Englishwoman and England is my home."

"You call this home!" The long Indian scarf attached to the shoulders of Laura's gray muslin gown floated through the air when she waved her hand dismissively. "Open your eyes, Judith, and look around you."

"It's not so bad." Judith defended the room with a touch of defiance. The closeness the sisters had shared the night Judith confessed her fear of Lord Lythes was gone. Turning her back on Laura, Judith walked to the bookshelf on the other side of the

163

fireplace and began to rearrange the large leather volumes.

"It's not so good either." Laura sighed and unconsciously rubbed the small of her back. She was exhausted, and the cold weather was taking its effect on her. Having lived in Louisiana for the past nine years, she had forgotten how cold January in England could be.

More thuds echoed through the thick panels of the library door, and one of the workers emitted a low growl and curse. Cook's bellow, then Morris's monotone could be heard above the noise.

"Papa and I divide our time between the town house on Calle di Conti and Ombres Azurées," Laura continued.

"How nice for you, sister dear." Judith's tones were positively icy; yet she wouldn't turn around to face her sister. "But I prefer a cottage in England to a mansion on a primitive frontier."

"New Orleans is hardly a primitive frontier." Laura smiled and moved to sit in one of the large chairs in front of the fireplace. The flames cast a gentle glow on her coral velvet jacket. "Besides, what will you do? Charlotte's allowance ceases with her death."

"I'm sure the earl will see fit to extend it to me." Judith lifted a hand and tugged the shawl more closely around her shoulders. "Besides, I have my own money coming quarterly from Beau."

"That doesn't make any difference. The allowance is a mere pittance. You can do no more than exist on it as you're doing now." Laura stood and moved to Judith, the soft swish of her muslin dress the only sound in the room. She laid her hand on Judith's shoulder. "Is this all you want for yourself? If you come to New Orleans, Papa will—"

164

Judith jerked away from Laura. "Don't tell me what Beau Talbot will do. I know. I remember well what my father did for me."

Slowly, Laura's hand dropped. "Judith, you didn't and still don't understand . . ."

Judith stalked across the room to pose proudly in front of the fireplace; her chin was aloft in defiance, her fists clenched to her sides. "I think we've had this conversation before, Laura. The content hasn't changed even after ten years."

Dully Laura returned to the chair and pulled her shawl around her shoulders. "Papa was doing only what he thought was best for you. If you'll remember correctly, Judith, you didn't go out of your way to endear yourself to anyone. You were a . . ."

"*Hellion* was the word I believe you used." Judith stared smugly at her sister.

Laura lifted her head and stared directly into Judith's face. "Exactly," she said, her tone implying *and you have not changed. You may be nine years older, but you are still as stubborn and unreasonable.*

Taken aback by Laura's adamancy, Judith started and hesitated fractionally before she said, "And you were a superior prig, and still are. You haven't changed one bit."

"Judith . . ." Laura's eyes narrowed; her brow furrowed in consternation. Again she sighed. *Why must every discussion we have end in an argument?*

When she spoke, Judith's voice was icy. "You've always tried to manipulate my life. And you're still doing it. You're trying to tell me what to do. What are you going to buy me this time?"

Laura's heart sunk to her feet. She paled and recoiled as if she had been struck. She had known the nine-year-old child was angry at life in general and had taken this anger out on her, but the idea that the

165

sapphire necklace had been a bribe had never entered her mind. Laura wondered if Judith still had it, but she would not ask.

For the first time since Charlotte's death, Laura thought about the gown that still lay folded in her trunk—the gift she had purchased for Judith. There it would remain for the time being. For a second Laura and Judith stared at each other, then Judith bent and picked up the coal scuttle.

Even as a child Judith had been obstinate, Laura thought, and age had only made it worse. Laura was hard pressed to keep from leaving the room and to leave Judith to the path she had chosen. But no matter how badly she hurt, Laura could not . . . would not abandon her sister a second time. Her gaze swept around the dismal room to the window and beyond the frosted panes to the loaded wagon in front of the house.

Pushing her own pain aside, Laura rose and moved closer to the fire. "Judith, Papa left you with Charlotte because you were so young. He thought she could do more for you than he could. He had to give all of his time to recoup his fortunes. After he'd gotten on his feet, he was willing to take Charlotte and you, but she wouldn't go. And he believed that *Grandmère* would offer you your rightful place in society."

"But he took you with him." The voice quivered; the eyes glittered with tears.

Laura pretended not to notice. She was afraid she would frighten Judith. Ever since Charlotte's death, Judith had withdrawn into a shell of icy indifference. She carefully avoided any sign of intimacy between the two of them.

"Yes," Laura continued in a soft voice laden with grief and guilt, "I was older and able to care for myself. After George renounced me, there was no chance for me in England. Not until the scandal had died down completely."

For a moment Judith stared at Laura. Her features softened, then hardened. "If you'd cared about me as you say you did, why didn't you insist that I come with you and Beau, sister dear?"

The question Laura had asked herself a thousand times during the past nine years! She sucked in her breath sharply. "I could have. But I didn't. You rejected everything I'd ever tried to do for you. How did I know you wouldn't reject my efforts again?"

"I was just a child," Judith flung out.

Laura straightened and shook her head in exasperation. "You were a child. And a mistake was made with you. But you've got to put that behind you. You can't let our mistake lead you to make a bigger one."

"I won't make a mistake."

"See that you don't. This is the most important decision of your life."

A sudden gust of wind whipped beneath the door to coil icy hands around Laura. She shivered and folded her arms over her chest. Neither her shawl nor her velvet spencer were enough to dispel the chill. She sat in the large wing chair that was closest to the fire but continued to stare at her sister.

Judith's gaze flitted from Laura to the library shelves. Again she turned her back to her sister and began to straighten the books. "You're asking me to come to America, but what about Beau? I don't see him over here asking me to leave the only home I've ever known."

"You didn't ask him to come, Judith. You wrote your letter to me. You've written all your letters to me. But still you remember how many times he's asked you to come to America."

"I couldn't leave Charlotte." The tones were adamant. "You saw the condition she was in when she died. That didn't happen overnight."

"No," Laura mused, a slight hardening in her voice, "and you never told me how bad she was." The night she had arrived in England she had broached Judith about this, but Judith had begged off. Now Laura demanded to know why Judith had not informed her of Charlotte's deteriorating health. "Why didn't you, Judith? I would have come and helped you with her."

Judith's hand dropped and she moved to her desk, careful not to look at Laura. "I didn't want to be whining and complaining all the time. Besides, I was handling it fine by myself."

"But didn't you ever consider that I would want to be here?" Laura was hurt. "Judith, no matter what Charlotte had done in the past, she was my mother too."

Judith lowered her head and shook it, but Laura would not be stopped. "You did wrong. You should have told me sooner that my mother was as sick as she was. You've kept me from her when she needed me. I'm only thankful that I was able to see her before it was too late."

Judith studied her hands. "I didn't think you'd care about either one of us."

"Of course I care. Charlotte was my mother, and you're my sister. I love you both."

Judith's head jerked up, and she stared at Laura. A bitter smile curled her lips. "What is love?"

Laura shook her head helplessly and frowned. That Judith asked the question was a poignant revelation of the lack of such emotion in her life. Guilt assailed her.

Eventually, she spoke. "I understand why you

didn't come, particularly in the last year or so. And you didn't let me know how bad she was. But don't you see? I've got to forgive and put all that behind me. And I am. Judith, you need us. You don't have anyone to protect you in England. You have to come to America with me."

Judith eased back in the chair and twined her fingers together in her lap. "I can apply to the earl. *Grandmère* said that she would introduce me to society."

The jade-green eyes narrowed to a speculative slit; they skimmed over the dull, worn dress. "You're nineteen years old. I was engaged when I was seventeen to George, a man I loved and respected. *Grandmère* has ignored you all these years. She might bring you out after all this time, but you can bet that you'll have to do exactly as she says. And marry when and where she wants you to."

"At least I'd be in England," was the swift reply.

"And Lord Lythes would still be around." The retort came as swiftly. "Neither *Grandmère* nor the earl protected Charlotte very well. Do you think they'll do any better for you?"

Judith rose and crossed the room to stare out the window into the snow-covered garden. Her gaze settled on the stone bench. "I don't know," she admitted.

"Yes, you do."

"The night Lythes attacked me was the most frightening, humiliating experience of my life."

The terror in her sister's voice compelled Laura to walk over and stand behind her. Again she laid her hand on Judith's shoulder. The tension in her sister's body communicated itself to her. Judith shivered and Laura rubbed her arms. She spoke reassuringly. "Believe me, Judith, I can understand how helpless a woman can feel when a man exerts his strength."

"You can't understand!" Judith shuddered. "No one can understand how horrible, how totally helpless a woman is when a man abuses her like he almost did me. You, least of all, sister, can understand how I feel."

"I of all people *most* understand how you feel." The whisper was almost lost in the spitting and sputtering of the fire.

"You?" Judith glanced over her shoulder. "How could you?"

Laura rubbed her hands together. "The incident and the man may be different, but the feelings of helplessness are just as real. Even though your bruises are physical and mine are emotional, men still took advantage of us."

While Clay had not taken advantage of Laura, her wounds were too new, too inflamed for her to reason correctly. Her face as white as the snow that covered the ground outside the cottage, she quietly told Judith about Clay.

"For heaven's sake, Laura . . ." Now it was Judith's turn to comfort. She embraced her sister and held her tightly.

"Oh, I know you think I'm in control." Laura's eyes were the only color in her face. "And most of the time I am, but when I'm around this man—this gambler—the most terrible feelings take control. For the first time in my life, I felt—helpless and afraid. Just as you did. Except that with emotions it's ten times worse."

"Oh, Laura. How could it have been worse?"

"When your emotions are involved, Judith, your very soul is touched." Laura laughed without mirth and pulled away from Judith. Suddenly cold, she moved toward the fire. "I don't care a flip about the

170

loss of my virginity," she added.

Judith's face went slack, and she gasped.

"I really don't," Laura averted. "After all, I'm twenty-six years old." Laura was disgusted when she remembered how soft she went in Clay's arms and begged him to possess her. Her voice hardened perceptibly. "What I care about is the loss of control. He destroyed my composure. He destroyed my confidence in my ability to be in control. He made me . . . feel."

Quite calmly she sat down, folded her hands in her lap, and tucked her feet beneath the chair. Her gaze locked with Judith's.

"Oh, Laura," Judith whispered.

The heart-cry touched Laura. Biting back the tears, she turned away and shrugged. She pressed the wrinkles out of her skirt. She regained her composure, and after a moment's silence said, "So you see, Judith, if you remain here, sooner or later Lord Lythes is going to drag you into his world just the way he dragged Charlotte. Just the way Clay Sutherland dragged me into his. He made me doubt myself. And I'll never forgive him for that. I really think I despise men."

"Oh, sister, you don't." Laura's soft declaration frightened Judith. "Remember how much you loved George?"

Laura tensed; her back straightened. Then she smiled and relaxed and draped her hands over the chair arms. Had she really loved George? She thought not. She loved what he could give her. Security. Title. An estate.

"George has never married. I suspect he still loves you," Judith said gently. "Why don't you see him again? Maybe it's not too late."

Laura settled more comfortably in the chair and

shook her head. "If he loved me, why did he turn his back on me when I needed him. No, I'll never be able to forgive him for that."

"You *can* forgive him," Judith insisted. "He's a victim of the same society. He's bound by the same laws that bind you." She stopped and grinned. "Why would you want me to enter that society? I don't want to have anything to do with it."

Laura's face tilted. "The laws may be binding, but everybody's life needs structure. I'm smart enough to know that there are wonderful things to be gotten from pleasant society. In New Orleans you'd have a chance for a new life . . ."

"The sort that you are having with Clay Sutherland?"

Laura's fingers curled around the chair arms. "Not at all," she denied. "Now we're talking about you and your problems. Leave Clay Sutherland alone. He's got no part in this."

"Oh, but he's very much a part of this, sister dear." Judith plunged to the attack. "You're offering protection to me? You can't protect your own self."

"I've put him out of my life, and I'm going to put him out of my mind." She breathed in deeply and lifted her hands, bridging them together as if she were uttering a prayer.

Judith shook her head. "Brave words, sister dear."

"At least I can call on Papa if I absolutely have to," Laura continued coolly, "but I won't have to call on Papa about this because I'll have everything under control."

"How very nice to be so nearly perfect."

"I'm surely not perfect. Just in control."

Judith knelt in front of Laura and looked directly into her eyes. "Must you always fight so hard for control? My God! You're human, Laura. And human beings have feelings. You'll suffocate if you don't allow them to come out. Break something. Scream! Cry! I'd suffocate if I had to live as you do."

If Judith only knew! Laura thought but said only, "Clay Sutherland is a thing of the past. I confided in you because I wanted you to understand that I have had my problems and have solved them."

"Oh, for heaven's sake." Judith rolled her eyes to the ceiling and leapt to her feet.

Ignoring her sister, Laura continued in the same quiet and controlled voice, "Forget about all that. We're talking about your future. And you have a future, Judith. Believe me. You've honestly never been given the chance to see if you could live in society. Now Papa and I want to give it to you with no strings attached. Papa would never tell you whom to marry. And you'd be safe. You'd be foolish not to take the opportunity. Or are you going to cower here until Lord Lythes comes for you?"

They stared at each other for a moment. Their thoughts were written in their eyes for each other to see. Randolph Carew was an opportunist, a sadist who would be back. If he were interested in Judith—and he was—he would not rest until he had her, until he had dragged her down to the same level that he had Charlotte. The silence grew between them.

Finally, Judith asked, "How can I believe you?"

"Judith, I've bared the inmost secret of my soul to you." Laura leaned forward. "You have to believe me. And you have to accept help from me. Because you really have no alternative. I promise that you'll have a chance."

Judith clenched her hands in front of her as if she were tearing fabric. Laura almost expected to hear again the ripping of the blue chintz dress. She covered them with her own. "Judith, please. Let's

173

give ourselves another opportunity to know each other as sisters should."

Judith nodded and smiled. "I can't go with you to America when you leave next week. I want to believe you, Laura. And I do. But I need more time to think about this."

Laura returned her smile. "Of course you do. Just don't think about it too long. Lord Lythes is only postponing his plans. Don't think he'll respect Charlotte's death any longer than a fortnight. He wants you, and if you remain within his reach, he'll have you—fair means or foul. You have to get away."

"You know, Laura, I'm luckier than you are. At least I have a place to run to. You have to run back to the place that you came from—and face your nemesis head-on."

At the thought of seeing Clay again . . . at the thought of never seeing him again, Laura shuddered. She could not imagine which would be the worse fate. She drew the huge wing chair closer to the fire and spread her hands over the golden flames. She sought their warmth, but inside she was cold.

Judith remained at the window. Slowly, she turned to face the frosted panes. The blue sun had melted the snow on the dark bench, and it stood a stark contrast to the purity of winter.

Chapter Eight

"I'm so glad to be home," Laura exclaimed as she sat in the carriage beside Celeste and waited for the servants to load her trunks. The ermine collar of her wine-colored velvet pelisse and her matching hat gently framed her face. Her smile was brilliant, her eyes glowing.

"And just in time for the Mardi Gras season," Celeste added, a twinkle in her eye. "We missed having you with us at Christmas, and when we received that letter from your *grandmère*, we thought we would not have you for Mardi Gras. We thought, *ma chère*, that you would not return at all."

"*Grandmère* should never have written such a letter." Laura slipped a gloved hand out of the ermine muff and caught her stepmother's hand. "But it was difficult for her to understand that I didn't want to live in England. They think America is a frontier and can't imagine anyone's preferring to live here rather than in London."

Celeste's eyes rounded. How dare anyone criticize New Orleans. "We are not primitive! We are one of the most cosmopolitan cities in the world. I don't know of many houses in Europe that could compare to Ombres Azurées."

"Of course not," Laura hastened to assure her.

"Your grandmother has always been a headstrong woman." Beau's deep, quiet voice joined the conversation. Sitting across from them, he draped one leg over the other and folded his arms across his chest. "She thought with your mother's death you would be willing to pick up your life where it had left off nine years ago. I guess now she'll be running Judith's."

"No." Laura's voice softened. "No one will run Judith's life but Judith. She's far older than her nineteen years, Papa. Life has matured her."

Beau squirmed uneasily.

Laura stared unrelentingly at him. "I wish you had gone with me, Papa. I'm sure you could have convinced her to return with us."

"You know I couldn't, Laura," Beau snapped. "Someone has to take care of business."

"Maurice could have seen after it for a few weeks, Papa." Laura leaned forward to place her hand on Beau's knee.

"We've already been through this, Laura." He had the grace to lower his head when both Laura and Celeste stared at him.

"You should have. Judith needed you."

"You were there."

"And I'm glad, but she wanted you, Papa. You should have seen her face when she learned that you hadn't come."

Again Beau shifted in the seat and ran his hand through his hair. He covered his embarrassment with anger. "If she wants to see me, why doesn't she come over here? Dear Lord, but I've begged her often enough. I've told her that Ombres Azurées is as much hers as it is yours."

"You've always assured her of money, Papa, but

176

Judith doesn't want charity. She wants love. Your love."

"Surely she knows I love her!" he exclaimed, incredulous.

"Why don't you write her, Beau?" Celeste suggested.

"Yes," Laura agreed. "Before I left England she promised she would come to New Orleans. But I don't know if she's prepared to live here or is merely coming for a visit."

"Visit!" Beau said. "I want her to live with us, Laura."

"I know," Laura answered, "but let's take it one step at a time, Papa. She's afraid of being suffocated by us. We must give her breathing room and allow her to make her own decisions. Beneath her hard surface she's still a little girl searching for the meaning of life. We must move slowly and gently with her."

Beau's face twisted in anguish. "My God, what have I done to my baby daughter? I should have gone. I should have gone and made her come back with you."

"No, *mon cher*." Celeste hurt for the man whom she loved so much. "We cannot make others do our bidding, no matter how good our motive may be. Nor can you undo the past. As *chère* Laura said, you must let Judith know you love her and want her to live with us. The decision to do so must be hers, *oui?*" The gentle brown eyes stared into pure sapphire-blue ones.

"*Oui.*"

Celeste turned to Laura. "Your grandmother mentioned that you were seeing George Beckworth. Is this true, *ma chère?*"

"Yes, I saw George," Laura answered.

177

The uncomfortable confrontation over, his composure regained, Beau was again leaning into the cushioned seat, one leg draped over the other. "I can't believe you'd see him after the way he treated you."

"Beau!" Celeste gently scolded and leaned forward to tap his knee with her fan.

"It's all right," Laura said. "And, yes, Papa, even after the way he treated me, I saw him. He came to Mama's funeral."

"Of all the gall!" Beau exclaimed. "From the tone of your grandmother's letter, I assume he is quite willing, in fact quite eager, to marry you now? Probably heard that you're going to inherit a fortune from me."

Laura stared into the eyes that were so reminiscent of her sister's. "Yes, he wanted to marry me, but I didn't want him."

Celeste's hand searched through the folds of material to find Laura's. "I am glad. Even though he has a title, you are much too good for him. A title is poor excuse for a good man and husband, *n'est-ce pas?*"

Laura's thoughts ran to Clay Sutherland. She lowered her eyelids for fear Celeste would read her thoughts. Memories of him so filled her mind and body that she could think of no other man. None could compare to him. None stirred her senses as he did; none made her blood roar like fire through her veins. No one but he made every other man in the room pale into insignificance.

"Roussel regrets that he was unable to come with us today," Celeste continued. "He missed you so much, *ma chère.*"

A shiver slid down Laura's spine. Vividly, she recalled the last time she had seen Roussel; as vividly she recalled the nightmare and his taloned hands

178

biting into her flesh. As clearly as if he were speaking to her, she heard his ominous threat.

"It is time you considered marriage, Laura," Beau said. "Roussel has been a patient man, but I don't know how much longer he will allow you to dangle him."

"I've never dangled Roussel," Laura denied. "When he proposed to me, Papa, I told him no. He's the one who has deluded himself."

"Laura," Celeste chided, "you are getting no younger. You must consider marriage."

Since Laura had set sail for England she had envisioned herself married, but never had her bridegroom or husband been Roussel. Always it was Clay Sutherland with his rugged dark features and sardonic smile.

"Have you never thought, *Maman,* that society is unfair."

Celeste and Beau looked at each other before she said, "Life is unfair, *ma chère.*"

A tall, slim man moved past the carriage, tipping his top hat. "Mam'selle."

"M'sieur Lambert," Laura said in greeting, smiling despite her irritation that the conversation had been stopped. "How delighted I am to see you again. May I present you to my parents?"

He smiled. *"Oui,* mam'selle, that will give me great pleasure." With long, slender fingers he brushed a shock of straight brown hair from his forehead.

Laura flung open the carriage door and said, "Papa, this is Edouard Lambert, the gentleman I sailed with from England, the one who is visiting with Roussel."

"Ah . . . yes." Beau scrutinized the man in front of him. "I'm surprised Roussel did not apprise us of your visit, m'sieur. You see, we are neighbors and good friends."

"I do not know M'sieur Giraumont personally," the Frenchman answered smoothly. "I only know of him. Because of the war, my departure from England was unexpectedly quick, and I did not have time to write M'sieur Giraumont of my arrival."

Beau nodded, but he was still wary. "The war indeed has thrown all of us into odd circumstances, m'sieur. For instance, I find it peculiar that you sailed on the *Laurel* from England."

If Edouard were perturbed, he never showed it. Quite calmly, he said, "Before I came to America, I visited with relatives in England."

"Since you're staying with Roussel, m'sieur, I'm sure we'll get to know each other better."

"Certainly."

"Now, M'sieur Lambert, I would like to introduce my wife, Madame Celeste Talbot."

Celeste smiled and extended her hand.

"Madame, *enchanté*." Edouard brushed a light kiss atop the cream-colored glove.

"M'sieur Lambert," Celeste said as she drew back her hand, "you couldn't have timed your visit to New Orleans any better. We are quickly approaching our Mardi Gras season."

"*Oui*, one of the most exciting times in New Orleans." Laura's face was as animated and beautiful as her voice. Edouard was unable to take his eyes off her.

Celeste smiled fondly, her eyes growing soft with memories. "It is exciting now, *oui*, but it was even more exciting when I was a child. Mardi Gras was indeed a celebration."

"But it is still wonderful," Laura insisted. "M'sieur Lambert, you must get Roussel to bring

180

you to one of our balls."

"I will, mam'selle," Lambert promised, his gaze locked to Laura's face.

Beau frowned at the Frenchman and cleared his throat. "Why are you here in New Orleans, M'sieur Lambert?"

Edouard's head turned and he stared blankly at Beau for a second. "I . . . er . . . have come at the request of my family, m'sieur. We—are thinking of moving from France . . . for political reasons."

"I take it you're a Bonapartist?" Beau said.

Edouard straightened. "My family supported the emperor. That is one of the reasons that we wish to leave France. If we remain after—" Unable to bring himself to say the words, he left the sentence hanging. "We shall be persecuted, m'sieur. We feel that it will be better for us to move."

Beau folded his arms across his chest. "Monetarily, it will be better for you to move."

Celeste said, "Do not speak so harshly and judgmentally, my husband."

Edouard nodded his head graciously and smiled. "Perhaps the words are harsh, madame, but nonetheless true. While I may be a Frenchman, I am also a realist. I supported Napoleon, but now I can do nothing. I wish my family . . . and my fortune to be safe. With Roussel's help I shall find property for sale, and—" A wave of his hand completed the sentence.

"Perhaps I can be of help." Beau offered, not because he admired Edouard Lambert but because he was a businessman first. Lambert's relocation in New Orleans as a planter meant more produce— more sugar or cotton or both—to be shipped through the Talbot lines. "If you are waiting here for Roussel, you may be waiting for hours. Business required him

181

to make a trip to Baton Rouge," Beau said.

"He doesn't know I'm here," Edouard answered. "I was fortunate to have gotten passage aboard your ship which has brought me here several weeks earlier than I expected. As soon as the congestion clears from the dock, I will hire a hack to take me to the Hotel New Orleans on Rue Royale. I shall send a letter to Roussel informing him of my arrival."

"We're traveling on Rue Royale. Ride with us," Beau said in invitation.

"I appreciate your offer, m'sieur," Edouard answered, "but I'm not going directly to the hotel. I must first stop by the Planters' Bank. I have some important papers which I wish to deposit."

"Then it's settled," Beau announced. "That's right on our way. What about your luggage?"

Before Laura quite knew what had happened, Edouard's trunk had been loaded atop the carriage, and he was sitting opposite her next to her father. They had not ridden far down Rue Royale when the coach stopped suddenly, throwing the women forward.

"What the—" Beau muttered, catching Celeste in his arms. After she resituated herself, he leaned out the window and yelled, "What happened?"

"Overturned wagon," the driver called back.

Squirming back into the thickly padded seat, Laura adjusted her hat and straightened her skirt. She peered through the window. A gathering crowd pressed around the wagon.

"Can you see anything?" Celeste asked.

"Nothing." Beau opened the carriage door and stepped down. "Wait here," he instructed. "Let me go check."

Soon he was lost in the crowd. Laura's gaze lifted. On the other side of the intersection another carriage stopped. Her heart skipped a beat; she recognized the blue and gold livery.

"My God! Someone help!" a voice in the crowd shouted. "A boy's caught under the wagon."

The door opened, and Clay leapt out. He stripped out of his jacket and tossed it to his driver. He shoved through the crowd.

"Get out of the way," he ordered to one, then said to another, "Make yourself useful. One of you go get a doctor. Get something so we can lever this wagon up."

Never stopping to think about what she was doing, forgetting Celeste and Edouard, Laura opened the door and jumped from the carriage. She elbowed her way through the crowd. Clay and her father knelt in a heap of cabbage beside the wagon.

"My legs," a small boy cried, his face pale with pain and fear.

Clay's hand curled around his shoulder, and he squeezed reassuringly. "Don't worry, son. We'll have you out from under here in a little while."

Several burly black dockworkers carrying huge planks on their shoulders pushed to the wagon. "Here you are, Mr. Sutherland," one of them said, a smile exposing two rows of even white teeth. "We'll have that little tyke out of there in just a minute."

Assessing the damage, Clay scooted around the wagon. "Thanks, Louis."

"I will help also, m'sieur," Edouard said. "Tell me what you wish for me to do."

Clay turned in surprise and stared at the Frenchman. His heavy and unfamiliar accent alerted Clay to his recent arrival in New Orleans. "I'm going to use the planks as levers to raise the wagon." Over his shoulder he called to Beau, "As soon as we lift the wagon high enough, Mr. Talbot, pull the boy free.

183

We won't have much time. The wagon may not be able to stand on its weight after the accident."

"I'll be ready," Beau gritted out.

With fluid motion Clay stripped off his cravat and shirt. He dropped them carelessly at his feet. Joining the dockworkers and Edouard, his hands clamped around one of the planks.

"Now," he shouted, and they pushed. But the wagon was too heavy and did not budge. "Harder," Clay grunted. The muscles in his biceps and shoulders flexed. His face turned red and the veins distended. "Harder."

The wagon creaked. The metal rim of the wheels grated on the bricked street. The crowd quieted. More produce toppled onto the street.

"A little higher," Beau called.

His palms flat on the top of the log, Clay took in a deep breath and pressed with all his strength. A thin sheen of perspiration covered his body. His tan breeches pulled tight across flexed buttocks and thigh muscles. His hair, a mass of riotous curls, tumbled about his face. Slowly, the wagon rose from the ground.

"A little more," Beau shouted. "A little more." Then: "I've got him."

"Get out of the way," Clay shouted as the wagon landed on its wheels, rocking from side to side.

Laura ran around the vehicle. Regardless of her expensive gown and fabric slippers, she knelt beside her father on the dirty bricks. She tossed her muff aside and stripped off her gloves. "It's going to be all right."

The boy lay there, a shock of red hair falling across his forehead. His freckles stood out against his pallid flesh. His tears had stopped, and his eyes were dull

184

and blank.

"Get me a knife." She held her hand out to her father. Her eyes never left the boy's face. "I need to cut your trousers so I can see how badly hurt your legs are."

Cold metal touched her palm, so did warm fingers that lingered momentarily. "Here, take mine." The warm, husky tones wrapped themselves around Laura, drawing her gaze against her will to the man who stood beside her. She looked into golden-brown eyes she remembered only too well.

"On second thought, let me." Clay knelt beside her. Taking the knife, he sliced the material on both breeches' legs.

Although Laura was aware of Clay, the boy's safety was her first concern. "What's your name?" Her hands examined up and down the leg from calf to thigh. She was unaware of the blood that soon spotted the front of her coat and soaked into the white silk dress beneath.

"John," the boy mumbled through clenched teeth.

"Can you feel this?" Her fingers bit into his calf muscle.

"Ouch!" He tried to flinch away from her, but Clay caught his shoulders and held him tightly. When Laura touched one of the deep cuts, he grimaced and groaned.

"No broken bones." Then gentle fingers examined the cuts. "How old are you, John?"

"Twelve," he grunted. "Are my legs gonna be okay? If they ain't, I don't know what I'll do. Mr. Simon ain't gonna like this. He'll—"

"He's not going to do anything to you," Laura promised. "And while the cuts are deep, they'll heal, given time. I don't think you've suffered any

185

permanent damage."

"Move aside," a gruff voice shouted. "That's my wagon."

"Hold the boy," Clay said to Beau. He rose slowly, the movement fluid and purposeful. The crowd fell aside to allow a short, squat man passage.

"Where's the boy?" the man demanded, hands falling to ample hips. His chest rose and fell beneath a dirty shirt as he caught his breath. Thin, faded britches strained across a bulging stomach.

"Are you Mr. Simon?"

The bloodshot eyes narrowed. "That's right. Durwood Simon. Came to get my wagon and the boy. I see the wagon and the vegetables. Where's the boy?"

"He's right here," Clay answered.

"Just let me get my hands on him," Simon threatened. "I'll whip the pure fire out of him. Can't take any better care of my property than this!"

"I don't think so." The words were soft, but Clay's stance, his expression, were indomitable. "He's hurt. Miss Talbot is tending to his cuts until a doctor arrives."

Chewing his cud of tobacco, Durwood Simon stared at Clay. Finally, he shrugged and walked around the wagon, kicking the strewn vegetables with the toe of his shoe. He stood behind Laura and glared at the boy. "One fine mess you've got me into, boy. All my food gone. My wagon in need of repair."

Clay's hand landed on the man's shoulder. His fingers dug into the flesh. "Go easy on the boy, mister. He's hurt pretty bad."

Simon jerked away from Clay's touch. He spun around and glared at him. "This here boy belongs to me, mister. He's my indentured servant. I have papers to prove it, and I'll treat him exactly like I want to. You or nobody else can tell me how to treat

186

him. Get up from there, John," he yelled. "You've caused enough commotion for one day."

"Yes, sir, Mr. Simon." The boy tried to push to his feet, but Beau held him securely.

"He can't," Laura cried. "He needs medical attention."

"Don't worry," Beau said to the boy. "We're going to take care of you."

"I'm gonna give him attention," the man snapped. "Get up from there, John."

Clay stepped in front of Simon but glanced down at Laura. "The boy doesn't do anything unless the lady tells him to."

Laura smiled wanly. "He needs to be moved somewhere so his cuts can be treated."

Clay looked at one of the dockworkers. "Louis, put the boy in my carriage."

When the black man picked John up, Simon shouted, "Put that boy down."

Louis looked from the vendor to Clay, who shook his head. "I'm taking him to the Golden Fleece," Clay said to Simon. "You can get him there after he's been treated by a doctor."

The produce vendor started toward Louis, but Clay blocked his path. "You'll have to kill me first."

"I just might do that," the man answered. His gaze followed the black man as he carried the boy toward Clay's carriage. Simon chewed his tobacco for a length of time, then ducked his head and spat.

Clay watched the spittle spread across the toe of his highly polished shoe. "I'm going to ignore that," he said. "I've already fought with your wagon."

"Don't reckon I want you to forget it," the man sneered. "Kinda figure you're scared to fight me. All talk and no do."

Clay's hand darted out, his fist curling around the

187

lapels of Simon's shirt. He jerked him to his toes and dragged him across the flagstones. Clay stared down into his face. "I don't give a damn what you think. All I care about is the boy. How much do you want for him?"

"What do you mean?" Simon grunted. He squirmed in Clay's grasp.

"I want to buy him."

The muddy eyes brightened at the prospect of making a dollar. "You're wanting me to sell him to you?"

"He's not going to be worth much to you while he's healing." Clay's grip relaxed, and Simon eased back on his heels.

"Don't know if I can do that," he said. "I'm right fond of the boy. We been together now for two years. Don't rightly know what I'd do without him."

"How much?" Clay's patience was running thin.

"Well, now—" Simon's gaze swept over the strewn produce to the damaged wagon. "Reckon I'll have to have about two hundred dollars."

"One hundred." Clay released the man completely. "And you have a deal."

Simon stumbled back a step before he regained his balance. "Don't reckon that's fair, mister. The boy means a lot more to me than—"

"One hundred." Clay's voice was as hard as his gaze.

"One hundred fifty," Simon said.

"One hundred."

Simon ran dirty palms down the front of his shirt. "Okay," he mumbled. "One hundred."

"Come to the Golden Fleece with the boy's papers. I'll give you your money then."

"I'll be there," Simon muttered. "You can count on that." Stooping, he began to pick up as much of

188

his produce as he could.

Laura gave scant regard to the bloodstains on her clothes and was brushing dirt from her coat when Clay said, "I believe this is yours."

Laura was not conscious of taking the muff he offered. Her father, the crowd, everything and everyone, faded into nothing as she gazed into the golden-brown eyes of the man standing in front of her. "Thank you," she murmured.

Clay smiled. "I wouldn't want your gown to be incomplete."

"I'm not talking about the muff," she said. "I'm talking about the child. That was kind of you."

Beau's lips thinned disapprovingly. His hand banded around Laura's upper arm. "Come, Laura, we must be on our way."

"The boy." Laura freed her arm from Beau's clasp. "Are you going to need me to—"

Clay's eyes softened. "Thank you for the offer, Miss Talbot. I'll get a doctor to look at him. Be assured, I'll take care of him."

"I am," Laura whispered, her heart going out to this man.

"I believe this is yours, m'sieur," Edouard said.

"Yes, it is." Clay's eyes skimmed the Frenchman while he took the knife. "Thank you."

"I must commend you, m'sieur—"

"Clay. Clay Sutherland."

"M'sieur Sutherland, you handled this incident quite well."

"Thank you." Clay's gaze shifted from Edouard to Laura. Curiosity glinted in the depth of his eyes.

"I am Edouard Lambert," the Frenchman said. "Newly arrived to your beautiful city."

"Well, Mr. Lambert," Clay returned, "let me welcome you to New Orleans. You've arrived just in

189

time for the—"

"I know." Edouard held up his hand. "I have arrived in time for the Mardi Gras season. Mademoiselle Talbot has been telling me all about the festivities." He looked at Laura and smiled. "She and I had the privilege of sailing from England together."

Clay cast Laura a sharp glance, which did not go unnoticed by Beau. Cutting the conversation short, he said, "We must be going. We need to get M'sieur Lambert to the bank before it closes for the day."

"While you're in New Orleans, Mr. Lambert," Clay said, "I invite you to join me and my customers at the Golden Fleece for many fun-filled nights." Clay then dipped his head to Laura and Beau. "Good day, Mistress Talbot, Mr. Talbot." He turned and walked toward his carriage, stopping along the way to pick up his shirt.

With greedy eyes Laura watched the material caress his skin as he slipped into it. As if he felt Laura's stare, Clay turned before he reached the carriage, the shirt unbuttoned and hanging loose, the tail flapping in the breeze. The white material was a pristine contrast to his tanned skin and black chest hair. Black curls gentled the indomitable lines and planes of his face.

"Laura, for God's sake," Beau muttered, clasping her arm once again and tugging, "let's get out of here."

Laura was aware of Clay's eyes on her as she walked back to the carriage between her father and Edouard Lambert.

"What happened, Laura?" Celeste gently brushed tendrils of hair from her cheeks.

"A produce wagon overturned," Beau answered cryptically. "A small boy was wedged underneath."

"The boy," Celeste said, "is he all right?"

190

"He's fine." Beau helped Laura into the carriage.

"Oh, Laura!" Celeste saw the soiled coat. "You have ruined your pelisse."

Laura looked down, aware for the first time of the bloodstains.

"And your gloves, Laura, where are your gloves?"

Not caring about her pelisse and gloves, Laura shook her head and shrugged. She scooted into the corner of the seat beside Celeste but heard nothing of the conversation as she gazed out the window for one last look at Clay. The crowd was thinning, and one by one carriages were moving around the produce wagon.

Clay's passed by. Framed in the window was Jena Benoit. The mulatto smiled and tipped her head in greeting.

Chapter Nine

"Laura, do sit down and quit pacing the floor."
Celeste lay her embroidery in her lap and patted the
sofa. "At the rate you're going, you'll have a hole
worn in my new carpet. Is something wrong?"

Laura walked to the window and stared into the
courtyard below. "I'm a little worried about the boy
who was injured in the accident."

Celeste looked at her and hiked one finely arched
brow. Then she resumed her sewing, the needle
dipping in and out of the linen cloth, colored thread
flying through the air. "I don't think you have a
worry. For what else he may be, M'sieur Sutherland
will look after the child."

"Yes, I know that. I would just like to see John.
And I guess I'm restless. My first night home and
Papa must work."

Celeste laughed softly. "I think it's good that
M'sieur Lambert is going to be with us this evening.
And you must, too, *ma chérie,* considering the way
you're dressed." The brown eyes swept over the white
silk dress with a low décolletage.

A little uncomfortable, Laura lifted her hand and
touched the Jade phoenix she wore around her neck.

Still she would not be deterred from her goal. "I'm sure M'sieur Lambert would find his evening more enjoyable if we were to show him New Orleans."

"I don't know, Laura," Celeste said. "Your father would not like your going out with M'sieur Lambert unchaperoned. It's so unconventional."

"But you could go with us, could you not?" Laura moved quickly to sit beside Celeste and took the embroidery out of her hands. Clasping them in her own, she squeezed.

The head shook, but the brown eyes lit up with interest. "Let us spend the evening here getting to know one another better. Besides, what would Roussel think of your going out with M'sieur Lambert? He would be jealous, *non?*"

"I'm not engaged to Roussel yet, no matter what you and Papa think. I don't owe him an explanation for what I do. Please."

Celeste withdrew her hands from Laura's. She lowered her head and began to trace a chain stitch with the tip of her nail. Her voice dropped to a wistful whisper, "If only your father did not have to meet Maurice tonight. I used to find myself jealous of your mother. Because of her I had to marry outside my church. I was afraid that one day your Papa would return to her and leave me alone."

"But you no longer have that fear, *Maman,*" Laura said gently. "And now you can have your marriage blessed in the church."

"*Oui,* your father and I discussed this before he left for the office. Now, *chère* Laura, I find that I am also jealous of the Talbot Shipping Line. I get tired of being Beau's second love."

Laura rubbed her stepmother's hands. "Perhaps it would do Papa good to know that you don't have to sit at home and wait for him, *non?* Why not spend an

193

enjoyable evening out?"

Mischievousness glinted in the depth of Celeste's chocolate-brown eyes that lifted to stare into Laura's face. Slowly, she nodded her head. *"Oui,* you have a point. A very good point. I think you and I shall take M'sieur Lambert out to see the city tonight. I have my allowance yet."

Momentarily, Laura's features darkened. She had been so intent on getting her own desire fulfilled, she had forgotten about Celeste's weakness with gambling. But her hesitation was temporary. Celeste had not gambled in years.

Laura withdrew to her corner of the carriage and drew her stole more closely around her shoulders. On the trip from England she had found Edouard to be an enjoyable companion, but she did not want him to get the wrong opinion. He was nothing more than a companion. She also felt guilty. She was using him tonight as an excuse to see Clay, but her conscience did not bother her enough for her to change her mind.

"Where are we going first?" Edouard asked, casually glancing out the window as the carriage briskly rolled down the bricked streets.

Laura said, "All afternoon I have been worried about the little boy who was in the accident. Do you mind if we stop by the Golden Fleece so I may check on him?"

Celeste's brow furrowed and she shook her head.

"Please," Laura coaxed softly. "Let me set my mind at ease."

Edouard's hand lifted, long, slender fingers caressing the white cravat at his throat. "Madame Talbot, I, too, would like to check on the child. Also

194

I have a great desire to see this Golden Fleece. You know, M'sieur Sutherland did give me a personal invitation."

"Very well." Celeste's lips thinned in disapproval. "Tell the driver, M'sieur Lambert."

Laura's heart was beating rapidly when she descended the coach at the Golden Fleece. She could not remember a time when she had been this excited. On Edouard's arm she entered the main salon and stood in awe of the blantant luxury. The room, ablaze with light, was filled with expensive and imported furniture, the upholstery done in muted tasteful colors. Four arched doorways led from the room; all were closed.

Three crystal chandeliers with hundreds of candles each hung suspended from the ceiling, their brilliance glittering off the sliding glass doors. On an elevated stage an orchestra played, soft music wafting through the room. On the far side, hidden behind an archway of stained glass doors, was a spiral staircase, gracefully curving from the salon to the second floor. Well built, the stairs were wide and easy to ascend. A polished mahogany rail glimmered in the candlelight from the chandeliers.

Gliding through one of the arched doorways, a beautiful woman approached them. Her bright red lips curved into a welcome smile, but her blue eyes were cool. "Good evening." Her voice was as icy as her stare. "I'm Roanna O'Brien, your hostess for the evening. The dining room is straight ahead; the ladies' salon to your left, the gentlemen's casino to your right. The saloon, m'sieur, is the door over there."

Her arm gracefully swung through the air as she pointed from one arched doorway to the other. The candlelight gleamed in jet-black hair that was pulled

195

from her face with pearl combs. Long curls cascaded down her back.

Her gaze flicked over the three of them. Celeste she quickly dismissed, her attention moving back and forth between Laura and Edouard. Finally, she spoke to Laura. "What is your pleasure for the evening, mam'selle?"

"I'm not here for pleasure, thank you." Laura's voice was as cool as her expression. "I'm introducing my friend, M'sieur Edouard Lambert, to New Orleans."

"Welcome to New Orleans, m'sieur," Roanna murmured. Her tone warmed, and suggestive blue eyes ran up and down his slight frame. "If I can assist in making your visit any more pleasant, please let me know."

Edouard smiled and bowed low. "Thank you, mam'selle, I will."

"Dining or gaming?" Roanna's expressive eyes swept from Laura to Celeste, the warmth leaving as quickly as it came. Her momentary display of friendliness was clearly reserved for the gentleman.

Before Celeste could answer, Laura asked, "Are you not coming with me, *Maman?*"

Celeste pulled Laura aside and said in a low voice, "If you don't mind, *chérie,* I would like to game a little."

Laura started to shake her head, but Celeste hurried on to say, "I promise I shall not spend more than my allowance. Besides, you're here to rescue me if my resolve should prove weak. It has been a long, long time since I have gamed."

Her stepmother's plea was so eloquent, Laura could not refuse. She smiled and squeezed Celeste's hands. "Absolutely no more than your allowance."

"I promise." Celeste's delicate face was animated

with excitement. She returned to the hostess. "Dining later. Gaming when the night is just beginning."

Roanna laughed, the sound deep and husky. "The ladies' salon, then, mam'selle?"

"Miss—" The title almost stuck in Laura's throat, but she managed to get it out. "Miss O'Brien, I wonder if it's possible for me to see M'sieur Sutherland?"

Roanna's eyes narrowed; her smile dimmed. "Is something wrong, mam'selle, that you wish to see the owner of the casino? I assure you I can handle any complaint you might have."

Laura was clearly displeased with the woman's impertinence. Unaccustomed to explaining herself to a domestic, she said in cold, hard tones, "Please inform M'sieur Sutherland that I'm here."

Roanna's lips twisted into a sarcastic smile; mockery glittered in the depth of her eyes. They seemed to say, *Another poor woman making a fool of herself over Clay Sutherland. I'm here to protect him from people like you.* "I'm sorry, but he can't be disturbed at the moment. He's in a meeting."

For the second time that evening the heat of embarrassment burned Laura's cheeks. But she had come this far and refused to be put off. After all, she told herself, she had a right to see John. She had nursed him on the street. And she had a right to see Clay if she so desired.

"Tell M'sieur Sutherland that Laura Talbot is here and would like to see him at his earliest convenience. I want to check on the little boy who was hurt in the accident today."

The smile widened, and mockery disappeared. In fact, Roanna's expression was almost friendly. "If it's John you're wanting to see, come with me. And you, M'sieur"— she turned to Edouard —"what is your pleasure tonight?"

For only a moment the black eyes were riveted to the blue ones. "Perhaps the saloon first, mam'selle, then the casino. I will wait here with Madame Talbot until you return. You can show Mademoiselle Talbot to the boy's room."

The smile never leaving her lips, Roanna nodded and moved across the room. Over her shoulder she said, "Miss Talbot, please follow me."

Laura turned, her feet moving silently over the hardwood floor, her gown whispering around her ankles as she followed the buxom brunette up the spiral stairs to the second floor. They walked across the receiving room, as opulent as the salon below and as tasteful and decorous, through one of the arched doors, into a brightly lit corridor. As she passed one of the closed doors, Laura heard a woman's husky laughter followed by Clay's

"That's Mr. Sutherland's office," Roanna said.

A meeting indeed! Laura paused and would have stopped, but Roanna was already knocking on another door farther down the corridor. "Here we are. John's room."

"Come in," a small voice answered.

Roanna opened the door and waved at the boy lying in the middle of a huge four-poster. "Miss Talbot has come to see you. Do you feel like having visitors?"

John's face lit up and he shoved up on the bed, grimacing when he hurt his legs. "Yes, ma'am." He swatted a lock of bright red hair out of his face.

Odd, Laura thought, following Roanna into the room, she'd never noticed today that he was red-headed, freckle-faced, and green-eyed. "Hello, John, Do you remember me?"

"Yes, ma'am!" He nodded his head, his face

creasing into one big grin. "Sure do. You're the one who doctored my legs. I didn't expect to see you again, ma'am."

Roanna quietly withdrew, shutting the door. Laura dragged a chair close to the bed and sat down. "I wanted to check to see if the physician had done a good job taking care of you."

"Sure did." John threw back the covers. He wore nothing but cut-off breeches, and his legs were propped on several pillows. Rather proudly he said, "'Course, they're turning black and blue, but the doctor said they would. They was badly bruised as well as cut up. He had to sew me up."

"He did a good job," Laura returned. "I think when the swelling has gone down and the color returns, you're going to be good as new."

"Sure hope so," John said, "but I don't rightly know, Miss Talbot. Leastways, while I'm getting better, I don't have to worry none about Mr. Simon."

"I don't think you'll ever have to worry about Mr. Simon."

"Well, now," John drawled, "I reckon Mr. Simon wasn't always a kindly man, but he did have his good side, Miss Talbot. I'm not so sure about Mr. Sutherland."

"Not so sure about what?" Laura asked.

She noted the simple elegance of the room. Certainly, there was nothing about the interior decorations to indicate this was a gambling house. Rather, it reminded her of the graciousness of a southern plantation home.

"Well, ma'am, he's done told me that I'm gonna have to get some schooling, and he made me take a bath today—even with my legs in the mess they was. Said he wasn't going to have me lying in one of his beds all dirty like I was. Said if I was his boy, I was going to learn to read and write. Said he was going to send me back east so's I could go to a military school when I got older."

Laura smiled. "Don't you think that's better than working in a produce stall with Mr. Simon?"

John scratched his head. "Don't rightly know, ma'am. I figure I don't have to read to count cabbage and lettuce and tomatoes."

"No, you don't, but do you wish to spend all your life counting vegetables?"

John curled his hand into a fist and rested his chin on it. After a pause he sighed. "To tell you the truth, I'm right scared. I never been that far away from home before. And I never been to school in my life. Reckon the other children will make fun of me?"

"Children can often be unkind, John, but that shouldn't stop you from getting an education. Only through education can you protect yourself."

"Rather have a knife or sword myself," John mumbled. "Mr. Simon was teaching me how to use the sword. He was pretty good with it too. Said he fought with the American Army against the British when he was a boy. I want to be a soldier when I grow up, Miss Laura."

Laura felt a tremor of pleasure skitter through her body when she remembered her foil with Clay. "I'll bet if you told M'sieur Sutherland you wanted to learn to use the sword or the knife, he'd teach you."

"You think so?" John's face lit up.

"He's really good."

"You've seen him in a duel?"

"I saw him practicing at Exhange Alley. When you're better, I'll wager he'll take you there."

John picked up one of the books on the night-stand, "Reading might not be so bad."

"It's not. Shall I read you a story?"

"Yeah." John quickly flipped through the pages. "I want you to read this one. I like this picture. He looks like a soldier."

Laura reached for the book and began to read the story about a young man who fought for American independence from Britain. By the time she finished the story, John was fast asleep. She laid the book on the table and pulled the covers over the boy.

"Good night, John," she whispered, and turned to walk out of the room. "One of these days your dream will come true. You'll be a soldier yet."

She was walking down the corridor when she noticed Clay's door ajar. She glanced inside to see Clay sitting behind his desk, smoking a cigar and writing. A lock of black hair swooped across his forehead, and his shirt was opened at the neck. As if aware of her presence, he looked up.

"Laura." His scowl turned into a smile of pleasure and transformed his chiseled features into dark, rugged handsomeness. He rose and moved from behind the desk.

The candlelight from the hall lingered in her hair, spinning the auburn strands into pure fire. The length was coiled into a chignon of curls, but loose curls escaped the confines of the hat she wore to form a natural halo around her face. Dark lashes framed the jade-green eyes.

"What are you doing here?"

She clutched her reticule a little more tightly. She licked lips suddenly gone dry and unconsciously stepped back. "I—was worried about John. I came to see him."

Clay came nearer; she could see the pulse beating at the base of his throat. "He's a bright boy. He wants to be a soldier."

Laura swallowed the knot that formed in her

throat. When she spoke, her voice was husky. "He told me that you're planning on sending him back to Virginia so he can go to school."

"A casino is no place to raise a child," he answered. "I'm going to send him to boarding school. He can spend the holidays with my folks."

"They won't mind?" Laura wondered about Clay's family.

"One more won't matter in a family as big as ours. My oldest sister will welcome him with open arms."

"I don't know anything about your family." She licked her dry lips.

"I'll tell you about them someday. Not now." Strong hands reached out and caught hers. "I'm glad you're here. I've been thinking about you. Come visit with me for a while."

"It's too late now. Perhaps earlier I would have."

Clay arched a brow in puzzlement.

"When I arrived you were in a *meeting*." When he said nothing and continued to look perplexed, she added, "I heard a woman's laughter when I passed your door on my way to John's room."

Clay's face relaxed. "Truly a *business* meeting, Laura Elyse Talbot. That was Annie Flannigan, one of my managers. We have a problem that needed to be worked out immediately." His clasp on her hands tightened. "Am I forgiven?

Even through the suede material of her gloves Laura felt the gentle pressure of Clay's thumb on her hand. "There's nothing to forgive."

"Then come visit with me for a little while." His eyes were earnest.

"I really can't stay." Laura had to get away from him; she realized that she was no match for Clay Sutherland. He had cast a spell over her. When she was around him, she was completely in his power.

Even now she had no will to pull her hands from his clasp. She told herself she should but made no effort. She felt that same aura around Clay that she had felt the night she had gone to the voodoo ritual with him. Unwittingly, she again became a part of that sexual current that flowed from him. "Celeste is waiting downstairs for me."

A muscle twitched in Clay's cheek, but his expression remained impassive. "By herself?"

"No, she's with Edouard," Laura found herself saying, and wondered why she was tampering with the truth.

Now Clay's visage clearly changed. The golden eyes narrowed to mere slits; his face set in uncompromising lines. When he spoke, his voice was cold and distant. "The man who was with you earlier today?"

Clay's anger fed strength into Laura. He had no right to question her friendships. Exactly who did he think he was? Ashamed of her momentary weakness, she said, "The same."

"Has he replaced Roussel in your affections, Miss Talbot?" Clay's fingers clamped around hers, and he pulled her through the door.

Stumbling toward him, Laura twisted but could not free her hands from his. Her chin lifted; the green eyes frosted with disdain. "Since Roussel has never had a place in my affections, M'sieur Sutherland, Edouard couldn't replace him. Perhaps he has replaced you."

Before she could imagine what he would do, Clay kicked the door shut, and, holding both her hands in one of his, leaned around her to lock it. Again Laura twisted in his grip but could not free herself. "Let me go."

"Not just yet. You came here for one thing, Laura

203

Elyse Talbot, and you're going to get it."

"I came here to check on John."

"That's what you're telling yourself, but both of us know differently." Piercing brown eyes surveyed her, conveying equal parts of anger and disgust . . . and lust. "I may be easily replaced in your bed, Laura Elyse Talbot, but it's not going to be by some dandy like Edouard Lambert . . . I guarantee you that."

He dragged her into his arms, his mouth moving unerringly toward hers. On her cheeks Laura felt the warmth of his breath and the faint odor of whiskey mixed with the expensive blend of cologne and aromatic tobacco. A shudder ran through her body, and she twisted her face aside. She refused to give in that easily. Surrender she would not!

Clay caught her chin in his hand and held it still. At last his mouth captured hers in a burning kiss. He groaned deeply in his throat. He lifted his face from hers to murmur, "Laura, sweet Laura, tell me you don't like my kisses."

His face lowered, his lips paying homage to the creamy swell of breast above the soft material of her bodice. She trembled in his arms as his large hand gently moved down the indentation of her spine. The strong fingers spread over the round, supple flesh of her buttocks.

"I've missed you. These four months that you've been gone have been longer than an eternity."

A flutter in Laura's stomach sent a throbbing, excited heat through her body to remind her that she had been a long time without Clay. Even without seeing him, without touching him, she remembered every inch of his magnificent body, and again she was inundated with yearning that he had awakened in her. For a second she felt light-headed and giddy. Her entire body was shaking uncontrollably. Tears sparkled in her eyes and spiked her long, curling lashes. Palms flat against Clay's chest, she shoved out of his arms and glared at him.

"Not so long that you didn't find yourself another woman." Laura was furious with herself when the confession tumbled out.

Clay grinned. "You found Edouard Lambert."

Now that she was a distance from him, Laura regained some of her composure. She reached up and straightened her bonnet with one hand; the other went behind her back and groped for the key to unlock the door. "Yes, I did find Edouard."

Clay's grin turned into rich, deep laughter. He held the key up. "Looking for this?"

"You can't keep me locked up in here forever." The calm words belied the excitement that churned in Laura's lower body.

He dropped the key into his shirt pocket, his hands sliding down to rest on lean, sinewy hips. "I can damn well do what I please, Miss Talbot. You're on Sutherland property now."

"Celeste and Edouard know that I'm up here." Her heart fluttered erratically, from fear or anticipation, she was not sure.

Golden-brown eyes glimmered; sensuous lips curled up at the corners. "You don't understand the charisma of the Golden Fleece, Miss Talbot. I make sure my guests are well taken care of, their needs and desires catered to. Both Edouard and Celeste are being entertained and will not be aware of the passing hour." He paused and moved toward her. "So why should we?"

Laura wanted to back away from Clay but had nowhere to go. Already the doorknob sank into the soft flesh of her buttocks. "I told you when I left for England that I would not be seeing you again."

"And already you've lied. You should be ashamed of yourself." The soft, caressive tones washed over Laura, slowly eroding her anger and resolve.

"Is Jena Benoit one of your employees?" she asked.

"Why do you ask?" The corner's of Clay's lips twitched.

"I was wondering if her being with you in your carriage today was also business."

"She was riding in my carriage but wasn't with me," Clay confessed. "Had you looked inside the carriage, you would have seen her escort. She was with a friend of mine."

He stood in front of her now, his face only inches away. He took the reticule from her hands and tossed it onto the sofa. He untied the ribbon on her bonnet and slipped it from her head. It fluttered from his hand to land at their feet. Regardless of who waited for her, Clay pulled the pins from her hair one by one and dropped them. When her hair hung free, he pushed his fingers through it.

"You're the only woman I want riding in my carriage with me. The only woman I want in my quarters . . . in my bed." His warm breath brushed against her flaming cheeks. His lips traced the pulsating cord of her throat. "I counted the days that you were gone; I marked them on the calendar. I waited for a letter but none came."

"No," Laura whispered, unable to take her eyes off his face. Her heart pounded in her chest and she knew Clay could hear it, that he could feel each pounding blow.

His hands slipped around her waist. He drew her closer. Laura found that she no longer had a desire to be free of his embrace. If anything, she wanted to be drawn closer and closer until they were one. Her arms circled his back, and her fingers dug into his shoulders. Beneath the softness of her palm she felt the whipcord strength. She lifted her face and welcomed Clay's lips which covered hers in a fierce, urgent kiss.

Every time Clay had held her in his arms and kissed her, Laura had felt the current flowing between them. Yet this kiss stunned her; liquid fire burned all the way through her veins, melting her body. She opened her mouth beneath his, and the passionate response set Clay's blood to boiling. His arms tightened, and he drew her closer if that were possible.

"I have dreamed of this moment ever since you left." Leaving her mouth, his lips tasted her chin, tracked her jawline, and lingered on the throbbing pulse at the base of her neck. "I knew you would come back to me."

"I did this time." Laura slid her fingers between the buttons to touch the warm textured flesh beneath the shirt.

Her words mocked him. They projected a time when she would not come to him.

"Laura Elyse Talbot." He murmured her name over and over again as his mouth traveled up again to explore the sweetness of her face and neck.

Laura felt his heart pounding against her palm; she felt the ragged rise and fall of his chest. "I really must go."

"I know." His mouth touched hers again; his lips and tongue moved intimately against, then within.

A thrill ran through Laura—a charged thrill that encompassed every fiber of her being. With the tip of his tongue he traced the line of her lips, then surged between them to savor the velvet flower of her inner mouth in a way that made her knees grow weak and her heart thunder all the louder. When his hands

207

began to wander freely over her lower back, Laura raised her arms and locked them around his neck. She pressed herself against him, eager to fill the yearning emptiness of her body.

He gently set her back and unbuttoned the bodice of her dress. He shoved the soft material aside to reveal the sheer beauty of her delicate loveliness. In the lamplight her skin looked like polished satin, smooth and flawless. His fingers stroked the full mounds until the nipples were pert. He lowered his face and caught one pink crest in his mouth, sucking gently one, then the other, to send Laura's emotions reeling.

When her fingers dug into his scalp and she moaned low in her throat, he slowed his motions, inflaming her entire body with frantic desire. Her hand slid from his head to clutch the material of his shirt. She closed her eyes and rolled her head against the door.

At this moment she was Clay Sutherland's for the taking.

"Meet me later." Clay's voice was ragged, his hands moving over her body.

His touch reminded Laura how little she had on beneath the sheer gown! The desire in his eyes rushed through his body and overflowed on her. He held her against him, her breasts pressing into his chest.

"I can't." Laura felt the hard length of his arousal and began to tremble anew. She lifted her face to stare at him. Her eyes were fevered with desire, her lips swollen from kissing. Her hair, in rich cascades of waves, fell around her face. "I must go before Celeste misses me."

"Yes."

His arms slackened and she pulled free. Drawing in deep breaths, he walked to a table against the wall.

Laura's gown rustled as she leaned down to pick up the pins and bonnet. She moved across tp the mirror to straighten her hair. Lifting the cut-glass decanter, Clay poured himself a healthy shot of whiskey which he downed in one swallow.

His back to her, he asked, "When can I see you again?"

After she pinned her hair atop her head and retied her bonnet, Laura remained at the mirror, staring at Clay's reflection. His shoulders were broad, muscle stretching the cambric material of his shirt. Once again his hair defied comb and brush to curl loosely around his face. "I don't know."

He set the glass on his desk, picked up the key, and walked to the door. "I want to see you Sunday afternoon."

"I don't know." Laura's mind refused to work; she was unable to think with him so near.

He caught her hands in his and squeezed. The gentle pressure gave her strength as well as reassurance. Leaning over, he kissed her gently on the forehead and felt her tremble beneath his touch. Inadvertently, Laura swayed closer.

"Sunday," he repeated, his lips never leaving her forehead.

The day after tomorrow, she thought. Against her fevered skin his breath felt like thick, oozing honey.

"I'll meet you at the deserted cottage by the old mill."

"My cottage?" She was surprised he knew about the cottage. Her cottage. The place where she went when she wanted to be alone and to think.

"The same."

Despite all her resolve, Laura was consumed with desire. She wanted far more than the whisper-light brush of Clay's mouth on her head. She wanted him

209

to possess every inch of her body. She wanted all of Clay Sutherland, and wanted him to have all of her. Sheer willpower pulled her head from his lips. She kept her face lowered, for her desires were written there for Clay to read. She would allow him to make love to her, but would never allow him to know how much power he had over her. Never!

"The cottage on Sunday," she whispered. Turning, she opened the door and stared into the face of a strange man.

"Cla—" Graham Bradford stood in the hallway, his right fist in the air. His puzzled glance went from Laura to Clay. Slowly, his hand dropped to his side.

A smile ghosted Clay's lips. "Graham Bradford, I'd like you to meet Miss Laura Talbot."

"Miss Talbot." Graham inclined his head.

"M'sieur Bradford."

Graham backed down the corridor. "I'll come back later, Clay."

"I was just leaving," Laura hastily assured him.

An older woman, her face thickly packed with cosmetics, raced down the hall, her dressing gown billowing to the sides. "Clay, I have to see you immediately. I'm not going to put up with Abner anymore. He has ruined—"

Graham held up his hands. "I'll be back later, Clay. It's plain to see you have your hands full now."

The woman looked down her nose at Laura, then lifted her chin and sniffed. "I suppose you want me to leave also, Clay."

Clay grinned. "No need, Fifine. I want to hear about your latest argument with the pianist. Miss Talbot and I had just completed our business." Long strides carried Clay back to his desk. He rang for a servant, then opened the wooden tobacco box and extracted a cigar.

"That's—right," Laura stammered. Embarrassed because she was blushing and stammering, Laura glared at Clay, who bent over the lamp to light his cigar. How dare he be so nonchalant! As if he were eager to be rid of her!

"You called, Mr. Sutherland?" Churnbarker appeared in the doorway, immaculately dressed in his black suit.

"I'd like you to escort Miss Talbot downstairs to the dining room. Take her to my private table. I'll be joining her in a few minutes, as soon as Fifine and I finish our discussion." Clay's voice was all business.

"As you wish." Without a blink of an eye Churnbarker turned to Laura. "Miss Talbot, please come with me."

Her gaze never leaving Clay's face, Laura said, "Thank you, M'sieur Sutherland, but no thank you. I've had dinner. I came to see John, and I've done that. Now I'll be on my way."

"Laura—"

Her chin tilted arrogantly, Laura swept out of the room ahead of Churnbarker. Furious with herself and with Clay, she fumed all the way down the corridor. When she reached the center of the receiving room, she froze. Jena Benoit stood at the top of the landing, her hand resting on the railing.

In the radiant glow of candlelight her hair gleamed blue-black, and a large gold hoop earring brushed against each cheek. An enigmatic smile curled her luscious lips. Through the thin, filmy muslin of her dress, devoid of petticoat, the long, sleek lines of her body were clearly visible. Ebony eyes slowly, carefully, studied Laura as she and Churnbarker approached.

"Good evening, Miss Benoit." Churnbarker never stopped walking, nor did he seem to notice the

211

woman's state of near nudity. "If you're looking for Mr. Sutherland, he's in his office."

"Thank you, Churnbarker." Jena's husky tones made even the mundane sensuous. She smiled at Laura, but when she spoke, her tones were cool. "Good evening, Mademoiselle Talbot . . . it is Talbot, is it not?"

"Yes, I am Mademoiselle Talbot," Laura said, and smiled, the gesture as cold as her voice. "I'm afraid you have me at a disadvantage. I don't know your name."

The mulatto's facial expression never changed, but her eyes were venomous. "Jena Benoit." She seemed to hiss the words. She parted her lips, her tongue darting out to graze them. "I'm a voodoo queen with great power, mam'selle. People have been known to die from my spells."

Laura shivered. The woman reminded her of a viper. "I don't believe in the power of voodoo."

"Perhaps you should, mam'selle."

The two stared at each other for a moment, then Jena laughed softly but dismissively and turned to walk away. When she reached the glass doors, she stopped. Over her shoulder she asked, "Churnbarker, did I leave my parasol in M'sieur Sutherland's apartment when I was here earlier?"

"Yes, ma'am. It's in the rack in the hall. Shall I get it for you?" Churnbarker turned at the landing to look at Jena.

"Non, I'll get it myself later . . . when my man and I are through."

Laura's eyes were smoldering when they reached the landing in the main salon. She had not liked Jena Benoit from the moment she first saw her; she liked her even less now. She was afraid of the woman. How could she have allowed Clay to touch her when he'd

212

been touching that woman! *Making love to that woman!* The very thought made Laura seethe. And he had lied to her. Jena Benoit had been with him earlier.

"Right this way, Miss Talbot."

"Thank you, Churnbarker, but I know my way around quite well." She was spoiling for a fight, and anyone would do.

For the first time Laura saw a dent in the servant's impassive demeanor. "But, miss, Mr. Sutherland told me to take you to his table in the dining room."

"I'm quite aware of what he said. Now please leave me."

Displeasure evident in every line of his countenance, Churnbarker bowed stiffly. "As you wish, madam." He walked away.

"As you wish, madam," Laura muttered under her breath as she headed not for the ladies' salon but for the casino. She would show Clay Sutherland a thing or two. He would rue the day he ordered Laura Elyse Talbot around without first consulting her wishes. She would teach him to mess with another woman!

What did she care anyway?

A guard, dressed in a conservative black suit, stopped her at the door. He crossed his hand over his chest. "This is the casino, ma'am. The ladies' salon is over there."

Laura's face became mutinous; her voice quite firm. "I'm not a simpleton, sir. I know quite well what this is. Now, will you move so that I may enter?"

The man's face reddened, and he looked flustered. "Ma'am, ladies don't—don't generally—"

Laura opened her reticule and pulled out a wad of bills. "I think the only requirement for entering a gambling hall, sir, is money. Is it not?"

He ran a finger around his collar as if it were biting into his neck.

"It's all right, Preston. I'll handle this." Clay's voice came from behind Laura. She tensed but did not turn around. She could hear his amusement. His hand curled around her upper arm firmly. Out of the corner of her eye she saw that he now wore his tailcoat and cravat. When he spoke, he lowered his voice so that only she could hear. "You heard the man, Laura, ladies don't frequent casinos. I have the salon for them. Now, come with me peacefully. I won't allow you to make a scene in my place of business. According to your society, I have very little honor; therefore, I must protect it at all costs."

Laura could only stare at him. The more she was around Clay Sutherland, the more she understood the true meaning of the word honor. But she refused to make such a confession to him.

"Are you feeling better?" The next morning Laura sat beside Celeste's bed, incense, candle fragrance, and scented water permeating the air.

Celeste lay quietly, a damp rag across her eyes. "These dreadful headaches. I do wish they'd go away. Has Berthe returned with the drink?"

"Not yet." Laura patted her stepmother's hands. "Don't you think you'd feel better if I opened the drapes and let some sunshine in?"

"Oh, no," came the pitiful wail. "Bright light would surely make my head explode."

Laura busied herself straightening the clutter on the dresser while she waited for Berthe to return with the tea. After she replaced the comb and brush to its box, she chanced to see her reflection in the mirror. She touched the dark smudges beneath her eyes.

"Oh, *chère* Laura." Celeste laid her hand over the washcloth. "Why did I ever let you convince me to go to the Golden Fleece last night. Your father is sure to find out."

"Yes." Promise and passion haunted the green eyes. "Are you worried?"

Laura barely heard the affirmative reply. She turned, her feet silently carrying her back to the bed.

"Your papa is going to think I have been a bad chaperone for you, Laura. I behaved quite irresponsibly. He is going to be so very angry with me."

"I am a woman, *Maman*. Twenty-six years old. I will tell Papa that you are not responsible for my actions. I do as I wish." *Except where Clay Sutherland is concerned!* After a lengthy pause she asked, "You didn't lose too heavily, did you?"

"No," Celeste mumbled truthfully. "I just don't want to face Beau's anger. Surely M'sieur Lambert will tell him we went, Laura. Surely he will."

"I'm quite certain he will. But never mind. By the time Papa gets home, he will have forgotten all about the incident."

"That's right. It will be days before he gets home."

The door opened, and Berthe walked into the room, a small serving tray in hand. "Tisane for Maîtresse Celeste."

While Berthe gave Celeste her tea, Laura took her mail and walked into the upstairs gallery. She stared at both letters, the handwriting on each quite feminine. The one she recognized as Judith's; the other she did not recognize at all. Moving to the banister, she stood in the morning sun and opened the first letter. She smiled as she read.

"Judith is coming," she shouted excitedly, her voice carrying down the corridor to her stepmother's room. "She says by the time we receive this letter, she'll be on her way."

Her voice much stronger now that she realized she would not have to confront Beau about her visit to the Golden Fleece, Celeste called back, "She will be here in time for the Mardi Gras season. How wonderful. We shall teach her how to mask. Who is the other letter from?"

The paper crackled in Laura's hand, her eyes skimming the unfamiliar handwriting. The answer was a long time in coming, but finally she said, "My—dressmaker."

Celeste never noticed the pause or the catch in Laura's voice. "Ah, yes, Mademoiselle LeBlanc is ready to begin your dresses for the costume balls."

Laura stared at the small card, the words *I warned you!* mocking her. A huge snake coiled around the edge of the card.

"We shall have her make some new dresses for Judith. A blue one to match her eyes. By the way, Laura, how did Judith like the blue dress you carried to her?"

Lifting her head, Laura stared at her stepmother. "I beg your pardon?"

"How did Judith like the blue dress you carried to her?"

Rubbing the card between her fingers and forcing her thoughts from Clay, Laura said, "She liked it, *Maman.* It's—one of the most beautiful that she's ever owned."

"I can hardly wait to see her in it." Celeste sighed and stretched. "Are her eyes truly the color of sapphires?"

"*Oui, Maman.*"

"As yours are the color of jade."

Laura lifted her hand, her fingers clasping the phoenix that hung from her neck. *"Oui."*

Chapter Ten

"Oh, Maîtresse," Jeanette wailed, her face ashen, "what are we going to do?"

This was Laura's first day back at Ombres Azurées since her return from England. Unpacked, her trunk sat at the foot of the bed. She stood at the side and stared at the grotesque doll lying in a puddle of blood on the white silk pillowcase. A huge pin was stuck through the chest. Although she trembled with fear, Laura forced herself to pick up the effigy and pull out the pin. Now she stared at a large, gaping hole—a hole where the doll's heart should have been. For long minutes she looked at her fingertips, wet and sticky with blood.

She threw the doll into the wastepaper basket and without thinking wiped her hand down her skirt, streaks of blood discoloring the checkered cambric. At the same time, a clap of thunder boomed through the room, closely followed by a flash of lightning.

"It's nothing," Laura announced. Still, Jena Benoit's warning rang in her ears.

"*Mais non*, Maîtresse," Jeanette murmured, her voice wavering. Her gazed was fixed on the soiled pillowcase. "It is something. It is you."

"How can you be sure?" Laura stared into the bottom of the wicker container. The doll seemed to be gloating as if it knew a secret she didn't.

"The dress, Maîtresse, did you not recognize the material? It is made from the suede glove you lost the other day. The gloves you wore with your pelisse."

Looking closer, Laura saw the wine-colored dress and the narrow collar of ermine. The band around her glove was now around the doll's throat. Automatically, her hand lifted, and her fingers—the same that had touched the blood—curled around the base of her neck.

"Someone wants you dead, Maîtresse."

"I hardly think so," Laura returned stoutly, refusing to give way to fear. Yet she shivered. "This is just a practical joke. Now see to it the linen is changed and lay me out a fresh gown."

"*Non.*" Jeanette shook her head.

"Why not?" Laura stared at the young servant incredulously.

"Please, Maîtresse," Jeanette pleaded, "pardon me. I will do all you ask, but the doll, she is no joke. She is real."

"Burn it, Jeanette." Fear was contagious, and Laura felt hers escalating.

Jeanette shook her head more vigorously. "I can't, Maîtresse. Really, I can't. We must let Berthe cast a spell for you. She can help us break the power of the curse."

"Surely you don't believe in this voodoo nonsense," Laura snapped, fear making her more curt than she intended. "I don't and won't hear any more about it."

"*Oui.* I have seen too much," the girl muttered. She fiddled nervously with the tail of her apron, her gaze darting around the room. "People die, Maîtresse. They do. I have seen it."

"Nonsense. This is nothing but rags and stuffing." Laura repeated, and lowered her hand into the basket. But for long seconds she stared at the strange creature, unable to touch it. Finally, she inhaled deeply and forced herself to pick it up the second time. It felt hot and wet to her hand. It seemed to breathe.

"And blood," Jeanette added.

"Chicken blood, I warrant." Laura strove for a nonchalance she was far from feeling, but she couldn't quite hide the tremor in her voice. "Come with me. You can watch me burn it."

"Please be careful." Jeanette begged, and followed Laura out of the room. "Do not take this too lightly."

"I'm not." Anger replaced Laura's fear. "I shall have a talk with Saloman to find out how someone could have gotten into my room unobserved."

"The spirits, Maîtresse," Jeanette explained, rushing behind Laura, her eyes darting around as if she expected to see one of them materialize at any moment and grab her. "They're the ones who did it. Nobody can stop spirits."

"This wasn't done by a spirit," Laura answered, a picture of Jena Benoit flashing through her mind.

Before she reached the landing, the door to Celeste's room opened and Berthe came out.

"Berthe," Jeanette cried out, and rushed up to the housekeeper, who laid a finger across her mouth and gently closed the door. In a whisper the maid said, "Look what Maîtresse found on her bed in a puddle of blood."

Berthe's eyes went from Jeanette to Laura, who held her hand out, the doll resting on her flattened, bloodied palm. The minute Berthe saw it, her eyes widened, then her face grew guarded and closed. She

219

reached for the doll, but Laura's fingers closed over it. She brought her hand back.

"No, Berthe, it was meant for me. I shall burn it."

Berthe's ebony eyes, filled with concern, settled on Laura. "Let me have it, *s'il vous plaît*. Let me dispose of this for you so that it does not come back to haunt you."

"No, Laura repeated, "I'll take care of it myself."

Jeanette held her fist up to her mouth, her startled, fearful eyes rotating back and forth between Laura and Berthe.

"Maîtresse," Berthe pleaded, "this is a grave matter, one of which you have little knowledge. You would be wise to let me have the doll."

"I said I'd take care of it, Berthe, and I will." Laura moved to the landing and stopped to turn. "At present I'm more concerned about the person who entered the house and put it on my pillow. I'm on my way to speak to Saloman about it right now."

"*Oui,*" Berthe agreed. "You should speak to him. We shall be most careful in the future, Maîtresse, that this will not happen again."

Getting no satisfaction from Saloman, Laura proceeded to the study. His feet stretched out, his hands twined together and resting on his stomach, Beau sat in one of the leather chairs in front of the roaring fire. When he heard the door open and shut, he turned his head.

Laura withdrew the effigy from her pocket and held it up. "Look at this, Papa."

Beau straightened up, his face twisting into a scowl. "Are the slaves practicing that damned voodoo nonsense? Where did it come from?"

"My pillow," Laura answered. "It was lying in a puddle of blood."

Beau's face paled. He walked to the table and with

shaking hands lifted the cut-glass whiskey decanter and poured himself a drink. "I'll have Donaldson's hide for this. We're not paying an overseer that exorbitant amount to let our slaves indulge in witchcraft. I won't have our lives threatened like this."

Laura walked closer to the fire. While the slaves might be responsible for putting the effigy on her pillow, she did not think they were responsible for its message. In her mind's eye she saw Jena Benoit standing on the landing of the stairs at the Golden Fleece. She could still see the woman's venomous gaze and hear the hiss of her voice. Laura wondered if the woman and snake could be one and the same.

The gray skies turned black. Thunder rolled and lightning flashed; the wind howled, slamming loose shutters against the cottage walls. Shadows filled the sitting room, the orange glow of Clay's cigar the only light. Still, Laura did not come. He turned from the window and walked to the small round table in the center of the sitting room. Angrily, he stubbed his cigar in the ashtray. Evidently, Laura did not plan to meet him. What a fool he had made of himself! Coming to this cottage and waiting for her like a lovesick kid! Dear God, why was he so obsessed with this woman?

But he had not counted on the sudden storm blowing in. He could not expect her to get out in such weather. He turned to pick up his hat when he heard the pounding of hooves. He dropped the hat and rushed across the room in long strides. Opening the door, he stepped onto the veranda and saw Laura leap from the horse. Quickly, she tied the reins around a sturdy bush as the bottom fell out of the sky, peppering the earth with large drops of rain.

"Hurry," he called, "or you're going to get wet."

A gust of wind picked up Laura's cape and swirled it through the air, the hood falling from her head. She rushed up the path, but not out of her fear of the brewing storm. She threw herself against Clay, her arms circling his body. Unable to say a word but grateful that he was here, she held him tightly.

"I thought perhaps you had forgotten about me." He inhaled her sweet scent.

"Just hold me, Clay," she whispered, and shivered convulsively as she thought of the doll. "Don't turn me loose."

"What's wrong?" His hands moved in soothing, circular rhythm over her upper back. He felt the tense muscles slowly relax.

Pulling away from him, the wind blowing tendrils of hair across her cheeks, Laura withdrew the doll from her pocket and held it out. "This."

Even in the dim light of early evening Clay recognized the voodoo doll. "Where did it come from," he demanded in a harsh voice, and took it from her unresisting fingers.

"My pillow. It was—in a pool of blood."

She shuddered when she remembered. She felt Clay's arm around her shoulder and allowed him to guide her into the cottage. He tossed the doll onto the nearby table.

"You—you know what it is?" she asked.

"Yes." He sat her down, then returned to the table and lit the lamp.

"Have you ever seen one before?"

Again the monosyllabic answer, "Yes." He filled a glass with wine.

"Jena did it," Laura said.

"You don't know that she did."

222

"I don't know that she did!" Laura shouted, and leapt to her feet, glaring at him. In equal part, hurt, anger, and fear vibrated in her voice. "That woman hates me. I could see it in her eyes last night."

He quickly moved to where she stood and laid a gentle hand on her shoulder. Pressing her into the chair, he handed her the glass. "Drink this. You'll feel better."

"Drink this, and I'll feel better. You must be jesting! You should have seen Jeanette's expression when she saw that—" Another shudder racked Laura's body, and she lifted the glass to her lips and gulped the wine. Appreciating the warmth that surged through her body, she settled her gaze on the doll. "She had stuck a pin through my—through my—"

Clay returned to the table and picked up the effigy. His thumb brushed over the large hole. "Not through your anything," he corrected her. "By no means must you believe this doll is you or that it has any power over you whatsoever. Always remember that whoever did this stuck the pin through the doll's chest."

"It's suppose to be me, Clay," she sobbed, and stood, the wineglass tumbling to the floor. "Somebody wants me dead."

Clay dropped the doll and rushed to gather her into his arms. "Don't cry," he whispered. "It's going to be all right. I'm not going to let anything happen to you. I promise, Laura Elyse."

Laura believed him; he was the kind of man a person did believe. Whatever else Clay Sutherland may be, he was strong and dependable. Feeling safe in his arms and glad for someone else to lean upon— a new experience for her—she snuggled against his chest. He would take care of her. Even with the storm

223

raging outside, the wind howling, and the rain pelting with torrential fury against the small cottage, she was safe in the pavilion of his arms. How easily she could love Clay Sutherland. How easily. She was unsure how long they stood there, but finally he pulled away and smiled down at her.

"Let me build a fire to chase away the chill and gloom."

She nodded although she was reluctant to let him go. No one had ever made her feel as safe as Clay did, as warm and protected. For some undefinable reason she trusted him implicitly. He knelt in front of the blackened fireplace. Quickly, in fluid motion he stacked the wood, strategically placing the kindling. The lamplight glimmered on his dark hair, a wave falling over his forehead; the light played on the tight stretch of fawn-colored trousers over sinewy thighs. Shoulder muscles rippled beneath the dark blue tailcoat.

When the fire was ablaze, he stood, dusted wood particles from his hands, and turned to her. A large smile lit his face. "If the weather had cooperated, I was going to take you on a picnic. I had Churnbarker pack us a lunch."

Shyly, Laura returned the smile. Such gentleness coming from Clay Sutherland was hard for her to accept. Yet she did and without question, without hesitation. "Could we not have one inside the cottage as well as outside?" she murmured.

"We could indeed."

"So much more cozy," she added.

First he took off his coat, laying it over the back of the sofa; then lifted his hands and removed his cravat, dropping it on top of the jacket. As he opened the top three buttons of his shirt, he moved until he was standing in front of her. "We had better eat, else we

224

won't, Laura Elyse. We're getting much too cozy." His lips came closer, hardly moving as he said, "It's leading to an intimacy that precludes such mundane activities as eating."

His mouth tentatively touched hers, their vapors becoming one. Slowly, her hands rose, and she cupped them behind his head, threading her fingers through the thickness of his hair. His hand gently plowed through the neatly waved furrows of her hairdo, releasing the silken mass so that it cascaded down her shoulders. Creating a space just for themselves, the kiss deepened.

Long after Clay lifted his lips from hers, they stood together, wrapped in each other's arms. She shoved her doubts aside, forgetting about the voodoo doll and Jena Benoit. She thought only of herself, only of the man who stood beside her.

"What did you bring?" she eventually asked.

Puzzled by her question, Clay pulled away from her and looked down.

Laura laughed quietly and reached up to unfasten her cape. Moving, she laid it on the sofa. The room was warm enough now for her to be without it. "The lunch?" What did Churnbarker pack?"

She gazed into Clay's face, knowing that she would see that beautiful, lopsided smile. "Fried chicken. Potato salad. Fresh baked bread and butter. A bottle of fine wine."

"I can almost smell it." She went back into his embrace, wrapping both arms around his waist and resting her cheek against his chest.

"Are you hungry?" he asked.

"Only for you."

His hands slowly moved up her back, inch by inch, until they were under the lace bolero she wore over her yellow batiste dress. His fingers gently touched the smooth warm flesh of her upper back and shoulders. Then he lowered his head, kissing her from the curve of her throat just below the ear to the end of her shoulders, and he felt her tremble against him.

"You smell good."

"My perfume. I bought it while I was in England."

"You and your perfume, but I like the smell of you better." He lifted his head and sniffed her hair. "It smells like a cool spring day. When I close my eyes I see the sun shining brightly, the blue sky above, and the big voluminous clouds as they float by."

"Perhaps you should have been a poet rather than a gambler. At least Irish rather than Scottish, so I could accuse you of having kissed the Blarney Stone."

Clay laughed with her, his words and laughter soothing all her aches away, chasing Jena and the voodoo doll from her thoughts. He touched his lips to hers lightly and tentatively. "Nay, lass," he drawled in thick brogue, "I didna kiss the Blarney Stone. All I tell ye be the truth."

Laura's face tilted up, her mouth open, her lips parted tremulously. Desperately, she clung to his confession. Desperately, her eyes moved from the dark, laughing eyes to his lips, and her soul hungered for one more taste.

Clay's face dipped nearer to hers, the strong lips serious in their quest. With reverent gentleness they touched hers, blessing her with a honeyed tenderness that caused her bones to melt. To keep from falling, she grabbed Clay around the waist, pressing herself to him. Her hips touched him, and her breasts lay against his chest. Then she pulled her shoulders away, lifted up her face, and offered her lips to him. She moved her mouth beneath his, her quivering response spontaneous and jubilant.

With a groan of surrender Clay's arms tightly circled around her, and for an eternity of seconds their bodies could have been no closer. Their breaths were as one, their heartbeats as one. The kiss deepened, and their lips parted even more, their mouths opening wider. Their tongues intermingled in the tentative forays of lovesweeps, and their sighs of pleasure lengthened into soft moans of desire.

His lips nuzzled from her lips to her ears to the sensitive area behind the lobe. They nibbled and nipped. But suddenly his hands were gone from her waist. She felt her loss. Closing her eyes, she wriggled closer to him, determined to find her warm, cozy spot. She rubbed her cheek against his chest.

Then she felt the fluttering touch of his hands at the nape of her neck and knew the tiny pearl buttons were slipping through the silk loops. The lace wisped against her shoulders, and she heard the faint swish as it landed on the nearest chair.

"Your skin is beautiful." His lips followed the line of material from the strap of her shoulder to the round neckline. "Soft and smooth."

His fingers crooked under the straps, tugging them off her shoulders but not revealing her breasts. She shivered not so much from his touch but from the hot molten desire that thickly poured through her veins. Again she was consumed with those passionate yearnings that refused to be disciplined, that refused to be denied.

Tonight she desired Clay Sutherland. There was no right and wrong, only desire. Her body remembered the touch of his hands, the whisper of his lips. She had lived for four months on her memories, but that wasn't enough. Now she needed something more tangible. She wanted to feel his heated caresses;

she wanted to hear his passionate endearments. She was ravenous for his loving.

"I want to kiss you, to hold you, to love you." Her lips nipped at the corners of his mouth, nibbling the laughter groove of his cheek. She covered his entire face in quicksilver kisses. Then their mouths touched, parted, and they were kissing each other deeply, their hands feverishly moving over each other's body.

"And you shall." Clay's voice was ragged and sharp.

He swept her into his arms and moved into the sole bedroom in the cottage. Furnished with belongings she had brought with her from England, this was Laura's private world that no one intruded upon, not even Beau and Celeste. Light from the sitting room filtered through the open door to gently touch each piece of expensive furniture and to linger on the beige linen bedspread. Lightning periodically flashed through the windows.

When Clay laid her on the bed, she rolled away from him and sat up. Her eyes never leaving his, she unbuttonerd the front of her dress and pulled the material aside, slipping it down her arms. In the muted glow of light the mounded beauty of her perfectly sculpted breasts were revealed in one flowing stroke.

Clay stood watching as she shed her clothes, dropping each garment to the side of the bed. She held her arms out to him. "Make love to me."

Clay shrugged out of the shirt and sat down in the small chair to remove his boots and socks; then he stood and moved closer to her, hands unbuttoning his breeches and undergarments. He stepped out of them.

Both of them were beautiful in their nakedness, in

their youth, and in their loving.

He sat on the edge of the bed, and she lifted her arms to circle his neck. She cupped the back of his head with her hands and brushed the skin of his abdomen with her breasts, each stroke of her flesh against his like the stroke of flint against a rock. Sparks shot off from each of them, creating the roaring blaze of desire that would surely flame around both of them.

Clay lowered his eyes, his lips moving down the hollow arch under her chin, on her neck, across her collarbone. He laid her on the bed, and in graceful movements they stretched out, his hands running the length of her legs. His mouth tenderly touched every inch of her flesh. His hands swept to the gateway of her femininity, and he kissed her breasts, his tongue inciting the sensitive tip.

"Laura," he murmured, his warm breath arousing her desires even more, "you're wonderful to love."

"So are you." She guided his mouth to hers, needing to fill her void, wanting her mouth full of the moist warmness of his, wanting her lower body filled with the firmness of his manhood. Motivated by passion, she held his face between her hands and invited the sweet spearing of his tongue into her mouth as his hand prepared her for him.

Tenderly, he made love to her, carrying her slowly beyond illusions and daydreams, beyond the bounds of memory to the highest pinnacle of joy and completeness. Their climax was the most fulfilling of all they had shared together. Not only had their bodies attained a physical oneness, their souls had mated.

They lay on the bed, their breathing quietly slowing as they listened to the wind howl around the small cottage and the rain pelt unmercifully against the tin roof. A tranquility permeated both of them, surrounding them with serene hush. They did not speak; they only clasped hands.

Eventually, Clay turned his head and looked at her. "We ought to be married."

"Why?" Laura asked dreamily.

Clay flopped on his side and laid his hand flat on her belly. His head bent, his face hidden, he said after a while, "You might become pregnant."

A part of Laura was disappointed; yet this was behavior she had come to expect from the Clay Sutherland that she was beginning to know so intimately. Truly at peace with the world tonight, she smiled. On the verge of recognizing her love for Clay, she said, "You're worried about my honor?"

Clay's fingers kneaded the soft flesh, the tips of his fingers brushing against the downy auburn hair at the juncture of her thighs. His head lifted and his hands stopped their movement; an invisible shutter closed over his eyes. He hesitated a moment before he shook his head. "No, I seldom think of honor. I was thinking of the baby. My baby."

The tone of voice, the withdrawal, hurt Laura, and she, too, retreated into a protective shell. For a moment she had forgotten they were merely lovers. While he might be concerned about his baby, he did not necessarily have to be concerned about her. The thought hurt her. Yet she could say nothing; she could not even fault him. She was the one who had established the rules of their relationship. She slipped off the bed and began fumbling for her clothes.

"I can take care of myself. Berthe knows what herbs will prevent conception."

"Do you find the idea of carrying my child so repugnant?" Clay's accusation was harsh and brutal;

like a whip they struck Laura and bit into her sensibilities. He slid off the bed and walked to where she stood. "I truly don't understand you, Laura. You want to make love to me but don't want my baby. You call yourself respectable. Yet you choose to have an affair of dishonor with me rather than marriage because I don't belong to your hypocritical society. You condemn me because I'm a gambler—a *lowlife* who collects debts people owe me, and you extol the man who would steal from me. You go so far as to call him a gentleman."

Clay's words pierced Laura to the quick. They were a mirror into which she did not wish to look. The reflection she saw was disgusting.

"If you do get pregnant"— his hands clamped on her shoulders and he forced her head up —"let me know. You may not want my child, but I do."

In an agonizing whisper Laura said, "Berthe will keep me from getting pregnant."

"If she doesn't," Clay insisted, "you had better let me know. Do you understand?"

Laura nodded. Her role of clandestine lover was more than she had bargained for. She was quickly discovering that beneath that exterior of calm and control she was a mass of emotion. She desired Clay to the exclusion of everything else in her life, and it was hard for her to remember what she must do in order to perpetuate the Talbot name in Creole society. For Laura, duty had always come first; so must it continue.

In the distance she heard Clay say, "I may offer Berthe a job at the casino. We could use her services." His voice was hard. He walked into the sitting room, returning in a few minutes with a cigar in his mouth. Still naked, he moved to the window and stared into the rain-thickened night.

231

Laura averted her gaze. "You could put your clothes on."

As when she'd first seen him, his face was obscured by a haze of smoke. "Why? You liked me naked a few minutes ago. What happened to change your mind?"

"It doesn't seem quite decent." She pulled the lace bolero over her shoulders and fumbled with the buttons at the back.

Cramming the cigar into the corner of his mouth, Clay moved behind her and pushed her hands away. "I've never considered making love indecent," he said as he fastened the bolero, "but then, I've never been a member of high society. I never cared to be because I considered it hypocritical. I've always preferred to be an outcast. But don't worry your pretty little head, Laura Elyse, by the standards you have chosen, what we're doing is considered to be quite the thing. As long as nobody knows what we're doing, everything is fine."

Laura did not feel indecent, yet she felt a twinge of guilt. Clay was telling the truth. The very rules by which she chose to live damned a woman who was openly intimate with a man out of wedlock. They branded such a woman a whore. They frowned on premarital sex. Yet according to this same elite group, a woman could have as many lovers as she chose as long as she was discreet . . . as long as no one found out. She felt the brush of his fingers over her back as he continued to button her bolero.

"There now, you're all covered up and decent again." His lips brushed against the back of her neck to send a shiver down her spine. "Shall we eat now? I'm famished."

"We have all night." Laura strove for the same casualness he displayed. Lovemaking was over, his sexual appetite assuaged, and he was ready for

232

food. "Why the hurry?"

"I wish I could stay all night," he answered, "but I can't. I have to get back to the casino. Tonight is one of our busiest. After we eat I'll escort you back to the plantation."

Again Laura was disappointed but said nothing. She had no reason to voice her displeasure. If Clay's following the rules she had instigated bothered her, she had no one to blame but herself. She picked up the picnic basket in the kitchen and carried it to the sitting room. Pulling the table closer to the fire, she spread the food, and they quietly ate. When he finished, Clay picked up his glass of wine and walked onto the veranda. The rain had slacked, but still an occasional bolt of lightning serrated the sky.

"I'm going to be gone for a few days," he said.

"Where?"

"Baton Rouge."

Already she missed him. She moved to the edge of the porch and held her hand out, letting the rain splash against her palm. "How long are you going to be gone?"

"Several weeks. Will you come with me?" He set the glass on the windowsill and moved to stand behind her.

"I can't," she answered. But she wanted to. His hands settled on her shoulders, and he pulled her against him.

"You mean you won't," he said softly. "We could arrange it so no one knows."

Laura turned in his arms. At that moment she would have denied him nothing. "I would love to go with you, Clay. Really I would. But Judith is coming to join us soon, and I need to make preparations. Besides, I've been gone too long from the plantation and the workers. I don't even know my own overseer.

233

If my slaves are involved in voodoo—" She left her sentence incomplete and shrugged her shoulders. "I must be here; I can't afford a revolt."

"I'm glad you have an overseer," he said. "You don't need to be running this damned plantation by yourself. You need someone to protect you. Why the hell Beau allows—"

"By someone, you mean a man," Laura said dryly.

"Yes, dammit, a man!"

She pressed her hand against his face, the faint beginnings of beard stubble rasping her palm. Joy raced through her bloodstream. "You're worried . . . about the effigy, aren't you?"

"Just the doll would be bad enough, but with the blood . . . Whoever did this, Laura, is serious."

"Do you believe in voodoo, Clay?"

"I don't disbelieve it," he answered evasively. "I stay away from it for the most part. When I'm forced into an encounter, I handle it with respect. Promise me that you won't leave the house by yourself?"

"I promise." His lips touched her tentatively, and she whispered, "Clay, stay with me tonight . . . please." Her hands slipped beneath the material of his shirt.

"Yes," he murmured, the word becoming the essence of their kiss.

On the day Clay left for Baton Rouge, Laura received a letter from Judith telling them of her coming visit and the date of her arrival. In the excitement of preparing for Judith's visit, Laura pushed the effigy incident aside but could not displace Clay from her thoughts as easily. The least little thing or word would remind her of him.

"Laura," Beau called from the front parlor of the town house, "are you ready yet?"

"I am," Laura answered as she tucked a curl beneath her bonnet. "But why the hurry, Papa? It's hours before the ship arrives."

"I know you women," he grumbled happily.

Celeste poked her head around the door. "Your Papa, he is quite happy that Judith is coming, no?"

Walking across the room to join her stepmother, Laura laughed softly. "*Oui*, but I would rather wait here in the cool house than outside in the heat."

Celeste looped her hand over Laura's arm. "We will do what your papa wishes," she said. "Today is his day. We shall let him meet Judith by himself. I do not know how she will greet him, and I do not wish for us to be spectators."

"Of course you're right," Laura said slowly. "I hadn't thought about that. Judith might not accept him."

"She was a baby when he left; now she is a woman who feels as if she has been abandoned. It will take a long time for her wounds to heal, *ma chère*. Surely you can remember how long it took for you."

"Yes," Laura said, "I remember. I regret that Judith didn't have someone like you to help her get over the hurt and bitterness."

Celeste smiled. "Thank you, dear Laura. Indeed, you are my daughter."

Hours later Laura paced the docks with her father and stepmother as they anxiously awaited the arrival of the tardy ship. Although Laura was aghast at the news of the pirate's attack, Beau brushed it aside as soon as he learned that all the passengers were safe. When the sails were in sight, Celeste tugged Laura's arm and the two of them returned to the carriage to wait.

Feeling extremely vulnerable, Judith was glad that

Laura was there with her when Beau introduced her stepmother. "Judith," Celeste said in a deeply accented voice, "I am so happy that you have come to see us."

"Thank you," Judith said, at a loss for words.

"Come," Beau said as he helped her into the carriage, "let's be on our way."

"By all means," Laura said. "Let's get out of this heat. I know Judith is dying for a glass of cold lemonade."

Her black wool dress scratching her skin reminded Judith exactly how sweltering the heat was in New Orleans. "I really would," she agreed.

Once the carriage rumbled down the street toward the town house, Laura turned to her father. "Papa," she said, "you must do something about those pirates. I don't know much about the Talbot lines, but even I know that it's not good for business, much less safe for passengers. I shudder to think what might have happened to Judith."

"Something needs to be done with that pirate in particular," Judith added. She could still see him ripping her clothes to shreds; she still felt his lips on hers and the length of his body pressed against her.

"I will, baby," Beau promised. "Right now let's put this behind us and think about happier things."

"I can't think of anything else," Judith answered. Indeed, the man's face kept swimming in front of her eyes. She wanted to wipe the smug smile from his face. "The man destroyed all my possessions."

"We'll get you more," Beau said.

"*Oui*, Judith"— Celeste beamed —"we will take care of you now. We are your family."

Judith's gaze settled on the pale woman who sat across from her. She opened her mouth to reply; however, Laura spoke first.

"She's right, Judith. Let Papa take care of this. He knows what to do, and he will."

Some of the anger seemed to drain out of Judith, and she shrugged her shoulders.

"Tonight is yours, baby," Beau said. "What would you like to do?"

Celeste laughed and clapped her hands together. "And tomorrow, Judith, we will go see Madame LeBlanc about making you some new dresses. Over here you will find your wool dress much too hot."

"Thank you, Celeste," Judith said, "but I'm rather fond of my dresses."

Even as she said the words, Judith knew they were a lie. She had treasured the new dresses she brought with her. For once in her life she had determined to be as beautiful as Laura, but that scoundrel of a pirate had destroyed that dream. Here she sat looking like a begger.

"Oh," Celeste murmured, "I did not mean to offend you, Judith. I only wanted—"

"I'm sorry," Judith said, and smiled. "I didn't mean to sound ungrateful."

"You didn't, my dear." Celeste leaned forward and patted her on the knee. "You're tired and hungry. Soon we'll be at the house. If you like, we can go on to Ombres Azurées."

"The plantation," Judith said more than asked.

"You'll love it," Laura said.

"I'm sure I will," Judith replied, then looked squarely at her father. "Did you mean it when you said tonight was my night?"

Beau nodded vigorously. "Sure did, baby."

"After we eat," Judith said, "I want to go see the offices of Talbot Shipping Line."

"Talbot Shipping Line," Laura and Celeste said together.

Judith smiled and crossed her arms over her breasts. "That's right," she said.

Although Laura missed Clay, she had no time to be lonely. She was spending her time with Judith, the two of them becoming intimately acquainted with Talbot Shipping Line much to their father's and Maurice Dufaure's irritation. Several days later Laura persuaded Judith to accompany her to Ombres Azurées.

On the second morning at the plantation Judith leaned against one of the columns on the front veranda. "You were right, Laura. New Orleans is beautiful."

"And Ombres Azurées in particular." Laura smiled. "If you feel like it, I'll take you on the grand tour today."

"Another day. I persuaded Papa to bring some ledgers home for me to study."

"I'm surprised that he did," Laura returned. "You know you're making both him and M'sieur Dufaure angry."

Judith smiled as a breeze lifted her red curls and brushed them against her cheeks. "They're going to have to get used to my being there, Laura. As long as I'm visiting here, I shall be working at the office."

"Hardly a visit." Laura sat in one of the cane-bottom rockers and gazed in satisfaction at the land— the land that she loved and would someday be hers. "Now that you're here, we expect you to stay. This is your home."

"No, I don't think so." Judith gazed into the distance. Although she was not quite as thin as she had been before her mother's death, her gray wool dress still hung loosely from her tall frame.

"What are you so pensive about?" Laura asked.

Judith lifted a shoulder and sighed. "I was thinking about the—the trip over here."

Laura sighed. Having endured the same trip, she could sympathize with her sister. But Laura was also astute enough to know that something else was niggling at Judith. "Is your concern the sailing and weather itself, or specifically, the pirates who boarded your ship?"

Eventually, Judith said, "The pirates. I have never experienced anything like it in my life, Laura. At first I was frightened; then I was angry. And I felt so helpless. There was nothing I could do against his brute strength."

"You're here now. That's what counts."

Judith spun around and shook her head in exasperation. "I don't think you understand. A pirate captured one of our ships—one of Beau Talbot's ships—and boarded it. He harassed the passengers, and no one stopped him. No one even tried, Laura. No one!"

"We're at war, Judith," Laura said.

"This wasn't war. This man wasn't fighting for either side, Laura. He was a pirate."

Laura sighed. "It's not going to do you any good to dwell on it, Judith."

Judith stared at her sister incredulously. "That man—that pirate—pushed the crew and passengers around, Laura. He tore my cabin up and destroyed all my clothes, all my new dresses." She flung her hands out and laughed without humor, her face gray and drawn. "He destroyed the dress you gave me, and it was so beautiful. I guess it serves me right. I ripped up the first blue dress you gave me and he—he cut this one to shreds and flung it around my cabin."

"Don't, Judith." Hearing Judith's anguish, Laura

rose and moved to her. She was glad that her sister was taking an interest in her clothing and hoped that Judith was making an attempt to become part of the family and to be accepted. "We'll buy you more clothes. I've already sent word to my seamstress and made an appointment for her to come fit you."

Eventually, Judith admitted, "It's not the clothes, Laura. It's the damned arrogance of the man."

Laura leaned back in the chair and studied her sister. "You keep saying *the man*, Judith. Is there one of these pirates you hate more than the others?"

Judith hesitated fractionally before she said, "Yes, there is. And one of these days I'll find him and repay him in kind for what he's done to me." Judith unconsciously lifted a hand and touched her lips.

Laura's eyes narrowed to mere slits as she observed the faraway look on Judith's face. Before she had only thought there was more to the story Judith was telling; more than anguish over losing a mere dress; now she knew. Softly, Laura asked, "And just what did he do to you, Judith?"

Judith's hands dropped. "That's . . . that's all."

"Then it can easily be forgotten. Papa will see that you have new dresses to replace the ones you lost. And now that you're rested up, we'll have a small party and introduce you to our friends. In fact, Papa and Celeste have already planned one for you."

"I need time to get to know the . . . family before we do that." Judith laughed bitterly. "I have the feeling that Celeste is interested only in introducing me to an eligible man."

Laura reached for the crystal pitcher sitting on the table in front of her and poured two glasses of lemonade. "You're right. *Maman* is a matchmaker."

"*Maman!*" Judith seemed to spit the words out with distaste. "How can you call her mother?"

240

Laura set the glass down and rose. Not quite as tall as her sister but every bit as assertive, she stared into the ice-blue eyes. "For the past seven years, since Celeste and Papa have been married, Celeste has been like a mother to me, Judith, and I love her dearly. She didn't take Charlotte's place. She didn't try or want to, but she became my *maman*. I won't hear you speak ill of her."

"I'm sorry." Judith brushed a fiery red curl from her cheek. "I don't mean to be so touchy. I just feel so out of place over here, Laura. I don't fit into the family."

"You will if you try," Laura returned.

"I am trying!" Judith's eyes glittered with tears.

Laura's voice softened. "Then you must give yourself time."

"I don't think so." Judith prowled the veranda restlessly. "We are so different, Laura. Can't you see, I'm totally British while you and Beau have become totally Creole."

"Living here has changed our viewpoints. That was inevitable. I'm sure yours will change also, given time."

"No, Laura, my loyalty will not change. I refuse to let you and Beau mold me into a copy of you. I'm Judith Claire Talbot-Harrow and shall always be."

"You're still a rebellious nine-year-old." Laura refused to let Judith arouse her temper.

"Perhaps." Judith picked up a glass of lemonade. She grinned at Laura, the gesture truly friendly and disarming. "Will you plead with our stepmother to give me a little more time?"

Judith drank greedily, the cool liquid tasting good to her parched throat. She wondered if she would ever get accustomed to the sultry heat of New Orleans.

"After all," she continued, plucking at her skirt

241

with one hand, "at present I would be an embarrassment to all of you. You will speak to Celeste?"

Laura nodded her head. "But I don't know that it will do any good. Celeste is an extremely persistent woman once she sets her mind to do something."

"If only she'll give me a few days. By that time I'll be living in town." Judith glanced at Laura. "I suppose Papa told you?"

"That you want to work with him at the office?" Judith nodded, and Laura leaned forward and began to tidy the tray. "I'm not sure that I approve of your working at the docks. It's so unladylike, so unconventional, Judith."

"But it's what I've always wanted to do, Laura. It's something I can excel in. Like Papa, I love the sea. This belongs to you, not to me." She waved her hand in an encompassing gesture and turned to Laura. "Can you understand?"

"Yes, I explained this to Papa when he asked me to talk you out of this notion."

Judith's eyes widened in surprise. "You're not?"

Laura's green eyes rested on Judith's face, entirely too thin but lovely all the same. Fiery red curls, defying restriction in a tight little chignon, wisped around her cheeks. "You've been cooped up all your life taking care of Charlotte. Now you want to try your wings. I know how important it is to you to find your own life and to prove yourself to Papa. While I don't think it's in a small, stuffy office at Talbot Shipping Line, I'm willing to let you find out for yourself."

"Perhaps you're right. We'll see." Judith sat a moment, posed on the edge of the chair. When Laura made no reply, she drew in a deep breath and said, "Did Papa tell you that I want to live in town . . . all the time?"

"No." Laura was clearly surprised.

Judith reached forward and caught Laura's hands in hers. "I know it's not the proper thing for a woman to do, Laura, but I'm suffocating here. Really I am. Beau and Celeste don't understand. You must. Please, give me some time and space."

"All right." A new understanding grew between the two sisters. "I'm glad you're here, Judith. Really I am."

"Me too."

Interlude II

Several mornings later Judith walked onto the veranda and smiled at Laura. "Good morning, sister. You promised to take me on a tour of Ombres Azurées. I'm ready to go."

Although Laura was surprised, she was pleased with Judith's request. Her gaze swept over the dark, nondescript wool dress. "Not quite." She smiled and called out, "Jeanette, please get Maîtresse Judith the proper coverings to protect her skin."

Judith grimaced. "Laura, surely all of that isn't necessary. My bonnet and parasol will do well enough."

"You're not accustomed to the heat, Judith. I insist that you wear it."

Judith's gaze raked over her sister. Against the humidity and sweltering heat of the early spring, Laura looked coolly elegant. Her hair was swirled into an elegant but functional chignon. Polished black boots complemented her taupe riding habit. Her broad-brimmed straw bonnet lay in one of the nearby rockers.

She walked to the edge of the porch and gazed into the sky. In the far distance she could see a mass of gray clouds. But for the moment the sun was shining brightly. "I know Celeste would agree with me."

"She probably wouldn't want me to go at all." Judith looked at the end of the porch. Sitting there was a wicker chaise longue, a cashmere shawl draped over the yellow floral cushions. "She's a great one for lying down in the middle of the day."

Laura, too, looked at the chaise. She said quietly, "Judith, Celeste has never worked a day in her life. She does what is expected of her and likes it."

"But you don't. You told me that you had to go around to visit all the workers' quarters and distribute food and clothing."

Before Laura could make comment, the door opened and Jeanette appeared with hat, mask, and heavy veiling. She placed them on the small table between the chairs.

Judith rolled her eyes disgustedly and looked at Laura. "You don't wear all that protection."

Laura grinned. "No, but I'm accustomed to the heat."

"If you swathe me from head to toe in muslin and linen, I'll pass out before we've gone a mile. I'll bet no one can breathe under all that."

"If you want to go, you'll have to figure out a way to breathe."

Recognizing the resolve in Laura's tone, Judith pushed her arm through the cream-colored duster that Jeanette held up. Then she slipped her hands into the white cotton gloves and stood while Jeanette arranged the coat. Then she picked up the hat and twirled it in her hands.

"You sound just like *Grandmère.*"

"That's right." Laura's grin widened. "And I'm the Countess of Ombres Azurées. You can be the Countess of the Talbot Line."

"On land and sea." Judith situated her hat and adjusted the cotton mask. "Right, sister dear?"

"Right."

Soon the gig was moving briskly along the road that threaded among the huge, moss-draped oak trees and stately pines. The Bayou d'Ombre was unusually large and deep, its waters a clear, sparkling blue. They passed the quarters, small stone cottages set in rows in which the slaves lived. The wind gently slapped brightly colored clothes hung on the line to dry. Men and women too old to work the fields sat in the shade of the porch, minding the house and watching the children who scampered about in the yard.

Laura introduced Judith to them, and they talked for a little while as Laura distributed sweets among the children. Then she drove Judith past the fields to see the crops of purple cane that shimmered and swayed in the morning breeze. They rode by the mill, where workers sang and the aroma of cane syrup permeated the air.

When Laura finally stopped the buggy, she and Judith sat in front of the small white cottage. Its color was a beautiful contrast to the vivid green of the forest and the colorful array of flowers among which it nestled. Lilac-blue wisteria hung in huge festoons off the oak trees. Pink honeysuckle bushes and dogwood trees abounded. Azaleas grew around the porch. All were in full bloom, their fragrance a sweet perfume.

A servant raced out of the house and tied the reins to the hitching post while Laura and Judith climbed out of the buggy. They walked through the small picket gate and up the boardwalk to the front porch. When they reached the sitting room, Judith quickly shed her bonnet and veils, dropping them into the arms of the waiting servant.

Laura moved to the casement window. "Isn't it beautiful?"

Judith followed. She fanned the lapels of her sweat-moistened dress in the air. Looking over Laura's shoulder, she said tentatively, "It's all so wild. It's not like any garden I've ever seen. Certainly not like an English garden."

"Perhaps that's why I love it so much," Laura confessed. "It's a challenge to keep it all under control."

Judith shook her head. "And they must grow so fast. I would think cutting back the same plants over and over would get awfully boring."

In the distance they heard the rumble of thunder, but neither seemed to notice. Slowly, the sky began to darken.

"I can't think of anything more boring than sitting in a stuffy office moving figures from one piece of paper to another. The land is never boring."

"How can you say that?" Judith swatted at a mosquito that kept singing around her head. "It's always the same."

"Oh, no." Laura's eyes glowed. "It's constantly generating new life. Crops are planted, they grow, they're harvested. A wonderful cycle—which I control."

"Just as I said. Boring."

Laura couldn't imagine anyone's wanting to spend their time poring over figures when they could be enjoying nature. "It's mine. And I'd do anything I had to to keep it."

"Are you sure you're not heading for disappointment?"

Laura looked at Judith.

"I understood the plantation was Celeste's."

Laura shook her head. "In point of fact, it's in Papa's name now." Judith looked surprised and Laura explained. "She insisted when they married." The maid entered, bearing a silver tray which she set on the low table in the center of the room. "She had so many outstanding debts that she was about to lose it."

"What kind of debts?"

Laura hesitated briefly. "Celeste likes to gamble."

Judith shrugged. "So did Charlotte."

"I don't like to gamble." Yet Laura remembered the incident in the Golden Fleece only the past week. When she was around Clay Sutherland her personality underwent a change. Again she vowed to keep her distance from the man, but knew she was lying to herself. Her weakness where this man was concerned troubled her. Although Celeste had told her that a woman could have a lover as long as she was discreet, Laura's conscience was plaguing her. Was discretion merely a mask for hypocrisy, she wondered.

So far none knew of her involvement with Clay, and she could only wonder why Roussel had said nothing about Clay's being on the ship the night she departed for England. She could only surmise that he would use the information at the time and place that it suited his purposes. Something about Roussel frightened her. His threat had been so quietly ominous."

"I don't like to drink," Judith eventually said.

"Would you like to see my retreat?"

"Yes, I'd like to very much."

Laura said, "I come here when I want to be alone. From here I can walk out to the fields; I can hear the Negroes singing. I see the bayou from my bedroom window. Here I read and work without making Celeste unhappy. I don't have to live my day on a

249

social routine. I can leave that to her."

Judith brushed the tips of her fingers through her sweat-moistened hair. "I know what you mean. I've worked hard for the past few years. I don't enjoy sitting around doing nothing. That's why I want to be part of the Talbot lines. I've planned on it. That's why I had my tutors instruct me in accounting and mathematics instead of watercolors and French."

Laura smiled at Judith and pointed to the picture of Ombres Azurées above the fireplace. "I'm quite proficient at watercolors and French."

Judith moved closer and looked at the picture. "Why, Laura, that's the plantation house to the life."

They smiled at each other, then Judith turned away restlessly. Crossing her arms over her chest, she walked around the small room, finally stopping in front of the window. "I want to live in town, Laura. I don't want to live here. I've been stuck in the country all my life. I don't like it."

"But if you go back to town and work for the Talbot lines, you'll have to stay in a cramped little office. How can you stand that?"

Judith flexed her fingers. "It's what I'll be working with. Figures and tangible objects that they stand for fascinate me. They're the exact sciences. I think I'd like to make money . . . on my own."

Laura stared at Judith. This sounded so unlike the image she had of her. "Why is money so important?"

Judith returned to the fireplace and gazed at the painting. "All my life, I've lived hemmed in on all sides by the wealth of Harrestone, but I've been a pauper."

Laura remembered the last time Judith had visited with their grandmother before Charlotte died. Even then she had been on a beggar's mission.

"I want to make money. Wealth makes a person

strong and respected. I want to be wealthy. I want that respect."

"I never thought we were anything alike. And yet we are." At this moment Laura truly identified with her sister; they were bound together by those invisible bonds of blood and love and purpose. She gazed at the picture, her eyes glinting with resolve. "The land is everything to me, the way money is to you. For me it's an exact science."

Not for a moment would she let anyone—not even Clay Sutherland—come between her and what she wanted. At times she mistook the emotions that raged through them as love, but Clay always straightened her out and let her know that it was merely passion. When George had let her down, when he had denied her the place in society which she wanted, she had promised herself that she would never be put in such a hurtful position again, and certainly not for lust.

"Why, Laura, I never realized—"

"The land I should have had was taken away from me." She spoke coolly with a detachment that precluded pain. Not for all the world would she let Judith know how deeply she had been hurt through the years. First, she had been denied Harrestone by the birth of little Harry; that she accepted. Then she had been denied Beckworth House when George had broken their engagement. Ombres Azurées would be hers. "I want this. It's my wealth and power."

Judith laughed softly and reached for her bonnet. "And you know who you sound like?" Her gaze caught Laura's. *"Grandmère."*

"Papa."

A new understanding between them, they smiled. Judith said, "We are sisters after all."

Chapter Eleven

When she reached the shade of the huge oaks that lined the road, Laura halted the gig. For an early spring morning, the weather was sultry, unusually so. A heat wave settled over the bayou country. The sun beat down unmercifully. Laura pulled her hat off. Her wet hair was plastered to her head. A fine film of perspiration and dust covered her face.

Judith had left for town two days before, and already Laura missed her. She was glad her sister had come from England to join them. During the brief time the two of them had been together at Ombres Azurées, they had grown close and had enjoyed each other's company. Laura would do anything to keep Judith in New Orleans with them. They were a family, and that's the way they would remain.

Swatting a mosquito from her face, Laura put her hat back on and picked up the reins. Once again the gig was moving briskly over the trodden path. As she neared the clearing, she slowed the horse's gait. The workers clustered together in a tight circle.

When they heard the buggy, they turned their heads and silently watched her approach; otherwise they did not move. Laura sensed that all was not well;

their expressions were guarded, their eyes hostile. As she approached, Joshua stepped from among the ranks. Leaning against him was Tomas, his young brother. Long, angry marks crisscrossed the lad's back.

Laura leapt from the gig. "What happened?"

"I had to punish one of the slaves." She heard Leroy Donaldson's voice long before he pushed through the workers. Coiled around his shoulder was a whip.

Anger surged through Laura. "I don't allow punishment like this, M'sieur Donaldson."

Donaldson tucked his thumbs beneath his suspenders. His lips twisted into an ugly sneer. "Reckon your paw don't feel that way, Miss Talbot. When he hired me, he told me to do what was necessary to keep these slaves under control. And I did just that."

"My father would never have given you permission to beat another human being as you've beaten this boy."

"You can't pamper 'em, ma'am, else a worker's gonna get fat and sassy." He tugged the brim of the battered hat lower on his forehead.

Joshua pressed closer to Laura. From beneath the brim of his hat he stared contemptuously at the overseer. At one word from Laura he would throw the overseer off Ombres Azurées. Seeing the Negro's protective move, Leroy Donaldson's beady black eyes narrowed. Nervously, he lifted his hand and rubbed it across his beard-stubbled chin. "I can understand how a woman might be squirmish about this, Miss Talbot, but if'n I'm gonna be your overseer, you're gonna hafta let me do my job."

The afternoon breeze caught Laura's veil and lifted it to reveal her cold expression. "Doing your job, Mr. Donaldson, does not include beating my slaves."

Donaldson's lips pulled wider to expose stained, uneven teeth. "Well now, missy, don't reckon I can agree to that. You see, where I've worked before, I've been given authority to—"

"I don't care where you worked before or under what conditions you worked. I am the authority on Ombres Azurées. The final authority. My word is law. My slaves are not to be beaten and abused."

Donaldson's eyes glinted open hostility. "Reckon I need to be a-speaking to your paw about this. I'm a man. I don't answer to no woman."

"You're fired, M'sieur Donaldson. Get out, and don't you ever set foot on Ombres Azurées again."

Donaldson's lips thinned; his nostrils flared. "Don't you reckon you better know what I whipped the boy about before you run me off." He turned, walked through the crowd, and bent down to pick up something. When he returned, he held his hand out.

Laura saw the effigy and gasped. Color drained from her face. As clearly as if it were happening at that moment, she saw the doll lying in a pool of blood on her pillow.

"Voodoo." He snorted. "And from the looks of it, Miss Talbot, I'd say this was supposed to be you. Do you recognize the material? Was it something you wore or owned?"

Of course it was. It was the other glove she lost the day she helped John.

The field workers slowly moved closer to tighten the circle around Laura and Donaldson. From somewhere in the crowd, a woman's voice howled in a frenzied wail. Simultaneously, the slaves began to clap their hands and moved aside to form an opening through which she danced. Another effigy landed at Donaldson's feet.

"And this one is you," she chanted. Her eyes were

closed, and her head bobbed from side to side in rhythm to the clapping. "If you're not careful, overseer man, you'll be dead before the day is over."

Fear distorted Donaldson's face; he spun around and with an agility at odds with his slovenly appearance, his whip snaked through the air to curl around the woman's neck. He jerked his wrist, the leather cutting into her windpipe. Her scream was muffled and cut short. She gasped for air; her eyes opened wide and bugged out. Her hands clawed at the leather vise.

"Stop it," Laura shouted.

But the man would not be stopped. No longer thinking rationally, he determined to choke the woman to death. Joshua pushed his brother aside and leapt at Donaldson. Laura looked for a weapon. She must do something. Her quirt was ineffective against his whip. She needed her gun! She raced to the buggy.

Donaldson was quicker than Joshua. At once he dodged and dropped the whip. The woman fell to her knees. Donaldson whisked a knife out of his waistband. Crouching, he flashed it through the air, the silver blade glimmering ominously in the sunlight.

"If any of you so much as lay a hand on me, I'll kill you," he snarled. "And no court is gonna do anything about it."

His eyes wide and fixed, Joshua never budged. His legs were straddled, his arms away from his body. Also crouching, he began to circle Donaldson. The other workers began to chant softly; they clapped their hands; they, too, circled the white man, their eyes riveted to him. A young black woman picked up the effigy and waved it through the air.

In an African and French dialect, she sang, "This

is you, white man. This is you, and you may die before the day is over."

"Don't!" Laura had returned, the gun in hand, but could not be heard above the noise of the workers.

Unable to see beyond the human circle of overt hostility, sweat beaded on Donaldson's upper lip. His eyes darted nervously about. The fieldhands were closing in on him. They chanted louder. Black hands on all sides clawed through the air. Frightened out of his wits, the overseer grabbed a young black girl by the neck and pulled her tightly against him. He held his knife against her throat.

"Let me out of here, or I'll kill her."

The fieldhands pressed closer. They had no fear. Only resolve gleamed in their eyes. Laura clawed her way through the workers to reach the center of the circle. But the blacks seemed to be oblivious to her. Caught up in their ritual, the chanting grew even louder.

Aiming the pistol, Laura shouted above the clamor. "Donaldson, turn her loose."

Crazed, the man was clearly beyond reason. His eyes dilated with fear. He pulled his hand back, the tip of the knife glimmering sinisterly.

"Donaldson, I said turn the girl loose."

The man turned to see Laura, to see the weapon pointed at him. His hand fell, and the blade sliced through the air, headed directly for Laura. Metal sang against the wind. Laura pulled the trigger as one of the slaves knocked her to the ground. Donaldson cried out in pain; he threw the girl away from him and clutched at his chest.

The slaves hushed their chanting and slowly backed away to stare at the dead man. An ever-increasing circle of blood discolored his chest. Shaking from head to toe, Laura dropped the rifle and pushed to her feet. Joshua knelt beside Donaldson and laid his hand over his mouth, then on his chest.

He looked at Laura. "He's dead, Maîtresse."

Laura wiped her arm across her forehead and said flatly, "See that he's buried. I must report his death to the authorities."

"Yes'm."

She walked over to Tomas and looked at his back. The cuts were deep and needed attention. She spoke to Joshua. "Send someone to the house to get some salve for his back. Don't work him until it's healed."

Laura then moved to the old woman who still crouched on the ground, one gnarled hand wrapped around the base of her throat. Laura knelt and removed the hand to examine the whip burn. "Here, Mandy. Let me tend to your wound."

The old woman shook her head. "I be all right, Maîtresse."

Laura helped Mandy to her feet. Then she bent and picked up the effigy that had fallen during the fracas. "Where did you get this?"

Mandy dropped her head and said nothing.

"Where did you get it?" Laura's voice was firmer this time, more demanding.

"I brought it to her." Tomas stepped forward.

Laura's gaze rested on the young boy. "Why?"

"It wasn't supposed to bring any harm." He looked at the dead man. "If he hadn't interfered, nothing bad would have happened."

"Is this supposed to be me?"

Unable to answer or to look into her face, the boy also lowered his head.

Fear climbed Laura's spine. Voodoo scared her. And since she'd been to Jena Benoit's ritual, strange things had begun to happen to her. Her nerves were like a tightly coiled spring. She felt dizzy and clammy. She turned to Joshua. "How long have my slaves been practicing voodoo?"

"I didn't know about it until today when they began the ritual," Joshua explained. "I was breaking it up when Donaldson arrived. When he found the doll, he went wild and began to beat Tomas. Then you showed up."

Mandy shuffled up to Laura. She spoke in broken French. "Berthe, she be stronger than any voodoo priestess. We have the ritual, but we know Berthe can undo the curse, Maîtresse."

Visions of a blood-soaked pillow nauseated Laura. "I suppose I'm to die now."

"Oh, no, Maîtresse," Tomas answered hastily. "This was merely to make you and M'sieur Roussel fall in love and marry."

Laura remembered the other doll. "That was M'sieur Roussel, not Donaldson?"

Tomas nodded his head vigorously. "We meant no harm, Maîtresse. We would not have done it had it been a curse."

"Who gave you the dolls?"

Long, tense minutes passed. Tomas looked from one of the workers to another. Their expressions never changed; they remained silent and impassive. Finally, Tomas said in a low voice, "Jena Benoit."

Not bothering to change from her riding habit in which she worked the plantation, Laura pulled the gig to a halt in front of the Golden Fleece and jumped out. The street was busy; vehicles moved in both directions but Laura observed nothing around her. She was unconcerned that this was the middle of the day and that she had burst into a gambling house, no matter that it was closed for business. She never

259

considered that someone might see and recognize her. Had she considered it, she would have gone in anyway.

Her boots clipped over the flagstones as determined steps carried her into the saloon. Sunlight poured into the room through the open doors and windows. Jena Benoit stood in the middle of the room, talking with a man. Both of them turned in surprise.

When Laura halted in front of the mulatto, she tossed the dolls at Jena's feet. "I believe these are yours."

His gaze shifting from one of the women to the other and to the effigies, the man stepped away. Jena gazed at them for a minute before she lifted her head. "Yes, they are."

Laura had been filled with equal parts of anger and fear before. When she had gone to Jena's home, she had learned that the mulatto was at the Golden Fleece. Her last vestige of fear left. Now she was nothing but a mass of fury, hot and molten, ready to explode.

"I found the first doll on my pillow in a puddle of blood," she said, "but I ignored that. It was meant for me alone, and I knew you were behind it. This time I'm not ignoring it. You're tampering with my workers. You're threatening Ombres Azurées, and I won't have that."

The expression on Jena's beautiful face never changed. The chocolate eyes darkened until they were almost black in color. Long fingernails, stained a deep bloodred, drummed against the tabletop. "And you, white woman, have tampered with a voodoo queen's man. I have warned you about my powers."

"I'm not afraid of you or your power or your

260

snakes." Laura's eyes blazed. "I'm giving you fair warning. Stay away from my plantation and my slaves. If I so much as suspect you've been near Ombres Azurées, I'll have you arrested and banished from New Orleans."

"You can't do that." The mulatto lost her composure. Hatred distorted her features.

In control now, Laura breathed deeply. "Not only can I, but I will. No one treats Laura Elyse Talbot with disdain. Not even a voodoo queen."

Laura turned to walk away.

Jena shook with rage. Her arm extended; her hand slowly clenched into a fist. "You will soon respect my powers, white woman."

Before Laura could guess her intention, Jena leapt on her back, her fingers digging into Laura's hair. Taken by surprise, Laura fell to her knees. She twisted her head and back; she hit at Jena, but the mulatto refused to turn loose.

The man abruptly plunged to the rescue. "Here, now, ladies," he said, grabbing Jena's shoulders and pulling her away from Laura, "let's stop this."

Jerking out of his arms, Jena spun around, lifted her foot, and belted him a heavy blow in the groin. He cried out in pain and fell to the ground.

Jena turned back to Laura. Lapsing into French, she said, "I'll kill you, white woman."

"Not if I have anything to say about it," Laura hissed in French also.

"Who do you think you are to order Jena Benoit around? Did you not see what happened to the girl who messed with my man?"

Laura sucked in air. "We're not talking about a man."

"Oh, yes, Laura Talbot, we are indeed. We're talking about Clay Sutherland."

They were, and each knew it. They had known it from the first night they had seen each other. Jena Benoit had staked her claim on Clay, and Laura had blatantly disregarded the boundary lines.

The women went at each other. They clawed and scratched. They tore clothing. They yelled obsceneties; they muttered oaths. Each returned blow for blow. But Laura was the larger woman. Accustomed to working outdoors, she had more stamina. Finally, she stood in the center of the room, her breasts heaving as she dragged air into her lungs. The bodice of her riding habit was torn, exposing the soft material of her chemise. Her hair hung in a tangled mess around her face. An angry cut ran down her cheek.

Jena lay on the floor, blood dribbling out of the corner of her mouth. Her breathing was heavy and ragged. She rolled over but made no effort to get to her feet. "You have not won, white woman. Clay Sutherland is not your man." Jena lapsed into English.

Laura brushed a strand of hair out of her face. "I told you this wasn't about Clay." She also spoke English.

Jena pushed up on her hands and spat blood out of her mouth. "I see the way you look at Clay Sutherland. I am not a fancy planter's daughter or wife, but I am intelligent. I know what the two of you are doing."

A shadow flickered through the room as someone walked in the front door, but neither woman was paying attention. They glared at each other, aware of no one but themselves.

"This fight was about Clay. I was fighting over my property, not a gambler."

"Tell yourself what you will, but I know better. I want Clay Sutherland. No other woman shall have him." Jena rose to her feet.

His face set, Clay strode fully into the saloon. His boots clicked a determined cadence on the hardwood floor. He tossed his hat on the nearest table and gazed from one woman to the other. His stance pulled the gray trousers tight across his sinewy legs. The black jacket molded his broad shoulders to perfection. Finally, his eyes settled on Laura.

The strand of hair flopped into her face again. She brushed it back. Clay's scrutiny made her aware of her disheveled appearance. It made her aware of him.

"You're defying all my preconceived notions of a plantation mistress, Mademoiselle Talbot." His lips twitched into a smile. "I can hardly imagine your being in a saloon brawl."

Pulling herself up a little straighter, Laura said, "This isn't quite that."

"No? Then what is it?"

Laura glared at the mulatto. In her anger Laura was beautiful. Her face was filled with soft color. Her eyes flashed. Her hand lifted to brush against the jade phoenix, revealed by the torn bodice. She turned her face. When Clay saw the jagged line running down her cheek, his smile vanished. His gaze unconsciously shifted to Jena's hands, to the long fingernails. He pulled his handkerchief from his pocket and walked to Laura. He gently pressed it against the streak of blood.

"Let's go upstairs," he said gently. "You can clean up before I take you home, and we can talk."

"No." His care and tenderness brought tears to Laura's eyes. She lifted her hand and laid it over his.

Willing to do anything to get her to stay, Clay said, "Then come upstairs and say hello to John. He'd love to see you."

Her voice husky, she said, "I'd love to see him, but not today, Clay. Tell him hello for me."

263

"Why won't you stay?"

"I have my gig outside."

"That's hardly a reason." Gently, he blotted the blood from her cheek.

She lifted imploring eyes. Her voice softened to a near whisper. "I need time, Clay, to straighten out my chaotic thoughts. I want to go to the cottage. I can't—I can't talk now."

Clay's eyes darkened. "I'd feel better if you'd let me drive you."

Laura shook her head and smiled. "You still think I need a man to take care of me?"

"Not just any man. You need me." Clay's voice was husky, his eyes anxiously roaming her bruised and battered face. He leaned over and gently brushed his lips against her forehead.

A tear slid past Laura's tightly closed lids. "Please, Clay, I must go."

Knowing that it was futile to argue with Laura, Clay walked her outdoors and helped her into the gig. He laid the reins in her hands. "You're going to be at the cottage?"

"Yes." Laura stared straight ahead.

"I'll see you later this evening."

"Not tonight." She looked down at him, her eyes sparkling. She laid her hand against his cheek. "I really do need time to think, Clay. I'll—send word."

He nodded and stepped back.

Laura drove home but felt none of the warmth of the afternoon sun. She saw none of its golden beauty. Tears spiked her lashes. Her life was knotted in such a mess, and she wondered how she was going to undo it. Tomas was coming later to trim the undergrowth around the house. Through him she would send word to Celeste that she was spending the night at the cottage. She did wish to be by herself. Perhaps she

264

could sort through the tangled mess.

Angry, Clay stared at Jena. "What was the fight about?"

She shrugged her shoulders, her eyes hastily scanning the floor for the telltale effigies. Somehow during the scuffle they had been kicked aside.

Clay prodded. "Laura wouldn't have come here without good reason."

Jena wiped the blood from the corner of her mouth. "She came to see you and was angry when she found me here."

Clay could hope so, but he knew differently. In broad daylight Laura would not defy society merely to come see him. He took a step and felt something strange and out of place hit against the toe of his boot. He looked down to see the grotesque doll peeking from beneath the table. He stooped and picked it up. His entire countenance exploded into fury. His head popped up.

"Yours?"

Jena hugged her arms to her chest. She looked everywhere but into his eyes. "I didn't mean to hurt her, Clay. I only wanted to scare her away from you."

Clay dropped the doll and moved to stand in front of Jena. His fingers banded around her upper arms, and he shook her until she looked at him. "Only wanted to frighten her," he mimicked. "Yet the first one you left at her house in a puddle of blood."

"It didn't mean anything," Jena shouted. "I didn't cast a spell. I simply had Tomas put it on her pillow in a cup of chicken blood. I wanted to frighten her away from you and into Giraumont's arms and bed. He has been buying spells for her. He bought the one I cast today."

265

"What kind?" He shook her again when she did not answer.

"He wants her to fall in love with him so they can be married quickly. It was a love spell, Clay. Really it was."

Jena's confession bothered Clay. Why was Roussel resorting to voodoo? Surely there was more to this than love, but what? "Leave Laura alone. If anything happens to her, I'll swear I'll come after you." He turned her loose and moved away.

"I didn't come here to see you. I brought news to Graham." She rubbed her arms. "Do you know when he'll be back?"

His back to her, Clay lifted a hand and massaged the base of his neck. He sighed. The events of the day tumbled in on him. "He won't."

"He's gone?" Jena asked.

"Dead."

Jena straightened up. "What happened?"

"His body was found in an overturned carriage on the outskirts of town this morning. The police are calling it an accidental death."

Softly, she said, "But you do not?"

"No, he was beaten to death." Clay shuddered when he recalled Graham's mutilated body. He walked to one of the tables that stood along the wall and opened the tobacco box. He selected a cigar and lit it.

"Does this end the investigation into the Bonapartists?" Jena asked.

Clay had struggled with this question ever since he had identified Graham's body at the police station. His greatest wish was to leave espionage behind him. That was why he had moved from Virginia in the first place. Yet Graham Bradford's death tangled him in the same web.

266

It angered Clay, but he knew he could not live with himself if he allowed his friend's death to go unsolved. He must work fast to find the operatives in New Orleans. He must find Graham's contact and must find him quickly.

Hidden behind a veil of smoke, he asked, "What have you learned?"

Jena smiled, and her dark eyes glittered maliciously. "Perhaps when I tell you, you will not feel so kindly about Laura Talbot.

Jena Benoit's cabin was nestled deep in the swamp, surrounded by alligator-infested water. A wooden bridge led from the land to her front porch. She paced back and forth in the sitting room. Every once in a while she would lift her hand and gingerly touch her right jaw. Only hours had passed, but it was discolored and swollen, a result of Laura's powerful left-hand swing. Muttering, Jena brooded over the day's events.

She looked at the bag of gold coins on the table and smiled, a hollow gesture. Giraumont had purchased a second spell. But Jena knew that Laura would never love a man like him. No woman would. Not once she had fallen in love with Clay Sutherland.

An aphrodisiac this time, Giraumont had suggested. One to be slipped into the house by one of the servants and put into Laura's chocolate.

Jena walked to the large wicker basket and lifted the lid. She smiled when she heard the soft hiss. "Don't worry, my lover," she crooned in French. "Soon you will be having fun. We will give Laura Talbot an aphrodisiac she will not soon forget."

Jena walked to the fireplace and stirred the thick, smelly liquid in the cauldron. Then she heard a noise. She lifted her head and strained to hear the smallest sound. She laughed softly. Paddles dipping in and out of the water. They had returned, bringing the last ingredient for her potion. Humming, she added more herbs to the mixture. She stirred it again.

Footsteps sounded on the porch, and two men entered the cabin. Both of them were tall and slender; their black bodies rippled with sleek muscles. They carried a heavy burden wrapped in a blanket.

"Over there." Jena pointed to the corner of the room.

The afternoon sun was settling low in the west, shadows falling on the boy who ran into town. The whip gashes on his back burned as perspiration trickled over them. Tears scalded his cheeks. His chest burned; his lungs felt as if they would surely burst. He was breathing deeply but was getting no air. Pain pierced his side. He clutched it with his hand.

Finally, Tomas turned onto Rue Royale. He staggered into the courtyard of the Golden Fleece. He pulled himself up the stairs and knocked on the door.

"M'sieur Sutherland," he gasped when the white man opened the door. "I must see him."

Churnbarker's eyes ran distastefully over the boy. "Mr. Sutherland can't be disturbed."

Tomas's hand flattened on the door and he pushed it open. Gaining a second wind, he dodged into the house, his eyes darting about. "M'sieur Sutherland," he yelled at the top of his voice. Up the stairs he ran and down the hall, Churnbarker right behind him. "Maîtresse Laura is in trouble. You must help her."

A door opened, and Clay rushed out of his office to bump into the boy. Clay caught him by the shoulders to keep him from falling.

"Maîtresse Laura," Tomas said between gasps, his fingers biting into his side, his face twisted in pain, "she's in trouble, m'sieur."

Clay led him into the office and shoved him into a chair. "Churnbarker, get him something cool to drink."

"Yes, sir," the faithful servant said between huffs.

"What about Laura?" Clay asked.

"I went to cut the bushes around the cottage, m'sieur. When I got there, I saw two men carrying a large bundle. They got into a pirogue and paddled down the bayou. I saw Maîtresse Laura's gig, but she wasn't at the cottage. I didn't find her anywhere."

"Did you recognize the men?"

Churnbarker returned with a glass of water. Tomas nodded his head as he drank deeply. He gasped. "They were Jena Benoit's priests."

Clay swore softly, regretting not for the first time that he had ever consented to take Laura to the voodoo ritual. "You're sure?"

Drinking more water, the boy again nodded his head.

"Do you know where they've taken her?"

"Her secret cabin in the swamps."

"How do you know about it?"

Tomas lowered his head. "I was going to be one of her priests."

"You're the one who put the doll and chicken blood on her pillow?"

Tomas's eyes rounded. "No spell went with it, m'sieur. I promise. Jena wanted only to frighten maîtresse. I would not have harmed her."

"How do I know I can trust you now?"

"Maîtresse Laura saved my life today, m'sieur. She kept the overseer from killing me. She is a good

269

maîtresse, and I do not want anything bad to happen to her."

"Take me to her."

Tomas leaned forward to set the glass on the edge of Clay's desk. He wiped a shaking hand across his mouth. "I'm not sure I can, m'sieur. I have never been there without being blindfolded."

Laura opened her eyes. The beamed ceiling was spinning above her head. Her lids shut again. She sniffed. An obnoxious odor filled the room. Strange noises assailed her ears. Her head hurt abominably. Forcibly, she lifted her lids a second time. She saw a blurry figure.

"So you're awake," the sultry voice said. "Good, it's time for me to give you your aphrodisiac. Roussel has paid me good for this potion, Mademoiselle Talbot."

The woman pushed a cup of the vile-smelling liquid beneath Laura's nose. Grabbing a handful of hair, Jena jerked Laura's head back. "Now drink."

Despite the dizziness and pain, Laura twisted her head furiously, the hot mixture scalding her chin, dribbling onto her dress.

"You will drink it." Jena moved away. "I promised Raoul that he could take his pleasure with you before you died. We want it willing, of course. It's a much greater pleasure for all of us."

Tears ran down Laura's cheeks. She could not hold out much longer. She was too weak to fight. "Is this—is this all over Clay?" Her mouth was dry, her tongue so large she could hardly talk. "I—I don't want him."

"If it were that simple," Jena said quietly, "I wouldn't have you here. But it's not. You see, Clay

270

Sutherland is enamored with you. Until you're gone . . . gone for good, he'll never look at me.''

Jena opened the door; however, before she walked out, she smiled at Laura. "If you're thinking of escaping, don't. My house is surrounded by swamp and alligators. There is only one way out, and that's being guarded.''

Later, as dusk settled over the Louisiana swamp, Laura stood and staggered from one window to the other. Swamp *was* all around her, but from the front window she could see the long boardwalk to land. Gingerly, she moved her pounding head. She looked from one end of the porch to the other. At one end Jena sat on the railing. She leaned against the building and had her eyes closed.

Again Laura's gaze darted back and forth as she searched for another guard. It had been a long time since she had heard a second voice. If she was going to escape, now was the time. She had nothing to lose either way. Should her escape fail, she would be killed. If she remained here, her fate was rape and murder.

Drawing in several deep and steadying breaths, she blinked her eyes to clear her vision. She eased her way to the door. Her hand closed over the handle and she tugged. She prayed the door would make no noise. Silently, it swished open. She gauged the distance from the porch to land. She saw the alligators dotting the waters. If she fell in, she had no chance.

But even they were preferable to Jena's choice of punishment.

Quietly, Laura moved onto the porch. One step. Two. Three. She was on the boardwalk and running. She thought she was running, but her body seemed to be moving so much slower than her mind. Too slow. Her head was much faster than her feet.

271

Jena's laughter followed her; it wrapped around her and like a rope began to tug her back to the cabin.

Laura fought. She caught the rail and pulled herself forward. She had to make it to shore. Soft thuds sounded behind her. Jena was coming. She was catching up with her. Another surge of anger propelled Laura a few more steps. She tripped over a loose board and fell.

Jena laughed again; she laughed louder and her hands closed over Laura's shoulder. "I had hoped to reward Raoul for faithful service," she grunted as she rolled Laura to the edge of the walkway, "but I don't think so now."

Laura's fingernails ripped and tore off as she fought for a grip on the rough planks. Splinters pricked her hands. Still, she would not turn loose.

Jena pushed harder. Laura slipped over the side, her feet hanging inches above the water. Several splashes echoed through the swamp. Alligators.

Laura's hands were tired; her shoulders ached. She could not hold on much longer. Jena began to stomp on her fingers. Out of the corner of her eye Laura saw the column that supported the railing. She turned loose of the walkway and lunged, wrapping her arms around the column. Closing her eyes against the terrific pain in her head, she swung her feet up.

Jena rushed to kneel beside Laura. She clawed at her hands. Laura lowered her head and bit Jena. She pulled her hand back and slapped Laura across the face. Momentarily blinded, Laura cried out in pain. When she felt her hands loosening their hold on the column, she lunged at Jena, the sudden force driving the voodoo priestess over the other side of the walkway.

Jena screamed but Laura was unable to move. Her head was splitting, and she could not see.

"Help me," Jena shouted. "Get me out of here."

Laura crawled to the other side of the walkway. She groped until she found the support column. Wrapping one arm around it, she yelled, "I can't see you. Swim to me and catch my arm. I'll help you up."

She heard Jena's frantic efforts. Her vision began to clear, and she saw the blurry form. She leaned farther down; she felt Jena's fingers graze hers. Then she heard the horrible scream . . . a long, agonizing scream. Swishing. Splashing. Thwacking. Then silence. Nothing but the night creatures of the forest.

Crying hysterically, Laura clutched the column and pulled to her feet. Never turning loose of the railing, she staggered the length of the bridge. In a state of shock she stumbled through the swamp, not knowing where she was going, not caring. The bushes tore her dress and scratched her arms and face. The harsh ground shredded her slippers from her feet.

Breathing raggedly, she collapsed at the foot of a huge cypress tree and leaned against the trunk. She was lost. She would never get home again. She would never see Ombres Azurées again. Nor her family. They would be worried. Celeste would be hysterical.

And Clay! What about Clay? All else paled into insignificance at the thought of never seeing him again. She would never feel the warmth and strength of his arms around her. She would not hear his laughter.

Hysterical herself, Laura began to laugh. Unable to stop herself, she laughed and laughed. Nothing was funny, yet she laughed. Somewhere out of the foggy region of her mind came sane thought. She must get up; she must keep moving. She rose and teetered. Finally, she balanced herself.

She heard the pirogue. She did not see it, but she

heard it. Shaking with fear, she hid behind the tree and peered through the dusky shadows. The water rippled first. Later she saw the bow, smoothly slicing the water aside. The pirogue neared. Two men! She saw two men.

She slapped her hand across her mouth to keep from screaming aloud. They were the ones who had kidnapped her from the cottage. Her thoughts in total shambles, she fled down the path in full view of the men. She stumbled and fell. She pushed up and ran again.

She heard the thuds of footsteps behind her. She heard the shouts. She ran faster. The forest was a mere blur around her. Her head pounded; her chest felt as if it were going to burst.

She looked over her shoulder. She saw no one, heard nothing, but she did not stop running. She staggered, regained her footing, and looked ahead.

She screamed as she collided into the chest of the man who had been chasing her.

Chapter Twelve

"Turn me loose," Laura screamed. Her head rolled back, and she beat on the man's chest with her fists. Then her fighting ceased, and she raked her injured fingers down the front of his shirt, leaving bloody tracks on the pristine white material. "Please let me go."

"Laura, darling, it's me." Clay held her tightly in his arms. He pressed his cheek against the top of her head. "I'm here. You're all right."

Laura's hysteria was a shield that kept her from hearing Clay. Night shadows kept her from seeing him clearly. She renewed her struggle. Her fists pounded his chest; her feet kicked against his shins. But the spurt of energy of short-lived. Exhausted, she slumped against him. He swept her into his arms and carried her through the woods. By the time he arrived at the pirogue, Tomas had spread blankets on the bottom. Clay lay her down.

His hands quickly examined her from head to toe to determine the extent of her injuries. He breathed in relief. None that he could ascertain . . . at least, none that were visible.

"Laura, where's Jena?"

"Jena?" she repeated blankly.

Clay turned to look at Tomas, who perched in the stern of the pirogue. "Did you find any sign of Jena?"

"No," the boy answered. "The cabin was empty."

"She's dead," Laura murmured. "I murdered her, Clay."

"No, darling, you didn't murder her."

"I did. I did," Laura insisted. "She was trying to kill me, and I—"

"It was self-defense, darling, not murder. Jena was trying to kill you."

"Yes." She gratefully accepted his assurance.

Clay knelt in the bow, and he and Tomas turned the pirogue around and headed back to New Orleans. In a semiconscious state Laura tossed restlessly and mumbled incoherently. Every so often her eyes would open, and she would look at Clay, silhouetted in the moonlight that filtered through the moss-laden trees. But there was no recognition. Her eyes were blank and unseeing. Night had settled in thickly and darkly when they docked below the city where Churnbarker waited with Clay's carriage.

"How is she, sir?" the servant asked.

"I'm fine," came Laura's dull answer as Clay swung her into his arms.

Clay called to the driver, "Take us to the Golden Fleece."

"No," Laura mumbled, "take me to the cottage. I must get home. Celeste will be worried."

Clay stopped walking. "You may need a doctor."

"No, you must take me to the cottage. My parents think I'm spending the night there."

"I'm going to take you to the Golden Fleece," Clay insisted. "I'll send word to your parents, telling them where you are." He turned to Tomas. "Get word to

276

her family that she's all right. Tell them to wait at Ombres Azurées for me. I'll bring her home later, when she's feeling better."

"Please, Clay, take me to the cottage," Laura begged for the third time, but Clay would not be dissuaded.

"Churnbarker, as soon as we arrive at the house, I want you to go get Dr. Burgaud."

"No! I don't want you to send for the doctor, Clay." Laura pushed away from his chest and stared through the muted lantern light into his set visage. "I'm fine. Really. And I don't want you to send word to my family. It's not because I'm ashamed of you, Clay. Really, it's not. Celeste will go into hysterics, and Papa will make a nasty scene. I don't want that right now."

Relieved by her confession, Clay nodded and sighed, then pulled her face back against his chest. "It's all right, sweetheart," he murmured. "I'll take care of everything. Don't worry about Celeste or your papa."

His words comforted her; they chased her fears away. She snuggled deeper into their protective warmth. "Jena sent her men to get me, Clay." Her voice was low and dull. "They forced me to drink something. Then they tied me up and—"

Clay held Laura in his arms through the long, rough journey into town. He listened as she told him all that had happened to her since she left the Golden Fleece earlier in the day. Tears rolled down his cheeks as she described her battle with Jena and the mulatto's death. Afterward he held Laura close to his chest and murmured words of love.

When the carriage stopped in the courtyard, he carried Laura upstairs to his apartment, finally to lay her in his bed. Pouring a glass of brandy, he handed it to her.

"Drink this. You'll feel better."

Pushing up on an elbow, Laura held the glass and stared at the golden-brown liquid. "I don't know that I want to drink anything ever again." She shivered and began to shake all over.

Clay sat down beside her and caught her in his arms. He took the snifter from her hands and pressed it to her lips. "Please drink it, my darling. I promise it won't hurt you."

Laura gulped down the liquor, glad for the fiery warmth that blazed a trail from her throat to her stomach. When she had finished the drink, she set the glass on the night table. She allowed Clay to take her clothes off and to press her into the softness of the bed. So sweet and wonderful was his touch. So tender and careful. He bathed her; he cleaned and doctored her cuts; he dressed her in one of his shirts. With tweezers he picked the splinters out of her hands. He tenderly examined each finger, the tips cut and bruised where she had fought to hang on to the walkway. He lifted her hand to his lips and softly kissed each fingertip.

His eyes were dark with pain and concern. "I'm sorry I introduced you to Jena. I had no idea it would turn out like this."

Laura slipped her hand from his and laid her palm against his cheek. "I'm not sorry for anything that we've shared. Jena Benoit was right. I was fighting as much for you as I was for Ombres Azurées."

Clay smiled tenderly. "I should hope so, my darling woman."

Tired, Laura lay back on the pillows he had bunched behind her. "I really need to go home, Clay.

I don't want Celeste to worry about my being gone for so long. She's liable to check on me at the cottage, and I'm too tired for a confrontation tonight."

Clay rose and walked to the table to pour himself a drink. He twirled the amber liquid in the glass. "Do you want Churnbarker to take you home?"

"No, I want you to." Laura slipped across the room and lay her hand over his shoulder.

Clay dropped his head, his gaze falling on the lacerated fingertips. "Are you sure?"

Laura nodded. "I'll get dressed."

She moved away, his shirttail swinging around her thighs. Clay's eyes darkened when he saw the length of beautiful legs exposed, the whiteness of the material a contrast with the creamy softness of her skin. At the bed she bent down to pick up her clothes.

"You can't wear those home. I'll see if one of the girls has a gown she can lend you."

Without waiting for her answer, Clay walked out of the bedroom and through the parlor. Later he returned, carrying a tray. Thrown across his shoulders were a red silk gown and white undergarments.

"Dinner. Churnbarker thought we could use some food. When you've eaten, we'll go to Ombres Azurées." He set the tray on the low table in the parlor.

Laura's stomach growled angrily to remind her she had not eaten since early morning. "Thank you, I can use some food."

Laura took the gown from him and closed the bedroom door. Why, she could not answer. He had seen her nudity many times over, and he had undressed and bathed her tonight. But at this particular moment she was feeling most vulnerable to Clay.

279

When she was dressed, she entered the parlor to find Clay sitting in one of the huge chairs, his booted feet propped on an ottoman. He was sipping a glass of whiskey. He turned his head, his eyes following her every movement.

She sat in the chair opposite him, on the other side of the table. She kept her face down, her gaze averted from his. He was blatantly handsome. The top buttons of his shirt were undone; the material fell open to reveal a wealth of crisp black hair. The gray britches stretched tightly over his thighs, a slight bulge reminding her of his masculinity.

"Are you hungry?" She picked up a slice of bread and liberally covered it with butter.

The brown eyes lingered at the swooping neckline of her dress. Laura could feel the heat rising in her body. She was on fire for him. She laid the bread down and dropped her trembling hands to her lap.

"Eat or you're going to be sick," he said. "No telling what kind of herbs Jena plied you with."

He turned his head and stared into the blackened fireplace. Cold and dark and gloomy.

The bread tasted like sawdust to Laura, the bite getting bigger and bigger by the second. Yet she chewed; she swallowed. Clay smoked his cigar and drank his glass of whiskey. Neither spoke. Clay seemed to be contented not to, and Laura was too uncertain of herself to do so.

"How's John?" Laura asked.

"He's doing good. He's able to walk on his leg without a crutch now."

"Are you still planning to send him back east?"

Clay nodded. "He's really excited about it. We're just waiting for my sister to answer my letter. She's going to get him situated in school." Clay smiled and

280

pointed at the tray. "Now eat before your food gets cold. We'll talk later."

A knock sounded in the outer part of the house. Churnbarker answered the door, his low monotone drifting into the parlor. Moments passed. Laura sipped on her milk, not because she was thirsty but because she needed something to occupy her hands.

"But, sir, you can't go in without my announcing you!" Churnbarker exclaimed.

"The hell I can't." Beau Talbot's voice thundered through the house. His palm flattened against the door and he shoved it open. "Sutherland, I've come here—"

Startled, Laura dropped her glass to the floor, milk puddling on the expensive imported rug. "Papa!"

Beau was truly dumbfounded. Finally, he mumbled, "What the hell are you doing here?"

Clay set his glass on the table and slowly rose to his feet. The sensuous lips curled into a wooden smile. "Good evening, Mr. Talbot. What a pleasant surprise."

"Not so pleasant, Sutherland."

Beau's angry eyes raked over Laura's appearance, the cuts and bruises on her face and arms. The dark circles around her eyes. The red gown was not familiar to him, but he recognized the expensive material and the gaudy color and design. He crossed the room and caught Laura's hands in his. When she winced in pain, he looked down and immediately turned her hands loose.

"*Mon Dieu*, Laura. What happened to you?"

She smelled the whiskey on his breath. Gazing at him curiously, she asked, "Didn't Tomas tell you?"

"Tell me what? I haven't seen the boy in days."

Laura's brow furrowed. "How did you know I

281

was here?"

"Roussel."

Laura was more confused than ever.

"Roussel returned from Baton Rouge today. He saw you here this afternoon, Laura." Emphatically, he jabbed his index finger toward the floor. "Here in this saloon in broad daylight. He heard about your brawl with Jena Benoit. From the looks of your face, you can't deny it."

"No," Laura admitted. "We fought."

"I was so sure Roussel had made a mistake, I rode to the plantation. Celeste said you were spending the night at your cottage. But you were gone. How could you, Laura?" His lips quivered with anger. "How could you have such scant regard for your reputation?"

"Because I had a greater regard for the safety of Ombres Azurées."

Beau's gaze raked contemptuously over Clay. "Tell me how the plantation fits into this."

Clay chuckled softly and walked to the table to refill his glass. "Would you care for a drink, Mr. Talbot?"

"I want nothing you have to offer, Sutherland."

Clay shrugged nonchalantly.

"M'sieur Sutherland saved my life."

"From Jena Benoit, I presume." Beau sneered.

Laura wrung her hands. "She tried to murder me. Two of her priests kidnapped me from the cottage and took me to her cabin in the swamp."

The confession that followed wiped the sneer from her father's face. He stepped toward Laura, but she backed away. In a quiet, controlled tone she told her father all that had happened, beginning with her first meeting of the voodoo queen and ending with

Jena's death.

Beau rushed to take her into his arms. "Baby, I'm so sorry. I didn't know. Come now. Let's go home." He guided her to the door.

Emotionally spent, Laura looked up at Beau. Tears swam in her eyes. "Aren't you going to thank Clay for saving me?"

Beau's blue eyes turned to pure slivers of ice; his lips thinned to a mere line. "I'm grateful he saved your life. But none of this would have happened had he not introduced you to that voodoo witch in the first place."

"Papa—" A tear escaped the corner of her eye to run down her cheek.

"Trust me to take care of this, Laura." His grip tightened around her shoulders as he looked over her head at Clay. "From now on, Sutherland, I want you to leave Laura alone. I don't want you ever to see her again."

Clay set the half-filled glass on the table. Through hooded eyes he stared at the distraught woman in front of him.

"That's up to Laura. She might not be willing to say good-bye to me so easily." His gaze locked with hers.

"Damn you!" Beau muttered.

Laura pulled away from Beau and walked to Clay. She never doubted that they were physically attracted to each other. But her fear was that they shared only desire, which was not a solid foundation for a relationship. Besides, she seemed to be the one most affected by the attraction.

So low that only Clay could hear, she asked, "Do you love me, Clay?"

Seconds turned into an eternity. All he had to do

was make a simple declaration of love. But he would not do that. That was not his way. "I'm not sure what love is, Laura, but I care for you."

Laura smiled sadly. She respected Clay for telling her the truth, but her heart ached badly. She could hardly endure the pain.

"May I call on you, Laura?" Clay asked. "I want to come through the front door, not the back. I'm tired of these clandestine meetings."

"So am I," she confessed. "But as I said earlier, I need time to think, Clay, and to sort things out. I'm tired right now—too tired to think."

Laura refused to return to Ombres Azurées with her father, choosing instead the solitude of the town house. By the time Judith came in from the docks, Laura had bathed and changed clothes and was standing on the balcony sipping a glass of wine.

Closing the door and laying a ledger on the entry table, Judith asked, "Are you by yourself?"

Laura nodded as she returned to the parlor and moved to the large table at the side of the room. Lifting the large lead-crystal pitcher, she poured Judith a glass of lemonade. "Do you mind?"

"No, why should I?" Judith asked, then added with a small smile, "After all, it's your house as much as it's mine."

"It doesn't seem that way," Laura said pensively. "You stay here more than you do at Ombres Azurées."

After a long swallow of the fruit drink, Judith set her glass on the table and undid the top three buttons of her dress. "It's not that I don't want to see you," she said, "but I don't feel comfortable out there."

"But you do here?" Laura sat in one of the chairs.

"I do." Judith sat down across from her sister and leaned forward. "But you didn't come here to discuss my not visiting Ombres Azurées, did you?"

"No," Laura confessed, "I wanted to see you."

Judith picked up her glass and leaned back on the divan, her eyes narrowed. "Is this another attempt to get me to go to Madame what's-her-name to be fitted for new dresses?"

Laura laughed lamely. "No, nothing ulterior."

Judith set her glass down and rose, moving to where Laura sat. She took the wineglass and set it on the nearest table. Gently, she said, "What's wrong, Laura?"

"Oh, Judith," Laura said, and fell into her sister's arms. Through her sobs she told Judith all the details about Jena Benoit's attempt on her life, about Clay's rescuing her, and of Beau's reaction. But she did not tell Judith that she and Clay were lovers. She did not want to share this with anyone yet.

All the time that she talked, Judith held her tightly, rocking her back and forth as if she were a baby. "It's all right," she crooned. "You're all right now."

A servant appeared in the door. "Dinner is served, Miss Judith."

"We'll be there in a minute," Judith answered, and Laura pushed out of her arms.

Wiping the tears from her eyes, she smiled and lay her palm against Judith's cheek. "Thanks for being here when I needed you."

Judith nodded her head. "Are you all right?"

"I'm fine," Laura assured her. "Now, go take your bath and change clothes, so we can eat. I'm famished."

285

"Me too." Judith rose and moved toward her bedroom. "We were so busy I didn't have time for lunch today."

"I'm proud of you, Judith," Laura said. "As much as you hate the hypocrisy of society, you're really making an effort to fit in."

Judith laughed sardonically. "Sometimes I wonder if it's worth the effort, sister."

"It is," Laura assured her. "Now go get dressed."

As her sister disappeared into the bedroom, Laura once again walked to the balcony and looked down on the city that was gently clothed in dusk. Her gaze strayed to the Golden Fleece.

Standing on the balcony after a restless night, Clay watched dawn streak the sky. He had been physically attracted to Laura from the first time he had seen her. She had presented him with a challenge. With no thought of the consequences, he had wanted to make love to her, to melt that icy reserve behind which she hid.

Well, he had done that, and he had done it for all the wrong reasons. He simply wanted to satisfy his male ego. He wanted the elation that comes with the conquest. But in doing so, he had unveiled a woman that enchanted him like none other had. Laura Elyse Talbot was a strange mixture of woman and child.

She had declared her love to him through her simple question. And like her fiancé so long ago who had failed to give her strength and support through her mother's scandal, Clay had failed to give Laura the support she needed the night before. Although his saying he cared carried more weight than most people's chatty I love yous, Laura would not

286

understand. He must see her to convince her of his sincerity, to let her know that his feelings for her were more than passion and desire.

But the next move was hers to make. Clay was unsure that his caring for Laura was enough. Within herself she had to come to an understanding of exactly what she wanted out of life and how much she was willing to sacrifice to get it. Perhaps she was unwilling to make the sacrifice.

The thought hurt Clay, but he faced it squarely. While he had no doubt Laura loved him, she might not be willing to sacrifice her position in Creole society for him. It was a decision she must make, and he could only wait to hear from her.

He walked to his desk and reached for a cigar. After he lit it, he stood looking at Graham Bradford's satchel on his desk. He opened it and took out the objects one by one. The watch. The gold chain. The deck of cards. Graham's clothing. Finally, Clay reached the cigars lying at the bottom of the satchel. He picked up one. For a man who did not smoke, Graham had a handful of cigars with tiny red, white, and blue bands around them. Clay laid them down and held his hand out. Only then did he notice the gray residue of dust. Only then did he know.

In less than an hour Clay entered a small tobacco shop off Front Street. The sun shone through the windows, illuminating the front of the store. The back was still hidden in shadows and flickering candlelight. Careful not to get his clothes dusty, he walked through the narrow aisle to the counter. A short time later the proprietor bustled through the rear door.

He bobbed his head energetically. "Good morning. What can I do for you this morning?"

287

"I came for some cigars."

"The ones in the red and yellow box are from—"

"—Havana, and these are from North Carolina." Clay pulled his handkerchief from his pocket and dusted the red and white box. Then he opened the lid and picked up the cigar, rolling it in his fingers. "I believe in supporting my country, don't you? The tobacco looks firm enough."

"Yes." The man took his glasses off and began to rub the lenses with his handkerchief. "Very good brand."

Reverting to strategies he had been taught during his years in the diplomatic service, Clay said, "My friend recommended your shop. He used to come here frequently to buy cigars. Perhaps you know him. Graham Bradford."

The man stuffed his handkerchief into his pocket and cocked his head to the side. "No. No, I don't recollect the name. I may know him by sight."

Clay returned the cigar to the box. His gaze moved up and down the counter. "Do you have any more besides these? A special blending of Virgina tobacco? It seems to me that my friend bought a different kind. A more expensive brand."

The man stared at Clay for an immeasurable period of time before he nodded his head toward the rear door. "Follow me. I keep my finer tobaccos in here."

Clay moved through the door into a small office. The sun filtered in through the tall, narrow window that was barred on the outside, but the rays were too weak to dispel the gloom. Crates lined the wall; papers cluttered the desk. Using a lever, the man pried the lid off one of the crates.

"Here's my finest. You're welcome to go through

them." He stepped aside.

Clay bent over the crate and began to dig through the cigar boxes. Then he saw it and smiled. Just as he supposed. What he should have known the first time he entered the shop months before. He had gotten rusty. "I'll take this one." He held the red, white, and blue box up.

"Who are you?" The man whipped the glasses off and immediately his drabness disappeared. The eyes were alert and perceptive; the stance guarded.

"Clay Sutherland, owner of the Golden Fleece." He tossed the cigar box onto the desk.

"Call me Reynolds." The man extended his hand and they shook. "Are you a friend of Bradford's?"

"More than friends. He and I have worked on several assignments together."

"What do you want from me?"

"I want to take Graham's place."

Reynolds rubbed his finger against the side of his nose. "How much do you know?"

Clay pulled a cigar from the inner pocket of his coat. He scratched a lucifer against the base of a rusted candle holder. "Not much. A French emissary is on his way to New Orleans to meet with the Bonapartist Creoles to discuss the possibility of Napoleon's moving his base of operation from France to New Orleans."

Reynolds nodded his head curtly. He cracked the door and looked around the shop. Satisfied that no one had entered, he then closed it and turned back to Clay. "Almost right but not quite. Napoleon is not planning to move his entire base of operation here immediately. He is sending key personnel and as much money as he can acquire to establish a second base."

289

Clay waved the match through the air, the flame flickering into a black nub. "We've heard rumors of this sort for years. What makes you think this time is any different?"

"The emissary is his brother."

Through the haze of smoke Clay hiked a brow. "Which one?"

"Joseph."

"Who's his contact?"

Reynolds scratched his head. "Bradford was working by himself. I know he was on to something, but he hadn't checked in with me for several days. I don't know what his latest leads were. If any."

"Graham got too close," Clay mused, wishing he had been able to talk to his friend before he died. "That's for sure."

"I figure he must have run into someone whom he recognized."

"Or someone who recognized him."

"When was the last time you talked with Graham?"

"Friday evening. He—came by the office and wanted to talk with me. At the time I couldn't. One of my entertainers was having problems with the pianist. By the time I was free, Graham was gone. I didn't see him again until I identified his body Monday afternoon."

The bell tinkled to announce the arrival of another customer. Reynolds walked to the door but paused before he opened it. "Why are you getting involved in this? Your friendship for Graham?"

"Possibly," Clay answered.

"Graham said something about a woman who might be involved with this. I don't suppose you know about her?"

Clay felt a tightening in his chest but merely shook his head.

"Don't let your emotions get involved." Reynolds slipped the thick lenses over his eyes and blinked his eyes owlishly. "Go out through the back. Be careful not to let anyone see you. I'll be here if you need me."

Clay returned to the casino and went directly to his office. Again he opened the luggage that contained Graham's belongings and dumped them on top of the desk. Although he had gone through them time and again, he went through them once more, object by object.

Clay walked around the desk and sat down. In the full spill of afternoon sunlight and with a magnifying glass, he went through the deck of cards to see if Graham had coded a message of any kind. He found nothing. Sighing, massaging the back of his neck with his hand and shifting in the chair, he reached for the cigars. He unwrapped each band and studied the inside. In turn pressing each one flat on the desk, he rubbed each with a lemony solution. Nothing happened.

Graham had left him no clues whotsoever. That was not like Graham. He was not a sloppy agent. Clay stood and walked to the window. His hand lifted and he lightly tapped his shirt pocket. He wanted a cigar but had none. He returned to the desk; the tobacco box was empty. He opened the bottom desk drawer and stared. Sitting there were cigars in a red, white, and blue box.

Eagerly, he pulled the box out and dumped the contents on his desk. One by one he unrolled the cigars and applied the mixture to the back of the bands in the hope he would find a message. This was no accident; Graham had planted the cigars.

291

They had to contain the clue. His hopes materialized. The solution caused pale writing to appear on one of them, a drawing of a pumpkin on the second.

Clay read the spidery words: Shadow Bayou. He felt as if a metal band had been twisted around his chest and was getting tighter by the minute. Never had he felt so constricted. Ombres Azurées. Laura's plantation was the Blue Shadows located on the Shadow Bayou. Of course, that did not necessarily mean she was implicated. But why else would her feelings be so ambivalent?

The pumpkin. If Clay remembered his French lessons at all, that pointed directly at Roussel Giraumont. He walked to the library shelf and ran his finger over the spines of several books. When he found his French dictionary, he extracted it and flipped through the pages. Pumpkin. Now he knew why the pumpkin had been so kind and understanding. He had an ulterior motive for wanting Ombres Azurées and it had to do with the bayou.

But something else niggled at Clay. Only too well he remembered how much this elite Creole society meant to Laura. He wandered over to his desk and picked up one of the cigars. After he lit it, he moved to the window and stared vacantly into the beauty of the garden below.

During her twenty-six years Laura had been English, French, and American. To which country was she loyal? He knew he ought to share this information with Reynolds since he was the master spy in this area, but he would not. And he knew why.

The sitting room was ablaze with light. All the candles were dressed and burning brightly. Celeste sat on the sofa, embroidering. Beau stood beside her. Laura paced in front of the fireplace; her coral silk dress rustled gently with her movement.

"Yes, Papa, I killed Leroy Donaldson. I had no choice. He was beating our slaves and causing an uprising." Laura was stiff from her fight with Jena two days before, but she was also angry at her father.

"My God, Laura, you could have been killed. That man has been trained to handle slaves. He knew what he was doing."

Laura's green eyes blazed. "You condone what he was doing?"

As usual Beau avoided a direct confrontation. His fist pounded the table. "First you, now Judith! Why won't you girls accept that you're women and not men? Why must you compete in a man's world?"

"Because it's the world in which we live. It's the only world we have."

Beau threw his hands up in the air in a gesture of defeat. "You're a puzzle to me, Laura. Until recently you have always behaved decorously. You've known your place in society and have maintained it with integrity and poise. You've changed since you met Clay Sutherland at Maurice's autumn ball. And you've changed for the worse."

"Yes," Laura admitted, "I have, and while the change may have begun with my meeting with Clay, it's not his fault. I've begun to see things in a different way, Papa. I don't know that it can necessarily be referred to as being 'worse.'"

As if he did not hear her, Beau said, "At first I was worried about Judith's not liking men. I find that may be a blessing. Maybe she has more sense than you do, after all."

Laura's eyes rounded and she drew back at the

anger and censure in her father's voice. Never during the nine years that she'd been living with him in America had she seen him this angry. For the first time, she was being compared unfavorably to her younger sister. And it hurt abominably.

Celeste laid her embroidery aside and moved to stand beside Beau. She laid a hand on his arm. *"Mon cher,* I have never seen you so angry at Laura before. You shouldn't be yelling at her like this. You were wrong. She is right."

"For God's sake, Celeste!" Beau grumbled, and walked to the table to pour himself a glass of whiskey. "What's a man to do when he's surrounded by headstrong women?"

Laura crossed the room.

Before she reached the door, Beau called, "Where are you going?"

She stopped. "To the cottage. I want to be alone."

"Forgive me, Laura." He sighed and set the glass down. He walked to where she stood and embraced her. "I don't know what came over me. Things aren't going so well at the office, and New Orleans has been in such a political turmoil."

"The Bonapartists again?" Celeste asked. The casual words belied the concern in her eyes.

"Not only them, but this blasted war with England. I don't think we have a thread of a chance of getting Napoleon over here," Beau muttered, "but the majority of my business acquaintances are so sure. They want him so much."

Horrified, Laura pulled away from Beau. "Papa, you can't! We are Americans. And we were English."

"I am French," said Celeste quietly and firmly.

Beau shook his head helplessly. "I'm not sure what I'm doing anymore. I'm worried about the Talbot line. I'm worried about you and Judith doing the right thing and making a good marriage. Well—after what the two of you have been through because of me and your mother.''

"It's all right, Papa," Laura said.

But the shadow of hurt did not pass from Laura's green eyes, nor did the tightness around the mouth ease. Although she uttered the apology, she did not feel it at the moment. Her heart was raw and bruised, and Beau was stepping all over it. For nine years she had been the only child, the only consideration. Would her position in the family be usurped yet again now that Judith was here? Laura understood the other times. This time she would not.

Celeste laid a detaining hand on Laura's arm. "Stay here at the house tonight. Let Berthe look after you again. You're still pale and weak."

Laura smiled wanly. "I'll take Jeanette and Tomas with me."

"You will be back in time for dinner tomorrow evening?" Celeste asked. "You know we are having guests."

"I'll be back." She began to walk again.

"Laura," Beau called.

She stopped at the door but did not turn around.

"Are you going to let us announce your engagement to Roussel?"

"No, Papa."

"You are going to marry Roussel?"

"No, Papa."

"It's that Sutherland bastard," Beau shouted "You're thinking about him. Next year you'll be telling me that you're going to marry him."

Laura said nothing. To argue with Beau was futile.

"Well, let me tell you. That man doesn't love you. He's only out for what he can get. He'll be crowing like a bantam if he should ever take you to bed. He loves what you stand for. He wants Ombres Azurées. He wants the respectability and power your name can bring him."

Celeste gasped in horror, and her hand flew to her face. "Beau! You should not say such things to Laura."

Hurt numbed Laura. Now she turned to look at her father with cold eyes. "You're saying I shouldn't be involved with Clay Sutherland because he doesn't love me, because he wants only what I stand for. Yet you ask me to marry Roussel when his motivations are the same as those you assign to Clay. Even worse, Papa, he actually tried to renege on a gambling debt he owed Clay."

Frustrated, Beau raked his hand through his graying hair. "It's different, Laura. Roussel is—"

"I know, Papa. Roussel is Creole French, descended from one of the founding families of New Orleans. He owns one of the largest plantations in the state. That makes him noble and honorable. Clay Sutherland is an American. He's a gambler and the owner of the Golden Fleece. Therefore, he has no honor or nobility."

Lifting her head and straightening her spine, Laura walked out of the room.

"Laura," Beau shouted, "you're twisting everything I say."

Laura never missed a step nor did she turn around.

Beau started to go after her, but Celeste caught his arm. "Leave her alone, my husband. She needs time to herself to think."

Laura was quiet as Tomas drove her and Jeanette

to the cottage. By the time she arrived, her anger was gone. She sat in the large chair in front of the fireplace and stared at the watercolor of Ombres Azurées. She was grateful to Beau. Because of their argument, she had sorted through her confusion.

She had always been searching for security and self-worth, never realizing they were inside her all the while, waiting for her to claim them. What Clay was did not matter to her. She loved him and wanted to give him the opportunity to love her.

Closing her eyes and leaning her head against the back of the chair, she thought about his passion and fire, the way her blood boiled hot when he looked at her. But more, she remembered his tenderness and concern, the way he had taken care of her time and again. Given time, he would come to love her as much as she loved him.

And love was strong—the strongest emotion in the world. If they loved, they could overcome any obstacle, any person; they could handle any situation that might arise from their marriage. Yes, their marriage!

Society was not going to hinder her from finding true happiness.

Smiling, she sprang from the chair. In a matter of minutes she was at her desk, writing a letter. When she was through, she called Tomas.

"Please, deliver this to M'sieur Sutherland at the Golden Fleece."

Night had fallen, and the small candle did little to dispel the darkness that descended on Reynolds's office. Shadows concealed the man who stood in front of the desk. Like the cigar vendor, this man was nondescript, a person easily lost in a crowd, easily forgotten. His name changed with his assignment. Now he was Jones. Several months ago he had been Brown. Two months from now he would be Smith or White.

Reynolds touched the corner of the envelope to the flame, the paper curling and turning black. He dropped it into the wastepaper basket and watched until it was no more than a pile of ashes.

"I hated to do that, Jones, but it's best for right now. Sutherland is getting too emotionally involved in this." He shook his head and sighed. "You're sure Laura Talbot has no idea that she's being watched?"

The man nodded his head. "Yes."

"You left Black to watch her?" When the man nodded again, Reynolds asked, "What about the boy?"

"I left as soon as I heard what she intended to do. I arrived at the Golden Fleece ahead of him. I was waiting in a servant's uniform. The boy will return to tell her the message has been delivered to Sutherland."

Reynolds breathed in deeply and nodded his head. "Good work."

"What if she decides to go to Sutherland herself?"

"Not to worry about that right now. I sent him on a wild-goose chase to get him out of the city. He'll be gone long enough. I told him that Graham had a contact by the name of Josiah Webb in Baton Rouge. I've just received a communication that confirms my suspicion that we have a double agent here in New Orleans. I just don't know who."

"Do you think Bradford did?"

"Yes, I'm sure of it. I firmly believe that's why Bradford's dead. And that's why I must take the precaution of having Sutherland and the Talbot woman watched. I can't take a chance that either of them will be killed. At the moment, they're the only clue we have to the French connection." Reynolds pulled a handkerchief from his pocket and picked up the glasses. He wiped the lenses, then held them in front of the candle. "And whoever this agent is, he's dangerous."

"Maurice Dufaure or Roussel Giraumont?"

Reynolds stuffed the handkerchief into his pocket and placed the spectacles on his face. The reflection of the candlelight on the lenses was rather ghostly. "I'm not sure. Maybe one or the other. Maybe both." After a lengthy pause he added, "Perhaps neither."

The days dragged for Laura. At first she eagerly awaited Clay's reply to her letter. When none came, her eagerness slowly turned into anxiety. She could only surmise that he did not care for her as he had said. But one thing was certain, his silence contradicted Beau's accusations. Clay Sutherland was not interested in her or in Ombres Azurées.

As the days turned into weeks, Laura lost herself in the running of the plantation. She worked from sunrise to sunset. She lost weight, and her face became gaunt and drawn. Her eyes were hollow, constantly underlined with dark semicircles of fatigue. At night she fell exhausted into bed but found no rest. Her nights were long, and if she slept, they were filled with nightmares.

The closer it came to the lenten season, the wilder Laura's imagination grew. Unable to cast thoughts of Clay Sutherland from her mind, she wondered what he was doing and with whom he was doing it.

At the most unexpected times she heard his husky laughter; she saw his lopsided smile. In every man she met she looked for the beautiful golden-brown eyes. She looked for the warmth and tenderness that was Clay Sutherland.

She could go to him. But she had pride. She wouldn't go crawling to any man. Still, Laura loved Clay, and deep in the recesses of her heart she knew he cared for her. Surely she would not allow pride to stand in the way of happiness.

Soon the city would be celebrating Shrove Tuesday. And not for a moment did Laura doubt the Golden Fleece would celebrate with a huge masquerade. She could mix and mingle with the crowds without the least worry of being recognized. Without groveling at his feet, without the loss of one tiny jot of pride, she could find out whether Clay Sutherland really cared about her or not.

And he deserves another chance, a small voice deep inside her insisted. *If he really cares for you, as he said he did, he'll recognize you! Then you can confess your love for him. If he does not recognize you . . .* Laura refused to think of Clay's not loving her.

The decision to go to Clay brought new life and energy to Laura. Exhilaration sang through her veins. The next morning she arose early but did not go to the fields. Rather, she dressed in her best muslin of softest green. Accompanied by Jeanette, she rode into town. Her first stop was at the docks. When the carriage stopped, Laura leaned out the window to spy her sister. Paper and quill in hand, Judith sat behind the folding desk at the foot of the gangplank and counted off barrels of sugar as workers rolled them past. Georges, her personal servant, stood behind, holding a parasol over her head to shade her from the sun.

"Judith," Laura called.

Judith lifted her head, smiled, and touched a gloved hand to wipe the perspiration from her forehead. Rising, she walked to the carriage and leaned against the door. "I'm surprised to see you," she said. "Nobody's been able to pry you away from the plantation for days."

"Shall I leave?" Laura kept her tone light, but inside she anxiously awaited her sister's reply.

"No," Judith answered gently. "I'm glad to see you, but I'm also curious. Exactly why have you come to town?"

"Soon it will be time for us to mask." Laura gazed at Judith's black wool dress that was dusty and stained with perspiration. "I thought perhaps you would like to go shopping with me to buy a costume or a new dress. Something you can wear to the masquerade balls."

"Oh, yes," Judith answered noncommittally, reaching up to brush a wet tendril of hair from her cheek. "The Beauvaliets *bal masqué.*"

Laura nodded. "Will you come shopping with me?"

Judith shook her head. "Not today. I have too much work to do."

Laura lay a gloved hand over Judith's fingers that curled over the window frame of the coach. "You are going to attend the masquerade with Beau and Celeste, are you not?"

Judith evaded the question with one of her own. "You're not coming?"

"I'm going, but . . . I shall be leaving before the evening is over. What about you?" Almost, Laura confided her plans for Shrove Tuesday to Judith, but

301

their relationship had not progressed that far.

Judith studied the toe of her shoe. "I . . . I don't think so, Laura. I don't want to . . . make a fool of myself. I don't know how to dance."

Laura's heart went out to her sister. "I promise no one will make a fool of you. We'll hire someone to come in and give you lessons in the latest step."

Judith raised her head. "And you'll laugh behind my back."

"I'd laugh *to* your face, but you have no worry about my laughing at all."

"What if I embarrass you and Papa in front of all those people?"

"I'm not concerned about your embarrassing us, Judith. I'm concerned about you."

The blue eyes, so like Beau Talbot's, surveyed Laura. "Yes, Laura, I believe you really are. You know, I'm quite envious of you. You never make a mistake, do you?"

Unable to meet her sister's candid gaze, Laura lowered her face. Evidently, Judith did not know about her saloon brawl with Jena Benoit. Beau had promised he would not speak about her indiscretion, and evidently he had not. Between him and Roussel the story had been hushed. Laura could only wonder at Roussel's reason for having kept his silence. She knew that soon his reason would be made known.

But no one had been able to ease the hurt and longing in her heart. Each day she missed Clay more than the day before; each day she wanted him more and wondered why he had chosen to ignore her.

A wagon loaded high with goods lumbered onto the docks, and Judith skipped back. "I must go now, or we'll be behind. Will Papa and I see you for supper tonight?"

"Not if I finish my shopping early. I wouldn't want Celeste to dine alone."

"Have fun!" Judith called, and waved as the carriage disappeared from the docks.

Laura's next stop was a small costume shop on Burgundy Street. The show window overflowed carnival delights. Papier-mâché donkey's heads with long ears, craniums of cows, of huge cats, of bears, of monkeys, of horned bulls. Behind them lay an assortment of masks. Some beautiful; some ugly; most of them bizarre.

Laura's eyes locked on the devil's mask, and she thought of Clay. Her gaze flickered to the spears and scepters, to the crimson cape. She leaned her forehead against the window, visions of Clay swimming in front of her eyes.

"Are you all right, Maîtresse?" Jeanette asked.

Lifting her head, Laura smiled. "Fine. I'm just a little tired. Come. Let's be on our way."

A little bell jangled as Laura and Jeanette opened the door and entered the shop. Behind the counter sat a middle-aged woman. Grossly obese, she wore a dirty gray canton flannel bedroom jacket and a faded black skirt. Her skin was oily, her coloring sallow. Her features had the undecided look of warm butter. Her dark hair was the result of raven-black dye.

At the sound she looked up. "Bonjour, mam'selle. Welcome to the Marbois Shop."

Laura smiled. "Bonjour, madame."

"Oh, Maîtresse," Jeanette whispered excitedly, "this is a truly delightful place."

Laura glanced around apprehensively. Every time she entered the Marbois Shop she had the feeling that some noxious insect was about to drop on her from among the folds of the hundreds of costumes that

303

drooped, listless, stringy, and dusty from the ceiling above her head. The air was heavy and musty.

"Madame Marbois, have you a special costume for me this year?" Laura asked.

"*Certainement*. Come with me."

Laura followed the woman through the shop into the sewing room at the back. Although burning candles hung in rusted holders on the four walls, the room was dingy, dark, and cluttered. The tables were stacked with material and patterns; they were surrounded by a pile of snips and patches of colored materials.

"Sit here, mam'selle." Madame Marbois brushed the pieces of fabric and paper out of the chair and shoved it to Laura. "I will show you our newest creations for this year's Mardi Gras season."

One by one the woman paraded the costumes in front of Laura, but none of them pleased her. Her eyes kept straying to the devil's mask and the crimson cape that lay beside it. With sudden inspiration she leaned forward.

"Madame Marbois, I wish to dress as Lucifer."

She screwed her face up and placed her hands on the roll of flesh that covered each hip joint. "But the devil, he is a man, *ma petite*."

"*Oui*, but I shall be a woman Lucifer," Laura answered. She reached for several bolts of material. "A dress out of this one; a cape from this. And I shall draw the mask which I want to wear."

Madame Marbois leaned over Laura's shoulder, breathing heavily as she watched her draw the intriguing mask. She chuckled. "This will be most provocative, *ma petite*. I pity the poor man who sees you dressed like this. His blood will boil in his veins."

Laura hoped so. Truly she did.

When Laura left the costume shop, she crossed the street and walked up a ways. She came to a small shop in whose front window sat a wax head coiffed with a peroxide wig. On either side were cosmetic sticks and hair switches of various colors.

On entering, she studied the display of wigs. Finally, she pointed to the top shelf. "That one, please."

The wigmaker moved to the rear of the store and returned with a large box. Placing it on the counter, he took out a beautiful blond wig. "So real, mam'selle," he murmured, and held it out for Laura to see, first one side, then the other. "No one will ever guess this is a wig."

"Yes, that's the one I want."

"And makeup?"

"Several sticks, please."

Her purchases in her arms, Laura walked out of the shop. She was glad that she had come. The gay, careless, rollicking carnival spirit suddenly gripped her, and her troubles slipped from her shoulders.

Yes, indeed, she would enjoy this Mardi Gras more than any other she had ever celebrated.

Chapter Thirteen

Giraumont quaffed his third glass of whiskey, not caring that several drops of it splashed onto his burgundy house jacket to stain and discolor the expensive silk material. He gazed out the library window toward Laura's plantation. "I must have Ombres Azurées."

Edouard crossed one leg over the other, then brushed a wrinkle out of his breeches. "You have been remiss, very remiss. Our plan is delayed because of you. Our emperor has trusted in you, and you have failed him. We have no time for such delays."

Giraumont's pudgy fingers squeezed tightly around the glass. "I can't get that English bitch to marry me."

"M'sieur Sutherland has no problem getting her cooperation, Roussel. Surely you *are* as much a man as he is." Edouard's shrill laughter mocked Giraumont.

Roussel spun around, the movement too quick for an obese man. He stumbled and would have fallen had he not caught the edge of the desk. "What are you implying?"

"Nothing." The dark eyes rested distastefully on

Giraumont's unshaved face and bloodshot eyes. "I am telling you another man is playing in your house. Or maybe it is not your house."

Roussel glowered at him but said nothing.

Edouard said, "If you cannot help me, I must go to someone else. You know what that means if I do?"

Visibly, Roussel sagged against the desk. With trembling hands he reached for the decanter and poured himself another drink. Nervous fingers traced the contours of his lips. If only Donaldson had not been such a stupid oaf. Now he had no one on Ombres Azurées to help him.

And Jena Benoit . . . the stupid little bitch had turned against him also. She was the one who sold information to Graham Bradford. He had come close—too close—to finding out the truth. How timely his death had been! His murder! Roussel emptied his glass. Even now he found it difficult to believe he had sunk to such depths. Roussel looked at Edouard and wondered if the man could read his mind.

"You shall have to return the money which we advanced you," Edouard continued smoothly. "It's imperative that . . . that our man gets here as soon as possible. Only he is empowered to make the final decision."

"I can and will help you." To give his words credence, Giraumont straightened his back. He had to fulfill his promise; he had already used the money to pay his gambling debt to Clay Sutherland. His only hope was marriage to Laura.

"You have no bayou and are too far away from the river."

Giraumont set his empty glass on the desk and rubbed his hands down the lapels of his jacket. "We will see a second base of operations established here

307

in New Orleans, and we will have full use of Shadow Bayou."

"Without Laura's help?"

"With Laura's help, my friend." Giraumont laughed, the sound sinister and ominous. "You see, Laura loves her *maman*."

A speculative gleam in his dark eyes, Edouard touched the tip of a slender finger to the corner of his mouth. He nodded his head slowly. *"Oui*, then Maîtresse Celeste is the one to help us."

Giraumont laughed again, causing even Edouard to shudder. "We shall see how much Laura loves her *maman*."

What are we going to do to test this love?"

"Maîtresse Celeste Devranche Talbot loves to gamble, my friend. We must insure that she has plenty of time for her favorite *divertissement*, one she has long been denied."

Edouard stood, slightly flexing his leg so that the wrinkles fell out of his breeches. "I work with you, Giraumont, because I have no choice. But I do not consider myself your friend. Do not refer to me as one."

Smoking a cigar, Clay leaned against a column and observed the people milling below. Every room was filled to overflowing. Mardi Gras. Shrove Tuesday. Tomorrow was a religious holiday—the first day of Lent. Yet the people thronged to the haunts of the devil . . . to his many *dens of iniquity*. Among them were the wealthiest and most influential citizens of New Orleans—all hidden behind masks.

His gaze swept over the ornate furnishings to the richly dressed hosts and hostesses who mingled below with the crowd. He had spared no amount of expense when he opened his establishment. Opulence was his intention. He solicited the wealthy; he catered to them. To assure their patronage he gave them a thin veneer of respectability.

His gaze once again skimmed the crowd, moving to the woman who stood framed in the arched entrance door. Her tall figure was covered by a billowing black cape. She tossed the hood off to reveal a wealth of golden-blond hair. The upper portion of her face was covered by an intriguing mask. Black and orange and red and yellow swirled together to look like tongues of fire. She must be an angel straight from the bowels of hell.

The cape slipped from her shoulders to expose a perfect figure clad in a low-cut, filmy crimson dress. A tiny black velvet ribbon was tied around her neck. Then she laughed, drawing his attention to her mouth. It was as red as her dress. Her lips were luscious. When she moved, the material clung to her legs like a second skin.

The woman looked up, and across the distance their gazes locked. Clay straightened. She took a step toward him, her smile growing larger, more seductive. He unconsciously moved toward her.

Clay's interest was piqued. The woman thoroughly attracted him. He was glad. For weeks he had been haunted by Laura Talbot, and it was past time to forget about her. At Reynolds's suggestion he went in search of a Josiah Webb, the man who was supposed to have been Graham's contact, but Clay had been unable to locate him. When he returned to New Orleans he expected to have heard something from Laura, but had not.

Evidently, he had been mistaken in thinking she cared about him. Or if she cared, she did not care

309

enough. Her position in Creole society meant more. She was not willing to make a sacrifice for him or for his love.

His gaze never wavering from the mystery woman, Clay smiled, slowly and deliberately descending the stairs. As deliberately, she walked toward him.

They met, and she held her gloved hand out. *"Bonsoir*, m'sieur." Her voice was thick and husky.

Wanting to see the color of her eyes, Clay peered through the narrow slits in the mask. The irises were barely discernible. He laughed softly, as if he were enjoying a secret. "Good evening, Mademoiselle Devil." He dropped his gaze to her left hand. "It is mademoiselle, is it not?"

"Oui." Laura's heart pounded when his gaze lifted and lingered on the creamy swell of her bosom, exposed by the low-cut dress.

"And are you a devil?" His eyes danced with mischievous delight.

"You might say I'm devil-ish." She laughed. "You like my costume, *oui?"*

The smiled widened. "Yes, and I like that you're a mademoiselle. I find husbands a difficult lot to deal with."

Momentarily, Laura's smile faltered, but she quickly regained her aplomb. Did he not recognize her? "How do you say? I do not speak English so well."

"What I have in mind, beautiful lady, doesn't require words."

Laura stiffened and wanted to slap his smug face. Clay did not recognize her; he thought she was a woman of the street.

"But I would like to know your name," he said. His voice was low and sultry, the sensuous tones caressing Laura.

310

"My—name?" Her confidence and resolve were quickly ebbing. Intellect was quickly replaced with emotionalism. Nothing in her daydreams had prepared her for the reality of meeting with Clay. Already she was turning to mush. Unconsciously, her hand lifted and touched the ribbon on her neck. Although she left the pendant at home, she thought of it. Without thinking, she said, "Phoenix."

"Hello, Phoenix." Again Clay's voice was low and resonant; it sent a shiver of anticipation down Laura's spine, as it was meant to. "I'm Clay Sutherland. Shall we go into the casino for a game of chance?"

His suggestion kindled another plan within Laura. She would not leave as she had originally intended. She would stay. She would flirt with him and tempt him. Then, when he thought he was going to make love to her, she would unmask and reveal herself to him. He would be revealed for a womanizing scoundrel.

"Are ladies permitted in the casino, m'sieur?"

Clay cupped Laura's elbow in his hand. His head lowered to hers; his lips brushed her ear when he said, "Indeed not."

Forgetting the role she was playing, Laura tensed. She tugged her bottom lip with her teeth. "Yet you are asking me to go in there?"

"You are a woman, mam'selle."

His gaze settled on her breasts, and Laura felt them tighten; the nipples hardened with desire. She had a sinking sensation in the bottom of her stomach.

"Much more to my liking than a lady."

"Then, m'sieur, while the lady in me says no, the woman says yes." Laura allowed him to guide her into the casino but realized she was out of her depth. Dismally, she wished she had heeded Celeste's

311

warning and had found herself a lover whom she could manipulate, one who loved her more than she loved. . . . Startled with her thoughts, Laura was not aware that Clay had stopped walking and stumbled into him.

Clay turned quickly, smoothly, his hands gently circling her upper arms to steady her. "Forgive me." The tones were pure seduction.

Frightened green eyes peered through the slits in the brilliant mask. She loved this man. She loved Clay Sutherland, and he thought she was someone else. He was seducing a woman of the night.

Equal parts of hurt and anger surged through Laura. Her first thought was to turn and run, to run from Clay Sutherland as fast as her feet would carry her. But that was the coward's way out. She would never run from a person or situation again. Whatever the consequences, she would face them.

Anger prevailed. Laura had begun this charade. She would finish it. She had been jilted by one man. She would not be victimized a second time.

The tips of his fingers trailed down her arm. Even through the gloves Laura could feel the burning touch. She shivered; then his hand caught hers, their fingers intertwining. She gazed into the beautiful golden-brown irises.

Throughout the evening he stayed near her and she flirted with him. She drank several glasses of wine. She played game after game . . . and won game after game. Heady, she felt as if she were walking on the edge of a dangerous precipice. She did not care.

"Lady Luck is with you tonight, my little Phoenix. You have been winning all evening. Now I would like a chance to recoup." A rakish smile dimpled his cheeks, and his eyes gazed at the creamy swell of her breasts.

As if she had received a blow to her stomach, Laura inhaled sharply. She was about to be caught in a swirling eddy that would drown her. Yet she continued to move toward it as if she had no other alternative. "What are you suggesting, m'sieur?"

"A private game of chance." He dared her to refuse. When she did not answer, he asked, "Are you afraid, mam'selle?" He laughed, the seductive tones wrapping themselves around Laura and drawing her all the closer to him.

Yes, I'm afraid, Laura silently answered. *And I'm hurt . . . hurting so badly I don't know what to do.*

"Surely not," Clay said. "Not the way your luck has been running this evening."

Laura pushed her fear aside. She had begun this game; she would finish it. She would unmask Clay Sutherland for the scoundrel he was. Breathlessly, she asked, "Where would we play this game, m'sieur?"

"In my apartment."

"Unchaperoned?"

"Not entirely. There are the servants."

"No one else, m'sieur? A wife perhaps?"

Clay chuckled; his eyes glinted dangerously. "No wife, mam'selle. They clutter up a man's life. I do have a ten-year-old ward staying with me temporarily, but he's safely tucked in bed now. He and his tutor, Mrs. Hazelwood, have adjoining rooms in another wing of the house . . . on the fourth floor."

Clay caught her arm loosely in his hand and guided her through the reception room, up the winding staircase to his apartment. He seated her, then poured each of them a glass of wine.

"What is this game you wish to play?" Laura asked.

"Dice," Clay answered. "First we lay our bets."

Slightly inebriated, Laura laughed. "Where are we playing this game, m'sieur?"

Clay looked into the bedroom but said, "Here. On the floor in front of the fireplace."

Laura slid from the chair and opened her reticule to dump her winnings on the floor beside her. She tilted her head provocatively and shoved the money to the center. "Now I lay my bet, m'sieur."

He smiled and shook his head. "This time, my mystery woman, I set the rules."

"But—" Laura looked at him quizzically.

"My wager." He imprisoned her fingers in his hand. "We'll play five games, winner must take three. All right?"

Tongues of fire leapt up Laura's arm. She licked her lips and nodded. He tossed the dice onto the floor and she stared at them while he outlined the rules. His fingers touched her chin, and he lifted her face.

"If I win, I take you to bed."

Laura's face never moved. When she spoke, her voice was a mere whisper. "If I win?"

He laughed softly. "You can take me to bed . . . my beautiful Phoenix."

"I'll play." Laura's heart thumped with exhilaration. There was no way she would lose. How right Clay Sutherland had been: Lady Luck was with her. She anticipated the moment when Clay Sutherland was in the throes of passion, and she would whisk off her mask to reveal herself to him. She would enjoy watching his face when he realized he was making love to Laura Talbot, not a woman of the night.

She drank another glass of wine . . . and another. They rolled the dice; they played several games in order for Laura to learn the rules; they flirted outrageously.

Laura won the first game; Clay the second. She

314

won the third, he the fourth. Her palms were sweaty, and her heart beat so fast she was getting dizzy. Her stomach was one massive knot. They were in the fifth and final game. On her knees she cupped the dice in her hands and shook them. She tossed the two dice; they skittered across the hardwood floor and danced around. They finally stopped.

"Seven!" Laura cried, and forgot about her deception. She forgot about the terms of their wager. "I won, Clay. I won."

Stretched out and propped up on his elbow, Clay smiled lazily. He took the dice into his palm, then tossed them in the nearest chair. He stood and lowered a hand to her. When her fingers gripped his, he pulled her up.

"In a way you did. In a way you didn't."

Laura was still so excited she was not thinking of the outcome of their game. "Of course I won. I threw a seven. You said—"

An arm slid around her waist; a finger rested on her mouth. "Seven is a winner in the beginning. A loser any other time."

"Nooo . . ."

"Yes." He laughed softly. "Now I shall take my winnings. I want to make love to my mystery woman."

At the same moment, Laura's well-laid plans and resolve deserted her. No matter what she had thought about doing, she could not go to bed with Clay knowing he wanted to make love to a strange woman, to a common street wench. She jumped back from him and darted for the door. Before she reached it, Clay was there barring her escape. He caught her wrist in a tight grip and shook his head.

"If one loses when she gambles, my little beauty, she must pay the price. If you knew me better, you

315

would be aware that I always collect my debts."

Laura moistened her lips. "The—stakes are too high."

"You should have thought of that sooner." His hand touched the drawstring at her bodice. With one flick he untied it, the material blousing out and falling below her waist. Under the thin chemise her breasts firmed.

"No," she said weakly, but her body betrayed her. Although she knew Clay wanted to make love with the strange woman, Laura Talbot wanted to make love to him. Desire obliterated her plan to unmask him and to show him for the scoundrel she thought him to be.

"Yes."

He caught the belt that secured the material at her waist and tugged. It, too, came untied. The red material pooled around their feet. He brushed the straps of the chemise from her shoulders. It fell on top of the dress. Laura stood before him naked.

"We'll save the mask for last. I want to make love to a mystery woman."

His gaze swept down her body to linger on the auburn mound of hair at the base of her stomach. His head lifted, and Laura found herself staring into the dark, sensuous eyes. She could not utter another word. His hands slid up to cup her breasts; his thumbs grazed the hardened tips. "I want to make love to you."

"Is it love, the mere taking of a mystery woman to your bed?" Laura heard herself whisper through numbed lips.

"Yes, my beautiful Phoenix, it is." His lips nipped the bottom curve of her face; they brushed up her cheek and rested at the corner of her mouth. "I've loved you from the very first moment that I laid eyes

316

on you and have been wanting to kiss your lips all evening." So saying, he set her away from him. "But I shall wait a little longer."

He unfastened his breeches, then pulled his shirt free and unbuttoned it. He dropped it to the floor at his feet. His trousers rested low on his hips. Dark, thickening abdominal hair was visible. Also visible was his hard fullness.

"No!" Her cry an anguished plea, Laura turned and tried to run from him, but he grabbed and pulled her against himself. Her breasts rubbed against his hot skin, against his coarse body hair. She wanted to give in to him. She must not submit to his will. Her hands coiled into fists. Clay Sutherland would not make love to her when he was infatuated with a woman who did not exist.

His arms tightened and he caught her fists between their bodies. "Yes, my darling."

A lone tear slipped from beneath the brilliant-colored mask to run down her cheek. "Please don't."

Clay flicked it off with his fingers, then reached up and caught the wig in his fist to pull it off her head. His smile was gentle as he said, "My dearest Laura, the gentleman in me says no, but the man in me says yes."

My dearest Laura. Never had her name sounded so beautiful.

"You knew," she breathed. "You knew it was me?"

"Yes." He untied the mask and threw it to the floor.

"All the time." Her eyes shimmered with tears.

"Not all the time." He swept her into his arms. "Not until I was close enough to see the green of your eyes. Did you think I would not recognize the woman whom I love?"

"You love me?" Laura asked.

317

"Yes." He walked into the bedroom and laid her on the bed.

"Then why didn't you answer my message?" she asked. "Why didn't you send me word?"

"What message?"

"The note I sent you the day after Jena and I fought. I knew I loved you then, Clay, but when I received no answer, I thought you didn't care for me."

Clay smiled tenderly. "I didn't get the note, sweetheart. If I had, I would have answered in person."

Tears of happiness sparkled in Laura's eyes. "I'm so glad I'm here tonight, or I would never have known—"

"I'm glad you're here, too. Now I don't have to put on a ridiculous costume to attend one of your balls."

Laura laughed. "Were you going to, Clay?"

He nodded. "I would have. I had to be certain that you didn't care for me."

Soon they were lying naked in bed, their arms and legs wrapped around each other, each caught in the maelstrom of their separate desires. After his declaration of love, Laura would deny him nothing.

His lips burned against her throat and breasts. His hands stroke her buttocks. His fingers parted the moist, intimate folds between her thighs and relentlessly caressed her until she was at the brink of ecstasy.

"I love you, Clay," she murmured.

In answer to her cry, Clay parted her legs. His body came down on hers. His penetration of her flesh was both a torment and a wondrous release. Faster and faster were his unsparing thrusts, and she answered him with equal frenzy. Her body arched to meet his.

318

They were of one mind, of one desire. Their coupling was more than a physical joining. Theirs was a union of soul, a uniting of hearts. Their passion brought them together again and again until violent tremors of fulfillment shook them simultaneously.

They were bound together by love.

As they slowly returned to reality, Laura clung to Clay. She would never turn him loose. They lay silent in each other's arms for a long while, only the sound of their measured breath breaking the stillness of the room.

Finally, Clay said, "Will you marry me?"

"Yes" was her tremulous reply.

Clay flipped over. "When?"

Deliciously in love, Laura laughed and cupped his face with her hands. "As soon as we can."

"I can't wait to make you my wife, Laura. I wish it could be tomorrow," he said on a soft sigh, "but I don't think it can be, darling."

"Of course, it can be." Laura leaned forward and fluffed the pillows behind her.

Clay shook his head. "We have to think about your parents. They're going to be heartbroken that you're marrying an American and a gambler."

"I know, darling," Laura said, "but I don't want to keep our love secret. It's wonderful, and I want the world to know."

"I do too." Clay leaned over and kissed her lips lightly. "But we're going to have break the news gently to Beau and Celeste. They'll—be hurt and disappointed, and it's going to take them a while to accept that you're not marrying that Creole aristocrat, Roussel Giraumont."

Clay rolled off the bed and pulled on his breeches. Then he lit a cigar and moved to the open window to smoke. Laura slipped out of bed and walked to where

Clay stood. She leaned against his back, running her nails down his spine.

"I'm glad you're not Creole aristocracy, my darling. Even more, I'm glad you're not one whit like Roussel."

Clay tossed the cigar out the window and caught Laura into his arms. He held her tightly, his cheek pressed against the crown of her head. "You don't know how jealous I've been of him."

Laura pulled her head back and laughed in amazement. "Of Roussel?"

"Don't laugh at me." He grinned down at her. "I remember when you defended his honor—when he owed me money, when you thought me dishonorable for trying to collect it. I was worried when I learned he was buying love potions from Jena Benoit."

Laura shuddered at the mention of Jena's name. "I didn't think you believed in voodoo?"

"I said I respect it," he corrected her.

"Evidently, it didn't work, but you needn't have been jealous of Roussel. He was never in love with me. He wants *Ombres Azurées*, and perhaps a son."

Clay splayed his hand on her stomach. "I don't believe that for a minute. But say it's true. As wealthy as he is, why would he want your plantation so badly that he'd go to a voodoo queen for potions?"

Without a pause Laura said, "The bayou. His plantation is situated in such a way that he doesn't have water frontage at all. That, my dearest darling, shows how little you know of agriculture. Water means savings both in time and finances."

"And by using the Bayou d'Ombre, one can travel day or night without anyone's knowing."

"Um-hmm."

Clay trailed his fingers seductively over her belly, and Laura trembled beneath his touch. "I'm glad

320

your cottage is on the bayou. That means we don't have to be separated until we are married. I can come to the cottage and be with you."

"Ah, yes," Laura murmured, "you do handle a pirogue quite proficiently, M'sieur Sutherland." As the clock on the mantel chimed the hour, she stirred in Clay's arms. "I need to return to the town house. The cannon will be sounding soon."

"Stay with me tonight. I'll take you home before the light of day."

When his lips touched hers, Laura knew she had no will to deny his request. And no reason. She loved Clay Sutherland and was going to marry him.

As Clay had promised, he had Laura at the town house on Calle di Conti before dawn. Blowing him a kiss, she ran through the courtyard and up the stairs. She moved quietly to keep from awakening the family, but the house was unusually quiet. Jeanette awakened and in whispered tones told her that Maîtresse Judith had returned quite early from the ball. Tabor O'Halloran had escorted her home. Laura was rather surprised. Beau Talbot liked Tabor, but Laura was unaware that he and Judith were seeing each other. M'sieur and Maîtresse Celeste had not come in yet. Laura smiled. Perhaps the evening had not been exciting for Judith, but it must have been for Papa and Celeste!

Wanting to tell someone about her and Clay, Laura thought about awakening Judith. While the sisters were moving toward a closer relationship, Judith still shied away from personal intimacy. Laura thought it better to wait. Going to her bedroom, she shed her clothes. They fell into a pile on the floor. She crawled between her sheets, but had not been asleep long before she was awakened by Jeanette. The maid hurried into the room, setting the candle on the nightstand.

"M'sieur and maîtresse arrived home a few minutes ago. M'sieur wishes to see you in the library as quickly as possible."

Laura sat up and yawned. "This early? What time is it?"

"Six o'clock. Much too early to be up." Jeanette giggled. "Especially when you have had such a long night."

Laura grinned and looked at the discarded costume in the chair. She lifted her hand and captured Clay's ring that hung on the black velvet ribbon. He had taken it off his little finger and had given it to her before he left.

"But I had a beautiful Mardi Gras."

"*Oui*, maîtresse." Jeanette knelt to place Laura's slippers on her feet.

Tying her robe around her, Laura hurried down the stairs into the library. Fully dressed, his hands braced against the mantel, her father stood in front of the fireplace and stared at the toes of his boots. The only light came from the candle on the center table.

"I'm sorry to awaken you." Beau Talbot's voice quavered. He removed his hand from the mantel. It shook violently, and he hastily braced it again. "But I wanted you to know that your *maman* and I have just arrived home."

Laura wondered why her father sounded so peculiar and why he was so edgy. "The Beauvaliets' *bal masqué* must have been a special one indeed to have kept you out all night."

He lifted his head and smiled weakly, but his eyes were dark and troubled. Having run the complete gamut of emotions from humiliation to anger to reconciliation, he was drained, his spirit crushed. "One I shall never forget no matter how many years I may live. Your sister . . ." He cleared his throat. "At the Beauvaliets' *bal masqué* Judith Claire announced that Tabor O'Halloran had seduced her." His hand balled into a fist. "He—took her virtue."

"Oh . . . Papa!" Laura sank into the nearest chair.

Beau settled dull, pain-filled eyes on her. "O'Halloran swept Judith into his arms and announced to one and all that she was his mistress. Then he left with her."

"I'm surprised," Laura murmured, brushing a strand of hair behind her ear. "I thought she hated the man. He's the pirate who—"

"Surprised! That's all you have to say about this?" Beau shouted, his fist slamming down on the mantel. "My God, Laura, don't you realize the significance of what I'm saying. Your sister—"

"Yes, Papa, I understand," Laura hastened to reassure her father. She had never seen her father so upset before.

"Neither of you girls have used any common sense in choosing your men," Beau muttered. "And now Judith has ruined our name by proclaiming her indiscretions to the Beauvaliets and everyone else at the party."

"She's young, Papa, and impulsive," Laura said, attempting to excuse her sister.

"Young and ignorant."

Laura ignored his comment. "How is Celeste taking it?"

Beau shook his head helplessly. "She took it much better than I. She insisted that we stay for the duration of the ball. That's why we were not home any sooner." He raked his hand through his already tousled hair and paced aimlessly around the room.

323

"But she doesn't realize the far-reaching consequences of Judith's actions, Laura. We could be ruined. As if the war isn't bad enough. Can you imagine how this will affect the planters? The very people Talbot Shipping depends on for its business. We're in financial straits enough without Judith's doing a foolish thing like this."

Laura's hand lay against the base of her throat. Concerned about her father, she said, "Judith's young, Papa. Too young to know better. And you know society. Given a little time and a lot of money, they tend to forget."

Beau Talbot glared at his daughter in disbelief. He struck the mantel again. "My honor has been ruined, Laura. I ought to call Tabor O'Halloran out. If only Celeste had not made me promise—"

"No, Papa," Laura quickly said, "you mustn't think such a thing. Let Tabor and Judith handle this. Surely there is more to it than meets the eye."

Laura was in a quandary. She wondered what Beau's reaction would be should she tell him about her wanting to marry Clay. While she had no desire to hide the truth in order to protect herself, she remembered her promise to Clay. He wanted to be with her when she announced to her parents that they were going to be married. Laura looked up to see Beau's shaking hands. He could still them only by placing them against another object.

At the moment she had to think of Beau and Celeste. She could not be selfish. As Beau had just stated, not only was their position in society endangered but their very livelihood. Laura would not bring more despair on her family than they were already suffering. She remembered only too well how Charlotte's confession had affected her.

At the same time, Laura did not fault Judith for

324

succumbing to Tabor's blandishments—although the news still surprised and puzzled her. Sadness settled over Laura as she realized that Judith had never confided in her about Tabor, yet he was definitely a part of Judith's life; otherwise, she would not have announced publicly that he seduced her. Once again Laura felt as if she had failed her baby sister. If only she had not been so caught up in her own life, she may have been able to curb Judith's impulsiveness that had led her to confess her indiscretion—if one could truly term it an indiscretion—at the *bal masqué*. Had the announcement affected only Judith, that would have been one thing, but this affected the entire family, and Laura admitted that it complicated her life immeasurably.

"Go to bed, Papa. I'm sure we can get this settled tomorrow."

"The more I think about it, the bigger it gets." Beau walked to the table on the far side of the room, picked up the crystal decanter, and with shaking hands poured himself a drink.

"That's why you need to go to bed." Laura rose and moved to the stairs. "When you're rested, things will be brighter."

"I don't know that things will ever be bright again."

"We've been through far worse than this, Papa." At the bottom of the stairs Laura turned to look at her father. Strands of hair whisked across his drawn face, and his shoulders were slumped. Why, she thought, he's an old man. Softly, she added, "We'll make it, Papa. I'm sure we'll make it somehow. Now, go to bed. I'll take care of Celeste myself."

Interlude III

Clad in her dressing gown, Laura eased out of Celeste's room, her hair fanning out behind her as she strode down the hall. Despite Celeste's assurance to Beau otherwise, Laura was still concerned about Judith's announcement and its effect on Celeste. She was in bed now with one of her severe migraine headaches. Laura had brewed tea, but nothing seemed to ease the pain. Finally, Laura had given her a small dosage of laudanum and had sat with her until she went to sleep.

Now, several hours later, Laura's nerves were frayed. She knocked softly on the bedroom door but received no answer. She listened and heard soft sounds; evidently, Judith was awake. She opened wide the door and entered the room to stare at her sister, who was dressing for work. Judith appeared to be totally unconcerned about the events of the preceding night.

"Judith Claire—" Laura's voice quavered with exhaustion. "Why did you do this?"

Her head down, Judith gave her full attention to her shoes. "I don't know. I really don't know. I thought I was doing the right thing. For everybody."

"You announced your seduction from the staircase! If only you had told me . . ." Laura spread her hands wide, her voice rising incredulously. She still could not believe Judith's foolishness.

Judith whirled around, straightening her collar. "Is that any worse than your getting into a brawl with a voodoo priestess in a saloon?"

"I was fighting for *Ombres Azurées*."

"You weren't thinking of your reputation when you got into that fight!" Judith fastened her second shoe.

Nettled by the accusatory tones, Laura said, "I couldn't help it. She attacked me."

"I couldn't help it either, Laura." Judith straightened and looked into the cheval glass. In the reflection her gaze locked with Laura's. "Perhaps I wasn't fighting for something as noble as Ombres Azurées, but my cause was no less just. I was deceived and tricked. I wanted to set the record straight. I wanted to expose Tabor O'Halloran for what he was."

"Instead, you exposed yourself." Laura turned her back to the mirror and walked away. She was too tired to fight anymore. "I don't know if New Orleans society will ever forgive us for this."

"They'll forgive *you*. And what they think doesn't matter to me."

Laura shook her head. "Of course it does."

"No, I don't care. An entire roomful of men and women stood and laughed while I was swept up and carried off against my will. It all seems like a nightmare. All I wanted was for everyone to know what he was and what he had done to me. I was the one hurt by him." She spread her hands in a plea for understanding; then she whipped them away into the folds of her skirt. Again she mumbled, "It all seems like a nightmare now."

"Oh, Judith"— Laura wanted to take Judith into her arms, but she seemed so angry and distant, so untouchable—"if only you had told me what you planned to do, I could have advised you."

"I don't know that I would have listened, Laura. He had done so much that was wrong and was getting away with it. I got so mad I couldn't stand it." Judith fumbled in the dresser drawer.

Laura's voice was soft. "At least I would have stayed and been there to stop him."

Surprised, Judith asked, "Would have stayed! Where were you?"

After a long, deliberate pause, Laura said, "I was at the Golden Fleece."

"With Clay Sutherland?"

"Yes."

"Do Beau and Celeste know?"

"Not yet."

"I don't know why they would be upset about your taking a gambler as a lover when they allowed a pirate to buy gowns for me."

"They probably wouldn't care so long as I handle the affair discreetly. That's the key in society. Discretion," Laura said rather bitterly. Since she had met Clay, her eyes were opening to the shortcomings of society.

Judith did not reply immediately. Her attention focused on her task, she pulled each glove on. Eventually she spoke. "I'm not going to live a social lie. That's why I warned you that society was not for me. I told you I didn't want to go to the ball." She began to move toward the door.

"The ball has nothing to do with this." Laura grabbed Judith's elbow; her sister's self-righteousness was rather irritating. "All you want to do is

329

check cargo on the docks with Georges holding your parasol as if you were queen of the Nile. Your decision to work on those damned docks precipitated this."

"I had no control over that either." Judith raised her voice and whirled away from Laura. "Maurice Dufaure refused to have me in the office, and Beau didn't want to stand up to him. Besides, it's honest work and I'm learning the business. And this didn't begin on the docks. Tabor O'Halloran boarded my ship in the middle of the Atlantic. He ruined everything I owned. And when I saw him—"

"You wouldn't have seen him if you hadn't been on those docks," Laura pointed out.

Judith avoided Laura's gaze and ignored her remark. Stubbornly, she continued. "When I saw him, I tried to have him arrested, but nobody would pay any attention to me."

Laura crossed her arms. "Yes, M'sieur Dufaure has told us how you behaved in the streets."

"Damn him. He had no business to tattle on me."

"He wasn't tattling. He's as interested in our reputation as we are. The business of Talbot Shipping depends upon goodwill and a good reputation. Besides . . ." She gave Judith a brief, reassuring smile. "He's worried about what could happen to you."

Judith laughed. "Laura, Maurice Dufaure would be overjoyed if I walked off the edge of the dock and sank like a stone to the bottom of the Mississippi." She stepped toward the door. "Besides, he's not your friend either. He's the one who told me you had gone to the voodoo ceremony. I didn't tell on you because I'm not a sneak. I never wanted to be a part of this anyway. You and Celeste forced me into it."

"No, Judith. We didn't. You agreed."

Her chin tilted defiantly, Judith stared at Laura for a long time before she sighed and hung her head. "I tried," she muttered. "I really tried, even though I didn't want to."

Laura's robe flowed behind her as she moved to the center of the room. "I thought we were ready to take our place in New Orleans society." She pirouetted as she had seen her mother do so many times in the past and flung out her hands. "You and I—the Talbot sisters! We could have dazzled them. As it is, neither one of us has exactly covered herself with glory."

Judith laughed. "Oh, Laura, we really have made a mess of this, haven't we? Just like our mother before us. What are you going to do about your masquerade with Clay?"

"I don't know."

"A gambler isn't eagerly welcomed into the ranks of the finest Creole families."

"I know. I know."

"On the other hand, you can have a discreet affair, as Celeste wants," Judith said. "Even though he isn't invited, he knows he's welcome just as pirates like Tabor and even Jean Lafitte know they can come to the balls. This is the city where everyone wears a mask."

"Not Clay. He wouldn't come where he's not invited."

"Since when do men like him need an invitation? He's like Lord Lythes. He doesn't care whether he's invited or not. He goes where he wants to."

There were times when Laura had not liked Clay, times when she would have compared other men to him, but she would not tolerate Judith's mentioning him in the same breath as Lythes. She headed for the door. "I'm not going to listen to you criticize him, Judith Claire."

331

Judith laughed and caught Laura's elbow as she stalked by. "Oh, yes, you are, sister dear. You started this conversation. Clay Sutherland is a man like any other. He's no better but no worse. You have to face a few home truths about him. Laura, listen to me." She transferred her hands to her sister's shoulders. "Every time someone says something you don't want to hear, you run away."

Laura pulled out of Judith's grasp. "I do not."

"You do too. And every time something goes wrong around here, you blame me when you're just as guilty as I am."

"I don't. How dare you say that!"

Judith threw up her hands. "I denounce a pirate at the Beauvaliets *bal masqué* and I've ruined the family. You have a secret affair with a gambler and that's all right." She began to pace back and forth across the room.

"You didn't denounce a pirate, little sister. You made public your indiscretion."

Judith stopped pacing and turned to look at Laura earnestly. "Why has it become my indiscretion and not his?"

Reluctantly, Laura spoke. "Because it's a rule of our society. A society that caters to the male. A gentleman does not carry the responsibility of proving his virtue. A lady does."

"But that's not fair."

Laura sat down and folded her hands in her lap. "No, it's not. Society's rules are frequently not fair, but they work for the majority." Laura paused, then said, "Judith, surely you can see the fight in the Golden Fleece is altogether different from the scene that you created."

"I don't see how," she stubbornly maintained. "There were just as many people present in the

332

saloon as in the ballroom. And probably many of them saw both scenes."

"I told you I was fighting to protect Ombres Azurées. I couldn't have the workers rebel against authority because of voodoo."

"So making a spectacle of yourself is all right for you because it's good and right, but when I do it, it's bad and wrong. Laura, can't you understand I was trying to make a point? Tabor O'Halloran is a lying, thieving pirate. I had to denounce him, or at least make an effort to."

Laura stared at Judith's pale face. Then her shoulders slumped. "We've ruined everything."

"If everything is so easily ruined, it must not have been worth much anyway."

"I just feel so bad about tearing down everything we've worked for ever since Papa came to New Orleans."

"I thought you said that marrying Celeste was the way Papa and you were accepted into society."

Green eyes pierced Judith. "That's the way we were accepted into society, but not the way we have stayed in society's good graces."

"Lord Lythes told me once that society is fake. The people in it are all liars in one way or another. No one shows his true colors. Everyone hides behind a mask of some kind. I didn't believe him until those men and women stood there as they did."

Laura suddenly smiled and nodded her head. "You're right, Judith."

Judith's jaw went slack in surprise. "I am?"

Laura's eyes widened as Judith took her hands and gave them a grateful squeeze. Then, after a moment's hesitation, she squeezed back.

Chapter Fourteen

"When did you discover this?" Her head bowed, Laura walked around the pirogue and looked for an identifying mark.

"This morning, Maîtresse. Last night I heard noises on the bayou. But I did not get up. It was Friday night, and I thought it was someone returning from the celebrations in town. This morning when I am clipping the bushes, I find this hidden in the undergrowth next to the bayou."

"It does not belong to any of us?"

Tomas gave his head a vigorous shake. "I do not recognize it. Maybe it belongs—belonged to M'sieur Donaldson."

"I shouldn't think so," Laura answered.

"Perhaps it belongs to a poacher," the boy suggested.

"That is more like it, Tomas."

"What do you want me to do with it, Maîtresse?"

"Go to the house and tell Joshua to send two men to the cottage. I will give them instructions."

A grin split the boy's face. "You're going to catch a poacher, Maîtresse?"

Laura grinned also. "I am indeed. I'll stay here

until you return, but you must hurry. I have to get back to the house to check on Maîtresse Celeste. She's not feeling well today."

Tomas was not gone long when Laura heard a rustle in the bushes. She ducked behind the trunk of a large tree and waited. A man whistled, the melody drifting through the forest. He appeared in the clearing and looked around.

"Edouard." Laura rushed from her hiding place. "What are you doing here?"

"What an unexpected pleasure to see you this afternoon, Mademoiselle Talbot. I am taking a walk to see the beauties of your country."

"It is beautiful." Laura's eyes softened as she looked around at the colorful array of flowers.

"I hope you do not mind that I am on your property."

"Not at all. Why would you ask?"

Edouard lifted a brow. "You were hiding behind the tree."

Laura laughed. "Tomas and I found a strange pirogue hidden by the bayou. We think we have a poacher."

Now Edouard laughed and tapped his chest with his finger. "And you thought I was that poacher?"

"I was taking no chances."

"I am glad that you are careful. Would you like to walk with me? We could talk, *non?*"

"I would love to," Laura said, "but I cannot. I must wait for Tomas to return. Would you like to walk up to the cottage for a cool drink of lemonade?"

"*Absolutement.* I would love that."

After Edouard left, Laura climbed into the gig and headed for the plantation house, returning for the first time since she had departed on the previous Thursday. Berthe was taking care of Celeste, and Beau was dividing his time between the plantation and town, working at the Talbot lines during the day and spending his evenings with Celeste. Judith had remained in town, retreating further into her shell, the tentative compromise between her and Laura still too new to create a bond between them.

Laura, too, had stayed away because she wanted Beau to have time to get over his humiliation and anger, but she could remain away no longer. He had said something about being home early today, and she hoped he was. She was concerned about the pirogue and had to tell him about it. Although she told Tomas she thought it was poachers, she was not convinced of that fact herself.

She also knew that she must tell Beau about her decision to marry Clay. She had been thinking about it a great deal during the past three days. Although the news would not please her parents, she was doing them, Clay, and herself a great disservice by not letting them know she loved Clay and was going to marry him. Clay would forgive her for telling their news without him. She wanted the world to know she loved Clay and that he loved her.

When Laura arrived at the house, she found her father in the sitting room. A glass of whiskey in hand, he sat in one of the wing chairs, his legs stretched out. He looked around when the door opened. Two liquor bottles sat on the table; one was empty, the other partially empty.

"Hello, Papa." Laura dreaded talking with her father when he was drunk, but he was seldom sober anymore. She laid her quirt on the table and slowly peeled off her gloves.

"And how is the plantation running, eldest

daughter?" he slurred. "Fine without Beau Talbot."

"I have something important to talk to you about, Papa." She moved to stand in front of her father. "Please put your whiskey aside and listen."

Beau straightened in the chair and set the glass on the nearby table. "And what is so important that you must come talk to your father?" He listened quietly as Laura told him about the pirogue. Picking up his glass, he stretched out again. "Probably nothing to be concerned about. You have someone watching. Whoever it is, we'll catch them."

Sighing, Laura walked to the fireplace and laid an arm on the mantel. "Also, Papa, I have something else I want to talk to you about."

Beau wheeled around in the chair and poured another glass of whiskey.

"I'm in love with Clay Sutherland. I'm going to marry him."

Beau leapt to his feet, the liquor sloshing out of the glass onto his wrinkled trousers. "And when did you make this decision?"

"He asked me to marry him Tuesday night, Papa, and I accepted."

Beau stared at her, his hand shaking. "You went to the Golden Fleece after you left the Beauvaliets? You were with him?"

Laura nodded. She held her back straight and faced her father squarely. "Yes."

Beau dropped the glass and walked up to her. "You slut!" He spat the words and slapped her face.

Laura staggered, her head jerking back from the blow, her hand automatically going to her cheek. This was the first time her father had ever hit her. Her eyes rounded, she stared at him but refused to quail. "I love him."

"You love him," Beau mimicked. Judith's announcement had pushed him to the edge; Laura's was pushing him over. "You're like a bitch, and this is your first time in heat. You'd go to bed with any man."

"Papa—" Although the only color in Laura's face was her large green eyes, she spoke calmly. "I don't want to hear anything you have to tell me now. When you're sober, we'll talk."

"I feel like an idiot, a man disgraced by both his daughters. Goddammit! Both of you are stubborn and rebellious. Judith screamed her filthy truths from the Beauvaliets' staircase, while you were in the Golden Fleece in bed with that—that gambler." He wagged his fist in her face. "And you never told me. You listened to me tell you about Judith, and you never said one word."

"I would have told you, but you were so upset over Judith. You were worried about the effects her action would have on the shipping line."

"Don't hide behind Judith's dress tail," he shouted.

"I'm not, and I'm not ashamed for my loving Clay and of my wanting to marry him."

Beau's bloodshot eyes pierced Laura. "Are you totally without honor?"

"No, I'm honorable." *Dear Lord, here they were playing with that hollow word again!* It was nothing but letters, devoid of meaning or significance.

"If you are, where is it? Tell me. Did you give your virginity to this commoner? Are you having an affair with him? Every one of our friends will know of this. What do you have to offer a decent man in marriage?"

If it were possible, Laura drew even straighter and taller. "Surely, there's more of me than my virginity. Would a decent man not be interested in me as a person? If I marry a *decent* man, I must be willing to overlook *his* past indiscretions. In fact, Papa, I'm told that I should be grateful that a *decent* man has had them. That he has learned from them and brings *experience* as well as syphilis to my bed."

"My God!" Horrified, Beau drew back. "How dare you use such language. Have you forgotten that you're a lady?"

"Just a moment ago you accused me of being a slut, Papa. Which am I?"

Outraged, Beau shook his head helplessly.

"Clay and Judith have been right all along," Laura continued. "Society makes hypocrites of all of us. I'll no longer be bound by rules that don't permit me to be happy."

Beau held a trembling hand out and pointed to the door. "Go to your room."

Laura lowered her hand to reveal her discolored cheek and smiled sadly. Her lips had begun to swell from the blow. "I'm not a child, Papa. You can no longer punish me by sending me to my room. You and Celeste are going to have to face the fact that Judith and I have chosen to live our own lives."

"Like mother, like daughters. Sluts. All three of you. At least, Judith is a child and didn't know better. You did." His eyes blazing with anger, Beau marched out of the room. He stopped in the doorway. "I want Clay Sutherland out of your life."

Laura shook her head. "I love him, Papa, and I'm going to marry him."

Beau's gaze settled on Laura's bruised cheek. "Laura, look what's happening to us since this man came into your life. Promise me you'll never see this man again."

"I'm going to marry him."

Beau's features contorted with anger. "Laura, if

340

you don't go to your room, I'll slap you again."

Shocked because her father had never treated her like this before, Laura moved past him. Although she knew he was overreacting to the situation because he was drunk, Laura still could not forgive him. With quiet dignity she said, "No, Papa, you won't. You'll never hit me again."

"Laura," Beau yelled to her retreating figure, "if you marry that man, I'll make sure you never get Ombres Azurées. Think this over. If you decide you're still going to marry the gambler, I want you to be the one to tell Celeste—if you're that callous."

Crushed but defiant to the last, Laura walked up the stairs to her stepmother's bedroom. It was difficult for her to comprehend how drastically her life had changed during the eight months since she had met Clay at Maurice Dufaure's autumn ball. Ironically, he had not changed her, but she had changed because of him. He had promised he would find the maiden beneath the veneer of ice, and he had. Willingly, she had allowed him to melt her reserve and to find the woman who was searching for love.

So much had happened during the past eight months to change Laura's life—Charlotte's death; her own visit to England to see the Harrow side of the family for the first time in nine years; Judith's coming to New Orleans. Now Beau. With a wave of her hand and a thump of her cane, *Grandmère* thought she could dismiss the intervening years and separation.

Laura's affair with Clay had changed her, but Judith's arrival had changed the family. At times Laura thought her father was getting closer to Judith than he was to her. She recalled his bragging about Judith's ability with figures and her knowledge of the sea and the shipping industry. Even now he seemed more understanding of Judith than he was

341

of her.

Yes, she was feeling pangs of jealousy.

And she yet had to talk with her stepmother. Laura truly loved Celeste and wished she did not have to confess her affair with Clay. How much easier it would have been if he and she could have begun courting and moved slowly and naturally into marriage. But that could not be. Beau knew about her night with Clay.

And Beau had promised to take Ombres Azurées away from her if she did not give up Clay.

Laura opened the door and walked into the darkened room. Candles burned in all the alcoves, and the air was heavy with incense.

Celeste turned her head on the pillow. "Is that you, Laura?"

"Yes, *Maman.*" Laura sat on the edge of the bed and took one of Celeste's hands in hers. "How are you feeling today?"

"Much better," Celeste answered weakly.

"Can I get you anything?" Laura asked.

"No, I've already had a cup of *tisane.* I shall be getting up later in the day. My headache is gone now."

"Are you still worried about Judith?"

"Yes, I am concerned about Judith, but not nearly so much as I am concerned about your papa. He does not remember how fickle society can be or how easily they can forget. He worries too much."

Now that her eyes had adjusted to the shadows, Laura could see her stepmother's face. "Have you been playing a game with us, *ma chère?*" she asked.

"Only a little." Celeste smiled. "Now, what did you come to talk to me about?"

Laura leaned over and picked up one of the folded cloths on the night table and doused it in the basin of water. After she wrung it out, she laid it on Celeste's forehead. *"Maman,* I'm in love with Clay Sutherland. I'm going to marry him."

"I knew that a long time ago, *ma chère,"* Celeste whispered. "And now, what will I do about your papa?"

"You must make him accept it, *Maman."*

Tears ran down the sides of Celeste's face. "I do not know if I can do that, Laura. I'm afraid your papa has been pushed too far. His pride will suffer only so much." She jerked the cloth from her face and sat up. "I must go to him. Get my wrapper for me."

"I'll come with you," Laura said.

"No, it is better if I talk to him alone."

Remembering her father's anger, Laura agreed with her stepmother. She went to her bedroom, and Celeste ran down the stairs into the library. When she opened the door, Beau stood in front of his desk. He lifted the lid of the flat rectangular mahogany box.

Standing in front of the open window, the sunlight glistened on the silver in his hair. His shoulders were rounding with age, and his stomach was developing a small paunch, but Celeste saw none of the irregularities of his physique. Beau Talbot was the man she loved, the person she loved above all others.

He extracted one of the small pistols by the ornate ivory handle and held it in his hand. The metal barrel shone in the sunlight.

"Beau!" Horrified, Celeste rushed across the room. What are you doing, *mon cher?* I told you Tuesday night to let Judith and that—that man work their own lives out. You promised me."

Beau disregarded the gentle tug on his arm and continued to inspect the pistols. "I promised you that I would not call Tabor O'Halloran out, dearest one,

343

but I said nothing about Clay Sutherland."

"*Mais non, mon cher. Mais non.*" The words were a mere whisper. Celeste's hand went to her mouth; she staggered as if a heavy weight had been settled on her shoulders.

"Laura wants to marry Clay Sutherland. Did she tell you?"

Celeste nodded. "Let her, Beau. It's her life."

"No, I will not allow her to disgrace our family. I am a man totally devoid of honor." Beau polished the handle of the gun and held it against the window. Squinting an eye, he searched for the minutest particle of dust. When he had inspected both of the pistols, he set them back in the box and fastened the lid.

"Knowing that my wife and Randolph Carew were having a scandalous affair, I was willing to take Charlotte back, but I wasn't willing to fight for my honor. I tucked my tail and ran. I allowed Judith to remain with the Harrows. Without so much as a word to the contrary, I let Tabor O'Halloran insult our honor."

The brown eyes opened wide; they sparkled with tears. Celeste shook her head, the gentle brown hair tumbling around her shoulders to give her a beautiful, haunting look. "*Non,* my darling."

Beau laid the gun on the desk and turned to pull Celeste into his arms. She felt good, and fit against his frame perfectly. He pressed her face against his chest and inhaled her perfume. "I'm not running anymore, *ma petite.* I will fight for Laura's honor.

"How has her honor been sullied?" Celeste sniffed. "She is marrying out of her class, but she is marrying, *mon cher.* Is that not enough for you?"

"I will not let her marry a commoner like Clay Sutherland. I would rather die first."

"You are no match for this man." Celeste pushed out of his arms, her hands clasping his upper arms. "He has a reputation, Beau. One that you cannot begin to match."

Beau's hand lifted and curled around her chin. His thumb traced the bottom line of her lip. "This is something I must do, my darling. Nothing . . . no one is going to stop me."

"Beau dearest," Celeste cried, "I do not want you to die. I need you."

Tenderly, Beau gazed at his wife. "If I do not do this, my darling, I am already dead and will be of little use to you." He leaned down to press his lips against hers in a warm kiss. Celeste sobbed and threw her arms around him. She held him tightly. Finally, he set her aside and opened the bottom drawer of his desk, from which he extracted a small cash box. He unlocked it and pulled out some money and a document. "In case—" He cleared his throat. "In case I do not return, I am taking care of everything for you and the girls."

Celeste lifted a hand and brushed the tears from her cheeks. She watched as he counted the money, returning some to the box. The remainder and the document he shoved into his coat pocket.

"Until the war with England is over and trade resumes, finances will be tight." He picked up the pistol case and tucked it under his arm. "With Laura and Judith pulling the purse strings as tightly as they can, the three of you can manage. The girls—while they haven't shown the best judgment in choosing their men—do have good business heads on their shoulders. They'll take care of you if anything should happen to me, my love."

Celeste reached for him again, but Beau held his arm out. "Don't make this any more difficult for me

345

than it is, sweetheart." He turned and walked out of the room, never looking back.

Celeste ran through the house and up the stairs, her silk wrapper billowing behind her petite figure. She thrust open the thick mahogany door and rushed into her stepdaughter's room. Her face was ashen.

"Laura," she cried. "Go to your papa at once. He's on his way to the Golden Fleece to challenge Clay Sutherland. You must stop him."

Laura sprang to her feet and ran down the stairs. Beau was walking down the hall to the front door. "Papa!"

He turned. His face looked as if it had been hewn from stone. Cold and impassive, the brown eyes pierced hers. No matter what the argument, no matter that he had slapped her in anger, Laura loved her father.

"Papa, you can't challenge Clay. You're no match for him."

"I can do nothing else." His voice was dull but resolved. "This has become a point of honor. I can do nothing else."

"Even if it is a matter of honor, Papa, it's my honor. I must fight for it, not you."

As if he had not heard her, Beau continued in his trancelike voice, "I will stop the wagging tongues. People will forgive Judith. She is young and inexperienced and English. She does not yet understand our ways. But they will not forgive you your indiscretion. You are one of us; you knew better. I will win back your honor."

Laura could not believe her father. She caught his shoulders and shook him. "Papa, this doesn't make sense to me. According to the rules of society, I have lost my honor by sleeping with Clay. Surely a duel will not restore my virtue. It will only add one more dishonor to our name. Or your death." *Or Clay's death!* Dear God, not Clay's death. Laura could not bear the thought of either.

Beau laid his large hand over Laura's and pressed it. His eyes softened but not his expression. "What I am doing is not for your or Judith's honor. I am doing this for myself. If I do not do this, I cannot hold my head up. And I'm too old to run anymore, Laura."

Tears scalded Laura's cheeks. "Please, don't do this, Papa. Please."

"Listen to her, Beau." Celeste caught his arm and tugged. *"Mon Dieu,* please listen."

Beau removed his wife's hands. "Leave me alone, Celeste. I failed Charlotte and the girls when they were smaller. I will not fail them or you now."

Saloman opened the front door. "The carriage is ready, M'sieur Talbot."

"Papa," Laura cried, "please don't go."

Beau Talbot turned and walked across the veranda.

"No, Beau," Celeste screamed, and ran after him, Laura following on her heels. She was crying so hard she could not see. "Don't go. Please, don't go."

As the footman opened the carriage door, Beau turned and gave each of them a sad smile. "I'll be back when it's settled."

"No!" Celeste screamed. She stumbled over the hem of her dress and fell to her knees.

Laura stooped and gently lifted her up. She held her in a tight embrace to comfort. "Please don't cry, *Maman.* It's going to be all right." Yet as Laura looked over Celeste's shoulders at the departing carriage, she could not contain her grief. She cried too.

How could it be all right? she wondered.

*　　*　　*

"You are an imbecile!" Edouard exclaimed, angrily pacing the library floor in Giraumont's plantation house the next morning. "Now that Laura has found the pirogue, she will have men watching the bayou, looking for poachers. Why did you hire such a clumsy oaf as Donaldson? Next Laura will be finding a letter of confession from him."

"He—couldn't write," Giraumont attempted to joke.

Edouard glared at him. "This is no time for levity, Roussel. Your time is running out."

Giraumont nervously tugged at his waistcoat. "I never expected her to be there," he kept repeating. "That's such a secluded branch of the bayou. I was so sure."

"It is good for you that I thought quickly and pretended to be taking a walk." He shook his head in disgust. "And what if that had been the emperor's brother and his most trusted advisers? Killed in America because one of these primitives thinks he's a poacher!" Now he threw his hands up. "That I must deal with such idiocy as this!"

Giraumont walked to the side table and poured himself a full glass of whiskey. After several bracing swallows, he said, "It doesn't appear to me that the French and their emperor are doing so well, my friend. Otherwise, he would not be looking to America for another base of operation, a place to run to if all does not go well in England."

Edouard looked at Giraumont with contempt; his lips thinned, and his nostrils flared in anger. "Have you succeeded in talking M'sieur Talbot into cooperating with us?"

A sinister smile played on Giraumont's lips. "Not yet. But I shall."

"We do not have time to wait on him." Exasperated, Edouard ran his fingers through his hair. "Who is your contact? I must speak directly with him. We must devise a new plan immediately."

Giraumont lifted the glass to his lips and drank freely as he thought. Still, he did not answer. He walked to the window and stared at the manicured gardens and hedges that decorated the front lawn. With interest he watched the carriage turn into the drive. The livery announced his visitor.

"M'sieur, we have no time to waste," Lambert repeated. "You must trust me or you must return the money."

Giraumont laughed nastily. "No, *mon ami,* you must trust me if you wish the emperor's brother to get safely into New Orleans. As you said a moment ago, time is running out . . . for you."

"You will do as I say," Lambert threatened.

Again Giraumont laughed. "Over here, M'sieur Lambert, I give the orders, not you. Our conversation must cease. I have company." When Beau Talbot entered the library a few minutes later, Giraumont smiled. "What a pleasant surprise, my friend."

"Not so pleasant I'm afraid," Beau answered. "I have a debt of honor to settle."

Roussel arched a brow and went to the table to fill two glasses with whiskey. "Do you wish me to be your second?"

"No, I have sent word to Maurice."

"I am puzzled, then, about the nature of your visit to me."

"Before I called Sutherland out, I wanted to settle my debt with you." He slipped his hand into his pocket to extract the document and money. These he laid on the desk, then sat down in the large chair. "If I should die, I do not wish to have my family burdened with more debts than they can manage. They do not

349

know of this one, and I should like it to remain a secret between you and me."

"Of course." Roussel handed Beau a glass of whiskey, then went to sit behind the desk. Smiling, he swept the money and the document into the drawer he'd just opened. "As you requested, I have told no one about the loan. But, my friend, tell me about your debt of honor."

"Surely marriage will restore Laura's honor." The hour was late, and Clay was tired. Standing in the center of the casino, he stared into Beau Talbot's face.

The crowd was silent. The games had ceased; the only movements were those of eyes vacillating between Beau and Clay. A few steps behind Beau stood Roussel Giraumont and Maurice Dufaure.

Beau drew to his full height, and his voice thundered through the large room. "I consider Laura's marriage to you an ever greater dishonor, Sutherland."

A muscle ticked in Clay's cheek, but he kept his voice quiet. Yet it carried more force than did Beau's. "I can't accept your challenge, Mr. Talbot. You're the father of the woman I'm going to marry."

Beau's hand flew through the air the second time, his glove striking Clay first on the right cheek, then on the left. "Defend yourself, sir. Unless you're a coward as well as a besmircher of innocent maidens, you'll give me satisfaction." His arm moved again, the gesture encompassing Giraumont and Dufaure. "These are my witnesses. M'sieur Dufaure will be my second."

Clay looked at Dufaure; the older man fidgeted under the hard stare but his eyes never moved. Clay then looked at Giraumont. Unable to meet Clay's cold stare, Giraumont squirmed and dropped his head. "Are neither of you going to talk sense into Mr. Talbot?" he asked.

"These men are my friends, not my keepers!" Beau exclaimed. "They do not tell me what I can or cannot do."

"Perhaps it is Roussel Giraumont who should be calling me out, Mr. Talbot?"

Surprise registered on Beau's face. Momentarily disconcerted, he looked from Dufaure to Giraumont as if seeking guidance.

"After all, I understand he's the man who wants to marry Laura," Clay continued.

Giraumont's expression went dark, and he clenched his fists to his side. "Had Laura and I had so much as an understanding, Sutherland, I would have called you out. But since we do not, it is M'sieur Talbot's duty to challenge you."

"Ah, yes," Clay drawled. "Another one of these duties of society."

"Exactly," Beau said. "A responsibility that you know nothing about, Sutherland."

"And God forbid that I ever do."

Clay's gaze skimmed the crowd. Already he could see their eyes glittering with excitement—the excitement that accompanied the making of the next bet and with finding a new game of chance. A stake of life or death was always much more challenging than mere cards or dice. Also, Clay's reputation was at stake. If he refused the challenge, he would be marked a coward. While that in itself did not bother him, its effect on his livelihood did.

"What is your answer, Sutherland?" Beau asked.

Seeing the satisfaction gleaming in the depths of Roussel's eyes and knowing that Beau had pushed himself . . . or had been pushed . . . beyond reason,

351

Clay sighed. "As you wish, Mr. Talbot. I'll give you satisfaction. Do you have a physician you prefer, or shall I provide one?"

"If you have no quarrel, I shall ask Dr. Herbert."

"Agreed," Clay said. "We shall meet at dawn."

"I do not wish to wait until dawn, Sutherland. I want to get this over with now."

"Not tonight. You're drunk." Clay stalled for time. "When I face a man, I want to make sure he's my match. Also, I want to make sure I can see my target. Shooting in the dark with only a lantern for light isn't to my liking. It's not sporting."

"What weapons will you choose?"

Again Clay hesitated; his brow furrowed. Eventually, he said, "Pistols. And you can choose our meeting place, Mr. Talbot. Send me word before dawn."

Beau bowed curtly. "As you wish."

Clay turned and walked upstairs. He was exhausted and still had to meet with Reynolds. Now this duel complicated matters even more. His and Laura's courtship—if one could rightly call it that—had been rocky from the beginning. In the morning at dawn he was going to face his beloved's father, and if they followed the duello, one of them would be dead.

Clay saw no way out of his dilemma. If he did not defend himself, his integrity would be ruined in the city. If he killed Beau, Laura would never forgive him. Surely she would not marry him. Either way he would have no future.

As he opened the door to his quarters, he heard a slight rustle. Immediately, he tensed, his eyes quickly scanning the firelit room. A woman stepped out of the shadows.

"Clay?"

352

"Laura."

Clay closed the door and strode across the room to take her into his arms. She lifted her face, and their lips met in a deep kiss. When finally he lifted his head, he cupped her face with his hands. His eyes were dark and somber; they mirrored his concern.

"Your father challenged me to a duel."

"I know. But he's drunk and angry. He didn't know what he was doing."

"He was drunk and angry, but he knew what he was doing."

"You can't fight him, Clay!"

"What alternative do I have?" he asked dully, then laughed bitterly at the irony of the situation. "My reputation and honor are at stake."

"Since when have you cared about your reputation and honor?"

Incredulous, Clay stared at Laura for immeasurable seconds. Then he brushed past her and walked to the desk. "Since I've been old enough to know how much reputation and honor count in this world we live in."

Laura ran and caught his arm, pulling him around. "Clay, please, you can't meet with Papa. He's no match for you. He hasn't used *épées* in years."

Clay gently disengaged her fingers and opened the black lacquered box. He spoke in a monotone. "We're using pistols."

"Clay, if you really love me, you won't do this. You don't have as much to lose as Papa does."

Clay did not look at Laura this time. He simply rolled the cigar in his fingers. Finally, he put it in his mouth and lit it. A thin line of white smoke swirled around his head. He smiled sadly; his brown eyes dulled. "If you loved me, you wouldn't think so little

353

of me. You would trust me."

Wounded, Laura drew back.

"You desire me, Laura, but you don't love me."

"How can you make such an accusation?"

"No accusation. Merely a statement of fact." He tipped his head and blew smoke rings.

"How do you expect me to react when the two men I care about most are going out to kill each other? Can't you understand how this is affecting me? I don't want either one of you hurt. Despite what you say, I love you."

"Then trust me."

Laura gazed into the somber brown eyes. "I do, I just don't—"

Clay rested a finger over her mouth. "Trust me to do what's right for all of us."

"All right," she murmured.

Clay laid the cigar in the ashtray and pulled Laura into his arms, holding her tightly. "It's too late for you to be traveling tonight."

"I know." She smiled quite demurely. "I planned to spend the night with you."

"Laura Elyse Talbot," Clay murmured, "I love you. You're what I've always looked for in a wife."

"And what is that, Mr. Sutherland?"

Clay grinned and tugged one of the curls that lay on her cheek. "To begin with, you're beautiful. Also, you're rich, influential, and belong to the select Creole society of New Orleans. You own one of the largest and most productive sugar cane plantations in the state."

Although Clay was teasing, Laura was hurt and troubled. She remembered Clay's words to Roussel the night of the autumn ball. She recalled her father's bitter and hateful accusations.

"Those aren't characteristics." She lifted her head

354

from his chest and searched his face. "They're possessions. Are they that important to you, Clay?"

"Yes," he replied quietly, "they're important to me. But they are not the reason that I love or want to marry you."

"You're wealthy, isn't that enough?"

"Not in our society. Wealth gives you a certain amount of power and influence, but the proper name and location of your home give you prestige."

Remembering her father's promise to disinherit her should she marry Clay, she asked, "Would you marry me if I were a nobody?"

"You couldn't be a nobody and be Laura Elyse Talbot. But yes, my darling, I would love you no matter what. And I would want to marry you."

Clay caught her close again, his hands moving up and down her back.

"Your love may be tested. Papa won't let me have Ombres Azurées if I marry you."

His hands stopped rubbing. "He wouldn't do that."

"Yes, he would," Laura said with certainty. "Whatever else Papa may be or do, he's not a liar."

"No," Clay agreed, "he's not."

Embracing each other, they stood quietly for a long time; then Laura thought about John. "Clay, I know you told John that you were going to send him back east, but if you want us to keep him here now that we're going to be married, I don't mind."

Clay smiled and held Laura tighter in his arms. "This is another reason why I love you so much, sweetheart. You're so unselfish. But my sister has already answered my letter. She wants John to come live with her. And I think that will be best for him. Anna has three boys herself, and John needs the companionship of boys his own age. He'll fit right in. Besides, he can come visit us during the summer holidays."

Laura stirred. "Tell me something about your family, Clay. I know so little about you."

Sweeping Laura into his arms, Clay carried her back to the bed. Laying her down, he stretched out beside her. "Right now, my darling, I have other things on my mind. The night is much too short for us to waste on talking, don't you think?"

The warm pressure of his lips and the gentle stroke of his hands on her body chased Laura's curiosity away. He dropped butterfly kisses against the corners of her mouth, against her eyelids, against her cheek and throat. His fingers stroked the nape of her neck and moved slowly down her spine, coming to rest in the small of her back. Soft pressure angled her body against his.

A painfully sweet longing swept over Laura. Her hands pressed against his chest. He was solid and he was here with her tonight. She knew not what tomorrow might bring. She wanted to run her fingers over his body, to feel the warmth of his skin next to hers. She wanted to know the taste and texture of him. Most of all, she wanted to make him tremble beneath her touch as she did beneath his.

Clay's lips captured hers in a wonderfully gentle kiss. It began with a brushstroke of lips, then a sweet joining of tongues. His hands moved in sensuous design up and down her back. His kiss deepened, and the tiny flames of desire burst into a passionate blaze. Laura locked her hands around his neck and tangled her fingers in the coarse black hair that met the collar of his shirt.

He lifted her into his arms and carried her to his bed. Stretching out beside her, he began a slow assault on the buttons of her dress. His eyes never left her, even when he slipped the material from her shoulders and his fingers brushed against the creamy mounds of her breasts. She had worn no chemise for her lovemaking. He caressed her breast.

"I have never seen such beauty," he murmured, his eyes following the movement of his hand. His fingers continued to stroke her breast, and his thumb played at the hardened tip. Bending his head, he brushed soft kisses along her throat. His lips traveled slowly to her breasts.

Desire coursed through Laura's veins. She pressed her hands against the tight muscles of his back and slid them up to his neck. One thumb rested against the pulse point of his throat.

"Now it's time for me to take your shirt off," Laura whispered.

With maddening slowness she worked at the buttons on his shirt. When it was open, she flattened her palms against his chest and brushed the material off his shoulders to reveal his bronzed skin. Dark hair curled across his chest.

Clay slipped her dress from her body and tossed it onto the floor. His eyes moved slowly down her smooth, satiny skin, lingered on the auburn triangle between her legs, then slowly wandered back to her face. His desires were written in his eyes for Laura to read.

In fluid motion he stood and unbuttoned his breeches. When he stood naked, Laura caught her breath. She had seen his masculinity unleashed, but always it filled her with a sense of power to know that she could do this to him.

He lay down again, his hand stroking the long, gentle curve of her hip and thigh. Laura wrapped her arms around Clay and pressed her breasts against his bare chest. Her lips touched his throat. "I love you,

357

my darling."

When Clay's hand moved between her legs, he knew she was ready. She was moist and warm. His fingers eased through the downy mound and touched the tender portal. His touch set her on fire.

Clay's lovemaking had always been wonderful and fulfilling for Laura, but tonight was unparalleled. The tenderness and sweetness was beyond description. Her body begged for his possession.

"Please, Clay, now."

"Yes, my darling."

His hand parted her legs, and he rose over her and slowly lowered himself. Their joining was as tender and sweet as the foreplay. They moved as one. Passion consumed them, and they gave themselves up to the wonder of love. Their rapture knew no bounds. Together they climbed the heights of ecstasy.

Later they lay together. Neither wanted to let go. Although their lovemaking had been overshadowed with grief, this was the most precious moment they had ever shared together. Each recognized for the first time that their hearts and souls had met and joined.

Chapter Fifteen

A smirking grin on his face, Maurice stood in front of his desk in the library. His small black eyes, sunk in a pox-scared face, focused on Roussel. He drummed the table with his long brown fingernails, the result of years of working with ink. "Things could not have worked out better had we planned them."

"What do you mean?" Roussel asked as he seated himself.

"We must make sure that neither Beau or Clay live to tell about this duel."

"Murder!" Giraumont's eyes bugged out, and he leaned forward. "Kill your own partner!"

"I want to own all of the Talbot Shipping Line, Roussel," Maurice said. "I still remember the day when it was Dufaure and Son Shipping Line. It will bear that name once again."

"But, Maurice, if Beau forces the duel, Sutherland will surely kill him in the morning. You will be rid of him."

"It is imperative that neither of these men live."

Giraumont nervously chewed on a fingernail. "I am not so sure of this."

Maurice went to Giraumont and laid a hand on his shoulder. "Both of us know that in the morning when Beau is sober, he will see matters in a different way. Even if he should insist on the duel, he lacks the skill to kill Sutherland, and Sutherland will not kill Beau. He wants to marry Laura. He will do his best to talk Beau out of the duel. Then both will be alive."

He removed his hand from Giraumont and moved away. "As long as Sutherland is alive, my friend, you will not marry Laura."

Giraumont chuckled. "Ah, yes, Maurice, I think Laura will marry me. I do not have to kill Sutherland for her."

"Do not underestimate Sutherland," Maurice cautioned. "If we plan this correctly, Roussel, everyone will believe Sutherland was the culprit. Then you and I will be able to control all the Talbot women."

Giraumont moistened his lips with his tongue. He had been drinking heavily all day, and his thinking was slow. "Maurice, I—I would like to see Sutherland dead, but I'm afraid of this."

"Don't be. Remember, we do what we must. Besides, my friend, since the death of Graham Bradford, Sutherland has begun snooping around. He doesn't believe Bradford's death was an accident."

Roussel nervously wiped his hand across his forehead. He jumped up from the chair and rushed to the table, where he poured himself some whiskey. He tipped the glass to his lips and drank freely.

"Even I must agree Bradford's death was strange," Maurice continued.

Giraumont lowered the glass. "I don't mind Sutherland's death, but I don't want to be connected with Beau's. *Mon Dieu*, Maurice, we'll be murderers!"

360

Maurice smiled. Giraumont was rather like a puppet. One only had to know which string to pull to manipulate him. "You and I will kill neither of them. We shall hire someone to do it for us."

Giraumont's hands shook badly. "What if someone finds out?"

"They won't. That's why I convinced Beau to have the duel in that remote area at the back of the plantation. No one will find the bodies until the field slaves pass on their way home in the afternoon."

"I don't know." Again Giraumont mopped the nervous perspiration from his face with his hand. "I don't like this, Maurice."

Maurice joined Giraumont at the table and filled a glass the second time with whiskey which he pressed into Giraumont's hands. "No one will even guess that we had anything to do with it."

"How—how are you going to do it?"

"I will hire two men to hide on either side of the dueling site. One will shoot Beau through the heart; the other will shoot Clay."

"What about Clay's second?"

Maurice shrugged. "We shall have to kill him also. It wouldn't do to have more than one witness alive."

"You?"

Maurice nodded. "You will be at *Ombres Azurées* visiting with Celeste and Laura and awaiting Beau's return from town. I will be the witness who lives to tell the story, and I shall tell the story I wish them to hear."

"You are forgetting the physician," Giraumont pointed out.

"We won't have one."

"But you must. That is—"

Maurice laughed softly and clapped Roussel on the back. "My friend, you are not thinking straight tonight. Beau is drunk. That's why he was so foolhardy. He will be quite sober when he awakens in the morning and will have a change of heart. I will see to that. He will arrive at the site with the intention of calling off the duel. Then when he and Sutherland least expect it, they shall be killed."

Giraumont set the glass down and jerked his handkerchief from his pocket. He wiped his face and the back of his neck as he paced the room. "You will murder them while they are standing there talking?"

"*Non,* I will have them killed. There is a difference, you know."

Roussel looked at Maurice imploringly. "What if—"

Maurice's smile widened. "No what ifs, Giraumont."

Giraumont ran his finger around the rim of his glass. "What if we fail?"

"My concern is not our failing," Maurice returned. "My concern is the English winning this war. The Americans are barbarians, but we will fare better under them than under the English." He heard the knock on the door and smiled. "That's my man now."

In a few minutes a dockworker entered the room, yellow hair falling across his forehead when he removed his hat. "Evening, Mr. Dufaure. You wanted to see me."

Dufaure reached into his pocket and pulled out several gold coins which he threw on the top of his desk. "I have a job for you."

"It must be an important one," the man said as he walked closer. "That's a lot of money."

"It is, Lejaune. I want you to kill three men."

The man picked up one of the coins and bit it. "Three men," he mused. "How are they to be killed?"

"In a duel in the morning at the Bayou d'Ombre on Ombres Azurées. You will need another man to help you. Their deaths must appear to be a result of the duel."

The man nodded and lifted a hand to wipe his chin.

"I have a spot where I want the two of you to hide. I want you to kill Beau Talbot, Clay Sutherland, and Sutherland's second." Maurice succinctly explained the way he wanted the three of them killed.

The man tucked the coins into his pocket, then grinned. "I don't mind killing 'em, Mr. Dufaure, but I figure I'm gonna need some more money. You're asking me to kill some mighty important people. Be easier just to arrange for them to die another way."

"No. I want their death to look like the result of a duel."

"Well," the man drawled, "to do this the way you want—to shoot all three in the heart—I'm gonna have to hire a second man. And I'll have to pay him extra."

Dufaure stared at the dirty, unkempt man for a long time before he walked behind his desk and pulled open the drawer. He tossed several more coins on the desk. "Roussel will take you to the place where we're to meet. You'll leave at once." As the man picked up the coins, Maurice tossed two more on the table. "When it's over, I want you to kill the man who helps you."

The dockworker grinned, exposing stained, uneven teeth. "I like you, Mr. Dufaure. It's a pleasure to do business with you."

"I presume you escorted Miss Talbot home before you answered my message."

Clay closed the door to Reynolds's office and sat

down on the other side of his desk. In the glow of candlelight he studied the master spy's face. "I did."

"You're still angry?"

"No, I'm angry at myself," Clay answered. "I should have known that you were sending me on a wild goose chase when you sent me to Baton Rouge."

"For your own good," Reynolds said briskly, playing with the glasses that lay on the desk.

"So you know about the duel?"

Surprised, Reynolds looked up. "I must be getting old. I didn't realize I had given myself away."

"I knew I was being watched, but wasn't sure by whom."

Reynolds pushed back in his chair, his face out of the arc of light. "Probably both sides. I'm having Laura Talbot watched also."

"Why?" Still wondering about Laura's involvement in the Napoleon conspiracy, Clay leaned forward.

"I've received word from Washington that a double agent is here in New Orleans. We have no name or description."

Clay sighed in relief. "And the only man who could have identified him is dead." He leaned forward and exclaimed, "Graham recognized the man. That's why he's dead. If only I had talked to him that night. That's what he wanted to tell me."

"You think so?"

Clay nodded and rose. "If you have nothing else to tell me, I'll be leaving. I have to rustle up a second for the duel in the morning."

"No matter what happens, Sutherland, you can't win this duel." Reynolds pushed to his feet. "No one can win in a situation like this."

"I'm going to talk Talbot out of it," Clay said. "He'll be sober in the morning. I think I can make him see reason.''

"No, I doubt that, and so do you. Talbot has been pushed over the edge . . . by Dufaure and Giraumont, I'll wager. He can't turn back now."

"I'll have to come up with an answer by dawn," Clay said flatly, thinking about Laura.

"I shouldn't tell you this, but—" Reynolds shrugged his shoulders. "I believe either Dufaure or Giraumont is the double agent. If I'm right, then this duel will provide them with an excuse to kill you."

Clay and the spy stared at each other for immeasurable seconds. "I get the feeling that you have a plan."

"No," Reynolds confessed on a sigh, "I'm not sure what Dufaure and Giraumont are up to. I don't know how they're going to handle this duel. But I'd like to send one of my men as your second, another as the physician."

Clay grinned. "You can provide the second. Talbot is getting the physician."

"What time shall my man meet you?"

"Four o'clock. At the Golden Fleece," Clay answered. "I'd like to meet him before I meet Beau."

Reynolds nodded.

"What's his name?"

"Jones."

"What Jones?"

"Just Jones."

A small breakfast party sat in chairs beneath the stately oaks on the lawn of Ombres Azurées. Although her eyes were dark with worry, Celeste carried out to perfection her role as hostess. Laura knew she had retreated into this world to block out her worries and cares. Now, sitting next to Judith, who came in answer to the note Laura had dispatched the night before by messenger, Celeste poured the lemonade and led the conversation.

Laura would make a comment every now and then, but her attention was not on the three men whom they entertained. She was worried about Beau, whom she had not seen since early the previous morning. Anxiously, her gaze kept returning to the oak-lined road that led to the house.

Her hand went to Clay's ring, which she still wore on a ribbon around her throat. He had asked her to trust him, and she did. He would find a way out of the duel. If he did not . . . she could not bear to think of the consequences. She could not imagine life without Clay. Her heart constricted, and her throat choked up.

"Surely, Roussel," Celeste said, her voice shrill with anxiety, "M'sieur Dufaure is quite happy to have Judith working for him. Beau tells me that she is learning the business quickly."

Giraumont nodded his head vigorously. "Yes. Yes, I'm sure she's doing quite well, but I still maintain, Madame Talbot, the office of a shipping line is not the place for a lady of Creole society. It's a wonder Beau is not fighting a duel over Judith's honor as well as Laura's."

Judith lowered her glass of lemonade and surveyed Giraumont with apparent contempt. Wiping her fingers on the linen napkin, she said coolly, "But then, M'sieur Giraumont, I'm not a lady of the Creole society. I'm English, and you'll do well to remember that."

Giraumont's mouthed pinched tight. "Since we're at war with England, I much prefer to forget that you're English. And you would do well to forget also."

Not liking the malevolent gaze Giraumont cast on Judith, Laura leaned forward to set her glass on the table. "Roussel, you'll do well to remember that you're speaking to Beau Talbot's daughter."

"Ah, yes," Roussel acquiesced. He squirmed nervously in the chair, and his gaze also darted to the road. He reached up to wipe the beads of perspiration from his upper lip.

"Why hasn't Papa returned?" Laura asked, putting into words everyone's concern. But other questions were turning over in her mind that she did not voice. *Where is Clay? Was he hurt? Was he able to dissuade her father?* "Surely the duel is over by now!"

When Celeste reached up and pressed the tips of her fingers to her temple, Laura asked, *"Maman,* are you feeling all right?"

"My headache," Celeste murmured, "it's returning, *ma chère.*" She rose but collapsed into the chair. "I—I must get to bed. I feel so bad."

The closest to her stepmother, Judith knelt in front of Celeste and began to rub her hands. Laura raced across the lawn in search of Berthe. She had not reached the front veranda when she heard the thundering of hooves. She turned to see Joshua's horse galloping toward the house. She turned and, driven by blind instinct, began to run down the road toward the slave. She saw the body slung over the horse in front of Joshua.

"Clay," she screamed, and ran all the faster.

Joshua pulled the horse to a stop and jumped down. Laura reached him, but he caught her. "Maîtresse," he said, "m'sieur is dead."

"No," Laura screamed. "No. Clay can't be dead." She jerked out of the man's arms and rushed to the horse. Her hand caught his head and she looked into her father's face. Then Laura was assailed with

367

guilt. Her first thoughts had been for Clay, not her father. She shook her head wildly.

She could not accept Beau's death. She laid her head on his chest and listened for his heartbeat; she heard nothing. She felt for the whisper of his breath on her hand; she felt nothing.

Joshua caught her shoulders and gently dragged her from the horse. "Maîtresse, we need to take him into the house to prepare him for burial."

One of the flatbed work wagons, driven by a slave, bounced down the road at a dangerously fast speed. Maurice Dufaure sat next to the driver, one hand holding on to the side of the seat, the other holding a blood-soaked handkerchief to his head. A horse, bearing a small, nondescript man, galloped behind. Several other slaves were hanging on to the sides of the wagon, their legs flailing through the air. The wagon came to a skidding halt inches away from Laura.

The slave leapt from the seat. "Maîtresse, I—"

The little man was beside her, his arm around her shoulder. "Mam'selle, I don't think you should—"

By this time the slaves had jumped down, and Laura saw the two bodies. The one she did not recognize; the other was Clay. Her heart seemed to stop beating. For the first time in her life the world came to an absolute stop around her. Nothing she had envisioned prepared her for the hurt that consumed her now. Clay was dead! Both her father and Clay were dead. For an eternity she stood there in numb shock, then pain welled up from the very bottom of her soul and exploded in a cry of anguish. Laura twisted away from the stranger and ran to the back of the wagon.

The man followed. This time his hands clamped like iron vises to her shoulders. He turned her around to face him; he shook her until she ceased her hysterics. Laura looked through the thick lenses, but she did not see the pale eyes. She stared blankly.

"I'm Dr. Renaud," the man said. "He's alive. Just barely. I have stopped the bleeding, but I must clean the wound. Do you hear me?"

Laura nodded.

"When he was shot, he fell and hit his head on a jagged stump. I fear he has a concussion. Do you understand what I am saying?"

Again she nodded.

"If you are to be of any use to him, mam'selle, you must collect your wits."

"Yes," Laura murmured, "I will, Doctor."

"Good." Renaud patted her shoulder and helped her into the wagon.

She scooted across the wooden bed and knelt beside Clay, her tears dropping onto his pale face. She caught his head in her hands, uncaring that her hands and dress were soon saturated in his blood.

Clay's lids fluttered opened. God, but he hurt. Fire burned through his chest. Every breath he drew was pure agony. His head was spinning. He was unable to see clearly. Through bleary eyes he saw a form leaning over him. He felt cool drops hitting his face.

"Oh, my darling," she sobbed.

"Laura," he murmured. He reached out and caught her hand. His fingers bit into hers. "What—what happened?" He coughed. His chest rattled, and blood ran down the corner of his mouth. "Beau?" he whispered. "How's Beau?"

Maurice turned in the seat. Blood streaked his face. "He's dead. You killed him, Sutherland. You and that fool second of yours managed to kill everyone but me. But for the grace of God I, too, would be dead!"

369

Clay's gaze flickered over to Maurice. He stared at Maurice for a second, at the blood-soaked cloth he held to his head. Then his eyes closed and his head rolled to the side. He was unconscious.

"No, this can't be!" Laura looked from Clay to the doctor. She caught Dr. Renaud by the shoulders and shook him. "You can't let Clay die. You can't."

Dr. Renaud pried Laura's fingers loose and reached down to lay his hand over Clay's chest. "He's still alive," he announced. "We must get him into the house."

The others arrived at the wagon. Celeste leaned on Giraumont. When she saw Beau's body, she screamed and fainted. Maurice Dufaure, the closest to her, dropped the cloth he held to his head and caught her as she fell.

"I'll take her to her room," he announced.

"What about your wound?" Judith shouted.

"It's superficial. I'm all right."

Judith nodded and raced to the house in front of Maurice, yelling, "Berthe, Celeste needs your attention immediately. Papa is dead."

The servant silently materialized, her hand moving in the sign of the cross. "*Oui*, Maîtresse." She led Maurice to the upstairs bedroom. Laura walked into the house, and Joshua followed, Clay in his arms.

"Put him in the guest bedroom across from mine," Laura directed; then she spoke to Jeanette, who hovered at the door. "Follow Dr. Renaud's instructions."

The maid nodded, and Dr. Renaud said, "Bring some water and rags and see that a fire is lit."

The young woman turned and raced out of the house to the kitchen in the back.

Outside, Roussel leaned against one of the porch columns. His lids were lowered, his dark lashes

370

fanning against his pallid skin. He lifted his hand to his mouth and chewed on his nails. When the door opened and Judith stepped onto the porch, he smiled limply.

"If there is anything I can do for you, mam'selle, please let me know."

Judith inclined her head curtly. "Thank you, Mr. Giraumont. I will."

Hastening to his carriage, Roussel strode across the porch and down the steps. Judith turned to Joshua, who stood a few feet behind her.

"Take the slaves back to the quarters."

Holding his hat in his hand, Joshua said, "I'm sorry about m'sieur, Maîtresse."

"Thank you. As soon as I make the funeral arrangements, I'll send word," Judith replied through numb lips.

Dusk settled its blue haze around the plantation. The wagon, loaded with the field slaves, lumbered down the path, and tears slowly tracked Judith's cheeks. So much she had not said to Papa; so much she had done to hurt him.

Laura sat in the parlor in the platform rocker and stared at Dr. Renaud. Her hair hung in wisps around her face; her dress was stained with perspiration and Clay's blood where she had helped the doctor clean his wound. She had not bothered to change clothes.

"You saw the duel?" she asked.

"No, ma'am," he murmured.

Laura looked at him curiously. "But I don't understand. You rode in with them. Were you not their physician?"

"I rode in with them but was not their physician," he answered. "I happened to be returning from a

371

house call when I heard the shooting. By the time I arrived, the duel was over."

"Clay shot my father."

Dr. Renaud uncrossed his legs, then crossed them again. "I am unsure what happened, Miss Talbot. Only M'sieur Dufaure can tell us that now. I heard a lot of shooting, but by the time I arrived, the four men were lying on the ground. I thought all of them were dead."

"Two are, M'sieur Renaud, and two are wounded. If someone had been a better shot, Clay would have also been dead." Laura rose and walked to the window to stare down the oak-lined road. "My father is dead, and the man I was going to marry is critically wounded. How do you think it feels to know that my fiancé killed my father?"

Before the physician could answer, a young black woman entered the room. "M'sieur Dufaure sends word that he must return to town, Maîtresse Laura."

Laura nodded. "Ask him to wait awhile. I'd like to talk with him before he leaves."

Dr. Renaud stood. "I'll be going, mam'selle. Shall I take the other body back to town and see to its burial?"

"Yes," Laura agreed quietly, "please."

Dr. Renaud clamped his hat on his head and walked to the door, where he met Dufaure. The two men paused and looked at each other, neither speaking. Dr. Renaud brushed past. Dufaure walked to the settee.

"I'm sorry I interrupted your conversation with the physician, Laura, but I really must get home." His hand went to his bandaged forehead. "I'm not feeling so well."

"Thank you for staying, m'sieur. I wanted to talk to you about the duel . . . and Papa." She sat down.

"You were with Papa before he—before he died. I wanted to know what he—" She pulled a handkerchief from her pocket and pressed it against her face. After a few minutes she said, "What did he say to you, M'sieur Dufaure?"

"You are wondering if perhaps he was still angry with you?" Maurice asked softly. Laura nodded and tears slid down her cheeks. "No, he was angry at himself, *ma chère*. He believed he had let his family down."

"Oh, m'sieur, if only I could undo the past." Laura's shoulders began to shake as she wept. Disregarding his pain and weakness from loss of blood, Maurice rose and hurried to the table across the room and poured brandy into a glass. When he returned, he pressed it into Laura's hands. "Drink this," he ordered briskly. "You'll feel better."

With no thought of disobeying, Laura gulped down the liquor, gasping and coughing as liquid fire burned its way to her stomach. "Clay promised he wouldn't kill Papa," she whispered. "He promised me."

Maurice sat on the edge of the settee and took Laura's hands into his. Looking into her dark, swollen eyes, he said, "Your papa told me that you love Sutherland and want to marry him."

Laura nodded.

"I believe you. You're that kind of woman, Laura, but you have been unwise in choosing the man to whom you gave your love. Clay Sutherland is interested only in Ombres Azurées. He'll get the plantation any way he can, Laura."

"No." She shook her head wildly, the wisps of hair brushing against her cheeks. "No, m'sieur, you're wrong. Clay loves me, not Ombres Azurées."

"I wish I were wrong, Laura, but I am not. What I

373

am going to tell you will hurt, *ma petite*, but it is for your own good." He captured her hands in his, but Laura quickly withdrew them. "Your papa was quite sober when he awakened this morning, and he was willing to call off the duel. We did not take a physician because we felt there would be no need for one. When we arrived, Beau told Sutherland that he had reconsidered the matter. He would not duel with the man his daughter loved and wanted to marry." Maurice paused to let Laura ponder the words. "But, Laura, he also told Sutherland that if the two of you married, he would not let you have Ombres Azurées."

"No, M'sieur Dufaure," Laura whispered, not wanting to hear the rest of the story.

"Yes, Laura, then Sutherland goaded your father into the duel. It mattered not to him that we had no physician. Clay shot Beau first, but your papa did not die so quickly. He shot and wounded Sutherland. The man who came with Sutherland was like a wild man after Clay was wounded. He aimed his pistols and shot. I had no choice but to kill him. By the time I reached your papa, he was dead."

"I cannot believe Clay would do that," Laura said.

"Believe me, Laura. He did." Then Maurice went on. "Your papa told Sutherland he was resolved that the two of you were getting married, and he would not stop the wedding. But he promised Clay that you would be disinherited. If you married Clay Sutherland, you would not get Ombres Azurées. And now your papa is dead, and Sutherland is alive. According to Beau's will, Ombres Azurées is yours now, Laura."

"No," Laura whispered, "that cannot be true. I know Clay. He would not kill for property."

"Perhaps not, my dear. Perhaps not. You know the man and his motives much better than I. But, please, *ma petite*, be careful." He smiled. "Now that Beau is

374

gone, Laura, I will be here for you . . . and Judith."

"Thank you, m'sieur."

Maurice rose. His hands twined together behind him, he said, "We must report this to the police, Laura."

"No!" Laura cried. "It was a duel, m'sieur. Papa challenged Clay."

"But your papa also called the duel off, and Sutherland killed him. That, *chère* Laura, is murder."

"Would it have been murder, m'sieur, if Papa had killed Clay?"

"I must leave," Maurice announced. "You my dear, are much too distraught to listen to reason. I'll be back to check on you tomorrow."

After Maurice left, Laura walked up the stairs and sat beside Clay's bed. He was still unconscious—from the blow to the head, Dr. Renaud had said. Clay's beard stubble was a dark contrast to his pale face. His breathing was ragged, his lungs congested. The bandage across his chest was already soaked with blood. While he was seriously hurt, he was not critically ill. He was fortunate that the bullet had gone clear through him. If she could keep his fever down and the wound from getting infected—and she could—he would recover quickly.

Night fell, and a lone candle flickered on the night table. Laura kept vigil. She sat looking at Clay, watching the shadows that played across his face. He had killed her father; still, she loved him. Maurice was a witness, and Dr. Renaud had appeared on the scene shortly afterward. Yet Laura could not bring herself to believe Clay killed her father for Ombres Azurées.

She would never have fallen in love with such a man. There was no doubt in her mind, she loved Clay

Sutherland. But the man she loved had killed her father. She reached up to touch the ring that hung on the velvet ribbon around her neck. Still, she would reserve final judgment until she heard Clay's side of the story. She owed him that.

Laura had accepted and lived by society's rules all her life. Now she had completely broken free of them. The duel, the highest form of integrity for the Creole gentry, had served to break the last tie. Both Clay Sutherland and her father had proved their honor. One was dead; the other might die, but their honor was intact. Little good it was doing either of them.

The door opened and Judith slipped into the room. She walked to the bed and looked down at Clay. "How is he?"

"He'll live if the fever stays down. Tonight and tomorrow will be the crucial period. How is Celeste?"

"Better. Berthe gave her a small dose of laudanum and is with her now. I'm—" Her voice broke. "I'm making the arrangements for the funeral."

Again the door opened, and one of the servants entered, a large basket over her arm. Quietly, she moved about the room, draping the windows, portraits, and mirrors in black. Ombres Azurées was in mourning.

Interlude IV

After the reading of Beau Talbot's will, Celeste once again took to her bed. Judith and Laura remained in the private sitting room. It was draped in mourning. Swags of black material hung over the windows; family portraits and mirrors were covered with black cheesecloth. Judith stood beside the window. Laura sat with her hands in her lap.

Lost in their own thoughts, neither was aware of the maid who entered the room to place a tray on the low table in front of Laura. She glanced at both of the women and sniffed. Her eyes were swollen and tear-stained. As she left the room, she hid her face in her apron.

Judith played with one of the swags. "I can't take all of this in. It's too much. Papa dead."

And Clay wounded. He lay in the upstairs bedroom.

Needing something to do with her hands and not wanting to think, Laura lifted the porcelain pot. "Will you have cream and sugar?"

Judith whirled around. "For God's sake, Laura. I don't want anything to drink. I don't want anything to eat."

Laura poured the thick chicory coffee into the delicate cups. The flesh around her eyes was bruised and swollen, her voice soft. "You might not want to, but we have to. We have to keep our strength. Remember, Papa's no longer here, so we have to do everything for ourselves."

Laura set down the pot on the tray and clasped her hands in her lap. Her gaze caught and locked with Judith's. In silence they stared at each other. Then Laura lost control and buried her face in her hands. "I don't think I can live with myself. I was the one who caused his death."

Judith threw up her hands. "No one causes another person's death, Laura, unless he actually murders him."

The black veil wisped around Laura's pale face, accenting the hollow green eyes. "Papa would never have challenged Clay if I hadn't been such a fool."

"That's silly, Laura." Judith prowled the room. "When two men decide to fight a duel, there are other things involved besides the obvious. I'm sure that you weren't the only thing."

Once again having regained her composure, Laura returned to her task. But when she spooned the sugar from the bowl, her hand began to shake. Grains of sugar spilled across the surface of the shiny tray. Laura dropped the spoon with a clatter. "I . . . can't do anything right. I can't even pour myself a cup of coffee."

Judith set down the figurine she was looking at and moved to Laura's side. She put her hand on her sister's shoulder. "Laura, you've always been able to do what was necessary. Remember, we took care of both our parents."

"But I might as well have shot him myself."

Judith's hand closed tighter and she gently rocked

378

her. "But you didn't, Laura. You've got to stop these thoughts. You of all people. After you've preached and preached: don't be sorry for yourself."

"I'm not. Can't you understand? I'll never be able to put the sight of his wounded body out of my mind. He was so still. I'd never seen him still. He was always so vital, so alive. His eyes were so blue. When Joshua brought him in, his eyes were closed. Oh, Judith, I'd never seen Papa asleep."

Tears trickled down Judith's cheeks. She pressed her thumb and third finger against the bridge of her nose. When she could speak, she said, "Stop that, Laura. Stop tearing yourself to pieces."

But the painful memories could not be contained. "They were just as blue as yours. I did it, Judith. *My* infatuation, *my* lack of judgment, *my* lack of control ended his life! Oh, God, if I could only do it over again."

Judith dropped down on the settee and pulled Laura into her arms. With trembling hands she patted and stroked the back of Laura's head while her sister cried against her shoulder. "Laura, be quiet. Don't think about it."

Judith held Laura until her crying was spent. Finally, Laura pushed away and reached into her pocket for a handkerchief to wipe her eyes. Judith stood up, pulling her own handkerchief from her sleeve. She walked across the room and jerked the black veiling from the mirror. She dabbed at her cheeks and tucked stray wisps of hair into her chignon. Dropping the veil over the mirror, she turned.

"Now, Laura, you're going to have to go on because all the people on Ombres Azurées depend on you. Just as Talbot Shipping depends on me to step in for Papa. You didn't kill him, but we mustn't let

379

all he worked for during his life slip away."

Laura pulled a fresh handkerchief from her pocket. "You're right, of course. That's why he left England. To build in the new world and make a success. We're fortunate that he let us take care of some of his things."

"Do you really think so?" Judith snapped bruskly. "I think Papa has put both of us in awkward, unpleasant situations."

"Judith!"

Judith nodded her head. "Well, he did. He left the fields and the mill to you, but you don't have a house to live in unless you stay in Celeste's good graces. He left the house and the land fronting the bayou to her. He wanted to make sure she was taken care of."

"Yes, but I don't mind. After all, Ombres Azurées was hers to begin with."

"Laura, you and I both know that Celeste would have lost all of this if not for Beau."

"He was such a good man." Now that Clay was on his way to full recovery, Laura could afford to be gracious to her father. She felt entirely to blame for Beau's death.

"You're missing the point."

Judith's criticism of Papa and Celeste jarred Laura out of her grief. Her lips compressed in disapproval. "You don't have anything to complain about. Papa left you his controlling interest in Talbot Shipping."

"With Maurice Dufaure to fight with me at every turn," Judith said dryly.

Laura remembered Maurice's kindness to them since Beau's death. "You should be glad of Maurice's guidance. He's had experience in business."

"He hates me!" Judith exclaimed adamantly.

"I find that difficult to believe. Maurice has always been one of our closest friends."

"Maybe yours, but not mine."

Laura picked up her cup of coffee and tasted. She wrinkled her face and set the cup down immediately. "This coffee is cold. I must ring for another pot."

Judith turned and walked to the window. She pulled aside the swag and drew the drapes. The day was cold and gray with very little sun. After she stared out for a while, she let the drapery fall back into place. Now grief and regret was settling around her.

"He should never have brought me here from England. I made so much misery for him these last few months."

"No, you didn't."

Judith nodded her head. "I embarrassed him in front of all his friends."

Laura wadded the handkerchief in her hands. "Maybe a little, but, Judith, having you here made him feel good about himself."

The maid quietly entered the room, and Laura ordered another pot of coffee.

Still at the window, Judith said, "I said horrible things to him. I always told him that I wanted to go back to England and I do, except . . . I just don't know."

Laura smiled in spite of her grief. "Well, I do." She filled the two demitasse cups with coffee, then rose and walked to a highboy across the room. She returned with a decanter of Beau's favorite whiskey. "I'll tell you what we're going to do."

She poured a thimbleful of whiskey into each of the cups and handed one to Judith, which she accepted reluctantly. They saluted each other.

Laura smiled. "To the Talbot sisters."

As long as they had each other, they were not alone.

Chapter Sixteen

Her hands twined together in her lap, Laura sat across from Maurice Dufaure in the black-draped parlor at Ombres Azurées. She was exhausted; mauve semicircles beneath her eyes stood out darkly against her pale face.

"No, m'sieur," she said, "he hasn't regained consciousness yet."

A gleam of satisfaction in his eyes, Maurice lowered his head and picked a piece of lint from his waistcoat. "I know it's been only a week since you buried your father, Laura. And I did hate to bother you, but the police were insistent. They want Sutherland to give them a full written report about the duel."

"I asked you not to go to the police, m'sieur." She spoke quietly, but she was angry and confused. She loved Clay, loved him with all her heart, and wanted him to live. And although she knew that with her father's death between them she and Clay had no future together, she did not want him charged with murder.

"I considered your request, Laura," Maurice replied, "but when your *maman* asked me to do otherwise, I could not refuse her."

Of course, Laura conceded silently, she was thinking only of herself. She sighed and bit back her tears. "It's all for nothing, m'sieur. Nothing will bring Papa back to us."

Maurice's expression darkened. "You cannot let your *maman* down. Her health is delicate, Laura, even more so since Beau died. Always you must remember, Laura, Sutherland killed your papa. You can never forget that. We are the ones who lived and must see that justice is done."

"You do not have to worry on my account," she said quietly. "I can never forget, m'sieur, no matter how much I wish I could. But I do not see how justice will be served for Clay to be convicted of murder. At the moment in the throes of her grief, *Maman* may think she wants that, but deep down she does not. She's not a vindictive woman."

Dufaure leaned forward, caught one of Laura's hands in his, and patted it most paternally. "I know all this distresses you, my dear, and I'm sorry. I am doing everything in my power to help you. Despite the anguish you are suffering, you must not let your emotions cloud your better judgment."

Laura withdrew her hands from Maurice. While she was grateful for his kindness since her father's death, she did not like his touching her. Even less she liked his open hostility to Clay. "Judgment seems so final, m'sieur, and so condemning. In the past few days we seem to have venerated my father— the person who instigated the duel in the first place— and have relegated Clay to a murderer. Now you seem determined that he will die also. Is not the death of one loved one enough?"

An invisible shield lowered over Dufaure's eyes. His expression guarded, he said, "I'm not overly fond of the Americans, Laura, but I'm a law-abiding citizen. Had your father's death been the result of an honorable duel, I would have let the matter stand. Beau Talbot was more than my partner. He was my friend. I will not allow his murderer to go free."

Like a bell out of control, Maurice's words rang through Laura's mind, each one louder than the other. She had begun to despise the word *honor* and all its hollow nuances.

After a while she said, "Either way, m'sieur, Beau Talbot's murderer will not go free. Every day of his life Clay Sutherland will be haunted by the ghost of Beau Talbot."

"*Mon Dieu*, Laura! You talk about venerating Beau; yet you sound as if you have venerated Clay Sutherland."

"No, m'sieur, I haven't. He's a man, and I love him. I also know how he thinks. He may have killed my father, but he is not without a conscience."

Maurice stood and went to the window, where he gazed at the front lawn. "I trust the plantation is doing all right, Laura?"

"We feel the effects of the war," Laura answered, "but if we're frugal, we can make it."

"I do not wish to be presumptuous," Maurice said, "but being your father's partner, I cannot help but know you're in a financial strait."

Laura rose, the lines of her black gown simple and elegant. The material rustled gently as she walked to the fireplace to straighten some small marble figurines on the mantel. Quite coolly she said, "Judith and I shall handle our own affairs, M'sieur Dufaure, and would appreciate your discretion in repeating such information to others."

Maurice wheeled around in mock remorse. "I am a friend of the family, Laura. I never meant to anger or

385

embarrass you. I only want you to know that I'm willing to buy out your interest in the shipping lines. This will provide you with the cash you need for the plantation."

Laura smiled bitterly. "And Roussel is our friend also, M'sieur Dufaure. Like you, he, too, is concerned about my finances. His solution is for us to marry and consolidate our plantations."

"Roussel and I mean you no harm. Please forgive us, my child. We merely wish to help the daughters of our dear friend." He shrugged and smiled. "You must overlook Roussel's eagerness for marriage, *ma chère*. He really does love and want to marry you."

Laura's face was guarded, as was her answer. "Perhaps."

"You must speak to Judith, Laura," Maurice insisted. "She will not listen to me. Persuade her that it is best for both of you if she sells her interest in the Talbot Shipping Line to me."

Remembering Judith's and her discussion at the cottage on that day so long ago, Laura said, "I'll tell Judith about it, m'sieur, but I can't promise that she'll even consider it. Papa would want us to carry on the Talbot name."

Laura thought about the wounded man lying in an upstairs room—the man she had intended to marry.

"Our name seems to be all we have left now."

After Maurice left, Laura walked up the stairs and into the bedroom across from hers. The drapes were opened and morning sunshine warmed the room. She neared the bed and looked at the man who lay there.

A two-day beard growth covered his lower face; his eyes were sunken and dark. His breathing was raspy and had been since he had been brought to the house.

When she had first seen him in the wagon, she had despaired of his living. But once again Clay Sutherland had proved himself a strong man with an equally strong will to live.

The door opened and Judith, also dressed in black, walked into the room, a tray in her hands. "How is he today?"

Laura tucked the sheet beneath his chin. "Better. And Celeste?"

Judith set the tray on the round reading table. "About the same. Berthe refuses to leave her. How about something cool to drink?"

"I would like that."

Judith seated herself in the chair next to the table and poured two glasses of lemonade.

"In such a short time," Laura said, "we have buried both our parents, and now it is only us, Judith. You and me."

Laura continued to stare at Clay. The day before yesterday her future had seemed so bright and beautiful. It was difficult for her to believe that one day—one incident—could bring so much change into her life.

"Yes," Judith answered, "it is left up to you and me to carry on Papa's name."

"That is what I told M'sieur Dufaure only minutes ago." Laura sat down and picked up her glass of lemonade.

Judith grimaced. "I don't like that man, Laura. I wish he wouldn't push himself on you. What did he want today?"

Laura gratefully drank her lemonade. When she returned the glass to the tray, she said, "He wanted me to persuade you to sell your interest in Talbot Shipping so I could save the plantation."

"He what!" Judith bounded to her feet and paced

the room.

"And for the same reason Roussel has asked me to marry him."

Judith's laugh was unpleasant. "The vultures are already swooping on the Talbot sisters."

"Yes," Laura murmured. How ironic that Judith would use such a metaphor to describe Maurice and Roussel. Laura vividly recalled the nightmare she had on the night her mother died.

Long after Judith had gone, Laura sat in the chair next to Clay's bed. She was grateful that he was alive, and she accepted his reasons for having killed her father. She no longer agreed with them herself, but she accepted that others did. Whether people wanted to or not, they could so easily become victims of society and its rules to the extent of losing their own indentity, to the extent of sacrificing their own principles. She had. Clay had.

Although Beau issued the challenge, although this was a point of honor for both men, Laura could not marry Clay now. Every time she looked at him she remembered that he had killed her father.

Clay moaned and turned, the covers slipping down to reveal his shoulders and chest. He threw a hand across the adjacent pillow—the hand on which he wore his ring. Laura automatically reached up, her fingers curling around the phoenix that once again hung around her neck. She had returned Clay's ring to his little finger. When he came to and saw it, he would understand.

Clay tried to sit up, but pain shot through his chest. He groaned and fell back against the pillows. The drapes were drawn, but the window was closed. He heard someone moving about the room and

388

turned his head. In the shadows he saw a skirt. Laura. His gaze lifted. The woman was tall and slender . . . too tall, too slender for Laura. Soon she stood beside the bed, looking down at him.

"I'm glad to see that you're awake."

His dark eyes studied her. He licked his dry lips and nodded his head. "Who are you?"

"Judith Talbot-Harrow, Laura's sister." She wrung out the washcloth and pressed it gently against Clay's mouth to dampen it.

"Where am I?"

"Ombres Azurées."

Against the pain he pushed up in bed, only then remembering his duel with Beau. "Where's Laura?"

"She's in her room resting."

"I want to talk to her."

"She doesn't wish to talk to you."

"Beau—" Clay's head was spinning. But suddenly a memory flashed through his mind. He was standing in the clearing at the Bayou d'Ombre. His eyes hurt; he was blinded by the sun. But he could remember no more. The memory was gone as quickly as it came. Angrily, he searched for it, but the harder he tried, the more it eluded his grasp. "What happened to Beau?"

Judith crossed her arms over her chest. She tried to keep emotion from her voice. "He's dead."

"Dead." Clay could not believe Beau was dead. His hand went to this throbbing head. As if the duel were occurring all over again, he heard the shot and felt the excruciating burning in his chest. More shots followed. He remembered squeezing the trigger. Yes, he pulled the trigger. Then Beau fell. Jones . . . what happened to Jones?

Frantically striving to recall the events of that day, Clay did not hear the door open. Still, the details of

389

the duel danced through his mind, taunting him but never coming close enough for total recall. "I didn't—I didn't kill him, did I?"

"Yes," Laura answered from the doorway. Judith spun around. Tears trickled down her sister's cheeks. "You killed him, Clay. You killed Papa."

Haunted brown eyes turned to Laura. "No. I swear I didn't kill your father. You must believe me."

"I wish I could believe you," she said, "but M'sieur Dufaure was a witness, Clay. He saw you kill Papa. Even Dr. Renaud testified that your pistol had been discharged."

He reached for her, but she did not move. His hand dropped to the bed. "Laura, things are fuzzy in my mind, but I would not have killed your father. I know myself well enough to know that."

"Nonetheless, Papa is dead, and the man who was your second is dead also." Laura tugged the bellpull. When the servant appeared at the door, she said, "Have someone bring me some clean water and linens." Then she turned to Clay. "I'll be back shortly to give you a bath and change your bed."

Laura walked out of the room into the hall, followed by Judith, who asked, "Are you going to call the magistrate?"

"No." Laura was too near tears to meet her sister's gaze. Although she had not recognized it, she had loved Clay from the first moment she saw him. Then her own foolishness and shallow values of society had stood in her way of admitting her feelings for him. Once she had removed those obstacles and had admitted her love for him, she discovered that she still could not have him. Forever the death of her father stood between them.

Judith laid a hand on Laura's shoulder and squeezed. "I understand how you must feel, Laura."

390

"Thank you," Laura murmured.

"Let me take care of him for you."

"I want to do it."

"All right," Judith said. "I'll check on Celeste."

Judith turned and moved toward her stepmother's room. Laura continued down the hall into her father's room, where she rummaged through his wardrobe for clean clothes for Clay. A shirt and pair of breeches in hand, she returned to the guest bedroom.

While Laura was gone, a maid delivered the water and linens to the room, but Clay paid her no attention. His brain was foggy, and he hurt—hurt too badly to think. Laura thought he had killed Beau. And his gun had been discharged. He remembered shooting. Yes, he shot his pistol . . . at Beau? Surely not. He closed his eyes and lay there; he delved through his mind for the elusive memories. They evaded him.

He heard Laura enter the room and opened his eyes. She filled the basin with water and doused a washcloth in it. When she wrung it out, she washed his face. He looked in added anguish at the haggard face and eyes that were bruised and swollen from crying. He grabbed her wrist but discovered he was too weak to stop her, too weak to argue with her. Laura stopped her movements and stared down at him, saying nothing. Sighing, he dropped his arm and closed his eyes. At the moment he could do nothing but regain his strength and remember. He lay quietly as she gave him a bath and shaved him.

"Laura," he was finally compelled to say as he racked his mind for a clearer picture of events, "I remember your father shooting me. The bullet tore into my chest. And as I fell, I pulled the trigger. Beau fell, but I—" He broke off and shook his head as if

391

that would make the memories fall into place. "I didn't kill him, Laura!" He caught her wrist this time and pulled her down on the bed beside him. "You must believe me. Your father shot me, but I didn't kill him."

"Perhaps you did not mean to." She smiled sadly. "Do not worry about it, Clay. Dr. Renaud said your memory would be fuzzy until your head wound healed. Let's give you some time."

"How did you know M'sieur Sutherland had regained consciousness?" Laura demanded, her gaze swinging from Maurice Dufaure to the portly policeman standing at his side.

"I told them," Celeste answered from behind Laura. "Judith was kind enough to let me know; she also told me that you did not intend to inform the police, so I took matters into my hands."

Laura spun around to see her stepmother walking down the stairs, one hand on the railing, the other clinging to Berthe's arm. Celeste's dark brown eyes were hollow circles in her pale face. They pooled with fresh tears.

"How could you, Laura? That man killed your papa."

"*Maman—*" Laura's heart went out to her step-mother. Every day she seemed to be more fragile. "Please don't upset yourself like this."

"I want that man punished for what he has done to us." Celeste began to sob hysterically, and Laura ran to her. "I want him to suffer as we are suffering."

Laura rang for Saloman and motioned Berthe to guide Celeste back to her bedroom. When the servant appeared in the door, Laura was at the bottom landing. "Take these gentlemen to M'sieur Sutherland's room while I see *Maman* back to bed."

"Oui, Maîtresse."

By the time Laura joined the men in the guest bedroom, Clay was sitting up in bed, wearing one of Beau's shirts and leaning back against fluffed pillows. The officer sat next to the bed, a small table in front of him.

"Now, M'sieur Sutherland—" The man dipped the quill into the small inkwell. "Tell me exactly what happened."

Clay glanced at Dufaure, who stood in front of the window in the afternoon sunlight. While he appeared to be indifferent, Clay recognized the man's interest. Maurice was controlled, every movement, every pose carefully thought out and executed. Intuitively, Clay knew to be cautious. He knew, for some reason, he was being tested and that his answer was of prime importance—perhaps a matter of life or death.

"All I remember is Beau's shooting me. The rest of the duel seems to be unclear." He lifted his hand and gingerly touched the back of his head where he had fallen against the tree stump. He shook his head and furrowed his brow. "Perhaps M'sieur Dufaure can shed some light on the subject. He was Beau Talbot's second."

"M'sieur Dufaure has already given us a statement," the magistrate said. "He claims that M'sieur Talbot awakened sober the next morning and regretted his decision of the evening before. Yet you forced M'sieur Talbot to duel, Mr. Sutherland. This is a serious matter."

Clay knew that was an outright lie, and he opened his mouth to protest. Then he looked from Dufaure to Laura. His sixth sense told him to remain silent. Again he hedged rather than point an accusing finger at Dufaure. "I—I can't believe I would do that, sir, but then, I can't remember what happened at all. Where's Jones? Did you get a statement from him?"

"Jones?" the magistrate asked. "I presume he was your second?"

"*Was* my second?"

"Yes, m'sieur," Maurice exclaimed. "When Jones thought both you and Beau were dead, he turned on me. Lucky for me that he was such a poor shoot. Otherwise I would have more than a head wound. I had to shoot him in self-defense."

Clay stared at the Frenchman. He sighed and reached up to rub his aching shoulder. He could not understand why Dufaure was lying, but lying he was. "Sir," he said to the magistrate, "at present I must accept Mr. Dufaure's statement as being true. I cannot remember; therefore, I can add nothing."

Observing the pinched look around Clay's mouth, Laura moved between the magistrate and the bed. "I think this is enough questioning today, gentlemen. M'sieur Sutherland is weak and needs to rest."

The officer folded the paper and inserted it into his jacket pocket. "M'sieur Sutherland, you are under arrest. As soon as you are able to travel, you will be removed to jail."

"On what charges?" Clay asked.

"Murder."

"No, m'sieur," Laura quietly said. "M'sieur Sutherland will not be charged with murder. I know for a fact that my father called him out."

"*Mon Dieu!*" Maurice exclaimed. "Have you no love or loyalty to your *maman?*"

Laura loved her stepmother, but no matter that Clay might have killed her father, she loved him too. She would protect him. She would not permit him to be charged with murder.

"M'sieur," she addressed the magistrate, "I am asking you to close the case. Please record it as a duel of honor. Surely you have more important cases to take your time?"

He looked from Laura to Dufaure and then back to Laura. "Please," she begged.

"*Oui*, mam'selle," he eventually said, "if that is the way you wish it to be. We have plenty of crimes to which we can turn our attention."

"This is my desire, m'sieur."

Maurice was scowling when he left Ombres Azurées.

Clad in a black wrapper, Celeste sat on the settee in the parlor, still draped with mourning. Her beautiful face was drawn, her eyes bruised and swollen from crying. She clutched a wadded handkerchief in her hands. "I never intended for it to be so," she whispered, and dabbed her hand against her eyes.

The months had dragged by, April gradually turning into August. She had needed something to do, to occupy her mind and to relieve her grief over Beau's death. She had not meant to start her gambling again. But M'sieur Lambert had been such a dear friend. When Laura was busy with the managing of the plantation and Judith with the shipping line, he was the one who had visited with Celeste, who had talked to her, who had listened. He had taken her into town and entertained her.

"It does not take debts long to mount when one is losing, madame." The bill collector sat in shadows, his features obscured by the darkness.

"I know," Celeste whispered.

This had happened before and Beau had been her savior. Now she had none. Beau was gone . . . gone forever . . . killed by Clay Sutherland. M'sieur Lambert had offered to advance her the money. Perhaps she should have taken it. But, no, she was not that kind of woman. She had kept thinking she would eventually win; her luck had to change.

"When one gambles, one must be prepared for the consequences be they good or bad."

"*Oui.*" She lifted the handkerchief and delicately touched the tip of her nose. Her voice broke, and she sniffed. "Please excuse the tears, m'sieur, I'm—I'm not over my husband's death."

"My condolences, madame." Anton Quigly rose. "But you must have the money to me no later than Monday. I cannot extend your payment date anymore. Ordinarily, I would be content to take the land and sell it, madame, but I am in such straits that I don't want or need property. I need money. Therefore, I shall put your markers on the market to the highest bidder."

"Would you consider letting me pay these over a period of time?"

"Since I've extended the date for your repayment, I can't afford to do that, ma'am. I want the amount in full."

"I—understand." Celeste pressed the handkerchief against her face.

Saloman showed the bill collector out, and Celeste continued to sit in the darkened parlor. Eventually, Berthe entered with a tray which she set on the low table in front of the settee. Picking up the pot, she poured the tea.

"I brought you something hot to drink, Maîtresse."

"*Merci,*" Celeste answered dully. She took the cup and swallowed but never tasted the tea. She knew her options were limited. Laura and Judith did not have

396

the money to give to her. If Laura were to marry Roussel . . . but she could not count on that. Laura was quite adamant in her refusal to consider his proposal. Her only alternative was Edouard Lambert. She sighed. She would go to him. She was not aware of anyone's entering the room or sitting down until she heard Roussel speak.

"Madame Talbot."

Celeste blinked and turned her head, peering through the shadows at the bulging figure in the chair. "Roussel, is that you?"

"*Oui.* I stopped by to see Laura, but I'm told she's at the quarters tending to the workers."

"*Oui,*" Celeste murmured, a bitter taint to her voice. "She's always doing something about the plantation. Her whole life is Ombres Azurées. She does not even have time for her *maman* now that her papa is dead." She succumbed to a new bout of crying. Her shoulders sagged, and she shook uncontrollably.

Roussel rose and went to her. He caught her in his arms and pressed her face to his chest. "What is wrong, madame?"

"Oh, Roussel," she wailed against the immaculate white shirt, "I've made such a fool of myself. I have gambled and lost and have no money with which to pay my markers. M'sieur Quigly was here but a moment ago. I have until Monday to bring him the money. If I don't, he's going to auction them." She held her tear-stained face away from him. "Whatever am I going to do?"

Roussel pressed her face against his chest again. Over her head he smiled and patted her back. "Do not worry about it, madame."

"But I do. We haven't the money, Roussel. M'sieur Lambert wanted to lend me the money, but I insisted

397

on signing the markers. What a fool I am!''

Roussel's eyes narrowed. "I'm glad you did not let a stranger advance you money, madame. And you are not a fool. Roussel Giraumont shall take care of everything for you.''

"You will lend me the money?''

Roussel hid his smile. "How much do you owe?''

When Celeste told him, Roussel's smile dimmed, but his eyes gleamed speculatively. "Better than that, madame, I am going to propose to Laura again. If she accepts, I shall give you the money to redeem your gambling debts.''

Celeste pushed away and sat up. Her face brightened visibly. "And Laura would need never know about my foolishness.''

Giraumont nodded. "She need never know. Give me a list of your creditors and the amounts you owe.''

For the first time since Anton Quigly's arrival, Celeste smiled; then she frowned. "What if Laura should decide not to marry you?''

Roussel smiled and his eyes gleamed. "She will not refuse, madame. But if it should happen, you will owe me. No one but you and I shall know of them. It will be our secret.''

Again Celeste smiled and walked to the bellpull and rang. "And I can repay you each month when I receive the allowance Beau provided me with.''

"Of course,'' he assured her.

"You do not know how happy you have made me. I shall send the list to you as I have it written out. Would you join me in a cup of tea?''

"I should be delighted, madame. Perhaps we can plan some of the details of the wedding.''

Clay peered through the narrow window in

Reynolds's office but observed no movement outside. Unconsciously, he reached up to massage his arm. Even after four months his shoulder hurt.

"You are fortunate indeed, my friend, that Dr. Renaud happened to be passing by."

Clay grinned. "Indeed I am. I'm just surprised that you showed up. I didn't expect you to."

"I didn't intend to, but the duel had me worried. It still does." Then, as if he had never rehearsed the sequences of events before, he said, "I followed you and Jones and was watching from a place of concealment. By the time I realized you were in crossfire, there was nothing I could do. The three of you were on the ground and dead for all I knew. My only alternative was to appear on the scene."

"Are you a doctor as well as a spy?"

Reynolds grinned. "My profession has trained me in many professions."

"I'm glad you're not only trained but proficient in them," Clay said. "Otherwise I would be dead too."

"Yes, you would." Reynolds rubbed his chin. "Later I returned to the scene of the duel and found signs that confirmed two men had been hiding on either side of the clearing. Someone set you and Beau up. Now the question is who."

"I haven't figured out why anyone would want either Beau or me dead badly enough to resort to two murders. I keep wondering what Beau knew that was so dangerous or what he was involved in."

Reynolds shrugged. "I can't answer. I'm not as fully informed on the French conspiracy as Graham was, and word hasn't yet reached me from Washington."

"I'm suspicious of this Edouard Lambert," Clay said. "Do you know anything about him?"

"I have a courier leaving for Washington tonight.

I'll ask him to check," Reynolds said. He picked up a sheet of paper and handed it to Clay. "Here. I thought you'd be interested in this report."

While Clay's eyes ran down the line of figures, Reynolds pulled his handkerchief from his pocket and wiped the lenses of his glasses. "Celeste Talbot's markers."

"Where did you get this?" Clay demanded.

"A contact brought them to me. He thought I would be interested in knowing that she owes money to nearly all the gambling casinos in New Orleans."

"Why you?"

"We have all the Talbots under surveillance."

Clay unconsciously wadded the paper. "Do you suspect all of them?"

"No, just one. Celeste. She and Lambert are being seen quite frequently around town." Reynolds laid his glasses on the table and stuffed the handkerchief into his pocket. Clay laid the paper on the desk. Reynolds looked up. "You can have it. I think the information will serve you better than me. I understand Lambert offered to lend Celeste the money for her gambling, but she refused. He also heads the list of those who would like to buy them when they're put on the market. Rumor also says Roussel Giraumont is trying to get a loan in order to buy up the markers."

"Why would he be getting a loan?"

"He invested heavily abroad, and his investments have been unwise. I understand he has a little capital on hand, but he's in financial trouble."

Now Clay knew why Giraumont was so insistent on marrying Laura. Her plantation would be sacrificed for his. Clay also figured that Giraumont would use Celeste's markers for no good. He did not trust the man . . . certainly not where Laura was concerned. Clay was also puzzled by Lambert's behavior. Lending Celeste money for her gambling far exceeded the bounds of friendship.

To protect Laura, Clay could take only one course of action. He folded the sheet of paper and inserted it in his coat pocket. "You can't really suspect Celeste Talbot?"

"As I said before, I'm not really working on the French conspiracy, but between you and—someone else—I have been drawn into this. The woman is suspicious. Consider: she's Creole aristocracy. The Devranche family was one of the founding families of New Orleans. The amount she owes is frightening. Think what could happen should the markers fall into the wrong hands. Perhaps unwillingly she would become a pawn in this game."

"Thanks for the information."

Reynolds shrugged. "Have you told Laura the real story about the duel? If you haven't, I would rather you didn't. It could hinder our investigation."

Clay sighed and shook his head. "No, at first I was tempted to tell her. But it sounded too preposterous even to my own ears. Beau doesn't have the kind of enemies who would kill him and his opponent in the middle of a duel. He's not the kind of man who would behave as he did at the duel. Despite what Maurice says, Beau was determined to have the duel even when the doctor did not show. Later, after I started thinking about it, I realized we had been set up. Someone carefully planned the murder of one of us."

"Or both of you?"

Clay nodded. "I've thought about that. So I decided my silence was my guarantee of life."

"Any idea who would want you dead?"

"Plenty, but they wouldn't go to such lengths."

A bell tinkled at the front of the shop, announcing the arrival of a customer. Reynolds picked up his spectacles and slipped them on his face. At the door he said, "I'll get word to you about Lambert as soon as I hear."

Clay slipped out the back door, careful that no one saw him leave. Almost unconsciously, his feet carried him to Front Street to the Talbot line building. Since the duel he frequently walked in that direction, and if he were not there one of his men was. He was obsessed with the idea that Dufaure was involved with Beau's death.

At first he had thought Dufaure was involved with the Bonapartists, but he had no evidence to substantiate such a belief. The man seemed to be wholly consumed with Talbot Shipping Line, as did Laura's sister. Clay figured that sooner or later Dufaure and the headstrong woman would come to blows.

A carriage rumbled past Clay. Dodging out of sight, he pressed closer to the building. Roussel Giraumont disembarked, looked around quickly, then darted into the building. Clay edged closer to the office until he stood beside an open window and listened to the conversation going on inside.

"Soon I'll have the leverage I need, and Laura Talbot will be my wife. I will own Ombres Azurées—all of it. The bank will let me know about the loan at the end of the week. They do seem disposed to lend me the money, since I have proof that Celeste is planning a wedding between Laura and me." Giraumont's voice drifted through the window.

"I wouldn't press my luck if that were all the leverage I had."

Roussel grinned. "Oh, it's not, Maurice. I have one more card up my sleeve which guarantees my winning the game, the plantation, and Laura."

"Congratulations!" Dufaure said sarcastically. "Do you care to tell me about it?"

"No, I don't."

Maurice cast Giraumont a quizzical look. "If Laura marries you, you'll be the biggest and most influential landowner in the entire state. Your financial worries will be over if you can manage to invest her money more wisely than you did yours."

Giraumont snorted. "And I'll have a soiled wife who's slept with a common gambler."

"What does it matter? You're not marrying for love."

"Every time I think of Laura's making love to Clay Sutherland, I want to kill him. It's too bad he didn't die in the duel."

Maurice laughed. "Perhaps you can do something about it yet, Roussel."

"No," Roussel answered, "killing is not for me, Maurice."

"What about the house?" Maurice asked. "Is that still in Celeste's name?"

"That and the immediate acreage that includes the bayou."

"I suppose you've taken measures to get it too."

Giraumont's laughter floated through the window. He had been rather trusting when he had first gotten involved with the movement to bring Napoleon to America, but not anymore. Edouard Lambert was moving behind his back to get control of Celeste's markers. And since the duel, Roussel did not trust Maurice. He would keep his own counsel. "I'm working on that also."

Clay heard a knock. Then a door opened. Judith Talbot said rather curtly, "M'sieur Dufaure, I don't mean to interrupt you, but I need to have these figures explained."

"Of course. Roussel was just leaving."

Wearing a green gown, her hair pulled into an elegant chignon, Laura sat on the settee. She was thinner than Clay had remembered, and her eyes had lost some of their sparkle.

"I wish you hadn't come," she said. "Nothing has changed since you left."

"I know, but I had to see you again." The brown eyes begged her to understand.

How handsome he was. The fawn-colored breeches fit tightly over his muscled legs; his black coat hugged his shoulders. The ecru and black paisley print cravat enhanced the bold, rugged lines of his face.

He leaned forward and caught her hand. "Laura, I love you."

The haunted eyes gazed at him. "I love you too. But love is not enough, Clay. My father's death will always be between us."

"Laura, believe in me. Please trust me."

Tears burned Laura's eyes. "That's what you told me the night before the duel."

Clay wanted to explain but could not. His chances of living were much greater as long as Dufaure and Giraumont thought he did not fully recall the details of the duel. Too much needed to be clarified before he confessed.

Also, he remembered the messages Graham had written on the cigar bands and wondered what role Laura played in the Napoleon conspiracy or what role Beau had played. And now he was concerned about Celeste's involvement. Clay could not afford to reveal his suspicions at the moment.

Eventually, he said, "I can't explain. All I can do is

ask you to trust me, Laura."

A maid entered with a tray which she set on the low table. When she left, Laura picked up the pot and poured two cups of coffee. "Roussel has asked me to marry him."

"You can't."

"I won't." She drank several swallows of her coffee. "He's desperate to marry me. If I do, he's promised to give me the money to buy the house from Celeste. He's promised to sign a prenuptial agreement stating that after our marriage I can retain all of Ombres Azurées in my name."

Clay raked his hand through his hair. Roussel was moving fast; Lambert could not be far behind. "Laura, for God's sake, don't consider marriage to Roussel. If you need money for the plantation, let me lend it to you. I'll do so with no conditions."

"Thank you, Clay." Laura picked up a linen napkin and blotted her lips. "But Judith and I will make it on our own."

His hand slipped into his pocket; his fingers curled around the slip of paper. He promised himself one thing: If Laura married Roussel Giraumont, she would do so because she wanted to, not because she was being blackmailed. He would see to that. He would protect her from opportunists like Roussel and Lambert.

Laura walked down the narrow path. Every now and again she would kick her foot to send pine needles flying through the air. She loved the forest. It was her domain. Since Beau's death she spent a great deal of her time in the solitude of the back acreage. At first she had come to grieve. She had grieved the loss of her papa and the only man she would ever love.

And she would love Clay Sutherland for the remainder of her life.

Celeste had refused to believe her and was adamant in her demand that Laura marry Giraumont. Laura had been relieved when her stepmother abruptly decided to go to Baton Rouge to visit with old family friends. Now she had some time to think and to decide what she wanted to do.

Since Laura had met Clay Sutherland, her values had undergone a change. While Ombres Azurées was important to her, she found that it alone was not enough. Something was lacking. She wanted more in life than mere land or wealth.

She stopped and leaned against a tree trunk. Without love her days seemed empty and shallow, her work a drudgery. She wondered if she could endure a life without Clay.

She began to walk again, her steps leading her deeper onto Giraumont property. She followed the narrow path—evidently a relatively new one—that led from her property on the other side of Bayou d'Ombre across the forest on the back portion of the Giraumont plantation. Tomas had pointed it out to her this morning, and she was curious to see where it took her.

When she reached a man-made clearing, she saw a small cottage—a new one—and hitched to the post outside was a horse. Curious, Laura moved closer. When she reached the front of the building, the door opened and Roussel stepped out.

He looked up in surprise. "Laura," he exclaimed, "what—a—what a surprise. I never expected to see you here." He rubbed his palms nervously down his chest.

Laura smiled. "The cottage is lovely, Roussel. I didn't know you had built this."

"Oh, yes," he said, and laughed unnaturally. "I copied yours. I, too, wanted a retreat."

"May I see it?" Laura asked.

"Of—course." Roussel stepped aside and allowed her to enter the room. He followed, hurriedly moving toward the desk and sweeping his papers together. Unnoticed by him, one fell to the floor. "I was doing some work here. I like the solitude."

"Yes, I know," Laura answered. "I like mine for the same reason." She walked to the windows behind his desk and gazed at the beautiful forest. She heard the crackle of paper and looked down. She was standing on the edge of one of his documents. She bent and picked it up. "Here," she said, "you dropped this."

Roussel jerked the map from her hands and quickly dropped it into a desk drawer, slamming it shut. "Thank you," he blustered. He moved to the table across the room and poured himself a glass of whiskey and took several swallows. "Are you ready to give me an answer, Laura?"

Laura turned to look at him. "I appreciate your offer of marriage, Roussel, and wish I could say yes. You've been most kind to me since Papa died, but I don't love you."

Roussel drained the glass and set it down. His voice was gruff when he said, "You don't have to love me, Laura. Love doesn't have to be a part of our agreement."

"I won't marry without love," she quietly affirmed.

Roussel smiled sinisterly and walked toward her. Liquor and anger made him forget caution. Yet when he spoke, his voice softened. "I had hoped I would not have to tell you about this, Laura, but your father owed me a great deal of money."

407

Laura looked at him suspiciously. "But I found no such note among his papers; neither did our solicitor."

"This was a private note, Laura, and quite legal. I had hoped I would not have to use it, but . . ." Roussel moved to the desk and opened a drawer. Riffling through it, he soon extracted a sheaf of papers which he threw on the desk. "I do not know where you father would have put his copies," he lied easily, "but this is mine. You can see that it's been duly signed by me, Beau, our witnesses, and my attorney, M'sieur Emeri Edgard. You may verify this with M'sieur Edgard if you wish."

Laura sank into the chair and read the document. She had no idea her father was this deeply in debt, and to Roussel. No wonder Beau had been pushing her into marriage with him.

"And this is not all, *chére* Laura," Roussel added sarcastically.

Still holding the papers in her hands, Laura looked up. "What do you mean, Roussel?"

"How do you think Celeste had been entertaining herself these past few months since Beau died and you've turned your entire attention to the plantation?" He laughed. "She's reverted to her old habits, *ma chére*."

"No," Laura whispered. Guilt settled its heavy cloak around her shoulders.

"Yes, dear Laura, and Celeste owes large amounts to many of the gambling establishments in the city. I know you do not have the money to buy the markers back, but I do. If you marry me, I have promised Celeste that I will buy them and the house remains hers intact. Also, my dear, you will not have to repay the money your father borrowed. We will consider this a mutual investment for *our plantation*."

Roussel took another step that brought him close enough that his foul-smelling breath splayed against Laura's skin.

"You do not have much time to make your decision. Anton Quigly has bought the markers from the casino owners, and if Celeste does not make her payment by Monday"—he paused and smiled sinisterly—"and that is only two days away, my dear, he will auction them off to anyone who has the money to buy them."

Laura's heart beat fearfully against the wall of her chest. Roussel was uttering no idle threat.

Chapter Seventeen

"Mr. Sutherland." A tall, burly man knocked on the door to Clay's office.

"Come in, Ralph." Clay leaned back in his chair and flexed his shoulders. He had been working on these figures all day, and still they did not balance.

"Someone here to see you," the deep voice announced. "A Miss Laura Talbot."

Clay's frown turned into a smile. He rose as the man opened the door wider and allowed Laura to precede him into the room. Clay moved from behind the desk and caught her extended hands in his. While the two of them looked at each other, Ralph quietly withdrew and closed the door.

"Hello, Laura."

Although she was still much too thin and her cheeks pale, Clay thought Laura was clearly the loveliest woman he had ever seen. If anything, grief had made her even more lovely. It had given her a haunting exquisiteness that forever denied her the frosty beauty she had once possessed. As always, her eyes were the focal point of her beauty, their color enhanced by the green dress she wore. They were large and alluring and seemed to sparkle with unshed tears. As if they knew a secret, they were mysterious and alluring.

"Hello, Clay," she murmured.

"I'm glad to see you." How foolish he sounded uttering such mundane words. But he was speechless, like a boy who had fallen in love for the first time.

Laura smiled. "I hope I'm not disturbing you."

"Not at all," he denied with a vigorous shake of his head. "And even if I were, I'd eagerly put business aside for you. May I get you something to drink? Lemonade? Tea? Coffee?"

Laura finally pulled her hands from his and sat in the chair in front of his desk. She took off her gloves. "No, thank you."

She laid her hands on her lap, their creamy beauty enhanced by the rich green fabric of her dress. Her fingers were long and slender. Clay recalled the feel of them upon his body; to stop the shudder that rippled his body, he moved to his desk and picked up his cigar. He squashed it in the ashtray.

"Clay," Laura began tentatively, her voice quavering slightly, "the other day . . . you told me that if I needed any money you would lend it to me."

In one sentence Laura turned Clay's happiness into disappointment. He moved around the desk and opened the tobacco box to extract a cigar. Lowering his head, he picked up a lucifer and raked it against the bottom of the candle holder.

Between puffs he said, "Yes, I did, Laura. I take it the purpose of your visit is to ask for a loan?"

"Yes." She twined her hands together.

Clay moved to the window, turning his back to her. "How much do you need?"

When she spoke the amount, Clay whirled around to stare at her incredulously. He had expected her to

411

call off the sum Celeste owed for her gambling debts, not this exorbitant amount.

"Why do you need it?" He laid the cigar in the ashtray.

Laura studied her hands intently. "I need it for the plantation."

"I assumed that," Clay answered dryly. "But if I'm going to lend you that amount of money, I'll need to know what it's going to be used for."

"I'll—I'll stand good for the money," she said, but Clay knew she could not. She raised her head desperately. "I must have the money, Clay. Really I must. I wouldn't be begging if I didn't. Begging doesn't come easy to me. While it may be a humbling experience, it's also humiliating."

Laura's plea tore at Clay's heart, but he was a businessman and knew he could not allow his sentiments to get in the way of sound judgment. Softly, he asked, "Have you tried the bank, Laura?"

"Yes," she murmured, "but they consider the plantation a poor risk at this time."

"What about the shipping line?"

"The controlling interest belongs to Judith . . . not me. I'm responsible for Ombres Azurées. Besides, she couldn't."

"What are you going to do with the money, Laura?"

Laura's face was stark, her eyes filled with fear. So much had tumbled on top of her recently, Clay could tell she was emotionally defenseless.

"I'm going to pay off Papa's debts."

"Will that leave you any capital on which to operate the plantation?"

"A little."

Clay caught her shoulders and lifted her to her feet. Her gloves and reticule fell to the floor. "Look at me,

Laura," he said gruffly in an attempt to get her attention and to jar her out of her grief. "This doesn't sound like you at all. Now, if we're going to do business, I expect you to handle it like a business-woman. Where's the old Laura Elyse Talbot I knew so well? The woman who would fight anyone for her plantation?"

"Oh, Clay!" She flung herself into his arms. "Because of me Celeste had begun gambling again. She owes—"

Clay held her closely, stroking her head as the words tumbled out of her mouth. She told him about Celeste's friendship with Edouard Lambert, the gambling debts, and her father's personal loan from Roussel. When the torrent of words and tears subsided, she remained in the warm circle of his arms. She had not felt this protected in a long time.

"Is retaining the house so important to you?" he asked.

"Yes," she murmured, soothed by his tender touch and the soft cadence of his voice. "The plantation is not Ombres Azurées without the house and the bayou."

The bayou! Clay was caught in the middle of duty and love. His greatest desire at the moment was to give Laura the money with absolutely no conditions, but he was concerned about Lambert and Girau-mont. He was unsure of Lambert's purpose, but he understood Giraumont's. The man would stop at nothing to have Ombres Azurées. Clay had to protect Laura from him . . . and Celeste from herself. "I'll give you the money," he said.

"Oh, Clay—" Laura was so relieved, she hugged him even tighter. "I don't know how I can ever thank you for this."

His hands slipped down her shoulders to her

upper arms, and he set her away from him the second time. "Save your thanks until you've heard the terms of the loan."

Laura looked at him quizzically. He turned and walked to the desk to pick up his cigar. The lucifer grated, the acrid odor of sulphur permeated the air, the flame touched the tip of the cigar. His back to her, he blew the smoke out.

"I'll have to have collateral for a loan of this magnitude, Laura."

"What—kind?"

He turned. "I want you to marry me."

Unable to utter a word, Laura could only stare.

"You and Celeste need someone to take care of you," he said gently. "Let me be the one."

She blinked back the tears. "We would have someone if Papa were still alive." She bent to retrieve her possessions. Pulling the drawstring of her reticule over her arm, she slipped her hands into the gloves. "I'll find someone else to lend me the money, Clay. Someone who can keep business and pleasure separated."

Clay's expression remained impassive, but his eyes remained warm and tender. "You don't have any choice in the matter, sweetheart."

The second glove part of the way on, Laura's movements stopped and she raised her hand to look at him.

"I own all Celeste's markers."

"You can't mean that!" Laura unconsciously moved to him.

"I bought them from Quigly, and, I'll have to add, the man made a healthy profit."

Laura jerked the remainder of the glove over her hand. "Tell me how much you paid him. I'll pay you back with interest as soon as I get a loan."

"I don't want the money," Clay said softly. "I want you. I want to marry you."

"I've explained why I won't marry you."

"You've given me silly excuses. Until you can truthfully say you don't love me, I won't leave you alone, Laura."

"I won't say it because it would be a lie." She paused, then said, "But neither do I want to marry you, not with the shadow of Papa's death between us."

"No marriage. No money."

"You're no different from Roussel," Laura finally said. She walked to the window and looked out, the sunlight glinting a fiery red in her hair. "Both of you are trying to blackmail me into marriage."

"No, Laura," Clay said, "I'm not like Giraumont at all. He doesn't love you. I do. He was trying to blackmail you because he wants your plantation."

"And you don't want Ombres Azurées?"

The golden-brown eyes caught and locked to hers. He had gone this far and would not back down now. No matter what she thought of him, he would not see her at the mercy of vultures like Dufaure and Giraumont . . . and Lambert.

"Yes, I do, Laura. And I want more. I want respectability, the kind that will come with my being married to you. You're one of New Orleans's finest marriage offers this season." He smiled, and his eyes suggestively traveled the length of her body. "Marriage to me can't be all bad. At least we're sexually compatible."

"If—if I agreed to marry you, it would be in name only."

Even as she uttered the words, Laura knew they were a lie. Did she really expect to live in the same house and be married to a man as physically

415

attractive as Clay Sutherland, to a man she loved, and not share his bed?

"I think not, Laura. You and I have been much too intimate for that." He smiled and reached out to brush an errant curl from her cheek. "You're much too passionate."

Laura's hand curled into a fist, and she stared at the bustling street below. "If I agree to marry you, will you sign a prenuptial agreement in which you deed the house and surrounding acreage to me?"

"No, I have nothing to gain by that. Once you have the property, you could get an annulment."

"You've been thorough, haven't you?"

Clay caught Laura's arms in his hands and turned her around to face him. "That's the kind of person I am, Laura. But I promise you'll have no reason for regret. As long as you're married to me, you'll have your Ombres Azurées."

Laura smiled woodenly. "When is the wedding?"

"As soon as possible, but not so soon that we can't have a large, beautiful wedding. I want all of New Orleans elite Creole society in attendance. And I want the ceremony solemnized in the church. I want pomp and pageantry."

Laura laughed bitterly. "You think Creole society will come to our wedding?"

"Yes, Laura, I do."

"Then you shall have it, M'sieur Sutherland," Laura promised, but he would not get her. He would have a bride but not a wife. She would taunt him with the nearness of her body, but she would never give herself to him. Never!

Interlude V

Talbot Shipping Line office
September 30, 1814

Her black muslin chiton wisping about her feet, Laura followed her sister into the office that had been Beau Talbot's. As soon as Judith closed the door, Laura lifted the veil from her face and draped it over her hat. She straightened the somber-colored Indian shawl about her shoulders and sat in the chair that Judith offered. Judith walked to the desk, where she dropped the lid on the inkwell and straightened invoices.

Quite calmly, as if she were discussing the weather, Laura said, "Judith, I'm going to be married."

"What?" Judith spun around to drop her pen on the desk, black ink splattering over the white paper and on the tips of her fingers. She seemed to slide into her father's chair and stared at her sister incredulously. "To Roussel?"

"No, to Clay Sutherland. I hope you'll wish me happy?"

"No." Judith still could not believe what she had heard. Needing something to do with her hands, she picked up a handkerchief on the desk and wiped her hands.

"Yes," came Laura's matter-of-fact reply.

Outraged, Judith tossed the cloth on the desk and sprang to her feet. Her hands clenched tightly. "The man who killed Papa? The man you wished in hell just a few months ago?"

Laura rested her head in her hand. Fighting her own battle, Laura refused to look at Judith. She had gone through the same argument with herself so many times, she knew the script by heart. "Don't make this any harder than it is. I know what I'm doing, Judith. I know what I have to do."

Judith stared at Laura for a long time. She moved closer to the chair and leaned down to put her arm around Laura's shoulder. "What you *have* to do? What could you possibly *have* to do?" She placed a quick kiss on Laura's temple.

In the same calm tones, tones of resolved acceptance, Laura said, "I have to save Ombres Azurées."

"Save the plantation?" Judith looked at Laura curiously. "I didn't know it needed to be saved."

"It does." Laura began to play with the fringe on her shawl, still not raising her head to look at Judith for fear she would begin crying. Neither would she tell Judith the embarrassing conditions of the marriage. "Clay . . . Sutherland has money to invest in it." After a poignant silence she added, "He might even be persuaded to invest some in Talbot Shipping."

Judith returned to her chair and gripped the arms tightly. "You don't marry your banker, sister dear!"

"Women marry for money all the time." Laura strove for a nonchalance that was far from her.

"A marriage of convenience? For Laura Talbot?"

418

"Are you suggesting a marriage for love, little sister?" Laura tried for levity, but her voice quavered. Her drawn face and black eyes belied the levity. She knew that her marriage to Clay would be far more than a convenience for her.

"Yes, Laura. At least for you. Love is important to you."

"Oh, don't be silly." Laura waved Judith's words aside. "Marriages in name only are all the fashion in our circle. They're more the thing than marriages for love. And much safer."

Judith rose and caught the fluttering hand. She knelt beside her sister. She was not going to be left out of this matter. "This isn't like you at all. You're not telling me the whole of this."

Now Laura looked squarely into Judith's eyes and confessed. "Clay Sutherland could own Ombres Azurées without ever marrying me."

Clearly, Judith was puzzled. "What are you talking about?"

Laura waited a moment before she said, "Celeste's gambling debts."

"Celeste!" Judith cursed angrily. "You told me she gambled occasionally, but I thought she'd been too grief-stricken since Beau died even to go out of the house."

Thinking perhaps she was to blame for Celeste's having taken up gambling again, she said softly, "She's been plunging heavily since Papa's death. I'm sure it's the way she exorcised her grief."

Judith backed away. "My God. Poor lady."

"Gambling has always been a weakness for her. Even before she married Papa. Her gambling debts were the primary reason she married out of her church. Later she really loved Papa."

"But this is all so terrible." Judith returned to the

desk and placed the quill to its holder. The stained paper she wadded and threw into an overflowing wastepaper basket. "How did Clay Sutherland manage to make this his business?"

"Clay bought up all of her markers."

"And now he wants to call them in on you?" Beneath her breath Judith muttered an imprecation.

Laura smiled wanly. "It's a simple matter of blackmail."

"Oh, sister." Kneeling, Judith reached out and took Laura's hand. Reassuringly, she squeezed. "I wish I could give you the money out of Talbot Shipping. But I don't have enough to give." Then with sudden inspiration she rushed on. "Is it possible that we could go to the bank? Surely they'll make us a loan on the land or the ships. They're worth more than enough money to cover Celeste's debts."

Her expression remaining dull, Laura shook her head. She laid a silencing finger over Judith's mouth. "Probably so. But Clay doesn't want the money. He wants me—the respectability that I represent—and Ombres Azurées."

"You're going to tie yourself to a man you hate because of your stepmother's gambling debts. That's crazy. This is the nineteenth century, not the seventeenth. A woman has recourse to the law, Laura." Judith rose and folded her arms across her chest.

"I can't let Clay hurt Celeste." Laura took umbrage at Judith's outburst. She did not hate Clay Sutherland. Far from it, she loved him. And she loved Celeste. Now that Beau was gone, she had to protect her. "And she's too wounded to be dragged through the courts. The law might cancel the debts, but the disclosure coming on top of all she's suffered would kill her."

"For mercy's sake, Laura, you love her." Judith flung her arms wide. "You want to take care of her. Beau intended that you should. But you can't give up your plans, your entire life. We're talking about marriage. That's supposed to be for life."

"Don't make me out to be a martyr, little sister. I'm doing what I must do to protect Celeste, but also to save Ombres Azurées."

For the past seven years this plantation had been her life, and how often she had said she would do whatever she had to do to keep it. Now had come the time of testing, and she was ready.

"When is this slave auction to take place?"

Laura turned, the morning sun glinting in her hair. "As soon as I can get ready. My bridegroom-to-be is demanding a huge wedding with all the pomp and circumstance that befits a member of Creole society."

Judith shook her head helplessly. "Laura, this breaks my heart."

At the same time, the sisters turned to each other. They embraced and hugged; they held on to each other as if each were afraid of being adrift and lost without the other.

"You mustn't talk that way," Laura murmured, her voice thick with tears. "Just be there to stand by me and help me get through it."

Judith gasped. Horrified, she pulled back and gazed into Laura's face. "Sister, I don't think I'll be able to attend."

"You must." Laura was prepared to marry Clay, but she wanted Judith with her. She needed support. "You're my only family. You're my maid of honor. Where else would you be?"

Her voice laden with remorse, Judith looked at the map above Beau's desk. "Laura, someone with the interest of the Talbot lines at heart is going to have to sail on the *White Hound.*"

The war had been devastating on the Talbot Shipping Line. Not only were the English preying on the ships but pirates also. But even Beau had not sailed on his ships recently. Laura could not understand why Judith must.

"Sail? A woman on a ship?" Laura questioned.

"It's not as if I were just a woman," Judith explained. "I'm the owner. The *White Cloud* has been taken by pirates. Her cargo was stolen. The crew was theatened. I can't let this happen again."

"You think you can do something about it!" Laura's problem was forgotten in the face of Judith's. She caught her sister by the shoulders and spun her around. "You're going among pirates. You'll be raped and murdered. Nothing is worth your life."

"Laura, I can't believe that the captains and crews are offering even token resistance anymore. With Beau Talbot dead, they don't have any faith in me as the owner and director of the line. Unless I'm willing to go where they go, to place myself in the same danger, they won't respect me."

Laura moved around the office, her anger growing. "I can understand your moving into a man's world. I'm in that world myself. I didn't want to be, but I am. But even in a man's world we have rules."

"Yes." Judith pressed her point. "And one rule is that the leader must not be afraid to lead. I was on board the *Portchester* when Tabor O'Halloran boarded her. The captain stood aside and let him do what he wanted. He struck sail. He didn't even try to outrun the *Banshee.* Much less fight off the pirates."

"But sailors can't be expected to fight cutthroats," Laura reasoned. "And Papa himself issued the orders that his crews were not to fight. He'd rather the pirates take the cargo and let the ship sail on unharmed."

"But this isn't a matter of the ship sailing on unharmed. The *Cloud* is lost to us. We've got to fight. I'm hiring extra men who won't be afraid of a gang of scurvy pirates."

"Then let *them* go," Laura insisted.

Judith shook her head. "No, Laura, I've got to go with them. To be their leader—if only in name. You're taking care of your problem your way. Tabor O'Halloran is mine, and I can't see any other way to handle it than by confronting it."

"But you could be killed." Fear, concern, and love in equal amounts were portrayed in her voice and expression.

"Tabor would never harm me," Judith assured her in a soft tone. "Don't forget. He liked Beau. And Beau liked him."

At this moment Laura was sure that Judith's interest in Tabor O'Halloran was more than business. Although she might not recognize the truth, she loved the man. Not only had he raided, plundered, and stolen one of the Talbot ships, he had done the same to the heart of Judith Claire Talbot-Harrow.

"So be it, sister," Laura said quietly.

Tears in their eyes, each understanding the other's inner struggles, the two women embraced and hugged each other tightly. Then Judith pulled away, and both of them grinned as they wiped the tears from their eyes. Judith opened the bottom drawer of Beau's desk and pulled out a bottle of whiskey and two glasses.

"Join me for a man's drink," she said, and poured a small amount of whiskey.

Judith lifted her glass. "To the new"— she paused

423

and smiled—"countess of Ombres Azurées."

Laura laughed with her. "To the new countess of the Talbot Shipping Line."

They drank their whiskey and looked at each other. Laura raised her hand again. Only this time her glass was empty—an echo of herself. Judith said, "To the Talbot sisters."

The salute rang hollow. Judith was a Talbot-Harrow, and Laura was soon to be Madame Clay Sutherland.

Chapter Eighteen

"I did not mean for this to happen, *ma chère*," Celeste cried, wringing her hands together. "I thought that you and Roussel—"

"I'm sure Roussel tried to get the markers, *Maman*," Laura returned quietly. "But Clay offered more, and M'sieur Quigly sold them to the highest bidder."

"*Non! Mais non!* You will not marry the man who murdered your papa!" Celeste's eyes blazed with anger. She strode across the room, her wrapper flaring to the sides as she walked.

"Clay didn't murder Papa," Laura said in defense of the man she loved. No matter that he was manipulating her into marriage, she absolutely refused to have anyone accuse him of murder.

Celeste paid her no attention. "Surely there is something we can do, Laura?"

"I'm doing what can be done. Clay doesn't want money for the markers. He wants marriage and Ombres Azurées."

Celeste continued to pace. Eventually, she sat down and folded her hands in her lap. "Laura, you are in this mess because of me and my foolishness.

Had I not gotten so caught up with M'sieur Lambert, I would not have begun gambling again. I am the one who must make amends here. All M'sieur Sutherland can get from me is the house and the land around the bayou," Celeste said with a flourish of her hand. "Let him have it. We shall build another house."

Laura smiled at her stepmother's brave words. "And shall we dig a bayou while we're at it?"

Celeste laughed with her. "Ah, *chérie*, you do have a point. But to marry Clay Sutherland. I cannot accept that, Laura."

"We also have to consider the loan Roussel made to Papa."

"I do not believe that," Celeste said. "Beau never mentioned it to me."

"But he had done it nevertheless, *Maman*. I saw the documents and spoke to Roussel's attorney and to the witnesses. And they were Papa's friends. They would not lie for Roussel."

Celeste was quiet for a long time, during which she stared at her stepdaughter. "Do you love Clay, Laura?"

"Yes," Laura answered, "I love him, *Maman*."

Celeste rose and moved to where Laura stood. She laid her hand on Laura's shoulder. "You must go with your heart, *ma chère*."

Laura moved slightly to clasp her stepmother's hands in hers. "But I'm not marrying him because I love him. I'm marrying him because that's the only way I can keep Ombres Azurées." *The only way I can protect you*, she silently finished.

After a long pause Celeste said, "I haven't changed my mind about Clay, but I'm a woman who can accept the inevitable. You've made up your mind to

426

this course of action, and you'll do it no matter what."

"Yes, I will."

"When is the wedding?"

"In two weeks."

"Two weeks?" Celeste exclaimed.

"That is enough time, *Maman*."

"Only if we hurry, *ma chère*. We must move my furniture to the cottage and get the house redecorated for you and Clay."

Remembering Charlotte, Laura said, "Absolutely not, *Maman*. You will not be moved out of the big house."

"Of course not." Celeste waved her hand through the air. "I shall move myself."

"There's no need," Laura protested. "This marriage is one of convenience. You can remain here in your suite."

Celeste shook her head. "*Non*, Laura. I will take Berthe with me and move to the cottage. A house is not big enough for two families. I need my own privacy, as do you and Clay."

The wedding was over, and Laura, still wearing her white wedding dress, stood in her bedroom in the master suite—the bedroom that had belonged to Celeste. The room had been completely renovated. New accessories, new draperies, even new furniture delivered from Europe by Clay's orders. Clay was in Papa's room. She could hear him stirring about. She looked at the door and grinned. The bolt was securely locked, which prohibited his coming and going at will.

She looked at the nightgown and dressing gown

427

spread across the bed. Pristine white lace that shimmered in the waning light of day. Laura's heart thumped loudly and heavily. She had been strong the past month, not giving in to his romantic overtures, but she had to admit Clay had not pressed her. He had played the role of the gentleman to the hilt. Today would be the test.

She walked to the dresser and took off her jewelry. She and Clay would be sleeping in the same house but not in the same bed. Clay Sutherland would rue the day he manipulated Laura Talbot into marriage—no matter what his reason.

She felt not the least bit of remorse, though perhaps she should. In return for the markers, Celeste had deeded the house to Clay, and he paid Beau's note to Roussel. Besides that, Clay had lavished money on the plantation house, and now it looked as if it were newly built. He had invested in new equipment for the planting and had paid off several outstanding debts. Yesterday he had moved all his personal belongings into his bedroom, also renovated to suit his taste.

Laura heard the soft knock on the door that opened into the hall. "Yes," she called.

"Dinner, Maîtresse," Jeanette said. She opened the door and wheeled the serving table into the room. "M'sieur said the two of you would be dining in your suite."

"Thank you, Jeanette," Laura said.

The connecting door between the two bedrooms rattled, but Laura ignored it. She did not intend to let Clay come into her room at will. He would use the hallway as did everyone else.

"What time shall I come back for the dishes?" the maid asked.

Clay strode down the hall. "Wait until morning,"

428

he answered for Laura. "We do not wish to be disturbed."

"*Oui,* m'sieur." Jeanette tucked her face to hide her grin as she scurried out of the room, closing the door behind her.

Laura looked up to see him lounging in the doorway. His coat was gone, and several of the topmost buttons on his shirt were undone. "It was nice of you to have dinner served," she said coolly.

Clay walked into the room and moved to the door that connected their bedroom. He flipped the bolt. "I want you to leave this open. I don't want to have to come to your room by way of the hall. We're married—*happily married*—and that's the way people are going to think of us. Our servants are not going to spread tales over the city of our having a marriage in name only."

"But, *my dear husband,* that is exactly what we will have. You manipulated me into marriage, but you will not manipulate me into bed. You wanted marriage. You have that. You're getting exactly what we agreed upon."

Clay folded his arms over his chest. "How long do you think you'll be able to hold out?" he asked.

Having no answer to his question—one that also plagued her—she said, "I'm not going to sleep with you."

"You don't have to sleep with me, but you will be my wife in every sense of the word."

"You can't make me." She wanted to move away from him but refused to do so. She was not going to let him know how much his proximity aroused her.

"I can, but I'm not. You'll come to me on your own." He smiled. "You might claim that you don't love me, and that you're angry because I manipulated you into marriage, but you sure as hell want me."

Laura's hands curled into fists at her side. She wanted with all her might to hate Clay Sutherland and to be able truthfully to deny his words, but she could not. She did desire him. He had awakened passions in her that only he could assuage. His mere presence created a yearning in her body.

And she knew that Clay Sutherland was right. He would not have to force her into his bed. She would go of her own free will. The thought angered Laura; it reinforced her weakness. When she was around Clay, she forgot he killed her father. She could almost believe he loved her and had not married her for Ombres Azurées. Almost but not quite.

"Are you ready to eat?" he asked.

Nodding her head, Laura moved to the table and sat down. As they ate, Clay talked as if nothing were amiss with their marriage. When he began to tell her about some ideas he had about the planting, Laura bristled.

"That's for me to do," she said.

Clay grinned. "We'll do it together, Laura. You can still administer the plantation, I merely want to be with you. I want to learn as much about the operation of it as possible."

When she had finished eating, Clay offered to pour her a second glass of wine. She shook her head and rose. "I remember what happened the last time you plied me with wine, m'sieur. Then I was as willing to play the game as you were, but not now. I'd like to be alone."

Clay stood also and moved to stand behind her. His breath touched the nape of her neck. It was warm and scented with wine. "Laura, our marriage can be beautiful if we want it to be."

Laura trembled. She closed her eyes and breathed deeply. Then she turned to stare into his face. "Clay,

430

let's get something straight from the beginning. I married you to save Celeste and my plantation. That was my only reason. While I may desire you, I refuse to pretend our marriage is anything other than a convenience for either of us."

Clay smiled and reached down to touch the lace on her collar. "All I'm asking for, love, is the convenience of marriage."

Laura's heart skipped a beat, but she remained still. "All my life I have been bound by society. Now I'm free. I don't have to live a lie, and I don't intend to. You and I have a business agreement, nothing more. That's the way it is; that's the way it's going to be."

He caught her chin in his fingers. "That's not the way you want it, my darling, and neither do I. You'll come to me sooner or later. I'm willing to wait."

He walked across the room through the connecting door which he did not close. In his room Clay took off his boots and shirt and lit a cigar. He sat in the wing chair in front of the darkened fireplace and smoked while he waited to see what Laura would do.

He had gone to great lengths to marry her, and he had done so because he loved and wanted to protect her from vultures who were ready to prey off her, and from herself. But if their marriage continued as it has begun, Clay knew that it was going to be hell.

He was astonished at the depth of emotion Laura aroused in him. He had desired women before and had taken his share of them. But he had never before been the victim of his own emotions. He wanted to shake his love into Laura. She accused him of manipulating her into marriage, little knowing that she had total control of his heart.

If he told her about the duel—the way it really took place—perhaps things between them would be different. But Reynolds had asked him not to do this. They did not know if Laura or Celeste or both were involved in the Napoleonic conspiracy. Clay knew he must intensify his investigation. He had to find Graham Bradford's murderer. This man held the key to the Talbots's involvement in the plot.

Night softly darkened the room. Clay lit a new candle and waited. He wanted Laura; he needed her but would not go to her. He wanted her to come to him.

Time passed. The bottom of the candle holder was filled with melted wax; the candle itself burned three quarters of the way down. Clay was filled with disappointment. He rose and walked to the bed, turning down the covers. Evidently, she was not coming.

He was unbuttoning his trousers when he heard the lock click. He stopped his movements and turned around to see Laura outlined in the doorway. The light in the room shone through her gown, silhouetting her slender, voluptuous form. Her hair was hanging in shimmering waves down her back.

Clay drew in a deep breath. Laura was gorgeous, and she was his wife. Slowly, she walked into the room, closer and closer to Clay. Her face was hauntingly beautiful, her green eyes shadowed.

Laura gazed at him. His trousers rode low on his hips. His dark abdominal hair was visible. Also visible was his hard fullness. Laura remembered another time when he had stood like this. The night he had made love to Phoenix and had proposed marriage to her. The night they declared their love for each other.

That night she had turned to run, but he had grabbed her and pulled her against his hot flesh. Tonight she had nowhere to run, and if she did, he would not come get her. She licked lips suddenly gone dry.

"I didn't think you would show up," he said. The trousers fell even lower.

Laura could not take her eyes off him. "Surely you knew I would."

"I hoped you would."

Laura knew that he was going to let her take the initiative. That in itself did not bother her. She wanted him with all her heart, but making love to him like this seemed so crass. Would he think she was prostituting herself? That she was making love to him as payment for the plantation?

It was not, of course. She loved him and wanted to make love to him. That was the only reason she was there in his room. She had hidden behind the skirttail of society once. Not again. She would be honest about her emotions.

"Clay," she whispered, "I want to make love to you."

He caught her hand and pressed her palm against his chest. "Can you tell, my darling, that I want you to."

"Not—not because of Ombres Azurées. Not because of a marriage agreement."

She wished she could see his face more clearly, but they were standing outside the circle of light. Laura wanted time to stand still and the world to consist of no one else but her and Clay. Gone were the strictures placed on her by society and family and friends. In the magical world she and Clay would create, she was free to make love to him and to accept whatever he was willing to give her.

"I want the plantation," she said "but I'm making love to you because I desire you."

"Those aren't exactly the words I wanted to hear,"

Clay said, holding her hands in his, "but I'm glad that you're doing it because you want to. I also want you to know that my desire for you has nothing to do with my wanting your plantation. I love you."

The words were Laura's undoing. They reached deeper than any caress they had ever shared. Overwhelmed by the sensations that rushed her body, she looked down to see her smaller hands completely covered with his larger ones. The roughness felt good to her. The gentle pressure gave her strength as well as assurance.

In comparison to his sun-browned hands, hers were creamy white. He leaned over and gently kissed her on the lips. Laura trembled. When he released her mouth without letting the kiss deepen, Laura knew he was going to let her initiate the moves tonight. She swayed closer to him. Her breasts, free of undergarments, brushed against his chest. She claimed his mouth with hers.

At that moment she realized that all her well-laid plans were for nought. The gentleness and restraint of the kiss shook her to the very depth of her soul. It affected her more than other passionate kisses she had shared with him. She wanted far more than the brush of his mouth on her forehead. She wanted him to possess every inch of her body. She wanted all of Clay Sutherland, and she wanted him to have all of her.

When Clay had kissed her before, Laura had felt the electrical current flow between them, but this kiss—new with tenderness and fraught with care—sent liquid fire through her bones. She opened her mouth beneath the gentle pressure of his.

Clay's arms tightened to draw her closer, and the kiss deepened. Laura had no desire to be free from Clay's embrace. If anything, she wanted to be drawn closer and closer until they were one. Her arms circled his back, and her fingers clung to his shoulders. Beneath the softness of her palm she felt the warm texture of skin.

His lips left her mouth to touch her chin, to trace her jawline, and at last to linger on the throbbing pulse at the base of her neck. As their lips touched again, as his lips and tongue moved intimately against, then within, her own, a thrill ran through her. With the tip of his tongue he traced the line of her lips, then surged between them to savor the velvet sweetness of her inner mouth in a way that made her knees grow weak and her heart thunder.

His hands wandered freely over her lower back. Laura pressed herself against him, eager to fill the yearning emptiness of her body. He pushed away and unbuttoned the wrapper and shoved the straps of her nightgown over her shoulders. Candlelight glistened against her skin to make it look like satin.

His fingers stroked her breasts until the nipples were pert. He then lowered his head and took one into his mouth, sucking gently at first one, then the other. Then he slowed his motions, until his tongue circled lazily a small, taut nipple to inflame her whole body with frantic desire. Laura arched her breasts forward and threw her head back, her auburn hair flowing over Clay's arm. She was utterly lost in the fire that blazed between them.

His head rose, and their lips touched in an urgent kiss that blazed into fiery passion. Clay filled the soft cavity with his probing tongue. As he explored the tender interior, his lips moved over hers, burning her with the intensity of his desire. As the same time his fingers cupped the back of her skull, the other hand dropped down her back to cup her naked buttocks.

Then he lifted her into his arms and gently swung

her onto the bed. As she watched, he stripped out of his trousers and stretched out beside her. His hand tangled in her silky hair.

"I'm so glad you're here, Laura," he murmured. "I have been so hungry for you."

"And I for you, my darling."

Refusing to be tormented by the loving foreplay any longer, Laura turned her head and her mouth captured his lips in a searing kiss that touched them both to their souls. Her hands roved his body hungrily, as did her mouth. She released his lips to claim his face, strewing kisses wherever her mouth moved, down his neck, across his collarbone. But always she returned to his welcome lips for the sustenance she had been denied for the past months.

Delicately, he cupped her breast in his hand and moved his palm lightly over the nipple. Instantly, it swelled and peaked beneath his touch. When both breasts had been thoroughly loved, he nibbled his way along her ribs, his hair brushing her tantalizingly. She moaned softly when his mouth stopped at her navel, and his warm breath oozed across her taut, flat, and quivering stomach. He rested his cheek against her skin.

The tips of his fingers began to move in the mound of auburn curls at the top of her thighs. Her hands tangled in his thick black hair, and she pulled his head back to hers. "Take me, Clay."

As he captured her mouth in his, he moved over her and plunged his strength into her. Laura received him deeply within herself. Moving together as one, they rose and fell with frenzied desperation, losing all reason and concept of time and place.

Higher and higher they climbed as deeper and deeper Clay delved into her velvety sheath. At the same time they reached the pinnacle of ultimate pleasure; they cried their victory together. When the wondrous moment was over, Laura slid her hands around Clay's neck and held him tightly. She nestled her cheek against his moist chest.

"I didn't know it could keep getting better and better," she murmured.

Clay laughed gently and also confessed, "I didn't know it could be as wonderful as this."

On a warm morning at the first of December, a month after her marriage to Clay, Laura awoke but did not open her eyes. She stretched on the bed. Clay was already gone to the fields, and she was sleeping late. How lazy she had become in a matter of weeks. But also what a deliciously wonderful feeling, she thought, and burrowed her face a little deeper into the softness of the pillow.

The month had passed quickly for Laura. She thought she hated Clay for the way he had begun to manipulate her life; yet each time they made love, each day they spent together, she found herself more tightly bound to him. She could not deny her love or physical attraction to him. She had no desire to spend her nights anywhere but in his bed.

Suddenly Laura sat up; she was nauseated. Without grabbing her wrapper, she slid off the bed and ran for the chamber pot. She barely had time to remove the lid before the retching began. She retched until her stomach muscles were contracting, and she thought she would die. When she was finished, she staggered back to the bed. She poured water into the basin and washed her face, then lay down, too weak to do anything.

She could not imagine why she was sick. Ordinarily, she did not have an upset stomach. She had eaten no new foods. Yet for the past two weeks she had been suffering twinges of nausea. However, this was the worst she had suffered, and it was not going away. She crawled to the head of the bed and rang the bell.

Jeanette came running. "You called, Maîtresse?" Before Laura could answer, the maid observed her pale face. "You are sick?"

"My stomach is upset," Laura told her. "Bring me a cup of tea."

Jeanette nodded. "I wish Berthe were here, Maîtresse. She would know what to do for you. Shall I go to the cottage to get her and Maîtresse Celeste."

"No," Laura returned weakly, her eyes closed. "If the tea doesn't work, we'll send for them. I don't want anyone fussing over me right now."

The maid quietly withdrew from the room, and Laura lay in the dark. She lay there, not daring to move for fear of retching again. Then she heard the door open, but the footsteps were heavier than those of Jeanette. They were masculine and booted. Her lids fluttered open and she saw Clay set a tray on the night table.

"Jeanette sent for me. She said you were ill." He poured her a cup of tea. "What's wrong?"

She shoved up in bed and took the cup. "I don't know. I'm sick at my stomach."

Clay stood still a moment before he asked, "How long has this been going on?"

Two swallows were all Laura wanted. She set the cup on the tray and lay back down. Closing her eyes, she said, "About two weeks, but this is the worst."

"How long has it been since you've menstruated?" he asked.

"Ah—I . . . don't know." Laura set up. Her lids flew open, and her eyes rounded. Before she thought she cried, "Oh my God, Clay! No, it can't be! I can't be pregnant."

"You most certainly could be." A big grin spread from ear to ear. He sat down on the side of the bed and caught Laura in his arms. But she began to fight him.

"Your cologne," she cried, and rolled off the bed, "it's making me sick." By the time she reached the chamber pot, she was retching again.

His brow furrowed in concern, Clay ran his hand through his hair and raced to the door. "Jeanette," he called. "Go get Berthe and Celeste. Tell them they're needed here to take care of Maîtresse Laura."

Clay washed off his after-shave cologne and stayed with Laura until Berthe arrived and ran him out of the room. "Maîtresse, she be coming later. She sent me ahead."

Clay walked to the library, where he poured himself a drink and lit a cigar, then sat in one of the wing chairs. A smile tugged at the corners of his lips. He was going to be a father. Laura was carrying his child. Pleasure raced through him. He wanted a child. He wanted his and Laura's child.

He was thrilled, but Laura was so sick. She did not seem to be happy about it at all. Her reaction was not as he would have expected or liked it to have been. He wondered if she was unhappy because she was pregnant—or was she unhappy that the child was his?

He had manipulated Laura into marriage. Now he regretted that move. He did not want her trapped into marriage but wanted her to come to him on her own. He must back off and give her some room.

He heard the knock on the door and answered. Saloman entered the room and handed Clay an envelope. "This just arrived, m'sieur."

As soon as the servant withdrew, Clay opened the

letter. Reynolds wanted to see him immediately. He had received some information from Washington that was vitally important to Clay. He threw his cigar into the fireplace and walked upstairs. Opening the door, he walked into her bedroom. Laura was almost asleep.

"I have to go into town on business," he said. "I'll be back as soon as I can."

"Um-hmm," she murmured, her lids never fluttering.

He leaned over and planted a kiss on her cheek. "Good-bye, my darling wife."

"No letters at all?" Laura demanded.

"No, Maîtresse," Jeanette said.

"Thank you."

"Shall I bring your breakfast now?"

Laura nodded and walked onto the second floor balcony. She was worried. Judith had been gone so long and she had received no word from her at all. Clay kept reassuring her that everything would be all right, that Tabor O'Halloran would take care of her fiesty little sister. Laura had no doubt of Judith's feelings for him, but still she worried because she was not quite sure of Tabor's feelings for Judith; nor was she sure what part he played in the war that waged in and around New Orleans, a city that was filled with intrigue. Despite Clay's reassurances otherwise, she wondered if perhaps Tabor O'Halloran was somehow behind the attempts on Judith's life. Laura would not rest until Judith returned home safely.

"Maîtresse"—Jeanette opened the door with one hand and entered the room, balancing a silver tray on the other—"a note from m'sieur."

Laura grinned. Gone for an entire week, Clay sent her a note every day, but she missed him and wanted him home with her. She worried that her initial surprise and reaction to her pregnancy had frightened him off. He left the very day she discovered she was with child.

Perhaps Clay did not want children; they had never discussed the issue. She also wondered if he would find her pregnant body repulsive. But she determined that she would not give him up without a fight. She loved Clay.

The door opened and Berthe entered the room. "How are you feeling today, Maîtresse?"

"Much better," Laura returned. She rummaged through the wardrobe for one of her favorite dresses. Finally, she picked a bright yellow one with green trim. "I think I'm going for a ride. I'll go over to the cottage and see *Maman*."

Berthe dropped her hands to her ample hips. "Your *maman* will be glad to see you, but I want you to be careful, Maîtresse. I don't want you losing that baby."

A tender warmth spread through Laura's body, and she put her hand over her belly. This baby was a part of her and Clay, a product of their love; she would do anything she had to in order to keep it. "No," she said, "I'm not going to lose it. I want our child too much."

She also wanted Clay too much to lose him. The past few months had been good for her. She had matured and changed in the process. Evidently, Clay still could not recall the events prior to the duel, but even so, Laura knew he had not deliberately shot her father. Perhaps he had shot the pistol but not at

441

her father.

As soon as she saw Clay again, she would tell him that Beau no longer stood between them.

"I wish Judith could be here with us," Celeste said as she snipped her crochet thread. "She will be so happy for you, *ma chère.*"

Laura nodded, and her smiled faded. "I'm worried about her, *Maman.* I haven't heard from her since she left two months ago."

"It was careless of me to mention her," Celeste said, and reached over to pat her hand. Her scissors slipped to the floor. "Forgive me, *ma chère.* Judith will be all right. If she can't take care of herself, Tabor O'Halloran will."

"You like Tabor?" Laura asked.

Celeste thought about the question for a minute, then said, "I don't know that I like him, but I do like him for Judith. He's the only kind of man she would respect. I feel the same way about Clay. At first I did not want you to marry him because of your papa, but now I know in my head as well as in my heart, he did not murder your papa."

Laura understood what her stepmother was saying. "I don't believe he killed Papa either, *Maman.*"

"Perhaps not," Celeste conceded but quickly pushed the subject aside. "Now let us think about some clothes for my first grandbaby. A girl, I think."

By mid-afternoon Celeste was ready for a nap and Laura straightened up the parlor. When she saw the scissors on the floor, she bent to pick them up. Remembering that Celeste's sewing basket was in the bedroom, she slipped them into her pocket. She would put them away later. Right now she wanted to go outdoors and enjoy the beautiful Indian summer day.

Caught up in plans for the baby, Laura was unaware of the distance she had walked. She was standing in a large covey of trees on the far reaches of the plantation, when she heard the pirogue. She stepped back into the thick foliage and watched as Roussel and Edouard disembarked and hid the craft in the thick underbrush.

They looked around to see if they were being watched. Then Edouard broke a branch off a bush and brushed the ground to erase any signs of their landing. Laura was truly puzzled by their behavior and remained hidden until they were out of sight.

She did not immediately follow them, in fact, even thought about not doing so, but curiosity got the best of her. About thirty minutes later she was moving down the small path that led to Roussel's cottage. When she arrived, she saw no signs of them. She must get to the windows on the far side. If they were open, she could see inside without them knowing she was there. Carefully, she made her way through the brush.

The windows were open, and Roussel and Edouard leaned over the desk. "This is the route the ship must take." Edouard thumped his index finger on the map. "No other."

Giraumont straightened and looked out the window. Laura ducked behind a large bush.

"I think we're going to have to get rid of Judith. She's getting in the way. She knows too much. Besides, after Clay Sutherland is killed, I don't want her in the way. I want the controlling interest in the Talbot Shipping Line as well as in Ombres Azurées."

Giraumont was still furious with Clay for having

bought Celeste's markers and for having paid Beau's loan the second time. But he was pleased with the cash he had on hand. He was no longer dependent on Lambert, and he enjoyed this liberation.

"*Mon Dieu!*" Edouard exclaimed. "Forget about the Talbot women and concentrate on the matter at hand. Concentrate on getting Napoleon's trusted officers here to New Orleans. They have information which we need."

"We shall get them here, m'sieur. None of their records will fall into the wrong hands. Your spy network will not be revealed in England. I promise," Roussel said. "But I will kill Judith Talbot-Harrow."

Frightened, Laura's heart beat furiously. She could hardly draw a breath. Crouching, she moved through the bushes until she was on the other side of the house. She was barely on the path when Edouard leapt from behind a tree in front of her. She looked into the barrel of a small pistol.

"Ah, Madame Sutherland," he said, "I do wish you had not chosen today to come visit us. You are creating unnecessary problems."

"What are you going to do with me?" Laura asked.

"Right now, let's turn around and walk to the cottage," he said. "We'll determine what to do with you later."

Also holding a pistol, Giraumont laughed as he held the door open for Edouard and Laura. "Well, M'sieur Lambert, it looks as if we do not have to go looking for M'sieur Sutherland. He will come looking for his wife. And I do have a score to settle with Sutherland. He'll think again before he messes up my plans."

Edouard nodded his head. Laying his weapon on the desk, he picked up a length of rope and tied Laura to one of the straight chairs. Using his handkerchief, he gagged her mouth. "I'm sorry, Laura," he said. "I really do like you. It's a shame that you and your husband are going to have to die."

Giraumont laughed. "Just think of all the money he's wasted to guarantee that Ombres Azurées will be his."

Chapter Nineteen

Edouard Lambert walked to the desk and gathered some papers which he slid into a portfolio. "I will make sure Sutherland learns we are holding his wife hostage. You stay here with Laura."

Roussel followed the Frenchman out the door, and the two of them stood on the front porch talking. Laura could hear only the low drone of their voices, not what they were saying. Because Edouard had not tied her too tightly, she was able to wiggle her left hand to the front. She slipped it into her dress pocket and found the pair of scissors. Holding them with her thumb and index finger, she began to cut at the rope.

"I am going now, Roussel," she heard Lambert say. "Watch her. She's crafty."

"I will," Giraumont called out. "Do not worry. She's not as crafty as I am."

The door closed, and she heard his heavy steps as he walked down the hall. Laura dropped the scissors into her pocket and quickly slid her arm behind her. She looked down at the rope and hoped Roussel would not come close enough to see the frayed ends.

"Well, Laura"—he rubbed his hands together as

he entered the room—"you have outsmarted yourself at last. Would you like me to take the gag out of your mouth so you can talk?" He walked closer to her. "I will."

The minute the handkerchief dropped from her mouth, Laura said, "You filthy—"

"Unh-unh!" He stuffed the cloth back into her mouth and wagged his index finger in the air. "A lady mustn't talk like that, Laura. But then, you're not a lady, are you? You're no better than a common whore. Of course you married Sutherland, but you were sleeping with him long before. I could have forgiven you, but you wouldn't allow me to."

Laura spit the handkerchief out. "Why, Roussel?" she asked.

He laced his hands together behind him. "Why what?"

"You and Lambert?"

"M'sieur Edouard Lambert is a emissary from Napoleon, my dear. He's over here making preparations for the emperor himself—and for some of Napoleon's most trusted advisers. Soon Louisiana will once again be under the French flag."

"You can't allow yourself to get caught up in this mania, Roussel. We're Americans now. We owe our allegiance to the United States."

"I owe no allegiance to the American government. I am one of the leaders of this mania, Laura. And I most certainly am caught up in it. If only you knew how much." He turned and walked to the window, then said in a tired voice, "I wish it could have been different. I'm not a murderer."

"Whatever do you mean?"

He sighed deeply but still did not turn to look at her. "For the cause I have been forced to kill, Laura. First there was that American spy. He found out who

447

Lambert really was. Edouard and I had to kill him. We tried to make it look like an accident, but Sutherland refused to believe it. He started investigating then. Now we have to kill him."

After a long pause Laura spoke. "You said first, Roussel. Am I to believe you have killed more than one person?"

His body shook as he nodded his head. "I would not have killed the second man. He was my friend, but I—I had to."

"Papa," Laura whispered, instinctively knowing Roussel was talking about Beau.

"Yes," he answered. "Maurice and I set it up to—"

"Maurice," Laura exclaimed. "Is he involved in this conspiracy also?"

Roussel hesitated a long time before he said, "Maurice killed Beau because Maurice wanted total control of the shipping lines. He thought he could get that easier from your sister."

"Maurice is going to kill Judith?"

"I'm afraid so."

Laura was more frightened than she had ever been before. Both Clay and Judith were in danger of losing their lives and she was helpless to warn them. She had to cut these ropes loose; she had to free herself. If only Roussel would leave the room.

But he did not. For a long time he sat at the desk and went through his papers. After a while he lifted a piece of paper and waved it through the air. "Your father's contract for our loan," he said. "You know, he had already paid it off the night before he died. He was so drunk he forgot to get a receipt; he even left all the papers here with me to give to you. Such a trusting soul."

"I hate you." Anger blazed in Laura's eyes.

"If you had cooperated with me, we could have

worked something out. You would not have to die."
He shoved back in the chair and rose. "I think I'll go
upstairs and rest for a while, my dear. I want to be
ready when your husband arrives."

"You'll never get Clay," Laura said. "He's smarter
than you."

Roussel stopped at the door and turned to her.
"Perhaps he is smarter, but he's more vulnerable,
Laura. You see, he loves you. When he learns that
you are here, he's going to forget to be careful. His
only thought is going to be to save you. You, my dear,
will be the death of him."

Laughing, he disappeared into another part of the
cottage. Tears ran down Laura's cheeks. She had
been the death of her father, now of Clay.

Night, like a heavy blanket, fell over the house, its
darkness broken only by moonbeams that filtered in
through the open window. Still Clay did not move
from the corner chair in the bedroom. Since he had
read the report Reynolds received, he had been
waiting. And he would wait longer. He held the
pistol lightly but not carelessly. He had heard the
horse gallop up the drive and knew the occupant
would soon arrive. He was ready. He heard someone
climb the stairs. Then he heard the clip of booted
footfalls in the hardwood corridor.

The door swished open, and in the silvery light
Clay could tell it was a man who entered. He closed
and locked the door, then moved to the night table to
set his portfolio down. Then there was an explosion
of light, followed by the acrid smell of sulfur. The
man, his back turned to Clay, touched the candle
with the match.

Clay's hand tightened around the pistol. "Good

evening, Mr. Lambert."

Edouard whirled around. "Sutherland! What are you doing here?"

"You know without asking," Clay said. Then: "Don't move, or I'll shoot. And believe me, I will shoot."

Lambert nodded. "How did you find out?"

"From Graham, whom you murdered."

"I did not kill Graham," he answered. "He followed me and Giraumont, and we captured him. I beat him to find out what he knew, but I did not kill him. His death was an accident."

"I don't believe you," Clay said.

Lambert shrugged. "Believe what you will. I had no reason to kill him. But after I learned of his death, I searched through his possessions. He left no clues."

"You didn't know your adversary as well as he knew you. He left me two cigar bands. Written on one was *Shadow Bayou.* On the other was *pumpkin.*"

Lambert laughed. "He was a good spy. So he figured out that I was working with Giraumont."

"Graham was better than good, Lambert. He was one of the best spies the American government has. He left me another clue, but it took me a long time to figure it out. Now that I have, I've put the entire puzzle together."

Again Lambert shrugged nonchalantly. "You're sounding quite mysterious, m'sieur. Please tell me. I would like to enjoy the story with you."

"I've known all along that we were dealing with a double agent, but I didn't know who it was. I figured it was either Giraumont or Dufaure, but I was wrong."

Lambert smiled. "I'm glad to see that you do make a mistake occasionally, M'sieur Sutherland."

"You're the double agent."

"M'sieur, I confess I am an emissary for Napoleon. Nothing more."

"No, you're not. You're an English spy. That's why Graham is dead. He recognized you the first night Laura brought you to the Golden Fleece. And you recognized him. That's why Graham had to be killed. He could expose you to us and to the Creoles. That's why he wrote his message on two bands when he could have easily used one."

Lambert waved his hand through the air. "And if this story of yours is true, m'sieur, how can you prove it?"

"You sent a dispatch today that we intercepted."

Lambert sagged.

"You have set the Creoles up, have you not? They think they are rescuing Napoleon's advisers and bringing them to safety when, in fact, they are leading them into a trap. English ships are waiting to capture all of them."

"You have captured me and have thwarted my government's plans, but the game is not over yet," Lambert said in perfect English. "Roussel and I have your lovely young bride as our prisoner. If I do not return by dawn, Roussel will kill her."

Fear chilled Clay's blood. He heard the ring of truth in Lambert's voice and knew this was no bluff. Laura was their prisoner. He rose and moved closer to the spy.

"You'll take me to her."

Lambert smiled. "Under certain conditions. Shall I outline them for you?"

"I'm not turning you loose."

"Then you'll not learn where she's being kept."

Clay reached out and grabbed Lambert by the shoulder, his hand fisting over the material of his coat. He swung him around. Pressing the pistol into his back, Clay pushed him out of the room.

"M'sieur," a maid called from the other end of the corridor, "is something wrong?"

"Get help," Lambert called out. "This man has broken into the house and taken me prisoner. He is going to kill me."

The servant screamed and dropped the linen she was carrying. Taking advantage of the confusion, Lambert broke loose from Clay and lunged for the stairs. He lost his balance, and the toe of his shoe caught in one of the banister supports. He fell down the stairs, landing on his head. He was dead when Clay reached him.

Clay stood and walked to the woman who cowered in the corner of the upstairs corridor. "Where is Mr. Giraumont?" he asked.

She shook her head, her dark eyes rounded. "I don't know, m'sieur. Since M'sieur Lambert arrived, he seldom stays home."

"A place," Clay said. "Tell me somewhere that he goes, someone that he visits." He was desperate to find Laura.

"I do not know, m'sieur." The woman was trembling.

Realizing that she was frightened, Clay sighed and raked his hand through his hair. "Please, think. Where could Mr. Giraumont be?"

Clay questioned all the house servants, but none of them knew where Roussel was. Finally, he sent one of them to town to notify Reynolds that Edouard Lambert was dead and Laura was being held prisoner by Giraumont. Then he left and headed for Ombres Azurées.

When he walked into the parlor, Celeste was pacing the floor. "Laura," she cried. "Where is she?"

"I don't know," he replied, wishing he could calm her, wishing he could calm himself.

Celeste paced the floor all the more. "She went for a walk when I lay down for my nap. I thought she had returned home. Then Jeanette and Tomas came looking for her when she didn't show up for dinner. Oh, Clay, what has happened to her?"

Rather than answer, Clay said, "She spent the afternoon with you?"

"*Oui*, we made plans for the baby." Her voice broke and she began to cry softly.

Clay went to her. "We'll find her," he promised.

Berthe entered the room with a tray and quickly poured Celeste a cup of tea. "Would you like some, Maître Sutherland?"

"No. I'm going to search for Laura." He walked to the door and called for Jeanette and Tomas. When the two of them entered, he asked, "Do you have any idea where your mistress went?"

"*Non*," Jeanette whispered.

Tomas shook his head.

"Think," Clay insisted. "Think of any place she could be."

"It's the curse," Jeanette cried. "Maîtresse made fun of the effigy."

Clay caught the young woman by the shoulders. "No, it's not voodoo." But even as he uttered the words, he wondered if this was Jena's hand reaching out to Laura from the grave.

"Where would your mistress have gone walking?"

"I know," Tomas shouted. "I know. I can take you there, m'sieur."

Night slowly turned into morning as the hours passed. Laura had worked blisters on her fingers as she cut through the thick rope. Every once in a while she would hear Roussel stirring upstairs, but no one came into the library. Then she felt the rope slack. She flexed her arms and it fell away. She was free to leave. She stood and the chair fell over, the noise echoing through the house. She froze, then heard the rush of feet.

"What's happening down there?" Roussel called out, his feet thumping against the stairs as he descended. As he neared, a wedge of light filtered into the room. Then he stood in the doorway, holding a lamp in his hand. "So you have freed yourself." He slowly advanced into the room and set the lamp on the nearest table. "But where are you going to run to? I have guards posted outside. You would get nowhere."

Laura looked around, her gaze stopping when she spied the sabers crossed over the mantel. Before Roussel quite knew what had happened, she raced across the room. While she pulled one down, he crossed his arms over his chest and smiled. Laura stood in the middle of the room, holding the sword.

Roussel laughed. "Ah, Laura, you do not frighten me. You have never used a saber before. Always you have used foils and *épées* when you have played at the fencing master's saloons."

"Do not press me, Roussel," Laura warned.

"But of course I shall," he said. "You have always wanted to be a man, but you've played his sport like a woman." For an obese man, Roussel moved quickly. Now it was his turn to surprise Laura. Before she knew what had happened, he had grabbed the other saber. "Now, my dear, let's see if you can play the game like a man. Perhaps die like a man."

Laura feared for her safety; more, she feared for her baby's safety, but she would not let Roussel know she

454

was afraid or with child. "You're evil, Roussel."

"Not evil," he answered. "Determined."

His saber swished through the air. A saber, not a foil or an *épée*. This time Laura heard no *en garde*. She dropped into position, for the first time looking her opponent—her adversary—directly in the eye. Gone were her mask and padding. At once she was afraid and excited. Her heart beat furiously, and she felt the rush of adrenaline.

The ping of metal sounded through the room as saber hit saber. Remembering all she was taught, Laura lunged. She surprised Roussel with her strength. He retreated from the attack.

They feinted; they parried. Attack. Parry. Riposte. The clash of metal rang through the house. The point of Roussel's saber touched Laura's shoulder, easily slicing through the material and her flesh. Fire shot through her arm.

As blood oozed out of the cut and discolored the sleeve, Laura gasped and stumbled backward. This was no game. It would not end in so many touches. For the first time, Laura realized she had taken up a blood sport. The bout would not end until one of them was dead. The truth hit her then: Roussel was trying his best to kill her. He caught her again; this time cutting only the material of her dress. The bodice fell below her waist, leaving her upper body covered only by a chemise.

Laura's left arm ached; her muscles burned; they quivered from exhaustion. But she remembered the most important lesson of all: she remembered to remain composed. As she thought about her foil with Clay, she smiled. Unconsciously, she became more graceful, her movements smoother.

She was in control once again.

She feinted. Panting by now, sweat dripping into

455

his eyes, Roussel parried. He should not have. He exposed his heart. Laura's first reaction was to withdraw, but she saw the hatred in his eyes. She knew he was after more than blood. He wanted her dead. She evaded the blade and disengaged to an open line. She extended her saber arm toward Roussel and lunged. She felt the blade penetrate his chest.

Roussel dropped his sword and caught the blade of hers with both hands. He gasped, blood spewing out of his mouth, and his eyes opened wide. As he fell to his knees, he muttered, "You . . . are . . . good—"

Then he fell over.

Tears running down her cheeks, Laura stood and stared at Roussel. When she heard a commotion outside, she grabbed his saber. The door opened, and Clay rushed into the room.

"Laura," he cried. "You're wounded."

"I'm fine now that you're here!" She dropped the saber and ran into his outstretched arms. "Oh, Clay, I can't believe you're here. How did you find me? Edouard is one of them. He's going to kill you."

"Yes, darling," he murmured, holding her tightly. Then he felt the wetness of her blood through his shirt. He pushed her away. "Let me see how badly you're injured."

"Just a few scratches." She smiled at him. "You ought to know that I'm not going to let a man get the better of me at fencing."

"The baby?"

Laura laughed through her tears. "He's fine, darling. Being our son, he couldn't be any less. He loves excitement."

"You're so sure it's a boy."

"I'm sure."

"That's my Laura Elyse." His lips touched hers in a wonderfully sweet kiss.

When he lifted his mouth from her, she said, "I love you, Clay. I love you. No matter what."

"Laura, I didn't kill your father." Now, at long last, he could confess to her what really happened on that fateful day.

"I know, my darling. Roussel told me. Forgive me for not—"

Clay laid a finger over her lips. "You never wavered in your love, my darling. That's what was important. I couldn't tell you what happened because I was involved in the investigation of Graham's murder."

"Edouard," she said, "he's involved in this too, Clay."

Joshua walked into the room and said, "Maître Sutherland, what do you want us to do with M'sieur Giraumont's guards?"

"Have them come get Giraumont's body and take it back to the plantation house. Take his men to their quarters," Clay answered. "They were following his orders. When you return to Ombres Azurées, tell Maîtresse Celeste that Laura is fine."

"Yes, sir."

The black man left, and Clay led Laura to the sofa. They sat down, but he would not turn her loose. As Roussel's slaves moved his body out of the room, Clay quietly told Laura about Lambert's involvement.

"And Roussel never knew Edouard was really working for the English?" Laura murmured when he had finished.

Clay shook his head. "Now that this is over, my dearest, I'm going to get you home. Then I need to make a report to Reynolds."

"You're going into town?"

When Clay nodded his head, she said, "You'll take me to Ombres Azurées but only long enough for me

457

to change clothes. I'm going to town with you, Clay Sutherland. You and I have been separated as much as I intend for us to be. Also, I've waited long enough for Judith to do what she must to save the Talbot lines. I'm going into town, and if she's not back or hasn't sent word, I'm going after her."

Gazing into Laura's eyes, Clay grinned. "I have a feeling that Judith Harrow-Talbot is in good hands, my darling."

"Tabor O'Halloran?" Laura asked, glad that it was not he who was endangering Judith's life. "Still, if she's not home, Clay."

"We'll go after her," Clay promised.

When he swung her into his arms, she rested her cheek against his chest and listened to the steady beat of his heart. Clay Sutherland was her husband, the father of her child, and her love.

Epilogue

"I feel like I'm looking into Beau's eyes." Judith picked up the baby and pressed kisses over his little face. "Michael, you are so sweet. You smell so good."

Standing at the crib, Laura laughed softly at her sister. "That's not Michael. That's Malcolm."

Judith held the baby out and looked at him; then she grinned at Laura. "The very least you could have done is have one with blue eyes and one with green, so I could tell them apart."

Laura caught Michael's tiny hand in hers. "Look at the name on his bracelet."

"So," Judith accused, "you can't tell them apart either?"

"I can, but Clay can't. He's still annoyed that they look more Talbot than Sutherland."

"I'm not surprised. *Grandmère* would tell him that the English strain is dominant." Judith laughed and swung Malcolm around. He chuckled and grabbed one of her fingers in his little fist.

"I've been thinking about taking them to England

for her to see. As soon as they're old enough, that is."
On her return from England, Laura planned to stop
in Virginia to see Clay's family. She wanted to meet
them, and she also wanted to see John.

"You'll have to take Celeste with you," Judith
said, "if you do. She couldn't stand for them to be
gone for all those months. She'd be afraid that they
won't be spoiled enough."

"That's where you come in, little sister." Laura
swung Michael through the air. "You have to give
her something else to spoil. When can we expect
another addition to the family?"

Judith concentrated on the baby for a moment,
then said, "Well, as Tabor so poetically puts it, the
cargo's been in the hatch now for three months, so
sometime in late fall we should be able to unload."

"Oh, Judith." Laura held Michael in one arm and
put the other around Judith.

About that time Clay opened the door and peered
into the nursery. "Looks as if we're being left out, old
man," he said over his shoulder to Tabor, who
followed.

"Here now." A smile spanning his face, Tabor
moved toward his wife. "Is this a private circle? Or
can a couple of more fellows get in?"

Laura beamed at her brother-in-law. "You wonderful man. Judith's just told me the good news."
Laura held Michael out to him. "Here. Get some
practice before the actual time comes."

Clay slapped Tabor on the back and laughed.
"Congratulations, Tabor. Looks like your adventures on the high seas are over for good."

"No more gambling for you either, my friend."

"Right. From now on everything's a sure thing."

Grinning, Judith handed Malcolm to Clay. "One
thing's for sure. His diaper needs changing."

460

Here's a taste of Deana James's *Masque of Sapphire*, on sale now from Zebra Books. Don't miss the adventures of Laura's sister, Judith, as she finds passion and adventure in the arms of a dashing privateer!

"You are still determined on this foolish visit to New Orleans?" The Dowager Countess of Harrestone poured tea with studied care. The harsh edge to her voice was the only evidence of her anger.

Judith reached to take the cup and saucer. "Yes, *Grandmère*."

The countess poured her own but set it aside. "You'll regret this, Judith Claire. You cannot expect to be welcomed into the family of a man who has had no contact with you for six years. If Laura has told you that you will, she is leading you along a primrose path, my girl."

Judith managed to set the tea down without sloshing it. "They have sent for me," she reminded her grandmother softly. "Beau has arranged passage for me on the *Portchester*."

The old woman sniffed contemptuously. "One of his oldest ships, I might tell you. Oh, you don't need to look surprised at me. I have kept up with my erstwhile son-in-law. Laura has written me faith-

461

fully. Such a good girl. And I have other ways. I am not without influence in the world."

"I'm sure," her granddaughter murmured.

"If you are so sure, then you must know that your place is here. You can never have any business in that savage country."

"I want to see for myself."

"Stubborn. Filled with detestable false pride. A place—an important place—could be made for you in society. I . . . I would like to have some member of my family with me. I am growing older." Her lips formed a tight slash in her wrinkled, powdered face.

Judith picked up the cup and saucer again. "I must make this visit."

"Perhaps next year," *Grandmère* snapped impatiently. "At this stage in your development, you can't help but fail. You know nothing about society. Nothing about proper behavior. It's true you'll be among parvenus of the worst sort. They'll despise you for your ancient lineage. And they'll be watching your every move. You'll embarrass yourself and them."

"Thank you, *Grandmère*."

"Stop that! No sarcasm, please. Sarcasm doesn't become a young woman. That's exactly what I'm talking about. I understand that your father has married a Frenchwoman." Her nostrils pinched more tightly together. "She won't want you around. You mark my words. She'll be eager for you to fail so she can throw you up to your father."

"Then you'll be glad to see me coming home sooner."

The old spotted hand crushed the fine Madeira napkin. Blue veins stood out on the back. "I'm telling you that you should not go at all. Not at all. Your place is here. I am willing—" She paused, relaxing her grip, smoothing the napkin across her lap. "I am eager to begin your education so that you can be introduced to society. I tell you, your place is here."

"I will go only for a visit. Laura was most insistent."

"And don't think your sister will be welcoming either. She's been the only chick for too long. She won't thank you for taking some of the attention away from her. And you, my girl, can't hope to compete with her on the social level. She's too experienced by half again."

Her words pelted Judith's self-esteem like hailstones. She could feel the tears prickling at the backs of her eyes. Her grandmother was certainly right about competing with Laura. But Judith's debut into society here would be the same. A whole bevy of magnificently beautiful young girls would quite put her in the shade. She blinked the tears back. "I won't be competing," she announced firmly. "I tell you I am merely going for a visit."

The *Banshee* aimed a burst from its forward cannon to cut across the bow of the *Portchester.*

"She's reefin', Cap'n." The first mate supplied the needless information as the flute's sails came rattling down.

"Right, Mr. Archer. Bring the *Banshee* around and give the order to board."

"Aye, sir."

Tabor O'Halloran lowered the spyglass; a feral grin bared even white teeth in his tanned face. "I'll lead the party, Mr. Archer. You take command."

"Right, sir."

The captain of the *Banshee* leapt down the steps to

main deck. A dozen men stood poised, grappling hooks swinging gently from the lines held in their hands. Another dozen waited behind and above them, ready to swing aboard once the brigantine came alongside the lumbering flute. Instead of taking a place beside them, O'Halloran stepped into the cabin.

Only a moment later he emerged with a bright red kerchief bound around his temples. The wind tangled the ends with the thick locks of his black hair. To his ordinary seaman's garb and black jackboots, he had added a red silk sash around his waist. Into it he had thrust a couple of horse pistols.

Flashing Mr. Archer a cheeky grin, he received an answering nod. The second mate emitted a derisive whistle between his teeth. Tabor lifted one black eyebrow in mock warning. "The captain's rank requires a certain style, after all. The flag, Mr. Pinckney. Let 'em know who we are."

"Aye, aye, sir."

The mate stepped to the masthead and pulled on the lines. A cheer went up from the men on the decks of the *Banshee* at the same time that a groan arose from the ten men on the deck of the flute. The black flag of the brigand fleet, feared from the Amazon to Nova Scotia, slithered up the mast and snapped open in the wind. But against this black background stood out a sharp white profile and stream of tangled red hair.

"Jesus Mary," the mate of the *Portchester* breathed. "The screaming skull. 'Tis the *Banshee*."

"It can't be," muttered the captain. "I'd heard he was dead."

As Tabor—very much alive—swung down onto

464

the deck and pulled one of the horse pistols from his sash, the *Portchester*'s captain held up his hands and stepped back. "Take whatever you want. You'll not get much more than the trouble of hauling it away."

Tabor swung the bore across the man's body and pointed toward the cabins aft. "Your cargo doesn't interest me, Captain. It's your passengers I came to see. The list, please."

The captain hesitated. His eyes darted toward the door that led to the companionway below deck. "Nobody of any importance," he muttered nervously.

"Perhaps I'm the best judge of that." Tabor motioned with the pistol to the second mate. "Fetch the books from the cabin, Pinky."

"I'm telling you, we're just carrying—"

"Save that for someone who'll believe you." Tabor grinned again, this time without mirth.

In a minute Mr. Pinckney returned. Tabor found the list. "Only three passengers," he noted. "One, a woman traveling alone. Two, a man and wife. Very interesting. Roust 'em out, Pinky, and let's see who we've got."

A woman screamed as Pinky pulled open the first door at the foot of the narrow stairs. The mate stepped back, glancing upward at his captain for reassurance. At a nod he drew his own pistol. "Would you please to step out on deck, ma'am?"

"No." The voice was punctuated with hysterical sobs. "Oh, no. Please. Edgar, save me."

"For God's sake, man," Edgar pleaded fervently. "I'll come out, but let her alone. She's had a terrible crossing. In the family way and all."

Pinky threw another quick look up at Tabor, who came partway down the steps. When the black head inclined fractionally, the mate nodded. "I guess that'll be all right."

The man called Edgar came out, his mouth twitching nervously. His face was white as chalk. "Don't shoot. I beg you, sir. Please. I have a little money." Watering eyes immediately spied Tabor, tricked out in sash and jackboots. He held up a leather purse. "Take it. Don't make my child an orphan. Don't make me walk the plank, sir."

From behind him Mr. Pinckney made a wry grimace. Tabor's eyesbrows rose, then drew together in a frown. The passenger gave a squeak and fell to his knees. Tabor stared disgustedly at the groveling figure.

"Get on to the next cabin, Pinky. Don't waste any more time."

The mate tried the knob of the door across the companionway. "Locked, Captain."

"Knock."

No answer came when the mate reversed the butt of his pistol and hit the heavy slab of mahoghany. He looked questioningly at Tabor.

"Break it in."

The captain of the *Portchester* came down the steps. "Captain, there's just one lady in there, and she's most likely fainted from fear. She's not a wealthy one. No jewelry. Just a little old lady." His next words reached Tabor's ears only. "She's a poor relation of some people in New Orleans. They paid for her passage, but she's got no money otherwise."

"I'll be the judge of that. Break it in, Pinky."

Bracing his back against the opposite wall of the narrow passage, the mate lifted his bare foot, its sole hard as any leather. With the full strength of his body he slammed it against the door just beside the lock. Metal spanged, wood splintered, and the door burst open.

No sound came from within the cabin. Tabor put a hand on the mate's arm when the man would have entered. "I'll handle this 'little old lady.'"

"Aye, Captain."

A couple of strides took him into the center of the tiny cabin before she struck. Judith Talbot-Harrow leapt from her place of concealment behind the narrow upright locker and swung the heavy pitcher with all her might.

The weighted crockery from the washstand caught Tabor across the side of the head. Had he not instinctively thrown up his shoulder, she would have knocked him unconscious. Only the scarf he had knotted at his temple prevented her blow from breaking the skin.

Nevertheless, the force staggered him. He pitched forward into the bunk, black spots swimming through his vision.

Judith whirled away from the fallen man. the hallway beyond her broken door was empty. Would no one come to help her? Would other pirates come through? On the bunk behind her the man muttered a curse. Whirling again, she found him pushing himself slowly up. Without hesitation she swung the pitcher.

If her blow had landed as intended, he would have been knocked unconscious. Tabor ducked completely as the heavy utensil arced toward him again. This time it smashed on the bunk frame above his head. The thick pottery shattered in all directions. Shards littered his thick black hair, his shoulders, the bunk, the floor.

Both fists ready to do battle, one clutching a brass-tricked horse pistol, he sprang at her.

Judith screamed in terror.

Lunging for her was a nightmare figure out of her

467

imagination. So this is how the infamous pirates of the Spanish Main must have looked. Out of the history books and the headlines of old newspapers he leapt to kidnap her and sell her into slavery in Barbary. He needed only the eye patch and wooden leg to be Captain Kidd or Blackbeard.

As she darted for the door, he caught her by the shoulder. She screeched again as he pulled her backward. "Here, now. Settle down. Settle . . . umph!"

Judith drove her shoulder into his midsection as he tried to turn her around. Pain jolted through her body. He was solid as a tree and as heavy. Although she had managed to knock the breath out of him, she had hurt herself more. Tears started in her eyes as she reeled away, tearing herself out of his grasp and stumbling for the door, where she thudded into Mr. Pinckney's chest.

"Grab her, Pinky," Tabor called, righting himself. "She's a tiger."

Obediently, the mate's arms, heavily muscled from years of hauling on lines and reefing in sails, closed around her in a bear hug that pinioned her so she could not move.

"Let me go. Damn you! Let me go," she spat out.

Tabor stepped up behind her so she was imprisoned between two male bodies, both much heavier and taller than she. "When you promise to stand still."

She twisted her head, the only part of her she could move effectively. "Monster! You'll be sorry for this."

He sank a hand into the fiery wreath of hair that fairly bristled about her head. "I'll make you sorrier than I'll ever be, lady, if you don't get some sense in your head." For emphasis he tugged roughly.

Judith's breath hissed through her teeth at the

pain. "Bully."

"Will you stand still if Pinky releases you?"

She set her teeth stubbornly, but he yanked again. "Yes!"

Tabor nodded to Mr. Pinckney, who moved back into the companionway with an obvious expression of relief.

Instantly, Judith stepped back only to blunder into Tabor's body. He caught her shoulder at the same time he slowly released his hold on her hair. The fiery strands seemed to spring after him. He had to shake his hand free of them. His grip on her tightened as he realized his pulse had accelerated. "Where is it?" he growled into her ear.

"Where is what?" She ground out her question through teeth clenched against the pain in her bruised shoulder.

He shook her roughly. "Don't make this hard on yourself. You know what I mean."

She cupped her hand around her elbow and flung back her head. "My money? I don't have even a pound. My jewelry? In the bottom of my trunk." She pointed to the large camelback of morocco, studded with brass. He looked at her doubtfully, but she met his expression with a scornful toss of her head.

The pain in her shoulder was growing steadily worse. She must have really hurt herself slamming into him that way. Whereas he appeared none the worse for her best efforts except for chips of pottery in his dark curly hair, she was feeling distinctly nauseated. She watched miserably as he turned the key she had left conveniently in the lock and threw the lid back.

The contents—dark, neatly folded garments—were unprepossessing in the extreme. Impatiently, he plucked out the first and tossed it aside.

"Wait!" She sprang forward to catch it before it billowed to the floor. It was one of her new dresses, purchased with money sent by her father. Indeed, the entire contents of the trunk, all she owned in the world, were her new clothes. Furthermore, they were more than she had owned in years. Of course, they were all black and dark colors, as befitted her mourning state, but new materials in the new styles.

As she had selected the materials, she had sternly turned her back on her favorite colors—the sapphire blues, the emerald greens, the aquamarines—as well as the soft yellows and more daring pinks. But when she had tried on the dresses for her fittings, she had found they looked well enough. The blacks especially had toned down her red hair and high coloring. Her eyes looked bluer than ever against the white of her skin.

While her clothes were not what she would have chosen had she been free to choose, they were fresh and crisp. No threads were broken in their seams. No frequent washings had dimmed their colors. No stench of the sickroom clung among their folds. Furthermore, they numbered more garments than she had had at any one time in her life. And they were new.

"Don't!" she cried as a second dress followed the first. "I'll find the jewelry for you."

His lips curled back from his white teeth in a feral grin. "And pull a loaded pistol out from among those rags. Not a chance." He tossed out another garment, this time over his other shoulder.

Her temper flared again at his insult to her clothes. "Stop it, you idiot. I don't have a loaded pistol. I swear." She winced as the dress of darkest forest-green fluttered down half on, half off the bunk.

Ignoring the rising heat in her voice, he rudely

shoved the other garments aside until he came to the jewel box. Lifting it out, he regarded it with suspicion before flipping open the lid. One glance at its contents and he contemptuously cast it aside.

The lacquerwood box with its delicate Chinese scene broke apart when it hit the cabin floor. With a cry Judith went down on her knees among the scattered pieces of her mother's jewelry. Long before the divorce, much of Charlotte's collection had been pawned to pay gambling debts. After dividing with Laura, Judith had only these few simple pieces.

Desperate to save the only things of value she had in the world, Judith fell on her knees. Her hand closed over her mother's favorite piece, a tiny gold ring set with a pearl and an emerald. She was too late to save her own gold locket with the sapphire in its heart. His heel crushed it as he turned. Only with anger could Judith control her pain. "Monster!"

If Tabor had hoped by his action to shock her into revealing the whereabouts of the payroll, he was doomed to disappointment. Blue eyes almost black with anger lanced at him. Fierce color had risen in her cheeks. Her lips looked hot and slightly swollen.

For a moment his original intent was forgotten. At the sight of her kneeling at his feet, his role of pirate of the Caribbean took possession of him. Tabor felt a sudden perverse stirring in his loins. His black eyes focused on her beautiful angry mouth. Down he dropped to one knee, his tanned face with its red kerchief banding the forehead only inches from her.

Instant awareness leapt between them. Even as she shrank back, his right arm whipped around her waist, lifting her to him. Their eyes locked. She raised her chin a notch. He kissed her. He did not have to force her. Her gasp of fright opened her mouth for his tongue to thrust into, filling her, penetrating her, making her his.

Only for a moment did she succumb, numb with virginal shock. Then memory flooded her consciousness. She was helpless in the grip of Lord Lythes. Her fighting blood surged through her veins. Her jaws clamped together hard.

He jerked his head back, snarling as her sharp teeth scraped his tongue. With an unintelligible curse he cuffed her on the shoulder. She fell backward, sprawling on the floor, her legs doubled under at the knee, her lower body arched. Though he knelt between her thighs, he could only glare at her, his hand clapped to his mouth. From behind it came an expletive, succinct but unintelligible.

She glared back, then scrambled away.

Swallowing hard, his tongue scraped and raw, he had to grate the next words out. "You'll save us both a lot of time if you'll just tell where it is."

"Where what is? I don't have anything except what you've destroyed." Her voice broke as she scanned the floor trying to locate the cherished pieces before they were trodden underfoot.

"That's trash," he observed. "Where's the real stuff?" He pushed back on his heels and stood up.

Angrily, she scooped up the large part of the jewelry and held it up to him. It did not fill her hands. "Will you please take this and get out? You're wasting time." Her voice was heavy with contempt. "Isn't there someone rich you ought to be robbing?"

Ignoring her, he looked around him with a frown. "Where's the payroll?"

"The what?"

He turned back to her trunk. Hoisting it by its handles, he lifted it and turned its contents out on the floor of the cabin.

"Stop! Don't!"

He paid no attention to her frantic pleas. The trunk felt no heavier than a normal empty trunk, but he could not be sure. "Pinky!"

"Aye, Captain."

As the mate entered the cabin, Judith scrambled to her feet. "Leave my things alone. Get out of here."

"Break it up."

"No. Oh, no."

Mr. Pinckney looked doubtfully from one to the other. "That, sir. I don't understand."

Tabor slid the trunk toward him. "Knock the bottom out of it. Let's see what she has stashed away."

"I don't have anything. Nothing." Judith flew at Tabor, who caught her wrists.

"Don't. It's new. I just bought it. Oh, don't."

At a nod from Tabor, Pinckney pulled the trunk half off the floor. Holding it by the handle, he smashed his foot down into the bottom of it.

"No! For heaven's sake. No!"

"Nothing there, Captain."

Her face contorted with rage, she doubled up her fist and swung it at Tabor. "Monster."

He caught her easily, twisting both hands behind her. "She's taken it out, then, and hidden it in the cabin."

"No. I haven't. I don't know . . ." She twisted impotently in his grip.

"Get Eben in here to help you. Turn this room upside down if you have to, but find it."

Tears trickled down her cheeks. "I don't have anything."

He pushed her into the narrow space between the bunk and the washstand. His broad shoulders partially obstructed her view, but she struggled furiously, managing to see around him as the men

473

tore the bedding from the bunk, pulled open the locker and the doors of the washstand, and sifted through her garments, tearing the hems and the linings.

The new blue dress Laura had given her caught on the hinge of the locker. Judith's cry of agony echoed the ripping cloth. At that she could no longer hold back the tears. "For pity's sake," she moaned. "Those clothes are all I have in world."

Staring down into the brilliant pleading eyes, he half raised his hand to halt the devastation, then clenched it into a fist. No matter how beautiful she was, she was still the enemy.

He hardened his heart. He had an honest man's contempt for spies. If she managed to carry the special payroll through to New Orleans, vaulable information could and would be purchased. The war would go on and on to the detriment of the struggling new United States.

He cleared his throat uncomfortably. "I'll give you this. You're a great actress. The War Office sure picked a good one when they made you the courier."

She hooted at the suggestion. "A courier! Me? For what? I've never even been to London until this month. I'm on my way to New Orleans to join my father and sister."

"And your father is?"

Her lips framed Beau Talbot's name. Then she clamped them shut. "Oh, no. I'm not going to tell you. Not you. You want to hold me for ransom."

At that he shrugged. She looked around her at the wreck of the cabin and pressed her fist against her mouth to hold back her distress. His eyes followed hers around the cabin. His forehead wrinkled in a frown. "Mr. Pinckney."

"Aye, Captain."

"Take a hard look at the cargo manifest. What about baggage in the hold?"

"I don't have any baggage in the hold." Bending carefully, as if in pain, Judith retrieved one of her mother's pearl earrings. Where the mate lay, she had no idea.

"Captain." Mr. Pinckney appeared in the doorway. "I think you'd better come hear this."

Relieved at the interruption, Tabor left her.

Pinckney stood aside for his superior to pass out into the companionway. When he would have motioned the sailor away from the door, Tabor remained where he could see Judith. As he watched she picked up another shiny object from the floor. Something dangled from it, then fell with a tiny clink. She mopped at her cheek.

"Captain O'Halloran," Pinckney muttered sotto voce. "I been thinking." The mate cleared his throat. "And if I'm right, you're not gonna like this."

"Somehow I'm not surprised."

"I've seen that Edgar somewhere's before."

Tabor's eyes narrowed suspiciously. "Are you sure?"

"Not much doubt. I'm thinking he was on board the *Halifax*, that day they took me and Roberts off the *Narragansett*. He was one of them fancy cadets."

"What!"

Pinckney winced. "He was a big jasper even then. He's still too big to be crawling around and licking ever'body's boots topside. I'd stake my share he's a naval officer."

The color drained from Tabor's face, leaving it waxen under the skin. His dark eyes flew from his mate's doleful countenance to the red-haired girl who sat on the bare box of the bed. He could not see her face. "Holy Mother," he muttered. Shoving

Pinckney back, he stepped into the companionway and closed Judith's door firmly behind him.

The screams of Edgar's "pregnant" wife quickly changed to curses as Tabor and his crew discovered the hiding place of the payroll. Taking the two into custody was a matter of minutes.

Screwing his courage to the sticking place, Tabor came back into Judith's cabin.

She looked up at him with dull eyes, the pieces of the jewel box in her lap. Her tiny store of treasure lay beside her on the bare bunk.

"I . . . er . . . that is, we found the . . . er . . . payroll."

She managed a defiant sneer. "Pardon me if I don't give a hearty cheer."

The tear stains on her cheeks made him sick. He came toward her, picking up her garments as he came, draping them over his arm. The black pelisse, its silk lining ripped out, he left lying on the floor. He looked around for the camelback trunk, then a dull flush rose in his face. It, too, lay in pieces, the bottom knocked out by Mr. Pinckney's foot, the lining ripped out of the top of the curved back.

Wordlessly, he draped the garments along its side so they no longer touched the littered floor. Pulling a heavy leather purse from his pocket, he turned to face her.

The hatred in her sapphire eyes drove him back a step. He swallowed. "I'm sorry for the damage we've done."

"You're sorry. Wonderful. That makes it all right." Bitterly, she dropped her eyes to the shattered pieces of wood in her lap before raising them again to his face.

He tried to rake his fingers through his tangled black hair, encountered the red scarf, and jerked it off angrily. He hated to be in this position.

"Well," she sneered after a moment. "What did you come back for? Rape?"

He sighed heavily. "Here." He shoved the purse into her hand.

She looked at it as if it were a dead rat. "What's this?"

"Money. There's ten twenty-dollar gold pieces."

She hit him in the face with it. "Get out!"

He staggered back. "Hey, just a minute!"

The pieces of the jewelry box clattered to the floor as she sprang up and strode to the door. "Get out of this room this instant. The very sight of you makes me sick."

"I was only . . ."

She flung open the door. "I've got a lot of work ahead of me and you're in the way. If you've got what you came for, leave me and this ship in peace and sail off over the horizon to new adventures."

He stooped and picked up the purse. Her attitude made him more than a little angry. If she couldn't be gracious about this . . . "Now, listen here. The captain told me that you're the poor relation of some people in New Orleans. You'll be needing this money." He took her hand and pressed the purse into it.

She looked at it and then back at him. Her eyes sparked fire as she spun and hurried out into the companionway. He followed her heels as she ran up the stairs to the deck. In front of the crews of both ships she flung the money down at his feet. "Will you get off this ship?" she demanded.

He thought he had never seen anything more beautiful in his life. The red hair shone in the sun. Her heavy black dress, rather than dimming the auburn color, made it all the more striking. Her eyes were blue as the sea and the sky. He picked up the purse for the second time. "Take it. Take it and I'll go." He stared deeply into her eyes.

She lifted her chin. "Never!" Whirling, she flung it as far and as hard as she could.

A concerted groan went up from the watching men as it arced out across the blue water and fell like a stone into the waves. Tabor could do nothing but gape at her.

Hands on hips, she faced him. "Give me another purse and I'll throw it overboard too. I promise you that. What would I use stolen money for? I wouldn't touch it."

Tabor staggered slightly and passed a hand over the lower half of his face. His eyes drank her in—her red hair, her flawless skin. More wonderful than her beauty was her spirit. Never had he expected to meet a spirit as wild and proud as his own. Heedless of the crews who stared incredulous at the pair, he advanced on her.

As a tremor racked her body, her eyes dilated, but they never faltered.

His big hands clasped her shoulders. Roughly, he pulled her forward. From thigh to mouth she was held hard against him. Then he bent his lips to hers.

The kiss was meant as a salute and a pledge, but her mind was too unsophisticated to comprehend it as such. To her it was an insult, punishing her as Lythes punished her, fueling her hatred, torturing her sensibilities in ways she could not identify. Finally, when she thought her control would break, when she feared she would give him the satisfaction of some kind of movement, he let her go.

His expression enigmatic, he sketched her a quick bow. "Let's go, men."

The remaining crew of the *Banshee* scrambled up

478

the lines and swung over onto their own deck. Last to go was Tabor O'Halloran. He leapt to the railing, one strong tanned hand clasping the line. "I'll see you again," he promised. "This is just the beginning."

She shuddered visibly. "I hope and pray I'll never see you again."

He grinned and swung onto the brigantine's deck as the last of the lines was cast off. Immediately, he leapt up the ladder to the quarterdeck. From its vantage he faced her as wind swelled the sails and the ship moved ahead of the flute.

Her temper reasserted itself. She ran to the rail of the flute. "If I ever see you again," she shouted, "I'll manage to find a pistol."

He raised his hand in farewell. "I would expect no less."